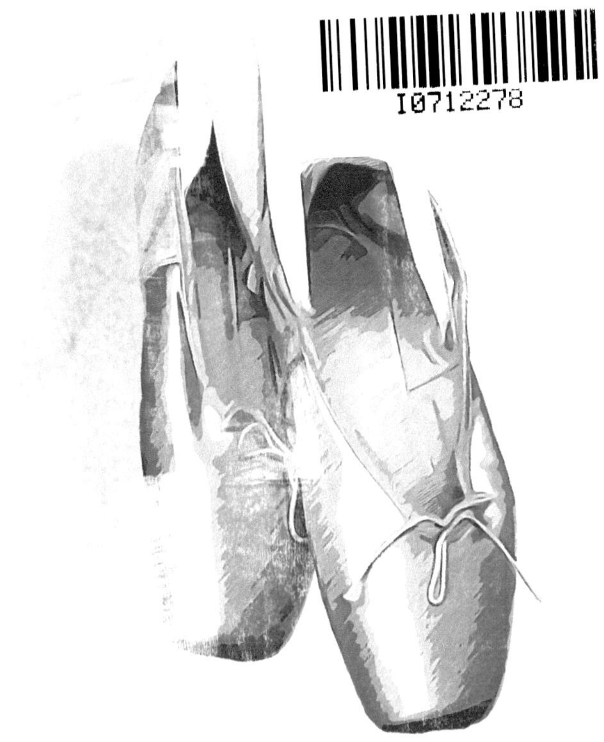

LAST SHOT

THE FIGHT GAME BOOK FOUR

NIKKI CASTLE

Cover Art: Haya In Designs

Formatting: Books and Moods

Editing: NiceGirlNaughtyEdits

To those that have to load up with a little extra armor.
You're seen, and you're loved.

Playlist

Numb the Pain — Clarx

Crazy Bitch — Buckcherry

Fighter — The Score

Take Me Away — New Medicine

deepfake — brakence

break my bones — Matt Hansen

BURNING IN DESIRE — Chris Grey

Drive You Insane — Daniel Di Angelo

more than friends — Isabel LaRosa

Fuck Em Only We Know — BANKS

Arch & Point — Miguel

IF THE WORLD — Josh Levi

We Go Down Together — Dove Cameron, Khalid

blame's on me — Alexander Stewart

RUNNING — NF

Silence — Marshmello, Khalid

AUTHOR'S NOTE

This book is a little different from the other books in the Fight Game series. Where those are mostly a fun, spicy time, this one contains references to some heavier topics. If you've read "3 Count," then you know Kane has some demons that he's contending with.

Listing those demons would spoil Kane's story, so for a full list of **Trigger Warnings**, flip to the Afterword at the end of this book.

I'M JUST ABOUT ready to leave when I hear it.

"Here we are! Welcome to my new apartment. What do you think?"

There's an obvious pause that sounds through the thin walls. Then…

"It's… cute," comes an older woman's hesitant voice. Then she hurriedly adds, "It's *so* cute! The exposed brick really brings the… um… the *farmhouse* look together. Very popular nowadays, I hear."

Another pause, and I can tell by the commentary and rich-lady tone what her next sentence is going to start with.

"But…"

There it is.

"…wouldn't you prefer to live in a better area? I know you're only planning to live here for a few months, but I looked up the city's crime rates, and this area doesn't seem the safest, honey. And you know I can get Richard to find you a nice little townhouse in Old City and have you moved in by tomorrow."

I slam the fridge door closed and force myself to swallow

the rapidly growing anger inside me.

I worked *damn hard* to get into this apartment building. When I moved in six months ago, I picked it *because* it was the nicest apartment I had ever seen, and in the best area of the city I could afford. And yet, this lady couldn't be more obvious about the fact that she thinks this is the slum of the city.

If only they could see what an actual shitty living situation looks like.

Memories of exactly that start to seep into my thoughts, so I reach for my water bottle and chug the whole thing in an effort to distract myself. By the time I'm tossing it forcefully into the trash can, I can hear my new neighbors talking again.

"—safe, I promise. I checked the crime rates, too, and they're no different from some of the areas you work in now. It's a city, Mom, just like New York City. And I didn't *want* Richard to set me up in a boujee house. I wanted to create a fresh start here on my own. I already hate that I had to dip into my trust fund for the deposit for this place."

My scoff is automatic, as is my headshake. *Looks like I guessed the rich thing right.*

I grab my backpack and sling it over my shoulder, pausing as I debate how to get past the Fresh Prince family. I don't feel like doing the meet-the-neighbor thing, especially with a spoiled rich girl and her parents. I'll just have to wait until I can hear them move into the back of the apartment so I can slip out.

Thankfully, it doesn't take long. I hear them discussing her décor options, an older male voice chiming in for the first time, and then their echoing steps start to wander. Eventually their muffled voices disappear into what I know is the one bedroom in the back, since the apartment is a mirror of my own.

Grabbing the keys to my bike, I quickly escape into the entryway that our apartments share and then down the steps to the street. By the time I've swung a leg over the bike and pulled a helmet over my head, there's still no sign of my new neighbor.

It isn't until I rev the engine that I see her.

And that relieved breath I just exhaled for avoiding a social situation gets immediately stuck in my chest.

The one I can only assume is my new neighbor steps out onto the landing at the top of the stairs, lifting a hand to shield her eyes from the bright sun when she does. I don't think she's noticed me on the other side of the street, which gives me a moment to shamelessly look her over.

With her hand casting a shadow over her face, her body is the first thing I notice. She's average height, though noticeably thin—not in a fragile kind of way, more like an incredibly lean kind of way, if the impressive line of muscles on her exposed legs are any indication. This girl is clearly an athlete.

And then her attention catches on me. She stops scanning the street, and she takes in the fact that I'm sitting on my bike across from her apartment building, my gaze glued to her. Thank God my helmet is already on and she can't see me clearly enough to know that.

Gingerly, she lifts the hand that was shielding her eyes and gives me a little wave.

Fuck, this girl's beautiful.

With her face uncovered, I can finally zero in on the details of her face. She looks young, her skin perfect and her smile too friendly. I have to tear my gaze away from her plump, pink lips and the intoxicating smile they're curved into. Instead, I watch as a few strands of her untamed, wavy brown hair flow into her face from a breeze, and as she shyly tucks them behind her ear while she waits for me to return her greeting.

I don't wave back.

I just rev my bike again and speed off, letting the wind on my skin cool the anger I feel at my own reaction to this girl who's too pretty for her own good and too different for mine.

An hour later, I'm walking into the gym without returning the nod I get from Jax behind the front desk. The nod I *always* get from him when I walk through the doors.

I don't understand why these idiots don't get that I'm not here to be their fucking friend.

Because it's not just Jax. The golden-haired pretty boy is also ready to make an effort to pull me into whatever conversation he's having with the black-haired jiu-jitsu kid who's always attached to his hip. Fortunately, it only takes a single hard stare and then turning away for that one to get the picture.

No one else dares to say anything to me. I've been here for months, and everyone besides those two have officially gotten the message that I'm here to train, and nothing else. This isn't a *team* sport, contrary to what these idiots think. When I get in the cage, it's just me, my fists, and my brain. I might have a coach yelling instructions, but it's up to me to follow them.

I'm on my own in there, just the way I like it.

I throw my bag on the edge of the mat and dig out my gloves and hand wraps. A lot of times I don't use the hand wraps, but those are days when I'm feeling particularly masochistic. Not only because it allows me to feel skull at the end of my punches, but also because the lack of protection sometimes rubs the skin off my knuckles. The pain serves as a reminder that I fought, and that I *won*.

As I start to wrap my hands, I watch Tristan shadowbox out of the corner of my eye. It didn't take long for me to begrudgingly admit to myself that he's the best fighter in the gym. And even though that doesn't mean he would win a fight to the death with me, it's clear he's the hardest worker in here and has a shit load of talent to back it up. There's a reason he got into the UFC and is working his way to the top of the food chain.

"Kane, once you're warmed up, I want you in the cage to do yesterday's drills with Tristan."

I turn toward Coach and give a stiff nod. I know better than to push back on authority figures, but it doesn't tamp down on the irritation that sparks in my chest every time I'm ordered around. I finish wrapping my hands and grab a jump rope to warm up.

Ten minutes later, I'm pulling on my gloves and glaring at Tristan where he's doing the same. He's relaxed, his muscles loose and his eyes lit up with a laugh at something his girlfriend says.

It turns my stomach.

No one should be that unbothered about fighting. This shit serves either one of two purposes: it's either a release—in which case the most you're allowed to feel is a sick sense of fascination—or a mode of survival. There's no in-between. This isn't *fun*.

There's no telling that to Tristan, though. Or anyone else in this godforsaken gym, really. They're all happy to be here, happy to hang out with their *teammates*, and happy to do this thing that is apparently a good time for them.

What a fucking joke.

Coach's voice snaps me out of my increasingly rage-filled thoughts. "Alright, so, Tristan, we're working that two-step retreat combo I showed you last week. Got it?"

"Yes, sir," Tristan immediately responds. He rolls out his shoulders one last time, and then starts to bounce around on the balls of his feet.

"Kane, just do what you usually do. Be aggressive."

As if I know any other way to fight.

But I nod to signal my understanding.

I don't need to stay loose the way I always see fighters doing at the beginning of a fight. I'm not stretching, not bouncing around to keep my body warm. You could wake me from a dead sleep in the middle of winter in a bedroom with no heat, and I'd still be ready to go at the sound of a bell. Fighting isn't physical, it's mental.

"Let's go," Coach barks, starting the ringside timer and interrupting my thoughts, thankfully before they can go down their usual dark path.

I dart forward, driven into Tristan's path with a bone-deep need to *break. Hurt. Kill.*

But he knows I'm coming, and he doesn't stay in one place

long enough for me to get a shot off.

"Let him tire himself out," Coach calls to Tristan. "Aggressive styles are exhausting, so as long as you're not constantly retreating, just use those lateral movements and evasions to keep from getting hurt."

Biting down hard on my mouthpiece, I tuck my chin and throw even harder, and faster. I'm mostly throwing punches, since that's what I'm comfortable with. And because Tristan is the hardest fighter in here to spar with, I'm reverting to my default of *just move forward and punch*. Which Tristan is entirely too familiar with.

It only takes him ninety seconds into the round to start picking apart my movements. He waits until I throw my big combos, and then he snaps out a quick counter that hits me where I'm still open. Where I haven't retained my guard because I'm that focused on *offense* instead of *defense*.

"Combo, combo!" Coach yells with only thirty seconds left. And even though I know that's his code word for *throw the combo we talked about before this round*, I'm still unable to avoid Tristan's movements.

As I push forward, he takes one step back, then another, and then quick as a snake, he's shifting left into the opposite stance and snapping a straight left at my chin.

It's not hard, but it stuns me. My head snaps back with the shot, and by the time I blink my focus back, the ten-second bell is sounding and Tristan is laying into me in order to steal the end of the round.

"Time!" Coach calls. "Back to your corners. Thirty second break."

My chest is heaving as I go back to my side of the cage, but it's not from exertion—though even if it was, it wouldn't affect a single aspect of my fighting. I fight the same way whether I'm in the best shape of my life or coming off a three-month recovery when the most I could do was upper body exercises. No, I'm breathing hard because the shock of Tristan's shot is wearing off and being replaced with unbridled rage.

It's a familiar emotion, with a familiar result every time. This kind of fury is a result of one thing only: the desperate need to survive.

"Round two, same thing," Coach instructs. "Kane, try to tighten those combos up a little when you're moving forward. Not so sloppy."

I don't even hear him, I'm staring at Tristan so intently. It's like there's a blanket of red in front of my eyes, and I'm waiting for it to move so I can charge forward at my target.

The bell rings. "Fight!"

The red lifts and, suddenly, I'm like a bull in the center of the stadium: singularly focused on slicing the matador into ribbons.

I can't even take the time to appreciate the way Tristan's eyes widen in surprise. The clear show of respect should make the animal within me beat its chest, but I'm too deep into the fight to let it mean anything. The only thing I'm capable of doing is throwing myself at Tristan with a bellow of aggression, chest heaving and punches flying.

For about ten seconds, every other punch lands. My gloves glance off his forehead, jaw, even jarring his body through the shot that lands on the forearm he has raised to protect himself.

For ten seconds, victory pumps through my blood. Victory that I was threatened, and I *survived*. My opponent is moving back, moving away from the threat I pose, and I've protected myself enough to live another day.

But as soon as those ten seconds are up, and Tristan gathers his wits enough to do more than just shell up and take my attack, those feelings crumble into dust in my lungs.

I don't realize until later that he uses the exact combo Coach gave him to beat me. That Tristan backing up wasn't him running away from me, but luring me into a false sense of security. Because the second I take another step forward, he's shifting into the other stance and firing a left cross directly at my chin.

And it's a *hard* shot. Rightfully so, because my intensity and power level in this round is exponentially higher than the last round. So of course, his rose too.

We call it a lightning knockout. It's not enough to put you unconscious on the ground, but your brain definitely shuts off.

I've had too many of these to count. I've always wondered if the reason my body prefers this kind of knockout to the real thing is because it's yet another survival tactic I've somehow internalized. Because if I go all the way out, I'll have no protection against any other damage coming my way.

Unfortunately, lightning knockouts come with their own danger. One I've managed to mostly keep at bay while I've been training at this gym.

At the feel of Tristan's punch landing on my face, a memory surfaces. Raised voices. Fear. The phantom sensation of a punch exactly like this one—

I crawl my way out of the pit of terror the same way I do every time I'm thrust into it. A switch flips inside of me, and I launch myself at Tristan with every single bit of fight I have left.

I start to pummel him. There's no other word for it. My eyes are crazed, my shots thrown out of fear, and I'm sunk so deep into this moment that I know without thinking that he'll have to kill me to get me to stop. I've been pushed so far that this is now a fight to the death.

I'm not sure what I notice first: the arms grabbing at me, or the panicked shouts ringing around the gym. But slowly, so slowly, reality filters into my consciousness.

Tristan's standing in front of me, still in his ready stance and looking entirely prepared to resume our fight. But there are hands clasping my arms and shoulders and even my waist. I jerk my head to the side and see Coach holding one arm, with Jax holding me back from behind. I don't care enough to see who's on my other side.

"Jesus," Jax gasps. "What the *fuck*, man?"

I don't answer. I can't.

I force myself to hold Coach's gaze with a blank stare and wait for his punishment.

His expression flickers with irritation, but for the most part, it's knowing. Though he has to push his rebuke through gritted teeth.

"If you can't keep your temper in check and your teammates safe, I won't let you on my mat," he says, in a voice low enough that only those standing next to me can hear. "I know you're new. And I know you did things differently where you come from. But the bottom line is, if you're a danger to this gym, I won't have you on the team. I'm not jeopardizing others because *you* are incapable of keeping your feelings leashed." He pauses to give me a hard stare, making sure he has my undivided attention. "Understood?"

"Yeah," I croak immediately.

Give me the punishment. I *want* it. With punishment comes numbness. And if the absence of feeling takes away the pain, then give me a burnout three times a day for the rest of my life. It's one of the only ways I've ever known peace.

"Good. Now get off my mat and give me 100 burpees and 1,000 kicks. On each side. If you can't work with your *teammates*"—he stresses the word in a way that lets me know he knows exactly how I feel about it—"then you get to do a solo workout. Get going."

Stepping toward the entrance to the cage, I shake off the remaining grips on my arms. I refuse to make eye contact with anyone—and there are a *lot* of people crowded around the cage, their mouths agape and their expressions shocked.

I turn my self-hatred outward and blow past every single one of them.

Fuck them.

I ALMOST DIDN'T get my parents out of my new apartment and settled in their hotel on time. I'm half-convinced the only reason I *did* get my mom to leave was because I have an appointment for something dance oriented. If there's one thing my parents will reorganize their entire lives for, it's dancing.

Glancing down at my phone, then back up at the building in front of me, I realize I should've calculated for extra time. Because there's no way I'm in the right spot.

2324 Pine St. *Address matches.*

It doesn't *look* like a place for dance, but then again, I've only ever seen ballet schools. Maybe these smaller studios can get away with different locations.

Taking a deep breath to steel myself, I walk up the stairs and push open the front doors.

And immediately come to a stop.

I can't figure out what to focus on first: the two men rolling around on the mat that stretches over the entire floor, or the pair punching each other on the far side of the room. The view, the sounds of grunting coming from both pairs, and the smell of Vaseline and Bengay are overwhelming to my senses.

This is definitely not a dance studio.

I must have made a startled sound when I walked in, because by the time I've finished taking in the sights and sounds before me, the wrestling duo has split apart and focused their attention on me. The larger one—a dark-haired man with piercing blue eyes and a distinct don't-fuck-with-me aura—stands up and walks over to the edge of the mat.

"Hi, can I help you?" he asks in a deep voice.

"Uh, I doubt it," is my honest response. This guy looks like he wouldn't be able to tell the difference between ballet and tap. "I'm looking for a dance studio, but clearly, this is the wrong spot."

For reasons I'm sure I'll never understand, the Adonis in front of me smirks at a woman standing along the chairs that line the edge of the room. Or why she rolls her eyes in return.

"You're close to the right spot," he says when he turns back to me. "Unfortunately, some websites still have the wrong address listed for the studio. It's in the building at the other end of the block."

"Oh," I breathe. "That's weird. Okay, well, thanks."

I'm just about to turn around to get out of this alternate dimension, when another man walks into the room from the other side of the building.

A shirtless, sweat-drenched, heavily-tattooed man with a scowl on his face that looks like it might be etched into his skin.

I'm caught completely off guard by the flash of heat that runs through me at the sight of him.

I've been surrounded by graceful, beautiful men my whole life. Not to say I've been living under a rock and haven't interacted with anyone who isn't a dancer, but my experience with most men—a singular boyfriend included—has been with a very particular type of man.

One who's the complete opposite of the man standing in front of me.

A man who immediately makes me want to know everything about him.

I must be staring because he notices me right away. His steps slow, and though he holds my gaze for a moment, it eventually drops and roves over my body.

It doesn't seem like it's in a sexual way, necessarily. He just looks curious, if curiosity came with a side of negativity. Because that scowl suddenly looks angrier than it did before he saw me.

I stare right back at the 6'2", 200-pound alpha. His focus reads like he expects me to wither at his attention, or maybe even his commanding and terrifying appearance, but I'm so mesmerized by him that I couldn't look away if I tried. I can only stare and hope my gaze doesn't read as mesmerized as I feel.

He gives me a second once-over, his brow furrowing slightly, this time seeming to draw a second conclusion. And when he realizes that I'm far from intimidated, he straightens and starts to move across the room again. I watch in awe as he grabs one of the dummies from the side, straddles it, and starts to rain life-ending punches onto the padded face.

The weird crackle of energy between us evaporates when I

hear a woman ask, "Did I hear someone asking about the dance studio?"

I turn in surprise to see a small blonde woman has walked out of the office, momentarily forgetting why I'm even here. But once her question registers, I answer, "Yeah, that's me. It had this as the address, but that's obviously wrong."

"Yeah, some websites still have the wrong one listed. I can walk you over there, though. I'm not taking class tonight, but I can at least show you around."

My eyebrows shoot to my hairline. "You go there. *And* you do this?"

She lets out a chuckle. "Punching things isn't really my thing. I'm only here because my boyfriend and sister train here."

With perfect timing, a man who can only be described as a Viking walks out of the office. He stops next to the petite blonde and wraps an arm around her shoulders. "Hey," he greets me with a smile. "I'm Jax. I'm the boyfriend."

"And I'm Hailey," chirps the blonde.

Out of the corner of my eye, I think I see the tattooed guy pause in his movements. It takes me a moment to remember to respond to the two in front of me. "Nice to meet you both. I'm Isabella."

"That's such a pretty name," Hailey says with an endearing sigh. "And so perfect for a ballet dancer." She smiles knowingly. "That's your main dance style, right?"

That's enough to finally bring a smile to my face. "I guess it's pretty obvious, huh?"

"It's okay, there are worse things to be obvious about," Hailey says with a laugh. "Come on, I'll walk you over to the studio."

I nod in silent thanks before taking another second to glance around what my brain is finally identifying as an MMA gym. My arrival has apparently disturbed the entire room, because every person in here has stopped their workout to stare at me. I feel slightly guilty about it, until my eyes lock with the tattooed guy's again.

We both freeze at the caught glance. I've stared enough at his body so instead, I mentally catalog his face—short, almost buzzed brown hair, a perpetual frown, and brown eyes that seem to say everything and nothing all at once. I'm experiencing the distinct sensation that he's catching and analyzing every thought, and every minuscule reaction, that's showing on my face right now.

I can't help the shiver that runs through me at being so… *naked* in front of someone. It makes me the first to break our eye contact, and I turn reluctantly toward Hailey.

She doesn't reveal whether or not she noticed my stare-down. She just gives me another warm smile and beckons me to follow her.

The gym door has barely slammed behind us when she asks, "So why the change from ballet?"

It takes me a second to answer her blunt question. Memories of agonizing pain, the flash of ambulance lights, the feeling of hopeless despair from a dream unrealized… in a flash they assault my brain. And though they only last for a second—I've gotten really good at tamping down on those feelings when they arise—they still leave me slightly breathless and battered.

Hailey's harmlessly curious glance encourages me to clear

my throat and answer her, though. I even go with a half-truth.

"I just needed a change of pace. I've been doing ballet for so long; I got burned out."

Hailey nods with understanding. "That makes sense. How long have you been dancing?"

"Since I could walk," I answer without any hesitation.

"Wow. You must be really good. Do you dance in the Philadelphia company? Or are you new to Philly?"

"New to Philly. I just moved here from New York a few days ago."

At that, I see out of the corner of my eye Hailey's head turn and her eyes go wide. I know exactly what she's about to say, so I purposefully don't meet her gaze, choosing instead to keep my focus ahead at the sidewalk.

"Did you dance in the New York City Ballet?"

I debate lying, but after a moment, I nod stiffly.

"Holy shit," she breathes. "So you're *really* good then."

I can't bring myself to react or say anything more. Even thinking about it this much is hard, but something about Hailey screams *caring but not pushy*, making it easier to expose some of myself.

Sure enough, Hailey seems to notice my stiff spine and the hard line of my lips, because she doesn't press for more information. She simply faces forward again. "It's right up here before the intersection."

I expect her to be silent as we walk the rest of the way, but instead, she says, "Jane is amazing with people that are new to hip-hop. You'll love her class. Just don't talk while she's teaching."

I think back to the glare of the company director in New York, and the vicious scoldings that would follow any chatter, mumbling, "Trust me, there's no chance of that happening."

When we reach the door to the dance studio, Hailey pushes it open and immediately calls out a hello. I step in behind her and see a woman wearing baggy pants and a crop top, talking to a group of young people who are hanging on her every word.

"Hey, Jane," Hailey calls. "I found a straggler at the gym again."

The woman turns away from the group and focuses her attention on me. "Oh yeah? Sorry about that. I can't for the life of me get that website to update our address. Are you new in town, or just new to dance?"

It takes me a second to admit, "Both. Or at least, I'm new to contemporary."

She smiles. "Ballet, right?"

I huff a laugh and glance at Hailey, who had made the same assumption just as quickly. She shrugs, smiling back at me. "I'm not very good at hiding it."

Flapping a hand at me, Jane says, "Never hide it. Clearly, it's who you are." She reaches a hand forward for me to shake. "I'm Jane, as Hailey said. I teach the contemporary classes."

I return the handshake. "I'm Isabella. I had to do a little bit of contemporary as part of my training at the school I came up with, but I always wanted to dive deeper into it. I'm going to apologize ahead of time for being annoyingly graceful."

Jane lets out a bark of laughter. "You'll fit in just fine here."

At that, the tension leaves my shoulders. Because I believe her. I didn't realize I was nervous about fitting in with a new group, about trying something new—especially something so close in theory to the thing that's filled up my entire life—until Jane's reassurance. I give her a grateful smile.

"Alright, I'm heading back to the gym then," Hailey says, bringing me back to the present. "I'll be in this week sometime for class. Maybe I'll see you then?"

I nod, returning her kind smile. "Yeah, I'll be here tomorrow too. Thanks a lot for walking me over."

"Don't mention it. Oh, and if you want, I can give you my number. You know, just in case you need it for 'dance' emergencies." She laughs, but I can only blink at her in surprise.

Dance can be a very alienating sport, especially at the competitive level I've been at for the past few years, so it's rare that anyone actually goes out of their way to be friendly.

"You don't even know me," I blurt out before I can reel it in. "Why are you being so nice to me?"

Hailey's expression softens. "I remember what it felt like to be on an island by yourself," she admits quietly, pursing her lips. "I wouldn't wish that on anyone."

I study her for a moment, wondering how this sweet, blonde-haired stranger appeared so suddenly in my life. But when I think about keeping to myself the way I normally would, I realize that *everything* in my life this past week, even the past year, has happened just as suddenly. And I remind myself that the whole reason I moved down here was to step out of my comfort bubble.

"That would be really helpful, actually. Thank you," I finally say, and this time, my smile is fully genuine.

Hailey's expression brightens at that. She grabs the offered phone and puts her number in, then waves goodbye with an energetic, "Enjoy your class!"

Then the door closes behind her, and I turn back to face this new and terrifying environment.

And when I walk out of the studio a little bit later, it's with a lightness that I haven't felt in a very long time.

CHAPTER 3
Isabella

WHEN I LOCK my apartment door behind me and start down the sidewalk, it's with my mental checklist of what I still need to do already buzzing around in my mind.

I'm not nearly as far along in my "new life" to-dos as I had intended to be. It's only been a week since I've moved to Philly, but I fully expected to accomplish more by now when I first came up with this insane temporary relocation idea.

I didn't expect needing a week to catch my breath after the whirlwind of the past year.

I'm mulling over finding the nearest laundromat, when my phone begins to ring with my mother's number. I swipe *Accept* as I lift it to my ear.

"Hey, Mom."

"Hi, sweetheart. How was the new dance studio?"

I adjust the bag on my shoulder as I start walking toward the dance studio. "It was good. It's a nice change of pace from Mrs. Thompson's classes, that's for sure. A lot less shouts of 'point your goddamn toes, Izzy.'"

My mom's laugh rings in my ears. "That's not hard to do. I

bet that woman said those words in her sleep."

I chuckle. "I'm not taking that bet."

"How are you settling into the apartment?" she asks in a more serious voice. "Have you explored at all? How's the area?"

I roll my eyes. "The area is fine, Mom. South Philly is a nice part of the city."

She sighs over the line. "I just worry about you. First time not living under my roof, and you decide to move to an entirely new city."

"I just needed a change of pace," I tell her quietly. "I didn't want to get away from *you*, I just needed… a new environment for a little bit."

"I know, honey. I understand that." Her voice takes on a happier pitch. "So is the apartment everything you wanted it to be?"

A proud smile stretches across my face. "Yeah. It's amazing."

"Good. I'm glad Freddy found you what you wanted. Lord knows I pay that man enough to get it right."

And just like that, my smile vanishes, and my moment of pride becomes nonexistent.

I shift the duffel bag on my shoulder, suddenly uncomfortable. The fact that my parents still handle things like this for me is a reminder of the exact reason I moved to Philadelphia in the first place.

Oblivious to my discomfort, my mom asks, "What about the job search? Any idea yet what you might want to do?"

Chewing on my lower lip, I debate telling her the truth. I haven't made any moves with a job search, but I *have* thought nonstop about what kind of job I might want. I have an idea for one that I'd have a good chance of getting but… I'm hesitant to say that out loud. Not because my mom isn't a supportive parent, but because I'm not ready to admit it to another person, to vocalize my hopes out loud.

"I'm still looking," I say instead.

"What about a teaching job at one of the ballet schools? I'm sure they'd love to have your knowledge at the front of the classroom. You could teach beginners, or even the kids again."

I wince at that thought. I loved teaching back in New York, but the thought of teaching here makes me slightly depressed. I moved away from the city I grew up in because I wanted a different life, something new to spend my days with. Teaching ballet would be an easy job to get and an even easier one to do, but I'm not quite ready to settle yet.

"Although in all honesty, you don't even really need a job. You've got plenty of money from the trust fund to just focus on getting comfortable in the city and enjoying yourself for a little while."

I need out of this conversation. Being reminded of my privilege is one thing, but having it thrown in my face is a whole other. I know my mom doesn't mean anything by it, but even the mention of it is enough to send my hope for this new phase of my life crashing into the ground.

"You've worked so hard your whole life, and you've had such a hard year. You deserve to relax and—"

"Mom, I've got to go. I have a call from the school coming in," I lie in a rush.

"Oh, okay. Good luck then, sweetheart, call me later."

"I will, Mom. I'll call you next week."

I hang up with a heavy exhale. And all the earlier feelings about my overwhelming to-do list come rushing back, this time accompanied by my nerves surrounding going down a very different career path.

I'm lost in my head the entire walk to the dance studio. By the time I reach the building, I think there's a permanent furrow in my forehead and I've chewed my lower lip raw.

I don't even notice Hailey until she calls my name.

"Hey!" she says, her face lighting up with the greeting. "You're back. Class went okay then?"

I focus my attention back on the present and return the smile as I walk over to her. "Better than okay. Jane is an incredible teacher. I couldn't wait to come back."

"Yeah, that's usually the reaction she gets. I'm glad it worked out for you." She continues to stretch as I set my gym bag down and pull out what I need for class. "So how are you settling into Philly? Was this the first dance school you checked out?"

I nod. "Yeah. Guess I got lucky. I only moved down here a week ago, so I'm still settling in, but my life has revolved around dance for long enough that I can't *not* have a place to dance. I just needed something that wasn't ballet."

She nods as I start my own stretches. "Are you doing ballet down here, too? Or did you stop that entirely?"

I glance down at my lap, hoping the turmoil doesn't show on my face. *She's just being friendly*, I remind myself.

"I didn't stop, I just… changed the direction of my career." I think about adding more, mentally debating if talking to *someone* about it would make me feel better, but then I see

Hailey's gaze dart down to where I'm subconsciously rubbing my left foot.

I let go of it as if burned.

"I'm going to check out the Philadelphia Ballet this week sometime," I finally force out. "I figure with so many changes going on in my life, it would help to have something I'm comfortable with."

Hailey nods, suddenly looking too distracted with the water bottle in her hand.

"Let me know if you want some company. I don't do ballet, but I'm sure the teachers there could always do with some entertainment."

That makes me laugh, and Hailey immediately looks relieved. It helps me forget all about the awkward conversation that I don't want to have.

We hear a clap from across the room. "Alright, ladies, let's get started," comes Jane's voice.

I enjoy this class just as much as I did yesterday's. When I first had this idea, I *really* wasn't sure how it was going to go, or if I would be back again. I've been an expert in this art for so long, I forgot what it was like to be a student. To show up in a new environment, pay someone to tell me what to do, and then be bad at something. It's refreshing.

But I'm also sore and groaning at the aches by the time class is over and Hailey and I start to stretch out.

"You know, I thought leaving the New York Ballet meant I'd finally be able to enjoy a nice, relaxed dance class," I say on a groan. "I don't think Jane got the memo."

Hailey chuckles from her place beside me. "If you're trying

to convince me that an amateur contemporary dance class is harder than the New York City Ballet, you're going to have to try a little harder. I've heard whispers about what the training is like up there and, honestly, I don't know how any of you do it. It seems grueling."

I deepen my stretch with a sigh. "It was. Sometimes I don't know how I did it for so long."

Hailey casts me a curious look. "I've just never understood how you could be *so immersed* in it for basically your entire life. I would've needed a side hobby or something just to give myself time away from everything."

Biting into my lower lip, I debate taking the opening Hailey has unwittingly given me. I'm not nearly ready to talk about everything that happened with my career, but talking to someone about the side hobby I picked up *because* of ballet is an easy way to practice opening up to someone.

"I actually got into yoga for that reason," I admit after a moment. "The stretching was obviously helpful and the practice itself was nice, but it was more of a mental help than anything. Quieted the stress a little."

"Oooh, that sounds like the perfect side hobby. Do you still do it?"

I nod my answer. Then, hesitantly, I add, "I actually got certified to teach yoga. After I... stopped ballet, it gave me something to focus on. To work toward. And, I don't know, maybe even something to do as a job."

If Hailey senses the weight of my words, she doesn't let it show. "We should bring you into the gym to teach a yoga class for the fighters. God, I can't even imagine how bad they would be at it," she says with a giggle.

I laugh along with her but don't respond. Her comment has me thinking about the MMA gym and the questions that have been rolling around in my head since I accidentally walked in. About the sport, the training, even the fighters themselves.

About one particular fighter.

"You said your sister fights, right?" I ask. "That's how you ended up at the gym?"

Hailey furrows her brow in concentration. "It's kind of a long story, but Jax, my boyfriend, is how my sister ended up at the gym. We all grew up together, and then Jax and I started dating last year. So long answer short, I go for both of them."

And with perfect timing, her boyfriend chooses that moment to walk into the room. He waves at a now-smiling Hailey, and then takes a seat in one of the chairs to wait for us to finish stretching out.

I study him for a moment. He's big, and his muscles are obvious, but I don't think I'd guess that he was a fighter at first glance. He doesn't look anything like the guy who was beating the bag to a pulp at the gym.

"Are fighters as violent as they seem?" I ask, trying to sound more curious than judgmental. "I just don't understand the sport beyond what I've seen on TV. I always figured fighting would appeal to dangerous people."

We both turn to look at the waiting area where Hailey's boyfriend is.

And watch as the blonde giant leans down to one of the

dancers to hear what she has to say. He reaches up to the nearby shelf and lifts a pair of ballet slippers off the ledge, passing them to the tiny dancer with a smile.

"Yeah, he's terrifying," Hailey says in a flat voice, her brow quirked when she looks back at me.

"Okay, clearly not him," I say with a chuckle. "But it's not the kind of sport you can pick up if you *don't* like violence, right? Why would someone willingly get into a ring with someone who wants to hurt them?"

Hailey sighs. "Okay, yes, MMA is inherently violent. But it's not nearly as bad as it seems. There hasn't been a death or a serious injury in the UFC since it was started. Football is actually way more dangerous, believe it or not. Nowadays, you have to be an intelligent, disciplined athlete to compete in MMA. You can't just be in it for the violence."

I let out a thoughtful hum, mulling over Hailey's words. I understand what she's saying, but it's difficult to reconcile her words with the memory of hate-filled punches being thrown at a heavy bag.

Hailey must notice because she says, "Tell you what. Come with me to the fights on Friday night. Do you remember that guy who was trying to punch a hole through the floor when you first walked into the gym? Kane? He has his first fight this weekend with Bulldog MMA, so everyone is going to show their support. Come with me. I'll introduce you to the world of MMA."

My nerves have me hesitating, but then I remind myself

that this is exactly the reason I moved down to Philly in the first place. To have new experiences.

While also trying to convince myself that it has nothing to do with the way my heart starts to race at even the mention of the guy fighting. *Kane.* What a ridiculously hot name.

"Okay," I tell Hailey with a small smile. "I'm in."

BY THE TIME I walk into the Philadelphia Ballet, it's taken me eight days to work up the courage to do it.

I haven't stepped foot into a ballet environment since I made the decision that changed my entire life. Quitting first the NYC Ballet, and then my job as a children's ballet teacher at the local school, was the hardest thing I had ever done. But I knew I couldn't dance at the level my company needed me at, and teaching the kids was just too hard of a reminder.

That day was eight months ago.

Now, stepping into a school again, it feels both like returning home *and* like opening up an old wound.

"Hi, can I help you?" the girl at the front desk greets with a smile.

"Hi, I called about registering?"

"Oh, that's right, Mrs. Martin said someone was coming by today. Can I schedule you for an audition?"

It should be a humbling question. It *is* humbling. It's been years since I've been in a ballet environment where I wasn't recognized, and although a lot of my peers in New York would be offended, the only thing I feel is the tension in my chest loosening. Because it means I don't have to be *Isabella, a soloist in the NYC Ballet*. I can just be… another dancer.

I open my mouth to answer *yes, I'd be happy to audition*, but I never get the chance.

"Rebecca, don't you know who you're talking to? That's Isabella Brooks. She doesn't need to audition. She'll be joining our Professional Program."

I turn a tight smile on the older woman walking toward us. I looked up the academy before coming in, of course, so I know she's the Artistic Director and main teacher for the school. I also know she had a very impressive career and an even more storied teaching history after she retired. I had assumed she'd recognize my name, but was mentally hoping she wouldn't.

"Mrs. Martin, it's so nice to meet you. Thank you for letting me come in."

"Of course, darling. Come over here, let's chat for a minute."

I take a deep breath and follow her into an office.

Mrs. Martin jumps right into asking the hard questions. Not that I expected anything different—I've learned that high-level teachers don't like to waste time.

"So, tell me why you're here. Why do you want to join the school?"

I, on the other hand, hesitate before answering. "I want to dance again. I miss it. I don't… feel like myself without it."

She nods. "So even without ballet as a career, you want to dance?"

My answering nod is tiny.

"And where do you stand with your injury? Is it fully healed?"

Injury. Like it's singular. Like I didn't have a number of injuries over a number of years that eventually weakened my left leg so much that I couldn't dance to my full potential.

But I know which one she's asking about. The big one that got the ballet community's attention. The one that happened right as I reached my long-time dream of becoming a soloist in the greatest ballet company in the country, right after the best performance of my career. *That* injury.

I clear my throat. "My foot is healed. They had to operate after the last stress fracture, but I completed all the rehab and can use it to full capacity."

I don't say that the reason I'm here, and not in New York, is because I can keep up with *her* dancers and not the ones in New York. That because the training here isn't as rigorous, it reduces what used to be the likely probability of yet another injury.

"And you're ready to dance with my dancers? I know we're not at the level of the NYCB, but I still expect a certain level of effort and consistency."

"Of course," I hurry to assure her. "I would never put in less than you expect of your dancers. I can promise you that." When she stays silent and waits for me to continue, I add, "I don't think I want to perform in any showcases, but I want to train. Here. With your school. If you'll have me."

Mrs. Martin studies me for a moment. I think I'm half expecting her to tell me she can't bring me on, when she says, "We'd be honored to have you, of course. I hope you know that was never a question. I just wanted to make sure you were here for the right reasons."

I give her a tight smile. "I completely understand."

She lets out a sigh and seems to relax. "Look, Isabella, I know what it's like to retire from dancing. I didn't experience it the way you did, but I know what it's like to be done with dancing and lost about what to do next. Are you sure you want to be here? Are you sure you're not just here because you don't know what else to do?"

That makes me frown. And think. God knows I dissected every one of my thoughts and feelings with my therapist after the injury, so there shouldn't be anything new here. But Mrs. Martin's question does make me double-check my reasons.

"I *am* a dancer," I say slowly. Purposefully. "Regardless of everything, it's a core piece of who I am. I don't *want* to be without it. But…" I nibble on my lower lip in thought. "But I don't want to be *only* a dancer. I moved to Philly because I wanted to find out who *else* I am, that's true. But I'm not running away from it. I'm not using it as a crutch to avoid finding out who I really am. If that's what you're asking."

Mrs. Martin nods once, her eyes searching mine. "That's what I'm asking. I want you to *want* to be here, yes, but I also want to make sure being here is the right decision for you. But only you can decide that."

"I want to be here. I *want* to dance. For you," I tell her firmly.

"Then that's all I needed to hear."

Slowly, the tension ebbs from my shoulders. I manage a small smile as genuine happiness bubbles in my chest. At the prospect of dancing again.

"Do you have any interest in teaching?" Mrs. Martin asks. "We could use the help with the children's program. Or even the adults."

That question I wasn't prepared for.

I mull over the idea for a moment. It would be so easy to accept her offer. So easy to settle into the same job I've always had, the one I can do in my sleep with no stress or struggles or worries about the longevity. It would probably be the smart thing, the responsible thing, to say yes.

But… that's not why I'm here. At the school or in the city. I left New York because I wanted a change. I wanted to try new things, and find a new path. Settling into the same job would be easy, but it would be exactly that: settling.

Which is why I've already worked up the courage to arrange an interview as a beginner yoga teacher.

"Thank you for the offer," I begin carefully. "I'd be happy to step in occasionally, but finding a job in a different community is one of the ways I *am* trying to distance myself from dance. I'm… actually hoping I get a job offer at my interview this afternoon."

Her smile softens at my answer. "That's amazing, I hope you do get it." She stands from her seat, and I hurry to follow suit. "If anything changes, just know my offer will always stand. But for now—" She reaches out to shake my hand. "Welcome to the Philadelphia Ballet, Isabella."

I got it. I actually got it.

I'm still reeling from the fact when I reach my building's

front door. My hands are shaking with excitement as I dig out my keys, and I'm so lost in my own pride, my own happiness, that it takes me several tries to even get the key in the door. By the time I do that, I hear the loud roar of a motorcycle parking in front of the building, only feet from where I'm standing.

I look over my shoulder in curiosity and freeze in place when I see Kane, who's sitting on his motorcycle and tugging a helmet off his head.

And *God,* if I thought he was hot at the gym, all sweat-drenched and with his tattoos on display, it's nothing compared to the sight of him straddling a bike.

I turn to face him completely. "What are you doing here?" I find myself blurting, too overwhelmed by the sight of him to be smooth.

Wrong thing to say, apparently, because his expression darkens.

"What, you think this place is too *nice* for me even though it's a *slum* for you?" he sneers.

I can only blink in confusion.

"I—what?"

He dismounts and grabs a gym bag from where it's stashed in one of the compartments. "Let me guess, you want to tell me that I look out of place, right?" When I only frown, he shakes his head. "I live here. Don't look so shocked that we can afford the same apartment, princess."

My cheeks warm with embarrassment, but not because I didn't think Kane could afford to live here. More like, my subconscious immediately jumped to the thought that he was here to see *me.*

"I wasn't surprised because I didn't think you could live here," I say, hoping he'll believe me. "I just... didn't expect to run into you. Small world and all that."

He scoffs and grabs his motorcycle helmet in his other hand. "Sure, let's go with that excuse."

There's hostility in his tone, but I'm too caught up in the fact that Kane, the hottest guy I've ever seen, is my *neighbor*. That I'm going to be seeing him regularly, that I'll be able to talk to him without seeming like the new girl who stops and lingers at the gym for no reason—

My thought process is cut off when Kane climbs the steps and stops in front of me, too close to be polite, his eyes flashing with something I'm too inexperienced to recognize, but too desperate to not get turned on by. His focus drops to my lips, only for a split second, but he seems to get angry with himself for even that. Locking eyes with mine, he says, "Tell me I'm wrong, princess."

I don't bother to correct him, since it's clear he's somehow already made up his mind about this. Instead, I ask, "Are you nervous for your fight on Friday?" I don't have to fake my concerned tone.

Kane jerks back as if slapped. His eyes are wide, the surprise clear on his face.

"I don't know how you do it," I ramble on. "I'd be so scared to do what you do. Do you get hurt when you fight? I'm assuming they have medics there in case something—"

He turns away from me, frustration emanating like waves from his tense body. It doesn't occur to me until later that he's unlocking the apartment door right next to mine.

I hurry to get my last words out. "If we're neighbors, then you should know if you ever need anything, I'm in apartment 2B—"

Kane slams the door in my face.

THE CLUB HAS already been open for hours by the time I get to work. When I walk inside, the music is blaring, and the strobe lights are everywhere. The usual aroma of perfume immediately invades my nostrils, just as it always does. I can make out one girl dancing on the pole in the center of the club.

I stride toward the couch room in the back, only taking the time to nod to Joe in the DJ booth on my way over. A silent greeting is the extent of my friendship with any of my coworkers, and even that's just because Joe and I agree on not wanting to be buddy-buddy with anyone we work with. We both just want to do our jobs and get a paycheck.

Not that I hate working here. Bouncing is an easy job for me most days, and with Joe playing a lot of the songs I like, it's a pretty laidback gig. I basically just listen to music and make sure no one gets fresh with the girls. If they do, I get to throw a few punches and manhandle a few drunks. And get paid to do it.

"It's pretty slow back here right now, but it should pick up soon," Marcus, the guy I'm taking over for, says as he stands from his place behind the monitors. "Indy and Natasha are coming in soon, so you know they're going to take over all the dances. Crystal is already pissed that she has to share a shift with them again."

I'm shaking my head as I slide my leather jacket off my shoulders. The girls are nice enough, and almost all of them tip me at the end of their shifts, but the catfights are my least favorite part of the job.

"I'll keep an eye out for her," I tell Marcus as I take my seat behind the high top.

He nods and starts to walk off. But then he remembers something and spins back around. "Oh, and just a heads up: there's a weird guy who's been on the floor for a while. I can't get a read on him, though."

"Weird, how?"

He scratches his chin as he answers. "I don't know. Not weird as in awkward, just weird as in *I don't know why he's here.* He's gotten a few dances from the girls, but he mostly just seems to want to talk to every dancer in here. Hasn't touched a drink, though, and I don't think he's on drugs. It's just weird because I can't figure out what he wants. Doesn't seem like the typical lonely guy who just wants company, because he's young and good-looking."

I look at the screen in front of me. It takes me three seconds to identify the people I've never seen before, and another two to spot the guy we're talking about.

"Black suit guy with his shirt unbuttoned down to his chest?"

Marcus nods. "Stands out like a sore thumb."

"I'll keep an eye on him. Can you tell Bobby on your way up front? He's manager tonight."

Another nod. "Sure thing. Good luck, man."

I don't bother responding to that. And Marcus doesn't expect me to. It's been six months of working here, and by now, everyone knows to only talk to me about work—anything else typically doesn't get an answer.

I settle into my shift, alternating between watching the monitors that cover the couch rooms, and taking money off the lonely bastards who look to a lap dance for some female affection.

It starts slow, but like Marcus predicted, it picks up as soon as a few more dancers start their shifts. Before long, all four rooms are filled, and my attention stays locked on the girls I'm responsible for.

"Crystal, get your hand out of his pants," I call out in a hard voice.

I see her pout on the screen in front of me. "I wasn't doing anything!" she protests.

"Crystal, I can *see* you. Keep his fucking clothes on."

Her pout stays glued to her face for the rest of the dance, but at least her hand stays off his zipper.

The couch rooms are steadily busy for the next few hours. My attention stays glued to the cameras covering the private dances, which means I haven't been able to look at the club floor. I wanted to have a better read on the weirdo in black by the time I switched to working security out there, but unfortunately, that's not how things happen.

Regardless, my focus zeroes in on him the second I take

up my place as the floater bouncer on the floor. There are the usual drunks and too-touchy assholes, but this guy is the one I'm watching.

Marcus was right, he talks to every girl who'll give him the time of day. He talks a mile a minute and looks at them almost expectantly at the end of his sermon, and every time, the girls give a polite smile and extricate themselves.

It occurs to me after a few minutes that he looks like he's trying to sell something. I don't know if it's a physical something or some kind of idea, but his physical mannerisms reek of used car salesman.

As soon as I make the observation, I see his face light up when the new girl in his lap eagerly nods at whatever he's saying.

My hackles are up even before I see him reach into his pocket. By the time he slides whatever's in his hand into the front of the girl's thong bottoms, I'm seeing red.

Flashes of images assault me before I can calm myself down. *Little bags of white powder in my mom's hand. Loud music and bottles of alcohol littered all over the living room. The massive beating that always came the day after.*

I'm striding across the room before I even realize I'm moving.

Gripping the guy by the shoulder, I jerk him off the chair and dump him on to the floor. I don't bother responding to the yelp the girl lets out as she tumbles off his lap and tries to right herself.

"What the *fuck*, dude?" the guy yells, hurrying back to his feet.

"What did you give her?" I roar, shoving him in the chest. "*What did you give her?*"

"Jesus, man, relax," he says, holding his hands up in surrender. "She just wanted to take the edge off a little."

I turn back to the new girl, taking in her blown-out pupils and the pounding pulse in her neck.

I couldn't stop myself from punching the guy in the face even if I wanted to. Even if I took a second to try to calm down, even if there was someone screaming at me to stop, I've never been able to control myself when it comes to my triggers. The memories don't allow it.

I'm cocking my fist back for a second punch, already knowing what the crunch of cartilage is going to feel like under my knuckles, when I feel myself pulled away from where black suit is stumbling into the chair I pulled him out of. I know it has to be one of the other bouncers, because they're the only guys strong enough to separate me from a guy giving drugs to a woman.

"Kane, man, *stop*," someone yells. "The cops are already on their way. He's going to press charges if you keep going."

"Fucking *let him*," I snarl, a burst of energy making me try again to break free of the bouncer's grip. "I'll kill him before they get here."

"Kane, *enough*," another voice barks. "What the *fuck*, man. I can't keep covering for you with this shit."

I feel powerless, unable to stop the violent urges from taking over, even as I hate myself for it in the same breath.

My boss lets out a frustrated exhale. "If you stop now, I can say it was his fault. But I can't protect you if you keep going."

"Hey!" the guy protests, clutching his bleeding nose. "*He* attacked *me!* How am I the one at fault here?"

"Shut up," the owner of the club and the bouncer still holding on to me snap in unison. My feelings about drugs might be extreme, but we all hate the random drug dealers that come in here just to make trouble.

Slowly, reluctantly, I come out of the haze I fell into so quickly. I shake Marcus's grip off me and turn to the dancer who was in the middle of all of this.

"Give it to me," I order.

She looks scared, like she's been forced down from whatever high she was riding before I rushed in here. But when I gesture impatiently with my hand, the look changes to pleading. Like she really doesn't want to part with the drugs.

"You don't need it," I tell her in a rare spout of words. "It's just an illusion; it doesn't change anything. *You don't need it.*"

I don't know if it's the words or the probably insane expression on my face, but she pulls the baggie of white powder out of her thong and places it in my waiting hand. I close my fingers around it and feel my chest loosen immediately.

Two uniformed officers pick that moment to walk onto the floor. I think I come down from an adrenaline high myself, because I don't remember much of the next few hours. I know the club empties as soon as the cops show up, and I know they talk to everyone involved about what happened. Looking back, the owner must have smoothed things over somehow, because I was barely questioned about anything.

All I know is everything happened around last call anyway, so it's 4 a.m. by the time everyone but the manager and I empty out of the club. Since I'm security on closing shift, I have to wait for the manager to count the cash before I can leave. And *of course*, on this night from hell, I get stuck with the one guy that has to recount everything six times. It's almost 6 a.m. by the time we're locking the doors behind us.

I have to fight to stay awake on the ride home. Between the late hour and the adrenaline dump, I almost ride into a ditch one or three times, before finally pulling up in front of my apartment building.

And yet, the second I walk into my apartment, I'm wide awake. I decide to make myself a bowl of cereal before forcing myself to lie down and at least attempt to get a few hours of sleep.

I've just barely slipped into unconsciousness when I hear a knock on my door.

My eyes snap open. *Who the fuck is that?*

I debate not opening it. But curiosity—and the knowledge that now I'm never going to get to sleep—have me getting up and walking to the front door. When I pull it open, my bright-eyed and bushy-tailed neighbor—Isabella, I heard her tell Jax and Hailey at the gym—is standing in front of me.

I hate the way my body instantly reacts to her. It doesn't matter that it's six in the morning and she's bare-faced and sleepy-looking, because all I can think of when I open the door is that she looks adorable.

That word shouldn't even be in my *vocabulary*.

"Hey, neighbor," she chirps, a sweet smile on her face. "I'm sorry to knock so early, but I heard you walking around, so I figured it was safe."

Adorable, but still irritating.

I don't respond. I just stare at her.

Her smile loses a little bit of its confidence. "Umm, I'm sorry to knock so early, or to knock at all, really, but I needed a favor, and I heard you up and walking around. I swear, these walls are paper-thin." She forces a laugh, sounding a little unsure of herself now. She opens her mouth to ramble some more, but finally seems to get a good look at me.

I'm sure I look like a mess right now. My hair is completely disheveled, my eyes are probably bloodshot from the long night, and I'm glaring at her with all the disbelief and annoyance that one expression can pack. Honestly, I'm surprised she's still standing on my doorstep.

But she's still brave enough to ask with a furrowed brow, "Did you… just get home?"

My disbelief grows by another mile. "How the fuck would that be any of your business?"

She has the good grace to blush. "You're right, that was rude. It's not my business at all, I'm sorry…" She trails off as I continue to stare at her. With a rough swallow, she works up the nerve to say what she came here to say.

"I was just coming over to see if you have any sugar I could borrow. I bought everything on my grocery list *except* for the one thing that I need for my coffee to turn me into a functioning human being in the morning." She lets out another nervous giggle, then glances up at me from under her eyelashes, waiting for my response.

I blink at her. Then…

"Are you fucking for real right now?"

Her blush deepens, but she's still not screaming and running away with her tail tucked between her legs. She must realize there isn't a chance in hell this conversation is going to get any better, so finally, fucking *finally*, she backs off.

"You know what, I'll just go buy some. Don't worry about it."

"I wasn't going to *worry* about it," I sneer.

I expect her to become flustered, but instead, she seems to hit a wall with her endless politeness. Apparently, the princess has a limit to how much of my attitude she'll put up with. She arches a perfectly plucked eyebrow and gives me a disapproving look. The words that come out of her mouth are prim and proper, but they come out an obvious bite. "Of course. Sorry to bother you so early. Have a good rest of your day."

She spins around and disappears into her own apartment. And I'm left with the scent of her floral shampoo and the sight of her ridiculously cute pajamas with bunnies on the butt.

I never end up falling back asleep.

CHAPTER 6
Isabella

On Friday night, I'm walking into a crowded arena with Hailey. The building is on fire with energy, the sounds of the crowd a dull roar, even though there isn't a fight going on right now. As a fighter makes a big entrance through smoke and lights, I hear a chant start on the other side of the building, rising in volume until I can't hear Hailey calling for me to follow her.

I wait patiently as she greets everyone in the section, where the rest of her gym is already congregated. I smile politely and wave at a few people, but for the most part, I'm too overwhelmed to take my attention off of everything going on around me. It's so *loud*, so different from the elegant setting of a theater on the night of a ballet performance. Both types of crowds might be readying for a show, but this one is not shying away from expressing their emotions during it.

It's never been more obvious that I am out of place here. And although I'm incredibly proud of the fact that I stepped out of my comfort zone, I'm still vibrating with nerves from standing in a foreign setting.

"So, how well do you know the guy fighting tonight?" I ask Hailey in an attempt to distract myself.

"Not very well," she answers. "Kane's new to the gym, so it's his first fight under the Bulldog MMA name. We'll see how he does. Jax says he's a bit of a loose cannon at the gym."

I hesitate, but I'm too curious to stop myself from asking another question. "So, what's his story? Why's he so… intense?"

Hailey snorts. "Intense is a tame way of putting it." She sighs before continuing. "To be honest, no one really knows. Jax said he just showed up at the gym one day a few months ago. Told Coach he was new to this part of Philly and looking for a local MMA gym. Didn't look at the prices, didn't ask about classes or Coach's pedigree, just asked if they're taking on MMA fighters and whether or not we had some big guys for him to work with. Took one look at Jax working out with Tristan, handed over a wad of cash, and asked where he needed to sign. He's barely said ten words since then."

I hear the concern in her voice. "Sounds like there might be some bad blood there now."

She sighs again, this one heavier than the last. "Not necessarily *bad* blood, but…" She straightens and turns to me. "Look, I know I told you the other day that fighters aren't just people looking for violence, but Kane… Kane seems to be the exception. He doesn't approach fighting the same way the other guys do. He doesn't care about taking the technique classes, or about getting better at the sport. Every time I see him working out, honest to God it feels like he's just looking for an excuse to punch someone."

That makes me frown. Not that I have a lot of experience

with physical fights—in *or* out of the cage—but I doubt someone would be looking to hurt other people for *no* reason.

I turn toward the fight currently going on in front of us. At some point, it went to the mat, so now one guy is on top of the other and raining down punches on his opponent's face. There's blood everywhere. And a few seconds later, the fight finally ends when the ref pulls a snarling and bloody victor off his opponent.

"They all have to like *some* violence," I comment. "You can't fault Kane for a quality they all need in order to get in that cage in the first place."

"That's true," Hailey says with a thoughtful nod.

We're silent as the ref raises the victor's hand, and during his interview. But when the cage clears out and the lights dim, a heavy metal song starting to blare through the speakers, I see Hailey start to squeeze her fingers together.

"Kane's next," she says in a tight voice.

Sure enough, Kane bursts through the smoke-filled entrance and runs down the pathway to the cage. He looks just as intimidating as he did that day I saw him in the gym, with his eyebrows pulled down into a scowl and his body vibrating with energy that just screams *I want to kill you.*

And that's even before he rips his shirt off and tries to push past the ref to get into the cage.

I suck in a breath at the sight of his sweaty, tattoo-covered body. A bolt of heat flashes through my body at the same time that my lungs demand more oxygen. There are no words for a man that looks like this.

The ref slows him down enough to do what seems to be

a pre-fight check, and then Kane is rushing past him and jumping up into the cage. And the entire time his opponent from the red corner makes his own entrance—a wildly different entrance from Kane, with the fighter smiling and bobbing his head to his own walkout song—Kane is pacing on his side of the cage, never stopping his movements and never taking his hard stare off his opponent.

It's mesmerizing.

"I really hope he listens to Coach," I hear Hailey murmur. "Everyone's pretty nervous he won't."

I manage to tear my gaze away from Kane to look at the guys standing on the other side of the cage behind their fighter. I recognize the guy who welcomed me into the gym, but not the older man next to him.

"The older guy is the head coach? You just call him Coach?"

Hailey lets out a shaky laugh. "Yeah. A lot of people don't even know his real name is Dominic. Everyone just knows him as Coach."

"Hmm. And what's the other guy's name?"

"Tristan. He's second-in-command at the gym. He's the best guy there—he fights in the UFC, the biggest MMA organization in the world—and he's the main coach after... well, after Coach."

I nod in understanding. "And your boyfriend, does he coach?"

I catch the wince on Hailey's face. "He does. He's retired from fighting, so he does a lot more of it nowadays. Normally, he'd be in there next to Coach—Tristan's pretty busy with training since he got into the UFC—but Jax and Kane don't exactly get along."

I let out a huff of laughter. "I thought you said there's no bad blood there."

Hailey echoes my laugh. "Something tells me Kane has bad blood with a lot of people." She pauses, then adds, "He broke Jax's nose during a warmup a few weeks ago. Since then, those two don't really train together."

To me that just sounds like part of the sport, but I don't say that out loud.

I have a million more questions about the gym—and about the man still pacing in the cage—but I don't get the chance to ask them, because the ref pulls the two fighters to the center of the mat. He says something to them, and Kane's opponent reaches his gloves out for a fist bump.

Kane doesn't move to return the gesture. He just backs up to the cage.

"God," I hear Hailey mutter. "This isn't going to be pretty."

"*FIGHT!*" the ref screams.

Kane rushes forward the second the bell rings. He doesn't settle into a rhythm the way other fighters seemed to do in the previous fights, he just… lays into his opponent.

"Settle into it, Kane, you don't have to throw everything at once!" I hear his coach yell from the corner.

Kane either doesn't hear or doesn't care.

He continues to swing wildly. After about fifteen seconds of this, his opponent, Red, seems to be done with playing defense. Still appearing calm, he starts to throw back at Kane.

His combos are different than Kane's. Where Kane seems to only want to throw punches, Red is throwing a variety of weapons. He throws kicks, knees, elbows... he's not just aiming for his opponent's face.

A few kicks aimed at Kane's leg manage to land. Red starts to time it so that when Kane steps forward, he smashes his shin into his thigh.

I wince because it looks like it would be painful, but Kane just hardens his jaw and pushes forward. It looks more like he's annoyed by a gnat than being beat in a fist fight.

"Kane, we have to defend those," his coach yells. "Remember, we're not just throwing hands."

Once again, Kane either doesn't hear or doesn't care. He goes right back to throwing big, wild punches.

I glance to his corner to see Tristan's head drop between his shoulders, his chest constricting with a heavy sigh.

My gaze darts back to Kane just in time to see his opponent land a punch to the body. Immediately, the crowd lets out a gasp, then a loud cheer. Dread coils in my gut.

And then he gets hit with another one. And this one's *hard*.

Kane stumbles back from the force of it, curling over his stomach. His face twists into a wince.

I gasp and clasp my hands together in front of my mouth. Fear churns inside me, and I want to look away, but I *can't*. My attention is glued to Kane as he struggles to stay upright, as his corner starts screaming for him to put his hands up because his opponent is about to charge. And I hope, more than I've ever hoped for anything in my life, that Kane doesn't get any more hurt.

But amid my fear, and as victory lights in Red's eyes, something seems to snap in Kane. It's like a switch has been flipped. His eyes blaze with rage and murder and hate and he bites down on his mouthpiece as he pushes forward to meet his opponent's attack. He starts to throw wild, crazy punches, blatantly ignoring his corner's instructions to tighten up and be smart about his attack.

Smart or not, it doesn't take long for one of Kane's shots to land flush.

The punch causes Red to wobble, and a dazed expression appears on his face.

A look of raw triumph flashes across Kane's.

The arena is *exploding* with cheers as Kane continues to pummel his disoriented opponent, but both Hailey and I— along with Kane's two cornermen—are too shocked to make even a single sound. We just watch as Kane lands one punch after the other.

It looks more like a bar brawl than an athletic sporting event.

Every shot affects Red more and more, his hands dropping lower with each one, but the last one knocks him out cold. He slumps to his knees as the lights go out in his eyes.

I breathe a sigh of relief that the fight is over, but apparently… it's not. Because Kane jumps on his unconscious opponent and drops all his weight into the punch he rains down on his face. Not once, but twice.

The referee is quick to step in and pull Kane off the stiff-as-a-board fighter. Thankfully, Kane goes easily.

"Oh my God," I breathe.

Hailey winces and hurries to tell me, "That's not as bad as it looks, I swear. Technically, they tell you to fight until the ref pulls you off your opponent. It's totally legal."

But that's not what prompted my comment. I've *never* seen this kind of savagery before, nothing even close to it, and I know I should absolutely be horrified by what I just witnessed.

And yet, all I feel is relief and pride that Kane came out the victor.

I watch as he strolls back to his corner to get some water from his coach. And if I thought a victory would change Kane's expression, would make him look any less angry at the world, that assumption is squashed with one glance at the big fighter.

He looks exactly the same as he did at the start of the fight. Scowling face, sweat-drenched, with his muscles vibrating with the promise of pain. He looks like he could—or *wants* to—go another few rounds with someone.

"Jesus, he's hot," I breathe.

"What'd you say?" Hailey asks.

I feel a blush heat my face at my blurted confession. "Nothing."

I pull my stare away from the cage and turn to her, just in time to see her gaze dart anxiously toward the back entrance.

"I told Jax I'd grab something from Tristan after Kane's fight," she says, and in her defense, she looks guilty. "Are you okay here for a few minutes while I run back there?"

I wave her off. "I'm fine. Go do what you need to do."

I only expect Hailey to be gone a few minutes, but fifteen minutes later, I'm still standing by myself, having watched the next two fighters make their way into the cage and who are now waiting for their fight to start.

But when the bell rings and the first shot lands, I feel a

massive presence take up space beside me.

I know who it is without even looking at him. I know because the thrill that runs through me is unlike anything I've ever felt before.

"Congrats on the win," I tell Kane in a genuine, though slightly nervous tone. It's not that I'm afraid of him after his fight, it's just that this schoolgirl crush is putting me completely out of my element, and I'm not really sure what to say to him right now.

He doesn't respond. The only reason I know he heard me is because I see him barely turn his head in my direction.

"Are you happy with how it went?" I ask, feeling like that might be a dumb question. But I think I'm a little too desperate to engage with him, especially after our last two conversations.

This time I get an eye roll, but still no words. Until he asks, "Why are you here?"

I suck in a breath at the sound of his voice, so gravelly that I feel it scrape over my bones in a shiver. It takes me a second to process his question.

"Same reason everyone else is," I answer breathily. "I just wanted to watch the fights."

He still hasn't really turned to look at me. But I see him scoff, right before he says, "Doesn't really seem like your scene, princess."

I look down at my outfit, taking in the sleek white pants and tan long-sleeved top that I decided to pair with simple black sandals for tonight. Then I look around myself, at the sea of leather and black that I'm surrounded by.

"I guess I do stand out a little," I say with a chuckle. "I wasn't sure what to wear. I've never been to one of these before."

"Obviously," he drawls, his attention still focused on the fight in front of us.

I readjust my purse strap in an attempt not to fidget. "Your fight was awesome," I blurt out.

That finally gets his attention. Turning toward me, he gives me a mean smile. "Did the blood turn you on, rich girl?"

I don't know how to answer that. My heart's beating too hard to let me, anyway.

Kane gives me a once-over, and sneers when he meets my eyes again. "Have you ever even seen a fight? Or has your life been so privileged that you *fight your battles with words?*" His tone is mocking when he says the last part.

I swallow the lump in my throat at the accusation. It would've been obvious to me even without seeing his fighting style that Kane has lived a hard life. No one is this closed off to the world, this angry at it, without a reason.

I don't know what that reason is, but my heart aches for Kane because of it.

"I've never seen any fights," I confirm with a shake of my head. "But the physicality of it is impressive, and I'm sure it takes a lot of skill to do what you—"

He cuts me off with a scoff and turns his attention forward again.

I'm fidgeting now, lost as to how I should navigate his hostility. It's obvious that Kane wants to be left alone—now and always—but with every look his way, the caretaker in me is bursting at the seams trying to get out. I can't *not* glance at Kane's bruised knuckles and ask, "Do you see a doctor after you fight? For your injuries?"

Kane barks out a cruel laugh. "A doctor? For *this?*"

My brow furrows in confusion. "Well, I'm sure the injury to your hand is normal, but you have a cut on your face. Don't you need stitches or something?"

He turns to me with a grin that is a little manic and a lot complicated.

"You have no idea, do you?"

I quirk an eyebrow. "About when I need stitches after I've been punched in the face? No, I don't. But let's not act like I don't know injuries. Your bloody bruises might come from fists and show on your face, but mine come from doing spins eight hours a day and show on my feet."

He takes his time tracking his gaze down my body, clearly taking in my athletic figure. I know he heard Hailey call me a dancer at the gym last week, so it's obvious that there are judgmental thoughts about ballet rolling around in his head right now.

After what feels like forever—and during which I never once allow myself to look away from his ogling—he turns his attention forward again.

"Sure, princess," he drawls. "Your sport is as physically grueling as mine."

I face forward with a sigh. "Are all fighters this stubborn?

You might have a few less scars if you weren't too proud to ask for help."

The air around us stills. Kane was quiet before, but the quiet that settles between us now is different. It's stifling in its enormity.

Eventually, I feel him turn away from me.

"No, I wouldn't," he says as he walks away.

I'M BACK IN the gym two days later.

When I walk through the front doors, Coach doesn't seem even a little bit surprised to see me. Even taking a weekend off from the physical activity was hard, but—and I'll never tell Isabella this—I did have to fix the cut I got. I didn't go to the hospital, but I did end up using the topical skin glue that I haven't had to purchase since I was a teenager.

"No sparring for one week," is all Coach says when he sees me. I grind my teeth in frustration, but I also know I have no grounds for argument. Instead, I force myself over to the heavy bag for some work.

By the time I get the go ahead to start sparring again, I'm walking around with fury in my heart and vengeance in my brain.

Coach calls for me halfway through my warmup. I've beaten the bag into a different shape, my shirt already drenched through with sweat.

"Kane, now that you've warmed up, you'll start with a shark tank in the cage," Coach calls from the other side of the gym. "You'll get a fresh new opponent every minute."

Despite it being the most hated drill because it's the most tiring, I don't even think to question the instruction. I just jump in the cage.

My first minute goes fine: they give me one of the newer pro fighters, someone who does well in his division but who's never been tested. But then the bell rings and my second fighter comes in.

It's a pretty back and forth round between Jax and I. We both land some hard shots, and we're both breathing heavily by the time the bell rings. Jax doesn't reach for a fist bump at the end of it, and I don't offer one.

Minute number three is against Tristan. I hold his stare until the bell rings, refusing to admit to myself that I have no shot at winning this round. I know exactly who Tristan West is, and I know how good he is at fighting; I know I'd win a fight to the death, but I also know that his skill got him into the UFC for a reason.

The bell rings and we trade a few punches, but it doesn't escape my notice that he's very obviously playing with me. His expression is lazy, and his combinations are simple, which means he doesn't think of me as much of an opponent.

That thought is enough to make me see red.

A furious growl vibrates through my chest as I dart forward with a vicious combination. He deflects the jab, barely slips the cross, but when I throw the left hook, the only defense he has is to cover the side of his head and take the shot.

Unfortunately, when I throw the punch, I extend my arm way too far and land it on an awkward angle. The second it hits,

I feel the muscle twinge in my shoulder.

I pull it back immediately, flattening the wince that wants to show on my face at the pain radiating up my arm.

"Kane, what's up with your shoulder?" I hear Coach yell from the outside of the cage.

"Nothing," I say through gritted teeth. "I'm fine. Keep going."

For the rest of the minute, I push myself through the motions. Even though my shoulder is on fire, I bite down on my mouthpiece and force myself to finish the round. Stopping any training exercise because you're in a little bit of pain is pussy shit, and I don't live by that—I work through anything that doesn't put me in the ground because that's what I have to do.

I barely make it through the round with Tristan. When the bell rings, I internally breathe a sigh of relief that the next guy is an amateur, and that he's too invested in technique to care about fights of will. I somehow overpower him even with an arm that feels like it's about to burn off my body.

"Kane, you're doing another round," Coach barks after the round ends.

I grind my jaw and nod stiffly.

Round One, I get Aiden. Easy money.

Round Two, Jax again. I barely survive his annoyance, but I make it.

Round Three, Tristan.

I don't make it out of that round.

Tristan smells my injury—as well as my refusal to acknowledge it—as soon as the bell rings. I know in the first ten seconds that I'm not going to survive the round.

"Kane, why the fuck aren't you throwing your left hook?" Coach's voice *reeks* of impatience.

"I'm trying to throw more right hands," I growl.

"Bullshit," he snaps. "You're ignoring your left arm. Why?" Before I can make up a lie, he's striding into the cage and grabbing my left elbow.

I manage to keep from shouting, but I can't swallow the pain-drenched groan that the touch forces out of me.

"That's what I thought," he says. "Why wouldn't you tell me you pulled the muscle?"

"I'm fine," I bite out, trying not to black out from the fiery pain shooting into my shoulder.

Coach shakes his head, disapproval emanating from his body.

"You're done," he says as he steps out of the cage. "Take a few days off to rest the shoulder. I don't want to see you back in here until you can throw a left hook without wincing."

"A few *days?*" I parrot incredulously, my voice rising. "I can't stay away that long, I'll go crazy." Imagining the tension that always seeps into my body if I go more than two days without punching something is enough to make my stomach roil. Even staying away from sparring for a few days was torture this week.

"Just let me take tomorrow off," I rush to argue. "And then when I come back, I'll just work my southpaw stance, no left hands. I'll let the arm rest."

"No. No sparring," he says without hesitation. "I can't keep you from working out, but stay out of this gym."

"Coach," I try, desperation bleeding into my tone that I'm not used to hearing.

He opens his mouth—likely to bark another *no*, if the expression on his face is anything to go by—but something in my voice makes him pause. His gaze drops to my shoulder where I'm subconsciously rubbing the sore muscle. I drop my hand as soon as I realize what I'm doing.

"Take tomorrow off," he says after a moment, and I immediately deflate in relief.

Except, he's not done.

"If you take tomorrow off, you can come back to the gym the day after, *on one condition*." He gives me a hard stare to emphasize his next words. "You sign up for a yoga class."

It takes a second for his words to register. "I… what?"

"Yoga," he repeats. "I want you to sign up. One class a week. You work out too much and you never stretch, which is why you're susceptible to these kinds of injuries. Yoga will help with that, and hopefully calm you down a bit, too. If you go for six weeks, I'll get you that matchup against Chevlin that you've been asking for."

"Wait, are you serious? You'd give me Chevlin?"

"*If* you do this, and *if* it works the way I think it will. Then yes, I'll set it up."

Fuck.

The idea of taking a yoga class makes my skin crawl, but I can't deny that this is a good deal. I've been begging Coach for that matchup since I showed up here. Stretching out on a mat once a week is a decent trade for the opportunity to pummel a shitty ex-teammate into the ground.

"Fine," I choke out. "I'll sign up tomorrow. So I'll be in here on Thursday."

He gives me a hard nod. "Fine. Now get out of here. Ice the shoulder, and *no punching anything*. Or any*one*."

I barely contain the offended growl that wants to tear out of me that he's treating me like this. Like a *child*. Just because I'm not a fucking pussy and crying to him about an injury.

I'm too angry to even say goodbye to anyone as I storm out. Not that I do normally, but I feel especially pissed at my "teammates" when there's pain radiating in my body and frustration welling in my heart.

I drink myself into a stupor that night.

If I can't work out tomorrow, I might as well enjoy the only vice I inherited from my mother.

It takes me less time than usual to get to the no-pain point—which I'm especially thankful for tonight, because my shoulder has really been killing me all day—and then the blackout point hits not long after that. When I wake up the next morning, it's with zero memories and the mother of all hangovers.

Having passed out on the couch, I push myself into a sitting position, immediately remembering yesterday's events when a searing pain shoots up my shoulder. I collapse back on to the cushions with a groan.

When I manage to push myself up with my other arm, I notice my laptop on the floor beside me. I try to remember why I was on it last night, but come up blank when my head starts to pound with every one of my heartbeats. I drag the piece of technology onto my lap with another groan.

As soon as the screen lights up, last night comes rushing back: *fucking yoga in Philadelphia.* That's the last search on my screen.

There are more studios than I thought there would be, which makes me grimace and quickly mark the one that's closest to me. What do I care if it's actually a good spot? I'm only doing this because Coach told me to. Might as well just pick the one that's first on the list.

I fill out the 'Contact Me' form and within a few hours, I'm confirmed for a spot in the beginner class this afternoon.

Fucking wonderful.

I kill time with some video games, but before I know it, I'm changing into workout clothes and packing up work clothes for my shift at the strip club afterward. It's a ten minute ride to the studio.

I don't even have to guess what my face looks like walking into the building—the reactions of the people I pass tell me exactly what I look like. Either their eyes widen, or they catch a glimpse of me and immediately jump back to create space between us. The reactions aren't uncommon in general, but in a place like this? I stick out like a sore thumb.

"Hi, can I help you?"

I turn to the chick sitting behind the desk and say gruffly, "Yeah, I signed up for the intro class today."

She smiles and moves her focus from my stiff posture to the computer screen in front of her. "Kane Whitaker?"

I don't have it in me to respond anymore. I am *thisclose* to walking out of this place as it is—screw Chevlin, I'm going to fight *Coach* for this.

I nod.

"You're right on time. Go ahead in, there are cubbies for your bag and extra mats if you need to borrow one for today. Your instructor should already be in there."

Another nod. Then I'm striding past more wide-eyed girls and walking into the yoga room.

Only to come face to face with Isabella.

"Fuck," I breathe.

I THINK A full minute passes before Kane snaps out of our weird, shocked haze first. "You've got to be shitting me," he says. "You go here?"

I start to fidget, my nerves over teaching only my second class immediately increasing.

Nodding, I mumble, "I'm teaching this class." I force a small smile, but that doesn't seem to help, because Kane's face tightens with visible frustration in response. I'd even say there's a little embarrassment if I thought the man was capable of it.

"Are you… taking the class?" I ask hesitantly. Not that yogis have a type, but Kane is the last person I expected to show up in my beginner yoga class.

"Why the fuck else would I be here?" he snaps back at me.

Before I can answer, I hear giggles on the other side of the room. Giggles clearly aimed at Kane.

His hands squeeze into fists, and yes, that's definitely embarrassment on his face.

Before I can think better of it, my head whips around to send the laughing girls a hard look. I don't say anything, and I'm not exactly glaring, but even still, it's probably not appropriate behavior as a teacher. And yet, I can't help my sudden need to protect *Kane*.

When I turn back to him, his expression has shifted. His brow is furrowed and he's looking at me like he's trying—and failing—to figure me out.

I take a deep breath to center myself before turning to the rest of the students around the room. "Alright, let's start to settle and get ready for class. Everyone set your mat down—or grab one from the back if you don't have one—and be ready to start in two minutes."

I try to keep my focus on the class as a whole, but my gaze keeps drifting back to Kane. I watch as he begrudgingly walks to the back of the room and grabs one of the extra mats. Clearly, he's not here because he wants to be, but whatever the reason for his attendance, it's important enough that he's forcing himself through the motions. I can admire that, and make a mental promise to myself to make sure he has a good class.

"Inhale deeply during these poses. Remember, we're grounding our body and using our breaths to do it. Focus on good breathing." My words are officially for the class, but they're directed toward Kane. Kane, who hasn't changed his breathing since we started, and who is clearly half-assing the movement of raising his hands on the inhale and lowering them on his exhale. He just looks like a grumpy bear waving his hands around for help.

"Take a big deep breath as you raise your hands up," I say quietly, trying to use my soothing yoga-voice to calm him.

"Expand your chest on the inhale, empty completely on the exhale. Breathe."

He must sense that my instructions are aimed toward him because I hear him grumble, "I know how to fucking breathe." And if I can hear it from all the way at the front of the room, then I can guarantee that everyone else in class heard it, too.

There are more collective giggles around the room, which only makes Kane's discomfort grow. I'm trying to figure out how to calm the class down, but before I can say anything, Kane seems to focus on his breathing. A moment later, I see his chest expand with a deep inhale.

I move class along to sun salutations, combining our breathing exercises with stretching. Kane still looks annoyed, but at least he's continuing to take deep breaths as he moves through the stretches. I'm able to focus on the other students, and manage to bring the aura of the class back to peaceful and welcoming.

Before long, I start in on our standing poses. This is usually where students start to fumble a bit and lose their serenity, so I work hard to keep them focused and positive. After working them through the three Warrior poses, I move into tree pose, and then begin my lap around the room to each of the students.

I chance a quick peek at Kane at the back of class. I know enough about martial arts to know that balance and flexibility are both important in the sport, and yet what I've seen of Kane's training so far doesn't make me think he cares as much about them as he should.

Sure enough, Kane's scowl has deepened as I've quietly assisted some of the other students. He's holding the one-legged pose, but barely—he's wobbling in place, looking seconds away from putting his foot down so he doesn't fall on his face. Taking a deep breath, I make my way over to him.

When he sees me coming, that frown becomes impossibly deeper. His leg drops at the same time that his hands do, until he's standing before me in a normal stance, his hands clenching into fists.

"Go again," I tell him softly.

For a moment, I think he's going to refuse and storm out, but then his jaw clenches and he lifts his foot again and places it on the inside of his thigh. He's steady enough to bring his hands together in front of him, but then he begins wobbling again.

I debate walking behind him to steady him the way I normally do with students, but something tells me Kane wouldn't appreciate having someone where he can't see them. So instead of gently clasping his hips from the back, I merely take a step into Kane's space and place my hands on him from the front.

His eyes widen a fraction of an inch. I only catch it because I'm so close to him. But when he doesn't drop the stance, doesn't move away from me, I'm emboldened enough to continue with my instruction.

"Try to keep your weight over your hips," I tell him quietly. "Your hips are the center of your body, so they naturally want to course-correct any balance issues. Just keep the weight of your upper body over your hips, and your standing foot centered."

Gently, so gently, I adjust his hips where they need to be. And as soon as he's centered, his wobbling stops.

"That's it," I whisper, a pleased smile coming unwittingly to my face. But when I glance up to look into Kane's, the smile disappears with a startled inhale.

Despite his height, his face is inches from mine. And he's staring at me with an expression that's clearly frustrated, a little bit curious, and a whole lot intense.

It gives me a chance to study him for a moment. His face is… a sad face. His lips are turned down in a permanent scowl, and I think I see an old scar on his forehead near his hairline. But that's not what sends ice through my veins.

He has no smile lines. None.

Not only is the skin around his eyes smooth, the wrinkles that should be starting to show around his mouth are turned down, in the opposite direction of where they should be going.

If Kane's seen any happiness in his life, there isn't a hint of it on his face.

A thud in the background suddenly jerks my attention away from Kane. My hands drop from his hips as I turn around, and I focus in on the embarrassed student who just lost her pose.

I try to swallow down the buzz of adrenaline that comes from being so close to Kane. "Alright, let's switch to our seated poses now," I call shakily, making my way back to the front of the classroom. "It's time to cool down our bodies. Have a seat on your mat and let's start with stretching into our pigeon pose."

Taking a seat on my own mat, I lead the class through the start of the cooldown. This is my favorite part of class, because it becomes evident how much more loose and comfortable students are since the beginning stretching poses. The aura of the classroom feels quiet, and peaceful, and it solidifies in my mind that I've made a difference in these people's days. That I've sent them home with a little less anxiety, and a little more peace, than what they came in with.

A sense of pride spreads through my chest. Pride for myself, that I made someone's day better in a way that has nothing to do with how well I can spin on the tips of my toes.

"When you're ready, let's finish with savasana," I call quietly after a few minutes. I wait for everyone to settle back into a cross-legged pose before saying, "Bring your hands together at your heart, lower your head to your heart, and acknowledge yourself for showing up to your mat today. Namaste."

The murmured response of *namaste* rings around the class, and then the sounds of everyone grabbing their waters and rolling up their mats can be heard around the room.

It takes me a minute to work up the courage to look toward Kane, to maybe even approach him and ask how he liked the class, but by the time I look up, he's gone.

It's Thursday night and I'm sitting on my couch, bored out of my mind and absentmindedly scrolling on my phone. I knew moving to a new city would come with its share of loneliness, but the extent of it still feels a little shocking. Going from a life where I'm constantly surrounded by teachers, a support system, and competitors everywhere, to living by myself and only having a single friend, is going to take some getting used to.

Yet with timing only the universe is capable of, my phone lights up with a text message.

HAILEY

Hey. Are you busy tonight?

ISABELLA

Not even a little. What's up?

HAILEY

I was thinking of getting a drink. Wanna come out with me?

My response is instant.

ISABELLA

Just tell me where and I'm there :)

Less than an hour later, I'm walking into a crowded bar. It only takes me a few seconds to spot Hailey at one of the high tops.

I smile and give her a wave, which she returns.

"I'm glad you decided to join me," she says when I've reached her. "I was going crazy spending another night at home in an empty house."

"Boo not home this week?" I ask.

"He's at a work conference," she explains, taking a sip of her Corona. She gestures at the bar. "What do you want? I've got first round."

I eye the bar nervously, looking for any kind of menu. I can probably count on one hand the number of times I've been to a bar, since drinking isn't high on the priority list of a professional dancer, which means I have no idea what to order. Eventually I answer with, "I'll just have what you're having."

Oblivious to my inner turmoil, Hailey nods and gestures at the waitress that's walking around taking orders.

"So how are you settling in?" she asks once she turns her attention back to me.

I let out a heavy breath. "Good, I guess. It's a lot. As embarrassing as it is to say, I've never lived on my own, so pretty much everything is new."

"That's not embarrassing. It took me forever to step out on my own. Everyone has their own path."

I give Hailey a grateful smile. "Don't get me wrong, I'm obviously incredibly thankful for my parents, but growing up with the lifestyle that I did left me slightly unprepared for the real world. I did the *dishes* for the first time in my life this week."

"Okay, yeah, that I can't relate to," Hailey mumbles. I let out a laugh at that.

When the waitress slides my drink in front of me, Hailey extends her beer toward me for a cheers.

"What are we celebrating?" I ask.

She pinches her lips thoughtfully for a moment, then says, "To not having to do dishes for over two decades, but to successfully figuring out how to do them anyway. Most husbands couldn't say the same."

My laugh is loud, and happy. Clinking my glass against hers, I take a sip of my first beer.

"Oh my God," I splutter once the liquid has gone down my throat. "That's not just beer, is it? What's *in* this?"

Hailey's grin is devilish. "That would be tequila."

I gape at her. "People mix liquor and beer?"

"Not usually," she says with a cackle. "But it's my personal favorite drink and I had a theory that you'd never had anything but wine before."

"Busted," I murmur, cautiously taking another sip. The second one isn't so bad—definitely less tequila in that one.

"So after up and moving to a new city on your own, you've found an apartment, signed up for a new hobby, and made a friend. I'd say you're off to a good start."

I twirl the beer bottle on the table in front of me. Hesitantly,

I voice the words I haven't actually said out loud yet.

"I actually got a job, too. I started teaching beginner yoga this week."

Hailey's jaw drops and her eyes go wide. "You just *got a job?* Why did we cheers to dishes if we could've been celebrating *that?*"

I shrug awkwardly.

"Well, now we *do* need to celebrate," Hailey says, stopping the waitress when she passes by us. "Can we get two shots of tequila please? With lime?"

"What?" I yelp. "I can't do a shot! I just had liquor for the first time in my life."

Hailey gives me a knowing look. "Are you telling me the whole reason you moved to Philly *isn't* because you wanted to try new things?"

I let out a sigh. "Touché."

Hailey grins in victory. Then something occurs to her, because her lips drop into a frown. "That timing is weird, though. Jax just told me Coach had Kane start doing yoga as a punishment. How insane would it be if he walked into one of your classes one day?"

Welp, that explains things.

Before I have to admit that that's already happened, the waitress appears with our shots.

"Okay, so we'll do a shooter and make it a legit first shot," Hailey explains, demonstrating as she talks. "Lick the salt, take the shot, and then bite the lime. Ready?"

I follow her lead and then take a second to steel myself. "Ready."

"Then cheers to getting a new job and being a total badass in a brand-new city."

Lick. Shot. Lime.

I don't know if it's her toast, or the bitter taste of tequila that has warmth spreading through my chest, but Hailey's doubled over laughing at my expression by the time I'm biting into the lime. "It's so bad the first time, there's no way to prepare you," she says apologetically.

"*Why* does anyone ever drink straight liquor?" I cough. "That was *awful*."

She shrugs. "It hits faster. You'll feel the buzz in a few minutes."

Just then, a guy walks up to our high top. He's young, and clearly dressed for an office job with his navy suit and styled hair. And with his button-up shirt rolled up to his elbows and a beer in his hand, he's casual enough to be extremely attractive.

He's wearing a flirtatious but genuine smile when he asks, "What are we celebrating, ladies? Can I buy the next round?"

Hailey shoots me a quick glance before responding for us. "We're good for right now, but thank you."

He nods, smile still comfortably in place. "Can I ask what we're celebrating anyway?"

I hesitate before deciding to answer. "I got a new job this week."

The guy's eyes light up with real happiness. "Congratulations! What's the job?"

"Yoga teacher," I answer with a proud smile.

His eyes dart the length of my body, so quick I almost don't notice it, before he says, "That's really cool. Seriously, congrats."

"Thank you."

He pauses to weigh my interest, but after a moment, decides to keep pushing the conversation, his attention now solely focused on me. I see Hailey bite off a smirk out of the corner of my eye.

"So yoga, huh?" he asks, leaning one forearm on the table in that typical casually attractive pose that men like. "That's sexy. How'd you get into that?"

I bite my lower lip in thought, then promptly take another sip of my drink. I'm very much *not* looking for a boyfriend right now, or even a hookup, so I need to tread carefully—especially because my experience with interested men is fairly limited, since for a lot of years I barely had enough time to sleep, let alone date. I did have a boyfriend for my first year at the NYC Ballet, but even that was only possible because he was a fellow dancer. And the only reason it started was because I was a nineteen-year-old girl that was curious about relationships.

I'm flying a little blind as far as expectations, but I'm not so naive that I don't realize my natural politeness might be interpreted as flirting back.

I decide on a neutral, "It was just something I picked up as a random hobby that happened to stick."

He doesn't seem deterred. "And yet you became good enough that it's now your job. That's impressive. I've always wanted to try a hot yoga class."

My smile becomes a little bit forced. "You should."

But before I need to start gently cutting the conversation off, I spot someone in my peripheral. I turn my attention in that direction and sure enough, Kane is standing at the bar.

He's already looking at me when my gaze settles on him. He's leaning against the bar top with a glass of clear liquid in his hand, looking just as hard as he always does. And with dark washed jeans and a tight black T-shirt that puts a lot of his ink on display, the combination is making him look ridiculously hot.

He lifts his glass to his lips to take a sip, his eyes never leaving mine. It isn't until he lowers the glass and sends the guy in front of me a judgmental look that our eye contact breaks. His lip visibly curls in disgust.

I raise an eyebrow at the look. Then, deciding to call him out on it, I call out, "Hey, Kane. Want to join us?"

There's a flash of surprise on his face, then he's back to looking like he just sucked down a glass of vinegar. Almost immediately, he turns his back on me to face the bar.

"Who is that?" the guy at our table asks. Both he and Hailey have turned to see what's caught my attention.

I take a sip of my beer, realizing the tequila buzz is starting to hit me. My skin feels warm, and I think I feel a little fearless.

"My neighbor," I respond.

That catches Hailey's attention. Her head snaps toward me and her mouth pops open. But before she can question me about it, her phone rings in her hand.

She glances at the screen before giving me a guilty look. "It's my sister," she says by way of explanation. "I'm sorry, I have to take this. I've been playing phone tag with her about something all day today." She glances at the guy at our table before meeting my eyes again. "You okay?"

I wave her off. "Go. I'm fine here."

She nods and answers the call, already walking out of the bar.

I turn back to the guy, fully intending to ditch him for Kane, but I'm saved from having to think up a polite excuse when his friends take that moment to wave him back to their group.

The guy gives them a nod before turning back to me. His look is hopeful, and even with my limited experience, I can guess what he's about to say.

"Want to join our group? It's my boy's birthday so I don't want to ditch him, but I'd like to keep talking to you, maybe buy you a drink when you're ready. Your friend is obviously welcome to join us, too," he hurries to add.

I give him a polite smile. "Not tonight, but thank you. I'm just going to hang out with my friend."

He nods, as if he already expected the answer. "Alright, well it was nice meeting you. Have a good rest of your night."

"You too," I say with another smile.

Once he walks off and I'm left by myself, my attention immediately travels back to Kane. He's turned around again, and he's giving me the same hard look he was before.

Just like at the gym the first time we met, I don't back down from that gaze.

In fact, I decide to call him out on the *don't touch me* vibes that he's radiating right now. Striding across the floor, I stand in at the bar right beside him and down the rest of my beer, surprised to realize it was so easy to drink.

"Another one?" the bartender asks before I've even put the

empty bottle down.

"Umm, actually I'd like to try something different," I answer, squinting at the rows of alcohol behind him. "Can you make me a tequila mixed drink?"

"Sure. Like a tequila sunrise?"

"That's fine."

"What kind of tequila do you want?"

"Umm, regular?"

I see his lip twitch with a smile at the same time that I hear a harsh bark of laughter beside me. I ignore Kane, willing my cheeks not to heat.

"I'll give you house, sweetheart," the bartender says, taking pity on me. I give him a grateful smile.

I choose to ignore the crack from Kane. Instead, I wait silently as the bartender prepares my drink. When he slides it in front of me, I take a sip and let out a pleased hum.

"Thank you," I tell him, sliding my card across the bar. "It's really good."

He winks, then moves away. Finally, I turn my head to give Kane my attention.

"So," I start casually. "How long is your coach punishing you with my yoga class?"

His eyebrows shoot up for a split second before he returns to his flat stare. He doesn't answer, which I expected. Instead, he asks, "So little Richie Rich is your type? I bet Mommy and Daddy would be thrilled. Could you be any more of a stereotypical rich girl?"

I cock my head and study him for a moment. It's so glaringly obvious that Kane's hostility is a defense mechanism that it doesn't really bother me anymore, even though it should be hurtful. Instead, I say evenly, "It's called being social, Kane. You should try it sometime."

He gestures around him. "I'm here, aren't I? I'm doing the same thing you are."

"Yeah, except you're glaring daggers at anyone that even *thinks* about approaching you. No one is going to want to talk to you that way. Don't you ever look for some female company?"

The look he gives me is heated to a thousand degrees. I swallow roughly, but I can't bring myself to look away from where he refuses to drop my gaze. *When did he get closer?*

After what feels like an eternity, he actually answers. "Don't worry, princess," he rumbles. "If I have female company, you'll know."

I hold his stare and, without missing a beat, I say, "You know, princess just makes it sound like you're flirting." Lowering my voice, I add in an almost-whisper, "Are you flirting with me, Kane?"

That's twice now I've surprised him. But then he's frowning as he studies me. When he speaks, his voice is careful. "Fine. Isabella."

I let a smile slowly stretch across my face, feeling entirely too pleased with myself.

"Look who cares enough to know my name," I purr.

His frown turns into a full-blown glare at that. But he's saved from having to reach for an answer he obviously doesn't have when there's some kind of commotion behind us.

Kane's eyes dart over my shoulder, and before I can compose myself enough to turn to look, several things happen at once.

There's a loud shout from someone.

A crash as someone hits the ground.

The colorful cursing of the bartender as he waves security over.

But I don't see any of that. Because all I see is Kane.

The second the shout sounds, the only thing I can focus on is Kane curling an arm around my waist and spinning me to his other side. My back presses against the bar top, and Kane presses against… me.

I gasp at the sudden change in position. With Kane's arm holding me tight against his body, we're flush against each other from chest to thighs. I swear I can even feel his heartbeat against mine.

But it's not just his rock-hard body pressed against me that has me unable to breathe. It's also the way he's looking at me.

Despite our close moment at the yoga studio, this is the first time I get a good look at his eyes. They're brown, which is why they didn't particularly stand out before, but now that he's mere inches away from my face, I can see the flecks of gold flashing like lightning around his pupils. And with his gaze now focused only on me, I can't help but wonder if that's a good descriptor of Kane as a person: shrouded by darkness at first glance, but with so much fiery light hidden beneath the surface.

I try to speak the words thank you. I can't remember for what, or how we got here, but it's so ingrained in me to show appreciation that I will my mouth to form the words.

Except, the second my lips move, and Kane's focus drops to them, I forget everything I wanted to say.

Kane doesn't seem to have that problem. It takes him a moment to tear his gaze from my mouth, but eventually he says in that deliciously deep voice, "You should pay more attention, *Isabella*. We wouldn't want you to get hurt."

And at the reminder of our conversation from only a minute ago, the haze clears from my head. I go to push on his chest to put some space between us, but immediately realize that my hands are already clutching his arms. I swallow roughly and push him away, forcing myself not to admire the feel of his rock-hard arms. He goes easily.

"Thank you," I tell him. "For… pulling me out of the way."

I can't decipher the look he gives me. I watch as he reaches into his pocket and pulls out a wad of cash, then steps past me to drop some bills on the bar.

He pauses beside me. Then his lips are at my ear, just barely brushing the skin as he whispers, "And for the record, you knew my name first, princess."

And then he's gone, leaving me with no breath and a rapidly beating heart.

I'm on edge when I step out of my apartment the next morning. More on edge than usual. Not because I have to work a double shift at the strip club today, or because my shoulder still hurts like a bitch from the bad shot I threw in training this week.

I'm in a bad mood because I can't get my new neighbor out of my fucking head.

Last night after the bar, I showered and changed instead of just passing out like I usually do, all because I still had her intoxicating scent in my nose. I scrubbed my chest because I could still feel her perfect tits pressed against me, and I brushed my teeth twice because I could already taste what it would be like to bite into that deliciously plump bottom lip of hers.

And yet, the thing that I *really* can't get out of my mind, even twelve hours later, is that she said *thank you*.

I'm an asshole. Certifiably. It's been a very long time since I've wanted to give a shit about anybody, which means there is no reason not to blunt my responses. Not only is it easier to say what I really mean, but it also keeps a very welcome wall between me and the rest of the world. Usually, it only takes a single conversation to get people to wise up to my disinterest and convince them I'm not worth the attention. Then I can be back in my own head and free of everyone else's bullshit.

Apparently, that doesn't apply to Isabella.

Because no matter how many times I push her, mock her, try to put distance between us… she pushes back. And somehow, she's doing it with a smile on her face.

It's infuriating and confusing all in one go.

I can't for the life of me figure out why she would care enough to even give me the time of day. I've offered her nothing, yet she keeps coming back.

Maybe she just wants a ride on the wild side.

Plenty of good girls have made it obvious to me that they just want a dirty fuck before they go back to their perfect lives, and normally I have no problem giving them just that. But that doesn't feel like the game Isabella's playing.

And *that* thought has me grinding my teeth so hard I expect them to crack.

Memories start to flood back from last night of her body pressed against mine. As much as I don't want to admit she's attractive, I can't deny that a) I'd be lying to myself, because b) my body definitely reacted to her last night. I had to angle my body in a way that she couldn't feel how hard she made me with her flirting. Though in hindsight, maybe I should've turned the heat all the way on and scared her off once and for all.

My mind drifts to what that would feel like. Thoughts of Isabella underneath me, moaning and begging for more, have my cock instantly turning to stone again.

Yeah, that would definitely scare her off.

And because the universe is hilarious, it chooses that moment to make Isabella appear before me.

I stop in my tracks on the sidewalk and glare through the laundromat window at the object of my annoyance. She's loading the last of her clothes into the washing machine, then squinting at all the knobs and buttons. She bites her lip after a moment, which I've noticed she does when she's thinking hard about something.

It just makes me want to bite her myself.

I watch as she pulls out the laundry detergent she brought, and slowly pours it into the tiny drawer at the top of the machine. She looks over the knobs again, clearly trying to figure out the right settings, and then she presses Start.

It's obvious she's never had to wash her own laundry before, but it's also obvious based on the clothes she wears and car she drives that even on her own, she's rich enough to have someone do them for her.

I remember the first time I did my own laundry. I was eight, and my mom was on such a bad bender that the idea of house chores never even entered her mind. So, I had to figure it out myself. It took me four tries to get the right settings, but eventually I walked out of the basement with clean, somewhat dry clothes. I was so proud of myself, I don't even remember the end of Mom's bender that week.

The memory, combined with the sight of Isabella going through the same experience—albeit for different reasons, thank God—has a bubble of admiration growing in my chest. She doesn't *need* to fumble her way through this, yet she's doing it anyway. Because she *wants* to learn.

She might not be the spoiled little rich girl I thought she was.

The annoyance from this morning wars with these feelings of admiration. I don't *want* to feel any of this. This girl should be an afterthought when I leave my apartment in the morning and pass by her front door. She shouldn't be present enough in my life to evoke any feeling, even something as mediocre as annoyance. And she *definitely* shouldn't be making me feel something as warm and fuzzy as admiration. Even the idea of that…

I feel the concoction of confusing emotions start to bubble in my stomach. I'm unsettled and growing angrier because of it, and I have no idea what to do with myself. I don't need or want this shit, and I want her *out* of my head.

And when Isabella spots me through the window and automatically smiles at me, I feel the implosion as it happens.

Ripping the door to the laundromat open, I stride over to where she's standing in front of the washing machine. She watches me as I move, her smile slowly slipping off her face. This isn't my usual avoidance of her, this is me *hunting* her.

She opens her mouth to say something, but it snaps shut when I stop in front of her—because I'm *way* too close. There's barely any space between us, and she has to look up to see my hard gaze.

She wants to keep pushing back? Keep appearing in my life despite the very obvious message that I want to be left alone? Fine, I'll give her the time of day. I'll give her my *attention*.

"Princess," I purr, feeling some of the roiling emotions inside me settle a bit when her expression turns into a familiar mask of nerves. "Funny seeing you here. Especially since we have a laundry room in the basement of our building."

Her cheeks pinken with embarrassment. *Good.*

"So how'd your night go?" I ask casually.

But she sees through my act, because her brow furrows at the unassuming question. And yet, she can't not answer. "It was fine."

I cock my head. "Richie Rich didn't please you enough?"

Her eyes go wide and her mouth pops open. I don't blame her. I'm completely in her space and her business right now, and I'm not pulling any punches.

"I didn't go *home* with him!" she protests. "How dare you imply—"

"I figured it wasn't your best night, because I didn't hear any sounds through our shared wall," I interrupt, as if she hasn't spoken.

"You were listening for it?" she asks, the disbelief evident in her tone.

I shrug, feigning nonchalance. "I had a bet going with myself. But I thought he'd at least make you moan a *little*."

She glares at me, annoyed despite the topic being hypothetical. She opens her mouth to snap back with something, but I don't give her the chance. I'm too eager to push her past any line she has, and finally break this thing between us that's fucking me up.

I crowd her back against the running washer with my body, so close to her now that I can plant my hands next to her head. But I'm not actually touching her.

Until I slide one thigh between her legs.

She gasps the second she feels it.

The sound makes me grin. "See? That wasn't so hard."

I shift my thigh, just slightly, just to tease her a little. The warmth of her pussy on my thigh—even through the leggings she's wearing—momentarily distracts me with a bolt of lust, but I force myself to focus on her face. Her expression is still one of shock, but now I can feel her squirming on my thigh.

"Poor little rich boy, doesn't know how to make you come," I taunt. I drive my knee forward until it hits the washer. Until I'm so close to her that I feel her tits brush against me on her every breath, and I can see just how wide her pupils have blown. When she bites down on her bottom lip, I'm so close that I could probably bite it myself if I ducked down just a little bit.

"I bet you could come just like this," I continue to taunt, my voice getting quieter with every inch that disappears between us. "Couldn't you?"

She shakes her head quickly with jerky, desperate movements.

I lean forward and press my lips to her ear. "What a pretty little liar you are," I whisper.

Not being able to see her seems to help my control. With her pink lips and wide-eyed innocence, coupled with the way she was looking up at me, she had me almost ready to groan and admit that I'm just as affected by this game. I wasn't expecting her essence to hit me this fucking hard.

But I'm determined to make her crack. To either admit that the reason she won't leave me alone is because she wants a ride on the wild side, or to scare her away *with* the idea of taking a ride on the wild side. Ten minutes ago I went into this hoping for option B, but right now I can't fucking remember why.

Because all I can think about is how sweet she'd feel taking my cock and screaming my name.

I'm so focused on getting a handle on my own urges that it takes me a second to clue into Isabella. It hits me that she's squirming on my leg and taking big gasping breaths. By the time I feel her hands scrabbling at my abs, I realize this has already gone way further than I ever intended.

I pull back to look down at Isabella, wide-eyed and slack jawed. And when her head drops back against the washer, her eyes closing and her hands fisting in my t-shirt as the sexiest fucking moan I've ever heard drips from her lips, all I can do is stare.

Stare and try to memorize the sight that is Isabella shuddering through her release.

I don't know if it takes seconds or minutes—I think I'm just as caught up in the orgasm as if *I* was the one coming. But eventually she sags against the machine, hands still gripping my shirt, and drops her forehead to the center of my chest.

In exhaustion? Embarrassment? Fuck, what the fuck do I do from here?

Before I can think better of it, I blurt out, "Did you just come?"

That seems to snap her out of the haze. She glances up at me, her cheeks reddening with embarrassment as she loosens her grip on my shirt.

"Your thigh was vibrating against the washer," she mumbles, so quietly I barely hear it. Then she's nudging me to back away from her.

I hurry to give her space. "Fuck, I didn't know. I didn't mean—" I swallow nervously, completely clueless about what else to say. I *never* wanted to push her that far.

And then I can only blink at her, still too stunned to do anything else. I'm waiting for her to yell, or slap me, or retaliate in any way that would be an entirely justified reaction to that kind of unwanted touch. It's exactly what I deserve.

And yet… she doesn't do any of that. She just looks down as she rights her sweatshirt and says, "You have *no* idea how annoying it is to know that you can do that without even trying."

I let out a bark of startled laughter.

Fuck, when was the last time someone made me laugh?

Isabella smiles, looking pleased with my reaction. Her cheeks are still pink, but she doesn't seem desperate to get away from me, or like she wants to punch me in the face. She just seems unsure of what to say.

Which, same.

"I'll leave you to it," I blurt awkwardly, and start to back away.

She seems amused by that but doesn't say anything.

So I turn and bolt.

IT TAKES ABOUT fifteen minutes for my day to go down the toilet.

First, the hot water heater is broken, which means a cold shower. Not the end of the world, because God knows as an athlete I've done plenty of cold plunges. But then I realize my coffee machine is broken. *That* is inexcusable.

I try to fix it but quickly realize I have zero handyman abilities. It doesn't help that a thought in the back of my head keeps nagging me, keeps reminding me that in New York, my reaction would've been *it doesn't matter, I'll just have the maid fix it today and have my driver stop for Starbucks on the way to the school.*

After a few minutes, I toss the screw in my hand on to the counter and make my breakfast instead.

I burn my eggs.

"I give up," I mutter angrily.

I manage to keep my sour mood to a minimum while I pack my clothes for the day and drive to the ballet school—stopping at Starbucks for a coffee and breakfast sandwich. I breathe a sigh of relief when I walk into the familiar environment.

Class is… effortless. When I tie my pointe shoes, I feel like I'm stepping into my own skin, and being the person I'm meant to be. All the stress from my move and my morning melts from my skin, and I feel excited to do what I've always felt I was meant to do.

I know my technique is exceptional today because Mrs. Martin gives me almost no critiques. The stiff-lipped old woman merely gives me a nod of approval.

Once class is over, I'm pulling on a few extra layers when I overhear some of the girls in the student program talking in a small group as they get ready for their class. I don't mean to listen, but my attention catches on their topic.

"I just wish I could *do* something," one of the young girls whines. "I've been killing myself with dance my whole life, done everything my teachers have said without question, and it *still* feels like it's not enough. I don't know what else to do. It's like your actual dance technique and style barely matters when you're trying to get into these big dance schools. But I *have* to get into that one. Everyone knows you can't get into the good companies later unless you went to one of their pre-approved schools."

"I'm sure you'll get a call back," another girl consoles. "You're the best dancer in this school, they'd be crazy not to give you an audition."

At that, one of the girls in the group shoots a glance my way. I duck my head to avoid her gaze.

I didn't exactly hide my dance status when I joined the Philly company. I was big enough that my name was recognized fairly often, so it didn't take long for whispers to spread that the girl who fell from grace with a horrific injury was now attending their school. But it wasn't a secret that pre-injury, I was better than every girl in here, with all the best connections.

Except, I had zero intention of flaunting any of that when I started here, since it felt like I had nothing to flaunt. I was just a washed-up dancer looking for a new place in the world.

But I know exactly what that glance means. And even though making friends feels a little foreign in this environment, what with dancers always competing with each other for a better spot, I make a split second decision to offer my help.

Straightening from where I've finished packing up my bag, I say loudly, "I can make a call, if you'd like."

The girl in question whips around to stare at me. "Are you serious?"

I nod. "I still have some contacts there. I can get you an audition."

Her eyes widen and her lips part in surprise. "Just like that? You can just *get* me an audition?"

I pause at her comment. I was just trying to make a nice gesture, show them I'm not here as competition—it didn't occur to me that I might be offering something that's unheard of for them.

I pick awkwardly at my sweater. "I mean, I graduated from there and was still visiting sometimes when… when everything happened. So I still have the contact information of the admission board." I force myself to stop fidgeting and give the girl a blank stare. "Do you want me to call them or not?"

An immediate blush heats her face. "Yes, please, that

would be great. Thank you so much, Isabella."

I nod. "You're welcome."

I can't get out of there fast enough. And it isn't until I get through lunch and walk into the yoga studio to teach my class that I realize why.

My boss Tanya is standing behind the reception desk when I walk in. She looks up and smiles when she sees me, but it doesn't quite reach her eyes.

"Hey," I greet her, adjusting my bag on my shoulder. "Everything okay?"

She nods, but it's stiff. "Yeah, everything's fine. I just wanted to talk to you about your paycheck onboarding. Did you log into that website I gave you and upload your financial information?"

For the second time today, I'm shuffling awkwardly.

"Umm, I did, but I didn't have some of the information on hand, so I couldn't submit it." I don't add that I'm waiting for my mom to provide the information.

Tanya gives me a hard look. "I need that filled out this week, Isabella. I can't pay you until that's in our system."

I give her an apologetic smile. "Of course, I understand. I'll get it done today."

She shoos me into the studio. Which is fine with me, because I feel the embarrassment coating my skin like oil.

I'm not used to having a job. And not because my parents have always paid for things, but because I've only ever been in schools and programs where I received a stipend to pay for my living expenses. I'm not used to actually working for a paycheck.

Which, at twenty-three years old, feels like an incredibly spoiled thing to say. Even though most of my peers in the company were the same way.

So Tanya pointing out that I don't even know how to set up my own direct deposit is yet another reminder that I haven't been living in the same world as everyone else. That I'm incompetent with basic things, and that I've only ever been good at one: dance.

Dance is… easy. It's the easiest thing I've ever done in my life. Not the performances, or the physical act of dancing—that's the hardest thing I've ever done—but *being* a dancer feels as easy and as natural as slipping on my pointe shoes. Doing everything in my power to move me even an inch closer to my goal of getting accepted to the New York City Ballet was obvious, and an easy choice. I never once felt like I was meant to do anything but dance.

So the fact that I don't know who to call for maintenance when my hot water doesn't work, and have no idea what my own social security number is in order to set up my job's financial onboarding…

Just emphasizes that the only thing I'm good at is dancing.

What am I even doing here? Why would I ever think I could do something that isn't *ballet? I should've just taken Mrs. Martin up on her offer of teaching at the school.*

I force those thoughts from my head as I walk into my classroom. Students are already chatting and warming up, and getting ready for class. It *should* make me feel better that a good number of women came to my class to learn from *me*, but with everything that's happened today, and all the annoying thoughts that have come with it, they're hardly helpful.

I don't even notice Kane walk into the room. It takes me getting halfway through the warmup to realize the enormous presence in the back is someone I know.

I haven't seen him since the laundromat "incident" a few days ago. Not that I've been chasing him down to try to talk about what happened, I just don't know if he's avoiding me, or if we just have opposite schedules—ever since I knocked on his door at 6 a.m. and discovered he was just getting home, I don't assume anything about his schedule. But I definitely didn't expect him to show up to my class again after how horrified he looked the other day at the laundromat. I thought for sure that was the end of his yoga practice, and that I'd only see him randomly in the building.

Seeing him again now makes a buzz of static energy run through me.

I have no idea what to do with Kane, so I put him out of my mind and focus on class. It only takes me a few minutes to settle into what I'm starting to feel is my teaching rhythm, and before long I'm completely in the zone.

Sixty minutes later, I end class with, "Namaste."

I hang out on the bench as everyone packs up and gets ready to leave. When there are only a few people lingering, I walk over to my bag to gather my own things.

It isn't until I've pulled my sweatshirt on, slung my yoga mat over my shoulder, and slid my phone in my pocket that I realize I'm missing my car keys.

I dig through my bag, unworried at the first pass, but my anxiety climbing by the second. By the third, I'm frantically ripping my bag apart, throwing water bottles and clothes and anything else in my bag all over the bench.

"Problem, princess?"

Tossing the wallet in my hand back into my bag, I straighten and plant my hands on my hips, a sulking expression etched on my face. "Of course not. Everything's just peachy."

A frown appears on Kane's face. He doesn't say anything, doesn't push me again to answer, but his hard stare is enough to tell me he's expecting something.

And for whatever reason, Kane standing there, patiently asking what's wrong—even though he's never given any indication that he would care—is enough to make the wall I've built around myself today crumble at my feet. My shoulders drop with a defeated breath.

"It's just been a bad day," I mumble. "It seems like everything is going wrong. And the cherry on top is that I can't find my keys. I have no idea what to do now." I shrug helplessly. "Guess I really am a princess."

And then, to my utter dismay, I start to tear up.

There's no way for Kane *not* to see it, so I don't bother to hide the way I wipe a single escaped tear from my cheek. I simply turn back to my bag and blindly start to rummage through it again.

"I don't know anyone who hasn't lost their keys at some point in their life," he murmurs.

Sniffing in answer, I chance a peek at him. *Is he trying to make me feel better right now?*

There's a pause, and I half expect him to realize his too-soft answer and immediately rush out of here. Instead, he says,

"Come on, I'll give you a ride on my way home."

"Why, so you can make me come on your lap again?"

It bursts out of me. I didn't even know that was a thought, let alone that I was going to say it out loud. Feeling my cheeks warm, I slowly lift my gaze to meet Kane's.

He's… *amused.* The corner of his lip is twitching with a smile, and his eyes are lit up with a twinkle.

"Is that the most vulgar thing you've ever said out loud?" he asks.

I straighten with a sigh. "Yes. And I don't like that you brought it out of me."

He huffs a laugh at that. I decide I *like* the sound of Kane's laugh.

When it's quiet again, I start to fidget with the bottom of my tank top. Eventually, I force myself to ask, "Are we going to talk about what happened?"

His stare heats to a thousand degrees. Just the sight of it has me growing damp between my legs, and suddenly I'm remembering the feel of him against me, his scent, his dirty words in my ear—

"No," he answers, interrupting my spiral of thoughts. "Not unless your answer is for me to leave you alone."

And then he waits. He waits for me to tell him off, to yell at him for touching me like that. He waits for me to say I didn't want it.

I don't tell him to leave me alone.

He studies me for a moment, then he nods. "Let's go then."

I rush to grab my bag because he's already pulling the door open and striding into the hallway.

And then I slam to a halt when I realize I completely forgot about Kane's mode of transportation.

"Um," I mumble when we reach the sidewalk. "I don't know if I can do this."

Kane just stares at me, like he has no idea why I'm freaking out. When I absolutely know he *does*, because I swear I can see a hint of a smirk on his mouth.

"What? It's transportation."

"It's a death trap on two wheels. Plus, I have a bag, and I don't have a helmet. So it's physically impossible for me to get on that thing."

Kane quirks an eyebrow and doesn't take his eyes off me as he opens a compartment on the back of the bike. He pulls out a helmet and gestures at the empty space he created.

Still, I fidget nervously. He waits patiently as I make up my mind, not rushing me as I look nervously around—expecting my keys to appear out of thin air?—but not quite managing to stop himself from saying with a teasing lilt, "Come on, princess, in the time it takes you to flag down a taxi, I could already have you home and sitting in a nice little lavender-scented bubble bath."

My eyes narrow at him. Finally, I hike my bag higher on my shoulder and grumble, "It's eucalyptus."

I don't get a reply, but I do catch his lip twitch with an almost-smile.

"Alright fine," I concede with a sigh. "But if I die, I'm dragging you to the hospital with me." Then I stuff my bag into the compartment and take the helmet from Kane's hands.

I pull it on my head and start to buckle the chin strap, but

I can't see what I'm doing, and I'm clearly fumbling it. It isn't until I let out a frustrated growl that Kane takes pity on me.

"Such a furious little ballerina," he murmurs, his lip curling into a smirk. He reaches to attach the strap for me.

I suck in a breath at his sudden closeness. His eyes are glued to my chin area as he works, which gives me free rein to let my gaze wander over his face.

The first time I saw him, I noticed his lack of smile lines. And I thought the absence of them was shocking. But now, looking at him when he has a smile on his face, I realize… *that's* what's shocking. Because Kane happy is a showstopper.

When he slots the buckle into place and lifts his eyes to meet mine, he must notice that he's showing me too much, because his expression immediately shutters into that familiar hard look. Then he's turning away to pull his own helmet on and climb on to the motorcycle.

Hesitantly, I brace a hand on his shoulder and ready myself to swing my leg over the back seat.

"So, this is just a spare helmet you carry around with you in case a damsel in distress needs a ride?" I ask unthinkingly, more focused on getting on the bike without tipping it over and making a fool of myself.

"You're pretty far from a damsel in distress, Isabella."

I smother a pleased smile at that, then work up my courage to push off the passenger foot pedal. A second later, I'm settled comfortably on the leather. "That hardly answered my question, Kane."

There's a pause before he replies.

"You're the first girl to ride bitch. Is that what you're

asking?"

I glare at the back of his head, even though the admission makes the butterflies in my stomach take off. "Has anyone ever told you that you're shockingly charming?"

He revs the engine. "It's practically my main descriptor."

I open my mouth to give him a *different* descriptor, but Kane revs the engine again and cuts off anything I want to say. I want to scold him for it, but suddenly, I'm more nervous about the fact that he's going to take off.

"Umm," I start, looking around my seat. "Where can I hold on? Is there an *oh shit* bar on this thing somewhere?"

I hear a soft chuckle in answer to my question, which is enough to snap my attention to the grizzly jerk currently holding my life in his hands.

"Sorry, princess, you're going to have to settle for my waist."

"Absolutely not," I splutter. "And if *that's* why you offered me a ride, then I might as well get off right now."

He shrugs, which draws my attention to his shoulders. "It's not, but suit yourself."

Slowly, hesitantly, I lift my hands to grip his shoulders. Shoulders are safe—there's nothing sexual about shoulders.

Except, when my palms slide over the rippling muscles and a shiver tears through me, that theory is soundly squashed.

And then Kane chooses that moment to shoot forward.

The force of it is so strong, and so sudden, that my body jerks backward before I can do anything. With a shriek, I dig my fingernails into Kane's shoulders and try with all my might to stay on.

Except, that was only a warning shot. Kane stops just

as quickly as he started, and the whiplash slides me forward and plasters me right up against his back. I don't question the instinct; I just scramble to wrap my arms tightly around his waist.

Kane's laugh is deep, and booming. The sound rings through my brain and fills my chest with warmth.

Of course, he has to ruin it as he starts to pull away from the curb—slower this time.

"Hang on and try not to come again."

CHAPTER 12
Kane

My ENTIRE SHIFT at the strip club, I can't get rid of the phantom feel of Isabella's arms around my waist.

It's fucking infuriating.

I know it was my idea, but I'm chalking that up to not being able to stand seeing her look like she's on the verge of tears. I have no experience with crying women—mostly because I never get close enough to them to experience it—but something about *Isabella* being upset hit me in the gut. I couldn't *not* offer the ride..

And yet, the second her arms wrapped around my waist, I couldn't get enough oxygen into my lungs. I thought her tentativeness was cute at first, and managed to laugh it off, but it took barely any time to slip into silence, just so I could focus on breathing through the feeling of her hands on my body. Because all I could think about was what they would feel like on my skin.

Part of me wonders if it's because I've never had a chick on my bike before. I know most guys get a motorcycle as a *way* to pick up women, but I've never wanted to be responsible for another person's life like that. I only got mine because bike rides were as close to therapy as I could get.

But the idea of leaving Isabella alone and upset in the yoga studio was worse than being careful on the bike for a short ride. At least if she's with me, I know *I* can protect her.

Unfortunately, that doesn't change the fact that I'm so annoyed with the direction of my obsessive thoughts, I have to go for a walk as soon as I get home, just to find a shred of peace. I drop my keys and bag off in my apartment, and then immediately take off down the street at a brisk pace.

I have no idea how long I walk for. Probably a while. I cycle through the memory of training this morning, and my shift at the club last night, but I'm constantly coming back to yoga today, and my ride around the city, and... Isabella. And every time my thoughts turn to her, I scowl to myself and walk another block.

I'm so lost in my thoughts that I almost don't pick up on the rustling sound in the alley I pass. But something about it catches my attention and makes me pause.

Frowning, I backtrack and peer into the alley. There's a dumpster halfway back, but other than that, I don't see anything. I take a hesitant step back in the direction I was heading.

Except, there it is again. The distinct rustling sound of trash bags.

Normally, I would assume it's someone homeless digging through the trash, but something is whispering in my subconscious to investigate further. Taking my knife out of my pocket and holding it firmly by my side, I take one, then two steps closer to the dumpster.

And that's when I hear it. A whining sound.

Fuck, that's not a human sound.

I rush the last few steps and throw the lid off the dumpster, then grab my phone so I can turn my flashlight on and shine it around the piles of trash.

There. I think that one moved.

I don't even hesitate. I vault over the metal side and land on top of a bag of something, and thankfully it's firm enough that I can keep my balance as I reach for the bag that's now very clearly wiggling.

It's bigger up-close than it looked at first. And when I pull it into my arms, it's definitely heavier than I thought it would be. Deciding that the easiest way to get it out of the dumpster is in the bag, I tighten my grip on the tied top of it and haul it over the side with me.

Landing in the dirt with a heavy thump, I gently place the bag on the ground, noticing for the first time that the bag stopped squirming as soon as I grabbed it. I hurry to untie the top, suddenly fearing the worst.

The dog lets out a single whimper when I free it from its prison. I back up to give it some space, knowing that a scared dog is very likely to bite.

But he doesn't snap at me. He barely even growls, he just… glares.

He's an adult dog, about fifty pounds, and his color is dark enough that it looks black in the night. He's obviously a pitbull, his skull and ears the typical pitbull shape. But none of that stands out to me.

He's missing one of his rear legs.

It doesn't seem to bother him, though. He's standing, looking perfectly balanced and comfortable in his own skin. And for several long moments, we just stare at each other.

Fuck. What do I do with a dog?

I could take him to the shelter. I know for a fact that Philly has one specifically for pitbulls.

But something in the back of my mind is telling me not to do that. At least not tonight. Because of all the strays that are probably dropped off at those places, I'm betting a dog missing a leg is going to be low on the adoptable list, and high on the euthanize one.

I take a tentative step toward the street. The dog still only stares at me, so I pat my leg and give a short whistle.

That makes his ears perk up. And when I take another step and give another whistle, the dog takes a tentative step of his own.

"Come on, boss, let's get you some food and water," I murmur in what I hope is a soothing voice. And either he recognizes the word food, or he senses I just want to help, because he takes a few more steps until he's standing beside me.

"Good boy," I breathe in relief. Deciding to push this a little further, I slowly extend my hand to let him sniff it. He does, although his demeanor is suspicious as he does it.

"Let's get you home and out of this shithole." And at the reminder that he was *literally left in a shithole*, my blood starts to boil in my veins.

I've seen a lot of fucked up shit in my life, and a lot of it has rolled off my shoulders, but animal abuse is something I won't fucking stand for. Lock me in a cage with the person who tied this creature into a tiny trash bag, and I guarantee they won't have a pulse by the time they're carried out.

I start to head in the direction of my apartment, suddenly thankful that it's only a short walk from here. He follows just behind me, and a few minutes later, we're climbing the steps to my second-floor apartment—missing leg be damned, because even that doesn't seem to bother this guy.

I immediately head to the kitchen for two bowls, and fill one with water while I look around for any food I could give him tonight. It's late, the pet stores all closed, so we'll just need to make do with what we have for right now.

Thankfully, I find half of a burger from my GrubHub order this week. I also throw in two hard-boiled eggs and voila, a meal for a dog.

He *scarfs* it down. I grit my teeth and force myself not to think about how long this poor dog has been starved to be eating like that.

While he's eating, I go in search of a blanket for him to sleep on. I set up a nice little nest for him in the bathroom, and by the time I walk back into the kitchen, he's devoured every scrap of food and has curled up in a ball on the carpet by the door.

I lure him into the bathroom with a piece of bacon, so that at the very least, I can wipe him down a little and check if there are any visible injuries or bugs on him. He holds still while I rub a damp towel over his fur, though he vibrates with nerves as I do it. Thankfully, though, I don't see any bugs or open wounds in his short fur—nothing beyond a few old scars that once again make me grind my jaw.

After I rub him down with a dry towel, he does settle on the blanket I set out for him, but when I go to close the door, he barks in panic and bolts past me back to the kitchen.

"Fuck," I mutter under my breath. *Guess we're giving the dog free roam of the house tonight.*

So instead of leading him into the bathroom again, I take the blanket and lay it out by the front door instead. It's not the worst thing in the world to have a scary dog like him be the first thing anyone sees, I'm just worried he's going to tear my house apart while I sleep.

But when I think of dropping him off at the shelter instead, the concern becomes nonexistent. I'd rather wake up to a torn-up couch than imagine him shaking in a crate at that place. Plus, it's not like there's anything valuable in my apartment— I'm too much of a minimalist and give too few shits for that.

"Alright, boss," I start, watching as he settles on the blanket. "Just… try not to do too much damage, alright? If you keep it clean, I'll get you a big breakfast tomorrow morning. Deal?"

When I only get a blank stare in response, I shake my head and turn to my own bedroom.

Guess we'll see.

Over the next few days, I go through all the steps you need to go through after rescuing a stray dog: I buy dog food, some treats, take him to the vet. He doesn't seem to have any interest in his dog bed or his toys, but I'm just glad he's eating. Also, that the vet gave him a clean bill of health after a round of vaccines and some heartworm medicine. And confirmed that his missing leg was a birth deformity, not an instance of animal abuse. Thank fucking God.

The only step I miss is actually taking him to a rescue shelter.

Because the more time I spend with him, the less I like the idea of giving him up.

We quickly settle into a new daily routine. My shifts at the strip club have me coming home in the middle of the night, but because I'm suddenly not dreading getting out of bed for another meaningless, repetitive day, I find myself starting my days earlier than usual.

I'm also having breakfast for the first time in my life that's not just coffee. I eat when the dog eats, and then we go for a long, lazy walk around the city. That's one thing I never really considered, that having a dog would get me more time to do one of the only things that clears my head. And with one long walk after breakfast and another between my training sessions and work shifts, we spend a lot of time exploring the city.

Plus, seeing the look of excitement on Oscar's face when I give him some chicken, or grab the leash to take him for a walk, gives *me* a burst of happiness.

It's on one of these before-work walks, when I'm thinking about how I'd like to introduce Oscar to a certain neighbor of mine, that I turn a corner and find none other than Isabella walking out of the corner store on our street.

She spots me at the same time, and we both freeze.

My mouth instantly dries at the sight of her. She's dressed

in tights, over-the-knee socks, shorts that are so small they can only be called boy shorts, and a baggy sweater to cover everything else up. It's all I can do not to gawk at her.

"Hey," she says with a smile as she steps out on to the sidewalk.

The smile immediately disarms me.

Fuck, how did that happen?

I'm so thrown off by the realization that I blurt out, "Why are you dressed like that?"

She looks amused as she gestures to her outfit. "Three guesses, Kane."

My eyes narrow. "Smartass," I mutter.

The corner of her lip twitches with a smirk, but it quickly spreads into a warm smile when her attention catches on the dog patiently sitting at my feet.

"Who's this?" she asks, and I'm glad to see she doesn't immediately approach a strange pitbull.

"He's a stray I just picked up," I answer.

"He's very handsome," she says, smile still in place. "Does he have a name?"

I hesitate before admitting, "I guess I've started calling him Oscar in my head." Isabella gives me a blank stare. "Like Oscar the Grouch," I explain. "Since I rescued him from a dumpster."

Her expression immediately shutters, and she looks at Oscar with sadness. "That's horrible. How could anyone be so cruel to an animal?"

She's visibly holding back from approaching him, though she can't seem to stop herself from dropping into a squat to be on Oscar's level. So I answer the question I know she's dying to ask. "I'd say you can pet him, but he doesn't seem to be great with strangers, so it's probably best if you stay—"

The words freeze in my throat when Oscar's ears swivel toward Isabella, and his tail starts wagging. I swear there's something like a pep in his step when he walks forward to greet her.

"Oh," she breathes in surprise. She extends her hand, her face lit up with happiness as Oscar first sniffs, then licks her. His tail wags even faster when she pets his head and scratches behind his ears. "You were saying?" she asks, giving me a smug smile.

My brow furrows as I stare down at the dog that has barked at no less than a dozen people since I found him. "Make a liar out of me, you little shit," I grumble.

And yet, I exhale a breath of relief over the exchange. Because as much as it makes me feel good that I seem to be the only person that Oscar tolerates, some part of me secretly likes that Isabella is also on that list.

She pets his head and scratches under his chin, and I'm shocked to see Oscar's eyes droop with pleasure. I'm distracted only by the sound of Isabella letting out a soft and delighted laugh at the sight.

After a few minutes, she visibly forces herself to pull away and stand up. She wipes her hands on her tights, uncaring about the dirt and dog drool now messing up her outfit.

I think I like her dirty.

"Alright, well, I'm heading home," she says, aiming a hesitant glance my way. "Are you just out walking him?"

I nod. "Yeah, but we've been out here for a while. He's

ready to go back." I frown when something occurs to me. "You walk around alone at night?"

"Sure. We're only two blocks away from the apartment building."

"Still a crime-filled city," I scold, the idea of Isabella walking around by herself at night in any city immediately making my skin itch. "Come on. We're walking that way anyway, we'll walk you home."

"Wha—? Wait, you don't have to do that," she stammers, but she trips after me to catch up as she says it. "Kane, I'm serious, that's not necessary—"

"Doesn't have to be necessary, I'm still doing it. Come on."

I hear her huff as she matches my stride. But she walks with me anyway, silent for the first few minutes.

She's too curious to let the silence stretch, though. No part of me is surprised when she blurts, "So when did you rescue Oscar?"

"About a week ago."

"Are you going to keep him?"

I let out a sigh. "I don't know. I really shouldn't. I don't have enough time for a dog, and I definitely don't have the right vehicle to transport him, so the right thing for both of us is probably to take him to a rescue shelter."

"So then why haven't you?"

I have no idea why I answer her. I've let plenty of her questions go unanswered, yet when I *do* indulge her curiosity, it just feels… safe.

"Dogs are the purest souls in the world," I muse. "They love despite everything, and all they want is for you to love them in return. It's hard to even stomach the thought of giving him away."

I look down to where Oscar is contentedly walking beside us. His gait is relaxed, his nose in the air, and he looks like there's no other place he'd rather be right now. My chest constricts at the thought of not having him around.

"Plus, with his deformity, there's a good chance he wouldn't be adopted out. The idea of him getting put down makes me slightly murderous."

Isabella's attention jerks down to Oscar at that. "His what? He's…?"

"The fact that you're not aware enough to notice my dog is missing a leg is making me feel better about the fact that I forced you to let me walk you home, princess," I say dryly.

Her gaze cuts to me with a glare. "Shut up, I was distracted by his cuteness." Then a sly smile tips her lips up. "*My* dog, huh?"

I frown when her point hits me, then cut a sharp look her way.

It doesn't even phase her. She lets out a low chuckle and turns her attention back to the sidewalk in front of us.

"So how many jobs *do* you have?" I ask, suddenly deciding that I don't want to be the only one answering probing questions. "Three dance schools and I'm assuming half a dozen jobs? You don't seem like the type that would be happy just sitting around."

"Just one job," she says with a laugh. She slants a sly look my way and adds, "My hands are full with telling grumpy men to breathe correctly."

I give her a scolding look, but that only seems to make her smile grow.

I hesitate to ask my next question, but it spills out of me anyway, remembering her conversation with her parents on the day she moved in. "What are you doing in Philly? You're new to the city, right?" But as soon as I voice it, I wince, worried my interest is too obvious.

My own concern disappears when I watch all the joy drop from Isabella's face.

I hate it. I hate myself for causing it.

But before I can backtrack, or cover it up, or say *something* to make it better, she's pulling in a shaky breath and answering my question.

"I got hurt... back in New York. It basically killed my ballet career overnight."

Her voice is full of sadness, of course, but there's also a coldness, like she's already accepted the fact and gone numb to it.

I know that numbness. I understand that numbness.

"I'm sorry to hear that," I tell her gruffly. Honestly.

She swallows roughly and nods. For a moment, I think that's going to be the end of our conversation, that we're going to finish the rest of the ten-minute walk in silence. But Isabella surprises me by continuing.

"My entire life has been about ballet. Every minute, every life decision, everything I've ever done or spent time on has been with the intent to get better at ballet. My parents sacrificed so much to get me the best of everything. They saw how much it meant to me to dance, so they rearranged their own lives to make my dream happen."

I hear a hitch in her voice, but I keep my eyes forward so she doesn't feel too uncomfortable to share whatever hard part comes next. Because I realize I really want to hear it. I want to hear about her life, and her passion, and what it's like to have parents that give a shit.

"In a way, my dream did actually come true," she says quietly. "I made it to the biggest ballet company in the country. And yet, one freak accident, one *singular* moment… and it was all gone. Just like that. Like none of it ever happened."

I don't know what that feels like. I don't even know what it's like to have *something*, let alone have everything and then lose it.

"So, a new city felt like the right move," she exhales in a rushed breath. "It's temporary as of right now, but I figured if I'm going to be starting over, I might as well do it in a new environment with new people." She glances sideways at me, and finally, she seems less tense. "Which is how I ended up with two jobs and thirteen hobbies," she jokes with a crooked smile.

I force a half-smile onto my own face, not wanting to kill her mood twice in two minutes.

"Personally, I could do without the job that has you yelling at me and bending me into positions no man should be in," I mutter.

I shouldn't be shocked by the sound of her laughter, but… I am. I can't remember the last time I made someone laugh. And the sound of *Isabella* doing it causes a warmth to blossom in my chest before I can tamp down on it.

"Don't you dare act like yoga hasn't completely benefited your fighting game," she says with a chuckle. "I bet your breathing has gotten better and the flexibility has helped your jiu-jitsu. Am I right?"

I don't bother giving her an answer, though she gives me a knowing grin anyway. I'm too busy quirking an eyebrow and asking, "Jiu-jitsu? Since when do you care about fighting enough to learn the terms?"

At that, the grin drops from her face and a blush lights it instead. She shrugs. "Hailey's always gushing about Jax and the gym, I guess I picked up a few phrases."

I quirk an eyebrow. "You sure it's not because you did a little research into the sport to see how yoga might be a benefit?"

Isabella turns her glare on me. "Absolutely not. Why would I care about that?"

I shrug and face forward, but there's a grin tugging at the edge of my lips.

She faces forward, as well. "I just figured I could stop your moaning if I showed you there's a benefit. Clearly I was right."

"Mhmm."

She lets out a huff. "What*ever.* I'll just stop caring about teaching you anything that might make it easier to twist people's arms behind their backs."

"Whatever you say, princess," I agree, finally letting my grin appear.

I can practically *see* the flames licking behind her eyes—she looks like she can't decide whether she wants to punch me or scold me for teasing her.

One of the options clearly wins out when she cocks her fist

back and playfully socks me in the shoulder.

It's so unexpected, I can't help it: I let out a loud bark of laughter, clutching the arm she just attacked.

Isabella looks like she wants to smile, too, but she startles and her gaze snaps to Oscar when he lets out a confused whine. "Sorry, buddy," she mutters, extending her hand to pet Oscar's head. "You know I wouldn't hurt your dad."

I'm still chuckling when Oscar, apparently contented with Isabella's apology, turns to me for confirmation.

"I'm good, boss," I tell him in as soothing a voice as I can muster. "Not thrilled about the fact that you didn't immediately jump to defend me, though. Is that the thanks I get for literally saving your life?"

When he gives me a look that can only be described as disbelieving, Isabella lets out a giggle. "He knows I'm right, that's why."

I turn my look on her.

Her laugh fades, though not completely. There's still an amused smile on her face.

Neither of us says a word when we reach our apartment building, or as we climb the steps to our floor. Our respective front doors are right beside each other, so when we finally stop in front of them, Isabella gestures to the door ahead of her. "Okay, this is me," she says awkwardly, her smile nervous.

I give her a gruff nod. She hesitates, looking like she wants to say something, but in the end, she heaves a sigh and drops to a squat so she can pet Oscar on his level.

"Goodbye, sweet boy," she coos. It takes her a while to pull herself away from where she's scratching behind his ear, smiling at the way his tongue lolls and his rear leg begins to thump. I don't mind waiting.

Eventually, she stands, once again looking nervous as she meets my gaze. "Thanks for walking me. I guess… I'll see you at yoga?"

I nod. I should turn away, should leave Isabella alone to her perfect life and go back to my own imperfect one, but something is keeping me in Isabella's orbit. I can't bring myself to leave it at that.

"Have a good night, Isabella."

Her eyes go wide at the sound of me finally uttering her name without condescension, without teasing, just… her name.

After a moment's hesitation, she whispers, "My friends call me Izzy."

I hold her gaze. I don't even think about it.

"I'm not going to call you Izzy."

Her eyes widen and I can practically see the thoughts pinging around in her brain—do I not want to be her friend? What does that mean? Where do we stand then?

Fuck if I know. I just know I don't want to be her friend.

After a moment, she smiles. And suddenly I'm too busy trying to breathe through the way the sight hits me in the chest.

CHAPTER 13
Isabella

TANYA

Hey, Izzy! Just wanted to pass on a message we got about you today. One of the girls from Tuesday's class sent us an email that she really loves the vibe of your class. She said she was scared to pick up a new hobby but you put her immediately at ease and made her feel welcome. Just wanted to pass the message along and say keep up the good work

It's been an hour, and I haven't been able to tamp down on the smile on my face and the giddy feeling in my chest. When that text came through, I was just getting home from my contemporary dance class and feeling good about my transition from one dance style to the other. It's only been three weeks, but I feel like I'm settling into a world that seemed so unattainable when I moved here.

Couple that with this text message from my employer confirming that I'm reaching success with another new area in my life, and I'm feeling an immense amount of pride.

I decide this day is worth celebrating with a pint of ice cream. It's getting late, and it's already dark out, but the corner store is only two blocks away and is way quicker than delivering. Grabbing my wallet and my phone, I head out of my apartment.

I breathe in the warm Philly air with a smile on my face. It's been so easy to fall in love with this city. It almost reminds me of home, like it's a smaller, more manageable version of New York. The food has been amazing—even through delivery services, because sitting alone in a restaurant is still out of my comfort zone—and I've made more friends than I would've expected to make by myself. The people have become the most pleasant surprise in this new life.

My brain starts with thoughts of my boss and coworkers at the yoga studio, how kind they've been and how much they've helped me get started in an entirely new endeavor. I think of Mrs. Martin, and how comforting it's been getting back into ballet. Hailey comes to mind, and the teachers and dancers at the dance studio. They've been so welcoming as I learn how to be a student again, and as I settle into a world that is so similar, yet so different, from what I'm used to.

And then I think about Kane—intoxicating, fascinating, unanticipated Kane.

Even the thought of my hot neighbor starts my heart racing. Within seconds, I'm lost in memories of Kane walking me home yesterday, of the ride I took on his bike, of the way I have dreams about him every night—

I don't notice the sound of footsteps behind me until a

hand grabs me and jerks me around.

"Whoa, *what*—"

I freeze when I get a look at the person who grabbed me.

"I—I'm s-sorry, I didn't mean to—"

"Give me all your money," the hooded man snarls. "And your phone."

I'm too stunned by the situation to truly understand the severity of it. My mind feels foggy, and I don't understand what he's asking.

"My what?" I ask in a daze. "You want my number?"

He lets out a bark of laughter. "Lady, you wish I'd take out an uptight cunt like you." His expression hardens and he gestures hurriedly at my purse. "Give me everything you have."

Enough brain power finally clicks into place that I realize he's not hitting on me. But I'm still only able to look down at myself in confusion. "My… what?"

"Jesus Christ," the guy growls, finally seeming to lose all of his patience. His arm snaps toward me. "Just give me that."

It's when his hand wraps around the strap of my purse and yanks, forcefully jerking me into his body, that I hear a new voice sound beside us.

"Let her go."

My attention turns toward the newcomer at the same time that the stranger's does. And I think we're both shocked to see Kane—all 6'2", two hundred pounds of him—standing at the corner of the street, a growling Oscar by his side.

"Get lost, man, this is between me and her," the hooded stranger snarls, though his eyes are darting to the pitbull. His words—and the tone they're spoken in—are enough to make me shrink back into my skin.

But not Kane. Kane just looks like he's taking an evening stroll in the city, his expression lax and Oscar's leash loose in his hand.

His eyes dart to me. He doesn't even hesitate before he says, "Whatever happens to her concerns me. So let's figure out a way to solve this without anyone getting hurt."

And while I'm frozen to the spot, his words seem to light a fire under the guy that still has a hand wrapped around my purse strap.

"Let me put it in a way you'll understand," he taunts.

And then he does something that makes me pale on the spot. That I'll never forget in a million years, no matter how badly I try to erase it.

With a gun pointing at Kane's head, the stranger growls, "Get lost or you'll be the one getting hurt."

I'm frozen. Slack-jawed, staring in disbelief at the scene in front of me.

Kane can't get hurt because of me, he just can't—

But just as I'm about to step between the two men, Kane's voice pierces my subconscious.

"Okay. You're in charge. I don't want any trouble. Here, take my wallet. I just don't want the girl to get hurt." He tosses his wallet at the guy's feet and steps back, one hand in the air in surrender, the other tugging Oscar further away from the scene. "Nobody wants anyone to get hurt, so just take the money and go. No one's stopping you."

The mugger's gaze snaps to me in disbelief. Like he can't believe he got a two-in-one, that he got *two*—

The second his attention strays toward me, Kane acts.

He leaps forward and knocks the gun out of the guy's hand, at the same time that Oscar charges to stand in front of me, his teeth bared and barking viciously. At the sound of the metal clattering to the ground, both my and the mugger's attention snaps to Kane.

Kane, who is already pressing his forearm to the stranger's throat against the brick wall of the building.

"You piece of fucking shit," he snarls, his face only an inch away from the guy. "You were going to hurt her? I could *kill* you."

And when his face contorts in rage, and Oscar's barks turn into blood-chilling growls, my instincts tell me to step in.

"Kane," I say softly. Pleadingly. "Please don't. Let's just call the cops. I'm okay, we can just—"

But at the word *cops*, the mugger's eyes go wild. And at the same time, Kane's attention strays to me. As he turns, Kane's forearm loosens from the guy's throat. Who immediately takes advantage of the situation and shoves Kane's body away from him, then turns to bolt down the street before either of us even realize what's happening. By the time Kane's gaze jerks away from me and toward the mugger, he's already turning around the corner and disappearing out of sight.

Kane doesn't even attempt to run after him. Oscar starts to chase, but before he can make it more than a few feet, Kane stops him with a hard command. Almost begrudgingly, the pitbull turns around and trots back to us, settling by my feet and giving my hand a lick.

Kane looks like he has half a thought to go after the guy,

but then he moves toward me with two quick steps, until he's close enough to lift his hand and grip my chin, his eyes boring into mine.

"Are you okay?" he demands in a voice that is somehow equal parts urgent and comforting. "Did he hurt you?"

"No," I say, breathless in my answer. "He didn't hurt me."

Even still, Kane takes a moment to look over my body, his touch shifting to cradle my face instead. It isn't until I grip his forearm with my own hand that his attention snaps back to my face.

"I'm okay, I promise," I whisper, unable to tear my gaze away from his.

He stares into my eyes for a beat, and then two, before he—almost begrudgingly—drops his hands from my face and takes a step back.

"We should… probably call the cops," he says in a stilted voice, squeezing his hands into fists by his side. He glances at me in a way that seems almost hesitant. "I'm assuming you want to call the cops?"

And with that question, it occurs to me that Kane is… trying to do the right thing.

I flash back to the expression he had on his face when he turned the corner and found a man physically threatening me. And I realize that Kane had several opportunities to deal with the man in a way that probably would have felt very normal to him. Very physical, very violent ways.

But he didn't. Because of me.

And now he's trying to do the *right thing*.

Because of *me*.

I suck in a breath at the realization. But I know he's still waiting for my reaction, so I answer quickly. "Yes, we should call the cops. I'll call."

He waits patiently as I dial 911. And even more patiently as I'm forwarded to the local precinct, as I give details about what just occurred. He doesn't move closer, he just stands there and gives me the impression that he's there for whatever I need him for.

It's almost more overwhelming than the attempted robbery.

"Yes, we can come down to the local precinct to give our statements," I say, ultimately ending my phone conversation. "We'll be there in a little bit."

When I hang up, I'm almost hesitant to meet Kane's gaze. He hasn't moved away for twenty minutes, and something tells me I'd have to send him away for that to happen.

"Do you… do you want to come to the police station with me?" I ask. He's staring at me the same way he was when the robbery first happened. "You don't have to, but I'm going to walk down—"

"I'll walk down with you," he interrupts. It takes him two seconds to get his phone out and type something, but then before he can put it back in his pocket, I see it ringing with a call. He hesitates, huffing out an agitated breath, then answers.

"Yeah," he answers tightly. "Yeah, I'm sure. Okay." A pause. "Thanks."

For a moment, I can only stare at him. I think Kane just called out of work, but I'm still too frozen to know what to do with that information. "Okay," I eventually blurt. "Let's… I'm… okay, let's walk this way."

Kane whistles for Oscar to follow him. He waits for me to begin walking, then steps beside me and silently matches my pace.

My phone says the precinct is a good ten-minute walk from where we are. We're silent for several minutes, and it takes way longer than I'd like to admit to work up the courage to ask him what I really want to know after tonight.

"You were... very calm during that whole thing," I say quietly.

"Panicking would've made him panic," he murmurs.

I chance another glance at him. "Even still, it's not the easiest thing to stay calm when there's a gun pointed at you."

My comment is enough to make the corner of Kane's lips twitch. He even gives me an amused look. "Have you had a lot of guns pointed at you, princess?"

I can feel my cheeks flame. "No, I can't say that I have." I hesitate, but force myself to ask, "Have you?"

That's enough to make the amusement drop from his face. He doesn't give me a verbal response, but the answer might as well be written all over his face.

"I'm sorry that's happened to you," I whisper, my eyes trained on the ground in front of me. But I can feel Kane's eyes on me after I say it.

His tone is disbelieving when he asks, "A guy just tried to mug you, and you're saying you feel bad for *me?*"

I nod. "No one should have to go through that even once, let alone multiple times. I'm sorry it happened to you."

He gently grabs my forearm in order to stop me and turn me toward him. "Are you sure you're okay?" he asks.

"Are you saying the fact that I'm sympathizing with your life experiences means I'm not okay?"

He only blinks at me and waits.

"I think I'm a little in shock," I admit in a whisper. Then hurry to add, "But I still meant what I said."

Kane studies me for a moment, his gaze traveling over my face. He must take my honesty at face value, because he eventually accepts it with a nod.

We spend the next two hours at the local police precinct. Most of the time is spent with me talking, giving my account of the altercation, with Oscar pressed against my leg in silent comfort. Kane stands against the back wall with his arms crossed, looking increasingly furious with every detail I recount.

Eventually, the cop asks Kane to describe what he saw. The guy is young, and clearly in awe of Kane from the moment we walk into the room. And as Kane begins to recount things as he experienced them, that awe only grows.

He's not the only one mesmerized. By the time Kane gets to the end, I'm probably staring at him like he's my own personal savior.

"Kane saved my life," I tell the cop. "If he hadn't shown up, I would've ended up dead on the sidewalk with a bullet in my head."

At even the thought, Kane's expression hardens. He doesn't seem to notice that he reaches for my chair and pulls me closer.

"You're lucky to have had him," the cop says with a comforting smile. Returning to his notes, he asks, "Can either of you describe what the man looked like?"

It takes us a few minutes of tentative sentences, but between the two of us, Kane and I describe what the guy looked like. By the end of it, none of us, including the cop taking our statement, have enough hope that our vague description will help them catch the guy.

"Can I take her home now?" Kane finally asks in a hard voice. "She's exhausted, and she needs to go home and get some sleep."

The cop startles and hurriedly closes his binder. "Of course. We should have everything we need for now." He shoots me a quizzical glance before adding, "Normally I would offer to have one of our officers escort her home, but I'm assuming you're just as safe with him."

Kane doesn't even hesitate in his response. "Not a chance I'm letting anyone else take her home." To which he gets a knowing smile from the young cop, and a dazed look from me.

I force my attention back to the police officer. "Please just call me if you identify anyone," I tell him.

He nods. "Absolutely. We'll call you if we need anything else. Get home safe, and please call us if you need anything else."

Kane barely waits for the end of the guy's sentiment before he's whistling at Oscar and pulling me in the direction of the exit.

And suddenly, I get the impression that this isn't the first time he's been in a police station, but that it might be the first time he's been on this side of the law.

THE WALK BACK to our street is quiet. I can tell by Isabella's stiff gait and bunched jaw that she's replaying the mugging, and it takes everything in me not to wrap an arm around her shoulder and shield her with my body.

But she doesn't need that. She needs to be reassured that she's confident and capable. I have no idea where that feeling comes from, but the knowledge is so obvious to me that I don't even think to question it. I just walk close enough to offer my unspoken protection, and I keep my mouth shut. Oscar walks on her other side in his own form of silent comfort.

It takes us less than ten minutes to reach Isabella's door. When she hesitates, I find myself saying, "I'll wait until you go inside and lock the door."

My words seem to cut through something in her brain, because she finally looks up at me.

"Can you—I mean, if it's not too much trouble, can you… come inside for a little bit?"

And if her stuttered words didn't convince me, her hopeful expression would have.

"I can do that."

I nod my chin at her front door. "Let's get you inside, princess," I say softly.

The familiar nickname—even though it's not spoken with my usual derision—is enough to snap her back to action. She immediately looks down at her keys, and starts to fumble with them in the lock. When she finally gets it open, she almost seems more nervous to be *in* her house than she was walking the street.

I study her out of the corner of my eye as I step inside, trying to determine if *I'm* the reason she's nervous—if maybe she regrets inviting me into her home.

But when she finally settles on the couch after tossing her bag on the kitchen counter, Oscar following her every move and settling right beside her, I realize she's fidgeting in her seat without even glancing at me.

After a moment, she notices me watching her and flattens her hands against her thighs. "Sorry," she says with a laugh. "I guess I'm still a little wound up."

And then my dog does that thing that only animals are capable of—when they sense the emotions of those around them, and immediately become their comfort. I watch in awe as he crawls closer to Isabella so he can drop his head into her lap, his tongue darting out to lick her hand.

Isabella smiles down at the dog. Her other hand pets his head, which makes his tail start to wag.

"Does he need anything?" she asks suddenly, her attention whipping over to me. "Do you need to get food for him? I can give him water."

I shake my head. "He already ate. He just needs a bowl of water. Though it doesn't look like he's going to move anytime soon."

Satisfied that Isabella isn't second-guessing letting me into her home, and that my dog is comfortably settled, I turn away from them and stride into Isabella's kitchen, taking in her apartment as I go.

Her apartment is a replica of mine, but you'd never know it at first glance. The layouts might be identical, but Isabella's home looks like an interior decorator came in and decorated it with an unlimited budget. Isabella's only been in the city a few weeks, and it already looks like she's made herself perfectly at home. I round her kitchen peninsula and reach immediately for the teapot I see sitting on her stove, glancing subtly around the home, taking everything in, and trying to hold back a whistle of appreciation at how nice everything is.

I take the teapot over to the kitchen sink and begin to fill it. I can't think of a single time in my life that I've ever made a cup of tea, but it's the only thing I can think of that might have a calming effect on Isabella.

Sure enough, Isabella's giving me a confused look from where she's frozen on the couch. But I see it click when she realizes what I'm doing, and then she's on her feet and stumbling toward me.

"No, you don't have to—" she starts.

"I know I don't," I interrupt her. The teapot full, I place it back on the stove and light it. Then I grab a mug from her girly little mug holder on the wall and place it on the counter.

My gaze lifts to meet hers. She's still standing frozen on

the other side of the counter, but I see a flicker of appreciation at my action. It doesn't outshine the nerves, though, so I try to put her at ease.

I slide the mug back toward myself. "Besides, the tea is for me. I can't end the day without a cup."

The startled laugh bursts out of her, and I couldn't help my answering smile even if I wanted to.

We're silent as I fill a Tupperware container with water for Oscar, and as we wait for the water to boil. But it's a comfortable silence. Isabella takes a seat at the counter, and she absentmindedly traces patterns on the marble as she lets me look around her house.

My attention is stuck on a black-and-white professional photo of Isabella dancing when the teapot starts to whistle. I have to rip my gaze away from the tantalizing lines of muscle that adorn her body as she holds some dance position that I probably can't pronounce.

I force myself to turn around and lift the teapot off the burner. I start to twist so I can ask Isabella what kind of tea she wants, but she beats me to it.

"Over your right shoulder. I could probably use some chamomile right now."

I finish making her tea, then I slide it in front of her.

"Thanks," she murmurs, shooting me a grateful smile. She cups her hands around the hot mug, waiting for it to cool down.

We're silent again, but this one feels fraught with tension. Normally I'm not one to initiate conversation, but I want her to feel better, so I find myself asking, "Want to talk about it?"

I see her hesitate again, like she knows I'm not a huge

talker.

But then it all spills out.

"I didn't think Philly was going to be any different from New York," she blurts out in a rush. "I mean, New York City is a million times bigger than Philly. And we're not exactly in a bad part of Philly, so it never even *occurred* to me that something like this could happen. How stupid is that? I don't even carry *pepper spray*, for god's sake!" It all comes out in a rush, like now that she started, she can't stop the word vomit.

I just listen, realizing I'm soaking up her thoughts like I would drops of water in a desert.

She continues, her gaze holding mine as she gestures wildly in the air as she talks.

"I never thought of my life in New York as scary, but I was so sure Philly would be way easier to deal with. I thought, it's a smaller city, easy to navigate, easy to figure out, easy to find a new life here. It couldn't *possibly* be scarier or harder than the insane life I had in New York: every minute of my day planned, everything provided for me, everything taken care of by others so I could focus completely on dance. I thought… that's what my life is going to be. There's nothing new, so nothing is scary. And then—" She sucks in a breath, hesitating, but then she forces herself to keep going. "And then my injury happened, and it was like everything became terrifying. I had no idea who I was—*no one* knew who I was without dance—and suddenly *all* I had was new: a new schedule, new hobbies, new ways to interact with people. And I thought, if everything is going to change, I might as well do it in a new place where I can fumble through it on my own without anyone watching."

She finally jerks her gaze away from mine, unable to meet my eyes.

"I don't know why it didn't occur to me that I might not be able to do it. I've been the privileged rich girl for as long as I can remember, and everything's *always* been taken care of for me. Why did I think living on my own wouldn't be the scariest thing ever? Why did I think *another* new thing—something that's huge, and risky, and clearly even dangerous—was the answer to my problems? And of course I get mugged only *four weeks* into my lease. If that isn't a sign, I don't know what is. I'm such an idiot for moving here, this was the biggest, stupidest mistake—"

"Stop," I finally growl, cutting her off.

She's not saying these things in a self-deprecating way, she honestly believes them.

And they're so laughably wrong that I can't stand it.

"Look, obviously today sucked," I tell her. She's still startled at my gruff reprimand, sitting frozen in her chair. "Anyone would be scared and questioning their new home after what happened today. But, Isabella, you couldn't be further from the truth with the rest of that bullshit. You're *more* than capable of living on your own. You've been here a month, and it took you, what, two weeks to get settled? To find a place to live, a job, a new dance studio? Not to mention, you made friends instantly. None of that shit is easy, and I'm assuming you did it without any trouble. Even without the added stress of your entire life changing because of your injury, that's not nothing. Far from it."

She ducks her head as she cradles the now-warm cup of

tea, but I see the blush that lights her face at my words. She looks like she doesn't know how to respond, so she lifts the mug to her lips and takes a sip instead.

And again, I feel the urge to lighten the mood and make her laugh.

I narrow my eyes and force a fake frown onto my face as I say, "And I'm never going to admit this again, but you actually have one of the best teaching styles I've ever seen—even though you are a pain in my ass during class."

It works. Another laugh sounds from her lips, and I ingest it like it's air I need to breathe.

"You're just so *bad* at it," she says, still laughing softly. But the look she gives me is thankful.

I ignore the tight feeling in my chest when it hits me that I actually made another person feel better. *She deserves that. She deserves to feel good about herself.*

We settle into another comfortable silence, and she continues to sip on her tea. The air has become serious again, and I can't stop myself from adding, "Today was just a blip, Isabella. I promise."

She studies me for a moment, then nods, her entire posture relaxing. I sense her hesitation with whatever she wants to say next.

"Is what happened today a normal part of your life?" she asks softly.

For a few seconds, I battle the urge to shut her down. The last thing I want to do is expose any part of my life— especially the parts before Philly—but when I see how much she's hanging on my response, and I realize my answer might actually help her recover from today, I deflate.

"Short answer is yes," I admit in a tight voice. I clear my throat and force myself to keep talking. "I grew up in a bad part of Baltimore, and I've been jumped more times than I can remember. You asked why I was calm today—that's why. I'm used to it."

She absorbs my answer with a thoughtful nod. Then, with nerves trembling in her voice, she asks, "Is that why you started training? You wanted to learn how to fight?"

My answer comes immediately and without thought. "I already knew how to fight," I say in a flat tone. "MMA was just an outlet."

I watch as Isabella accepts my answer, as she visibly decides not to push me anymore.

For some reason, I find myself adding to my answer anyway.

"I had a… hard childhood," I admit in that same tight voice. "I had to become a fighter to survive. Training just keeps the anger at bay for a little while."

Her gaze softens at my comment. I automatically tense, expecting the usual reaction of pity—I fucking hate pitying looks—but I see none of that in Isabella's eyes. Nothing but normal, human empathy.

My muscles only relax an inch, but it's everything. I haven't admitted that part of my life to anyone in years.

"I got tired of always having to fight," I add. "I needed to get away from it all."

"Or maybe you were tired of surviving," she says absentmindedly, her gaze on where she's twirling her empty mug. "Maybe you wanted to learn how to live, instead."

For a moment, all I can do is stare at her. It's obvious she said it without thinking, and even now, she doesn't realize that what she said might've been monumental.

Her words ring on repeat in my brain, so much so that it takes me a second to realize Isabella is swaying in her seat. She's clearly exhausted, and crashing from everything that happened today, and I notice with a start that it's well past midnight.

"It's late," I say quietly, reaching for her mug so I can place it in the sink. "You should go to bed." Walking around the counter, I gently lift her out of her seat, but then hesitate when I realize that I might be pushing my boundaries a little with taking her to bed—after all, she only now even let me into her home.

"I'm going to sleep on the couch," she slurs. "I don't have a TV in my bedroom, and I have a feeling I won't be able to sleep without a distraction."

Well, that solves my inner turmoil, at least.

I lead her back to the couch and reach for the blanket that's draped over the back of it so I can place it on her once she's lying down. Oscar hasn't moved from his place on the couch since we arrived, but he shifts a little bit now and settles on top of Isabella's feet. She hums contentedly at the warmth, a small smile playing on her lips.

I hesitate because I think I hate leaving her alone after today, but I also know I can't stay. We barely know each other.

Liar. You told her more today than you've ever told even those close to you.

I shake my head and turn away anyway. But I'm stopped

when Isabella grabs my hand.

"Wait," she says, forcing her eyes to open. "Can you… watch something with me? Just for a little while," she tacks on hurriedly.

And I realize that it doesn't matter that I barely know her, there's less and less that I *wouldn't* do for this girl.

"Just for a little," I agree softly.

She relaxes back into the couch, another pleased smile appearing on her lips. I grab the remote from the coffee table and settle into the single seat next to the couch.

"Do you want to watch anything in particular?" I ask as I click the TV on and pull up the menu.

When I don't get an answer, I turn and see Isabella fast asleep, that smile still etched onto her face.

Hours pass before I can bring myself to leave her alone. When I finally lock and triple-check her door, the sky is pink with the breaking dawn.

CHAPTER 15
Isabella

When I wake up, I'm staring at a TV. I rarely fall asleep on the couch, so it takes a few seconds of dazedly looking around before I remember where I am.

I fell asleep on the couch last night.

Kane was here.

Kane stayed with me after I almost got mugged yesterday.

I turn my attention to the accent chair next to my couch. I remember him standing in front of it, but I was out before his butt even hit the seat, so I don't remember anything else. And yet, when I look at the chair, I see a deep Kane-imprint in the cushion.

A smile comes unbidden to my lips. I can't help it—even though yesterday was the second-scariest day of my life, Kane's presence in it was still the most comforting thing I could've asked for. Not only did he save me, but he stayed with me afterward, too.

I squeeze my eyes shut and think about the conversation we had in my kitchen.

He opened up to me. He told me about his life experiences, about his childhood.

He made me feel better.

He made jokes.

I laugh to myself about that last one. Who knew Kane had a sense of humor?

I'm so pleased with my discovery that it takes me a minute to pull myself together and focus my brain. I force my thoughts away from Kane, and instead start to think about my day: what I have to do, where I need to teach, the training I need to go through.

In some ways it's reminiscent of my pre-injury life, but in other ways… it's not.

I make it through two days on autopilot before something shakes me out of it. It's during a dance class with Hailey that I'm eventually reminded of what happened, and when I once again word-vomit my thoughts. She doesn't even blink, which makes me think she's either used to muggings in Philly, or that Kane said something at the gym.

I'm way more confident in the first option than the second.

But after I leave the dance studio that day, I find my thumb hovering over the number for the police precinct.

I couldn't tell you how long it took me to hit *Call.*

But I can tell you how long the phone call was.

Ninety seconds. Just long enough for me to ask him if there were any developments, or any suspects, and for him to tell me that nothing has changed since I last saw him.

When I hang up, I feel dejected. Even though I knew Kane and I didn't give the cops any description they could realistically work off of, I still had my hopes up that they had gotten lucky and found the mugger.

You're living in an imaginary world, Isabella. The real world doesn't work that way.

I shake the thoughts from my head. I know I told Kane that I thought I was sheltered and naïve, but his response somehow convinced me in fifteen seconds that I was wrong to feel that way. That I *did* have a handle on the world, and that I wasn't an idiot when it came to what happened to us.

I manage to distract myself from the negative thoughts while I get ready to teach a yoga class. And yet, when I walk into the studio, I'm still very much on edge.

I'm distracted and shaking with the overwhelming emotions when my students start to show up. I try to busy myself with setting the perfect temperature, the perfect playlist, while I wait for everyone to set up their mats. It isn't until I literally run into Kane that I realize how futile my efforts were.

Because it only takes one look at him to calm my nerves.

He notices right away. Whether it's because of our joint experience or because my emotions are plastered over my skin, I have no idea. But he can tell.

"Are you okay?" he asks in a low murmur. His hands are still on my arms, still holding me steady. And I realize it's the first time in two days that I've felt grounded.

"I'm fine," I croak out. "Sorry, I wasn't looking where I was going."

His eyes narrow suspiciously, but he must decide against pushing me because the only push he gives me is to rub his hands over my arms for a nanosecond before pulling them back to his sides.

"Okay," is all he says.

I shine a smile at him that I'm sure screams *fake* before pushing past him to unnecessarily fill up my already-full water bottle. I waste time until the clock tells me to start class.

I'm on autopilot during the hour. I can't remember what I teach, and it's a testament to my dedication to yoga that I can go through the motions without any thought. But I do it. And it isn't until it's over that I even realize I did it.

The first thing to snap me out of it is noticing Kane standing at the water fountain. It's odd enough that he didn't leave as soon as we were finished, but it's even more odd that he fills his water bottle and then stands nearby to make small talk with the girl who steps up after him.

He's hesitating. He's waiting for something.

The second I make the observation, I watch him firm his resolve and lock his gaze on me. My breath catches, my feet freeze where they are, and I watch in helpless wonder as he starts toward me.

"Hey," he says in a tight voice.

I swallow roughly. "Hey, back," I answer.

"I wanted to offer some self-defense lessons," he eventually says. "I figure the other day was stressful, and it can't ever hurt to learn, so—" He cuts himself off. "I just thought I'd make the offer. If you were interested."

I hesitate to accept, and he notices. It's probably what makes him add quietly, "I know when it happened to me, learning to protect myself made it easier to deal with the fear of it happening again."

And that decides it. Not just the truth of his statement, but also the fact that he's making this offer because he's concerned about me.

"Okay," I blurt out before I can lose my nerve. "When?"

He seems relieved at my acceptance. "Come to the gym after lunch tomorrow."

I give him a shaky smile. "Okay. I'll be there."

"Okay," he parrots, his shoulders relaxing. "I'll see you tomorrow then."

I don't stop thinking about his offer for the rest of the day. The only thing that puts a pause on my obsessing is walking out of my apartment the next morning to find a gift bag on my doormat.

Confused, I reach down to pick it up. There's no tissue paper, or note, or anything else that you'd normally find in a gift bag, so I peek inside to figure out what it is and who might have left it.

As soon as I see what's inside, a smile stretches across my face, so wide it almost hurts. I've received plenty of gorgeous, expensive gifts in my life, but none as thoughtful as this one. And knowing someone thought of me, that they deliberately went out to buy something that would make my life even a little bit easier, fills my chest with an overwhelming sense of happiness.

I put the pepper spray in my purse and leave to start my day, my steps lighter than they've felt in a long time.

When I walk into the gym, I'm surprised to find it empty.

I'm not sure what I pictured when Kane offered his gym

as the location for our lesson, but I realize I never considered it would just be the two of us when I accepted. Not because I'm scared of him, but because I've never seen the gym anything less than filled with sweaty, grunting people.

I'm just about to call out his name when I hear the sounds of fists hitting a heavy bag in the other room.

I follow the sounds to the door at the end of the mat. When I hesitantly push it open, I come face to face with a very shirtless, and very sweaty, Kane.

I'm just as mesmerized by the sight as I was the first time I saw him.

For a moment, it's all I can do to stare at him. To watch as his muscles ripple with every punch, as his sweat shines over every fine inch of him. He's two hundred pounds of perfect, *male* specimen, and I can't tear my eyes away from him.

It's also the first time I can take my time admiring his appearance. I've been wanting to ask him about his tattoos, simply because he has so *many*, but since they're visible to me right now, I let my gaze drop over his body.

All of his ink is black. One of his arms is covered in a full sleeve, some kind of cohesive image from chest to hand that features a detailed dragon in the center of it. His chest and stomach are a mix of images and what look like quotes, and he even has a tattoo of an olive branch at the base of his throat. I can't see his back from here, but I know he's got a full back tattoo that stretches into whatever the tree is that's on his ribs. The only part of him that's not tattooed is his legs.

I have no idea how long I salivate over the sight of Kane: maybe a second, maybe a thousand. But when his gaze eventually meets mine, it still doesn't feel like long enough.

"I didn't hear you come in," he says, his tone apologetic. He wipes the sweat from his eyes with his boxing glove. "Come in. I'm just finishing up."

When I finally force myself down the stairs, I see him striding toward his gym bag and grabbing a towel from it. He hurriedly runs it all over his arms and chest. Then he's reaching for an extra t-shirt, and I realize I'm disappointed when he pulls it over his head.

"I got a little carried away with my workout," he admits sheepishly. "I wasn't planning on being sweaty for our lesson."

I force down the urge to let my ridiculous crush turn me into a drooling idiot. "It's okay," I rush out. "I'm an athlete too, I'm not scared of sweat."

My comment causes his eyebrow to rise, and for his gaze to slide over my body.

"Trust me, I know," he says in an absentminded murmur.

And just like that, heat lights in my body and I can't stand still. *This may have been a risky idea.*

"Come on, princess. Let's get started."

Definitely a risky idea.

I make my way down the steps to the mat area, trying desperately to not give away how excited I am about spending time physically close to Kane. Dropping my bag on one of the chairs, I toe my shoes off and step onto the mat.

"So, the biggest part of self-defense is awareness," Kane starts, taking up his place in front of me. There's still plenty of space between us, but you'd never know it based on how my body is vibrating from his proximity. "That's why no headphones in, no walking down bad streets, and you need to have eyes and ears open regardless of where you're walking."

I nod, knowing all of this is common sense but also remembering that I was lost in my thoughts—of Kane, ironically—when I was attacked. I don't tell him that, though.

"Even if someone is already in front of you, awareness also means being *aware* of their body language, how close they are, what their intentions might be. So even if I'm just standing in front of you talking, you have to be aware of what I *look* like. Am I staring at you? Do I look agitated? Does it look like I want to be closer to you?"

God, I hope so.

I can't bring myself to speak. I just stare at Kane, silently begging for all of that to be true. Even the memory of Kane pressing against my body has my breath coming quickly, and I know if he comes closer to me right now, the lesson is going out the window because I'm not pushing back.

"So, when I start to crowd you," he continues, his voice low, "you're already ready for it. Ready to react." He takes a step closer, and then another.

I'm frozen, unable to move or look away from his gaze.

"Put your hand out straight and tell me to stop," he says.

I extend a hand, albeit shakily. "Stop," I say. "Don't come any closer."

Kane nods approvingly. But then he takes another step, and now he's close enough to bump against my hand.

His heart beats rapidly under my hand, the only sign that he's just as affected by our proximity as I am.

"Tell me again," he says quietly.

I swallow and force out the words, "Step back. Move away from me."

My words sound unbelievable, even to me.

"Good girl," Kane praises, those two words doing more to me than my first boyfriend managed to do in an entire year. I think Kane knows it, too, because his lip twitches when I feel my cheeks flame.

He steps back again, and the distance is like a fan blowing against my heated body. I suck in a shaky breath and remind myself that this is a self-defense lesson, not… Kane's version of foreplay.

"Ideally, that's enough to make someone back off," Kane says—but only after he straightens and seems to refocus. "But if it doesn't, there are some moves you can easily learn to do. They're nothing crazy, no flashy 'technique' I need to teach you, it's just a matter of doing enough reps that they become a natural response to somebody crowding your space."

"Hailey said Jax taught her how to bitch slap," I tell him. "She said it's safer than learning how to punch?"

Kane thinks about that for a moment. "She's probably right. Punches can often break your hand." He doesn't seem to realize that he starts to flex his hand as he says it. As if remembering what a broken hand feels like.

That, and the reminder it brings with it that Kane has been forced to fight multiple times in his life, is like a bucket of ice-cold water.

"I want you to practice reacting to being grabbed," he continues. "The easiest is a knee to the balls, so I just want you to do that. Okay?"

I nod. I've never raised a hand to anyone in my life, but I'm pretty sure I can handle throwing a knee.

Except that when Kane presses forward, when he forces his way past my outstretched hand and grabs my arms, my rational brain goes out the window and my panic takes over.

The mugger's hands grab me, his fingers tightening around my muscles and squeezing so hard, I know they'll leave bruises. I smell his stale, disgusting breath in my face and I know I'm in trouble. He's going to hurt me, maybe even kill me, and there's nothing I can do—

I'm snapped out of the flashback when the grips on my arm go from bruising to comforting. When I hear my name murmured in a soothing tone.

"Isabella," I hear in a quiet voice. "It's okay. Isabella."

When I come to, I realize Kane is standing in front of me. Gently rubbing my arms and calling my name. And yet, when he sees my attention settle on him, he lets me go and steps back to give me space.

"I'm sorry," I blurt. "When you grabbed me, I… I mean, I thought…"

"It's okay," he reiterates. "I get it, trust me. I—" He hesitates before he admits the next part. "I get flashbacks sometimes, too. They're totally normal."

For some reason, his comment soothes me—makes me feel like I'm not alone. So much so that I find the courage to ask, "Do—do they get better?"

"Over time, yeah. But it helped a lot to learn self-defense. It's more of a mental exercise than a physical one, but I swear it helps."

I look down at my clenched fists. "So… do you see your opponent and then picture them when you train? Or how does it help?"

It seems like he identifies something in my expression because he moves forward and steps into my personal space.

"Let's do this," he starts. Then he gently grips my forearms and lifts them up so they're not hanging by my side, but guarding the center of my chest. "I'm going to rush you, and when I don't respond to you holding your space, react the way your body tells you to. Slap me, kick me, do whatever your *body* tells you to do when dealing with a threat. Don't worry about me, just react the way you think you should. And *take control* of the memory."

His words are so empowering that I find myself giving a firm nod before I can think too hard.

Seeming pleased by my quick capitulation, he takes a few steps back to start from the normal—and safe—stranger distance. Then, as soon as he senses I'm ready, he slowly starts to move forward.

When he gets too close for comfort, but before he can touch me, I put my hand up and say firmly, "Stop."

He doesn't stop. He keeps coming, his slow pace *screaming* 'predator.'

"I said stop," I repeat. "Don't come any closer."

Still, he ignores me. When his chest hits my outstretched hand, he continues to plow forward, forcing my elbow to bend and completely overwhelming me with his presence.

And that's even before his arms come around me to grip me firmly by the arms, effectively pinning them to my sides.

Then the flashback comes.

Crazy eyes, unshaven face, spittle flying from his lips as he barks at me to give him everything I have…

I don't think, I just do.

My knee comes up and slams into his groin. And the second he doubles over, I aim a vicious slap at his face.

Immediately, I feel a sense of triumph. Before the flashback fully fades, I experience *victory*, of the accomplishment that taking down my attacker comes with.

But after a moment, it does fade. And instead of the mugger, I see Kane on his knees, hunched over as he cups between his legs.

"Oh my God," I breathe in horror. "Oh my God, *Kane.*" I drop to the mat in front of him, my hands lifting up toward him but never landing anywhere because I don't know how to help. "I'm so sorry. I had no idea I was going to do that, I didn't want to hurt you—"

I'm cut off by the sound of his laughter. His head tips back, and now that his dark hair isn't hiding his face from me, I see the look of pure glee on it.

"That was amazing," he laughs. "If I wasn't prepared to catch that knee to my thigh, you definitely would have smashed the fuck out of my nuts."

For a moment, all I can do is gawk at him. But when he finally meets my eyes, letting me experience the full force of his amusement—and that he's being honest—I huff a nervous laugh.

But that, too, only lasts for a moment. Because then I notice the red welt fading on his cheek.

I gasp and lightly touch it with my fingers. "I hit you," I whisper in disbelief.

Kane's laugh has faded. He holds my gaze and says, "Yes you did."

The air between us sparks. Suddenly, I'm all too aware of the tension between us, of the fact that we're close and that I'm still touching him. That he's unflinchingly holding my gaze.

I pull my hand back as if burned. Ripping my gaze from his, I stand to my feet and dart a look at the door to the front of the gym.

"I should get going," I hear myself babble. "I have dance class tonight."

Kane unfolds his big body as he, too, gets to his feet. He's sobered and is back to his usual intense aura. And yet, I hear him ask, "Want me to walk you over?"

The underlying question goes unspoken.

Are you still scared? Did the lesson help the anxiety?

I force myself to consider his question. I know with absolute certainty that he's not offering just to be polite, that he would absolutely walk me to the end of the block if I admitted I was still scared.

I feel… a little nervous to walk in the city by myself, but it's been downgraded from anxious. And nerves feel like they're a healthy reaction to a tiny girl walking in a big city alone, so that's probably not even a result of the mugging. In fact, I probably should've been nervous *before* the mugging.

"I'm okay," I finally answer. A tentative smile stretches across my face, the memory of Kane's gift chasing away any leftover gloom. "And I have my pepper spray."

And as I leave the gym with a glance back at Kane, I think that maybe facing my fears really was worth it.

CHAPTER 16
Kane

I'm punching a dummy on the mat the next time I see Isabella.

"Well, this looks familiar," I hear her say in a dry tone.

I straighten from the bag and wipe my face with the bottom of my shirt, smirking in satisfaction when I see her eyes go black at the sight of my abs.

"What can I say, I'm a simple man," I tell her. "Whether I'm working or playing, I'm hitting things."

Shocked out of her teasing, she focuses on my answer and cocks her head. "I don't think I ever asked. What do you do? Like for work?"

"Three guesses," I deadpan. And almost chuckle when a slow grin spreads across her face.

"Bouncing?"

"Bingo. At a strip club."

She laughs. "I should've known. I bet you're a nightmare for bar patrons. Do they ever get in fights with you?"

I shrug. "Sometimes. First night I ever worked the club, this cocky realtor got in my face and I had to throw him down the stairs."

Isabella gapes at me. "You *had* to?"

Another shrug. "It was my first night. I had to prove my worth."

Isabella lets out a disbelieving giggle at that. "Do you ever run into them on the street and think, *Oh look, that's the guy I threw out last night?*"

My lip twitches with a smug grin. "Actually, that first guy? The one I threw down the stairs? His face is on a huge billboard on 95. I see him every day."

"Oh my *God*, are you talking about Jack Bueregard? The guy with that outrageous real estate billboard coming down from Northeast Philly?"

Isabella and I turn to find a slack-jawed Aiden, his eyes wide as saucers. I didn't even hear him come into the room.

Which is surprising, because that fucker is obnoxious.

"Is that the guy you're talking about?" he presses. "Because I've always wondered if he's as much of a tool as he looks."

"He is," I confirm dryly.

Aiden lets out a loud cackle. "That's amazing. And you threw him down a flight of stairs? God, I can't wait to tell Max. We're always laughing about how douchey he looks on that damn billboard when we drive back from the boxing gym."

I only grunt in response. I don't admit that I do the same.

I don't realize that Isabella and I were chatting like old friends—and that I was *enjoying* it—until Aiden glances between us with a look of bewilderment. "Why are we talking about Angry Man's bouncing mishaps?"

I quirk an eyebrow before I can stop it. *"Angry Man?"*

He shrugs, looking completely unapologetic. "If the shoe

fits."

"You're an idiot," I grumble.

"So people tell me," he says with a sigh.

"Why are we calling Aiden an idiot today?" Jax asks, appearing from the office behind Isabella. Hailey trails behind him, almost entirely hidden from view behind her boyfriend's massive stature.

"He admitted to Kane that he calls him Angry Man," comes Hailey's sister's tired voice as she emerges from the locker room. She also smacks Aiden in the back of the head as she passes him on her way to the mat, almost as an afterthought.

"Ow," he mutters, rubbing his head and glaring at Remy. "I was just making small talk. He's been here for weeks, and none of us have ever talked to him. I was trying to break the ice." He turns his attention to Isabella. "I didn't know he even cared to exchange words. Apparently, I'm just not his *type*."

Isabella blushes as everyone's attention zeroes in on her. She trips over an answer, hurrying to downplay the situation.

"I was just asking what Kane does for work," she says, face still bright red.

"And that could've been answered with a simple 'he throws people down stairs,'" Aiden says pointedly. "Yet, somehow, you got a whole story."

Isabella glares at him. The sight of it–especially not aimed at *me*–makes a grin form on my lips.

Fuck, she's sexy.

Isabella quirks an eyebrow in Aiden's direction. "Should I ask him to throw *you* down the stairs?"

"Well, that's not very live laugh love of you," I murmur

quietly, my smirk coming out in full force.

I regret the words as soon as they come out of my mouth, because my not-quite-so-quiet comment has every person's shock zeroing in on me.

"Did you... did you just make a *joke*?" Aiden asks incredulously. His head whips back to Isabella. "What did you *do* to him?"

I can only cough into my fist and glare at him, promising, without words, a very painful training session.

"Alright everybody, enough chit chat," Jax interrupts, clapping his hands together. I can't tell if he's purposefully trying to save me from an Aiden interrogation, or if he's just trying to start class, but either way, I breathe a sigh of relief.

"Izzy, you ready to go?" I hear Hailey ask.

I see Jax frown at the nickname. "Sorry, I should've asked. Do you prefer to go by Izzy?"

A light blush stains Isabella's cheeks, and she sends a glance my way. I know she's remembering our conversation about her name, even as she tries to shrug it off. "It's the nickname everyone uses for me. Isabella is too much of a mouthful."

No, it's not. Fuck no, it's not.

But I don't say that out loud. I don't correct her that Isabella is the *only* thing she should be called, that the nickname "Izzy" isn't even in the realm of something fitting for her. I simply give her a hard stare to convey a message along the lines of *bullshit*, and then I'm turning to walk down the mat into the bag room.

I don't catch Hailey's knowing look, or the way Isabella lets out the breath she was holding as she waited for me to say something.

It's late when I get home. Tristan put us all through the wringer tonight, making us do an entire bag workout *before* throwing us into a shark tank drill.

It's rare that I'm not exhausted after a workout, since I prefer to push my body to the brink, but it's not often that I'm so tired, I can barely gather enough energy to take Oscar for a walk. Thank God I'm not working tonight, because there's a good chance I would fall asleep if they put me on camera watch duty.

I force myself to feed Oscar, take a shower as he's eating, and then take him for a short walk after he's done. By the time I get back to my apartment, it's almost 7 p.m. I have to drag myself into the kitchen to make some semblance of dinner.

But just as I'm pulling a strip steak out of the fridge and readying to throw it in a pan, I hear my phone ring.

Frowning, I reach for the iPhone on my counter. *Unknown number.*

It's weird enough that someone's calling me this late, but for it to be a random, non-800 number is even weirder.

I swipe the green button on the screen. "Hello?"

"Kane."

An icy chill runs through me from just that—from nothing but my name.

I swallow the rock lodged in my throat. "Mom. What do you want?"

A laugh sounds from the other end of the line. It's gritty,

and rough-sounding. Like she hasn't laughed a real laugh in years. She probably hasn't.

"What, not even a hello?" she asks.

I don't bother responding.

"You always were such a stupid boy," she says in a cruel voice. "You run away from me, but don't bother to change your number? Why are you even surprised I'm calling you?"

I don't tell her that it's because I can't remember the last time she called me. That her preferred method of contact is showing up on my doorstep after she's tracked me down with the type of determination that only addicts are capable of when they want something.

"What do you want?" I repeat.

"That's it? That's all you want to ask me? After three years, I don't even get a *how are you, Mom?*"

My eyes slide closed as I battle with what I *should* do, vs. what she always makes me *want* to do.

I lose the battle. Every single fucking time. A twenty-six-year-old grown man, and within ten seconds, I'm succumbing to the toxic, manipulative, fucked up will of my mother, the same way I did when I was a child.

"How are you?"

Another laugh, though this time I can hear the poisonous victory in the sound. "I'm okay, baby. I moved out of West Baltimore, so I even managed to clean up for a while."

Which could be her way of saying she stopped using, but not drinking. It doesn't change the fact that I hear the slur in her words, though, or that she used the past tense of the word.

"That's great, Mom," I say in a flat voice. "I'm happy for

you."

"I even got married," she continues. "You had a real stepfather."

"*Had?*" I latch onto that word immediately.

A pause on the other end of the line, and I can hear her fidgeting with something. I know what's coming before she even says it.

"He left," she finally admits. "Guess he wasn't man enough to stick around. Just like your father."

Which, guessing from her defensive words, translates to *he caught her with another man*. Mom always did manage to sabotage her own happiness.

"I'm sorry to hear that," I force out. "So where are you living now?" Not that I care, but she's taking this conversation in a specific direction and I want to get there as soon as possible so I can hang up as soon as possible.

Another pause. "I'm staying with a friend of mine for now."

Code for: *I got kicked out of wherever I was living and now I'm sleeping with anyone who will take me in.*

Suddenly, I'm sick of this entire fucking conversation. I'm sick of reliving my past, my past that's *on repeat*, and I want to vomit from the knowledge that I managed to get away from it for three years. None of which did any fucking good, because, of course, *here we are again*.

"Mom, I have to go," I say hurriedly. "Thanks for calling. I'll talk to you later."

"Don't you dare hang up on me, boy," she snarls.

And there she is, the real woman beneath the mother's mask.

"I just told you I got a divorce and I'm crashing on

someone's couch, and you can't even offer me a place to stay? I'm your *mother*, for fuck's sake. Have some goddamn respect."

That's all it takes to revert me back to the scared little boy that used to hide in the coat closet at his mother's request. The one that is trained to do whatever she says, either because of her manipulation, or for fear of repercussion. By her hand or someone else's.

I can hear her slurred voice just as clearly in my head today. *Leave mommy alone for a little bit, Kane. After everything I do for you, I need some adult time. I deserve that.*

"What do you want from me?" I ask. "What is it this time, Mom? Money? Drugs? I can't offer you a place to stay that's better than where you are now."

"Oh, no?" she asks.

And at her smug tone, my blood chills.

"You don't think Philly is just a little better than Baltimore?"

My eyes slide closed, my chest starting to rise and fall with rapid, panicked breaths.

"You really thought I wouldn't find out, didn't you," she says with a cold laugh. "Well, let me tell you something: you're not as hard to figure out as you think you are. If I'm stupid, you're right there with me. Because I know *exactly* where you're living."

Fuck.

Fuck.

I thought leaving the city would be enough to lose her. I wasn't exactly hiding from her, or at least not so much that a little Internet research couldn't find me, but I really thought she'd never leave Baltimore, not even to abuse and dry up her own kid. I should've known her desperation and cruelty know no bounds.

"I saw a fight poster for your last fight," she says with a cruel laugh, just to drive the stake in a little harder. "Your opponent was from your old gym in Baltimore, remember? Your face was plastered all over your old stomping grounds down here. *That's* how easy it was to follow you to Philly and your new gym."

"What do you want?" I repeat. "I don't have anything for you. I'm just as stuck in the dumps as you are. It wouldn't be worth it to come up here."

"Bullshit," she snarls. "You've got a nice, cushy job now. I bet that club pays well. It has to, if you've got your own apartment in a good area of the city. Although, I'm sure it helps that you're funneling drugs and sex through the dancers. Isn't that right, Kane?"

For a moment, I can only blink in shock. "I… what? What're you talking about? I don't do that shit. *They* don't do that shit. The club's clean."

She laughs, the sound a dark, disturbed sound. And all I want to do is slam the phone down and crack it into a million pieces.

"Are you sure about that?" she asks. "What if someone slipped it to your boss that you were doing both of those things? Does he trust you enough to believe you if you deny it? Does *anyone* trust you enough to believe you?"

Godfuckingdamnit. I'm so fucking sick of living like this. Of being threatened, both physically and where my home and well-being are concerned. I want away from this fucking life, from this *fear*—

"Don't worry, I'm not coming up there anytime soon." Her words cut through my haze of thoughts. "I just wanted to make sure you understood that it works in your best interest to have *my* best interests at heart. And that I might be calling you soon for that help." She pauses, and I half expect her to be doing it just to drag out the torture. "Be ready to help your poor mother, Kane. She's done so much for you in your life. The least you could do is help her in her time of need."

I don't respond. I *can't.*

"Bye, baby. Enjoy your night."

Click.

I pull the phone away from my ear in stunned silence. And it doesn't feel like three years has passed since the last time I felt like this. It feels like it was only yesterday.

My brain feels frozen, my body moving on autopilot as I reach to turn the stove off. Suddenly, despite not eating all day, hunger is the last thing I'm feeling. Suddenly, the only thing I feel is thirst.

I reach for the bottle of vodka.

CHAPTER 17
Isabella

I'm breaking in my new pointe shoes when I get the phone call.

"Hey, Hailey," I say cheerfully. "I was just about to text you. Are you coming to class tonight?"

"Um, no," I hear, and right away I can tell there's something off in her voice.

I straighten. "What's wrong? What happened?"

She pauses, and in the quiet, I can hear raised voices and loud thuds in the background. Now I'm panicked and about to repeat the question louder, but before I get the chance, she asks, "Have you talked to Kane recently?"

Hearing his name in the context of whatever chaos is going on around her immediately chills my blood.

"I don't know how to answer that," I tell her. "What's going on? Just tell me."

Another pause. "Kane's kind of freaking out at the gym right now. No one knows what set him off, and Coach isn't here, and Tristan and Jax can't seem to calm him down. He's about to hurt himself with how hard he's going. I figured if anyone would know anything, it would be you."

I wrack my brain for something, anything, to explain a Kane freakout. God knows I've seen him edgy and violent, but I've never actually seen him snap—I have no idea what would set him off.

"He hasn't said anything to me," I finally respond. "I don't know why he'd be freaking out."

"Damnit," I hear Hailey mutter. More shouting in the background, and this time Kane's voice is distinct, and clearly panicked. "You're the only one any of us have ever seen talk to Kane, so I thought you might know something. And I know you're his neighbor. But I guess it was a long shot."

I blink in confusion. Because yes, I've heard people at the gym say Kane doesn't talk to them, but right now is when it really hits me that *I'm the only person Kane talks to*. That Hailey called *me* to help Kane.

It only takes me half a second to make a decision.

"I'm coming over there," I say hurriedly, standing up and tossing my things in my gym bag. "I'll be there in five minutes."

I make it in two.

I'm still breathing hard when I skitter to a stop at the gym entrance, as I throw the door open and rush inside.

But the sight that greets me stops me in my tracks.

In a way, it directly mimics the first time I met Kane. He's shirtless and drenched in sweat, and he's straddling a heavy bag on the edge of the mat and raining punches down on it.

The only difference is the first time I saw him, he stopped when he saw me. Now, he's so lost in his thoughts that he doesn't stop when I walk in. He doesn't stop when Tristan and

Jax each latch onto an arm and try to pull him off the bag that he's beaten into exploding, clothes and sand littering the mat all around him.

He's blind to everything and everyone. He just continues to punch what's left of the bag, the power with which he's throwing clearly coming from a place of pain and desperation.

I'm stunned into silence at the sight. I always knew Kane was capable of violence—even without seeing him fight, it would only take one look at him to know that fact—but this… this is something I never could've pictured. And it breaks my heart to see it.

A deep desire to help him grips me. Not because he did the same for me after the mugging, but because I want to help *him*.

"Kane," I call out, but my voice is quiet and a little breathless. I clear my throat and try again, this time louder. "Kane, stop."

He doesn't hear me. The only reaction I get is Tristan and Jax jerking their gazes toward me, but it's only for a split second, because they have to go right back to trying to restrain Kane. So, I grit my teeth and move toward him instead.

"Isabella," Jax says nervously. "I don't think you should be—"

"I don't care," I say, never taking my eyes off Kane. I step in front of him and reach forward to place a hand on his shoulder, feeling his muscles ripple as he throws his punches. "Kane, look at me," I say softly.

He stills instantly. His chest heaving, he slowly raises his head to meet my gaze.

I suck in a breath at the sight of pain—*so much pain*—in his eyes. Suddenly, I'm not looking at an angry, grown man, but a sad, broken boy. One so lost in a memory that he's not aware of his actions. Of his current reality.

"Kane," I breathe. But it says everything.

I step closer and move my hand from his shoulder to the side of his face.

"It's okay," I say in a whisper. I hold his gaze, letting him see the truth in my words and urging him to let me in. "You're okay. Everything's okay."

He swallows roughly at the words, and I see a little more of him settle back into the present moment.

I drop my hand from his face and reach for one of his hands, undoing the Velcro around his wrist and gently tugging the glove off his hand. Then I do the other one. And when I'm done, I fold his hand in mine and meet his eyes.

"Let's get out of here," I say quietly.

His nod comes without any hesitation.

I turn and start to pull him in the direction of the exit, but suddenly become aware of the fact that everyone in the gym is gaping at us. Tristan and Jax look completely shell-shocked, and even Hailey—who is obviously the most aware of my connection with Kane—is wide-eyed and silent.

I debate saying something—a joke, an apology for the mess, something—but realize it doesn't actually matter. Kane is all that matters. So, I don't say anything, I just pull him over to his bag so he can grab what he needs, and then I hustle him into the locker rooms.

When he returns after his shower, he looks calmer. Everyone else has returned to their workouts, clearly trying to return to normalcy despite the interruption. They can't help sneaking glances at us, though.

Kane ignores them and grabs my hand. Then he's pulling me out of the gym and onto the back of his bike.

After he confirms that the extra helmet is snug on my head, he swings his leg over the bike and revs the engine. "Where are we going?" His voice is rough, though I'm not sure if it's from disuse or lots of yelling.

I climb on behind him and wrap my arms around his waist without any hesitation. "Spruce Street Harbor Park. Where we're going is right next to it."

He nods once and then pulls out into traffic.

We're silent on the way, this ride vastly different from the last one we took. Where that ride was playful, this one is tense—where last time I squeezed him as tightly as I could to avoid falling off, this time I'm rubbing soothing circles over his chest to relax his tense body.

It works, a little. By the time we reach our destination, it no longer feels like I'm holding on to a marble statue.

I'm the first to hop off the bike. I take my helmet off as he takes off his, and as soon as he's settled everything, I take his hand and guide him in the direction of the river's edge.

"Where are we going?" he asks, his demand harsh.

"We're just walking," I answer simply, without looking at him. When I pull him after me, he follows. But when we reach the sidewalk and start walking, he slides his hand from mine. I don't take it personally.

I discovered Spruce Street Harbor Park when I was wandering around Philly my first week here. It's a cute little park with hammocks and weekend events, and a path along the water's edge all the way down to the Naval Yard. During the day it's almost entirely empty. When I first got here and was stressing about what to do with my life, I would come down here just to be by myself.

Kane seems like he could use a little of that right now.

My heart is still beating so hard against my ribs. Hailey's call scared me more than I knew, and only now, when I'm looking for a calming environment, do I realize just how much it affected me.

I like Kane. I shouldn't, because he's brash and rude and clearly has no interest in making friends, but the more I'm around him, the more I realize all of that is just a front. Behind that mile-high brick wall and the artillery defending it, Kane is so much more than people give him credit for. At his core, he's quick-witted and hard-working and, despite how badly he wants to deny it, he cares about other people. There's no other reason he would have taken care of me after the mugging and *then* given me peace of mind with the pepper spray and self-defense lesson.

I also think of Oscar, and about how Kane saved his life. Rescuing him out of that dumpster was one thing, but keeping him because he knew Oscar wouldn't have a chance of getting adopted is a whole other. As much as he tries to hide it, Kane is a caretaker.

Which is why I ran to the gym. Beyond the snippets that Kane's given me about a rough childhood, I don't know much about him. And yet, something tells me he doesn't—or hasn't—had a lot of people look out for him. The way he lives his life and approaches people screams loner. And while that might work day to day, everyone needs someone they can trust and lean on.

I don't know if I'll be that for Kane—if he even *wants* me to be that for him—but there's not a chance in hell I'm not going to at least offer it.

"Why'd you come to the gym?" he asks suddenly.

I don't look at him, don't react in any way when he voices the question. I'll answer anything he wants to know, and I'll be honest about it, but I refuse to make a big deal out of anything that might startle him.

"Hailey called me," I answer simply.

I can sense his confusion. "Why?"

"She knows I'm your neighbor," I say with a shrug.

He's silent after that.

We walk along the river's edge on the sidewalk, occasionally passing by other people, but for the most part, it's just us. The sound of the water is soothing, and it allows our silence to be comfortable instead of awkward.

"I don't know what those guys have against working hard," he says eventually, his voice hard and clearly defensive. "So I beat a heavy bag to a pulp, so what? Most coaches would be thrilled about it."

I don't comment on it. I just let him talk.

I feel him glance at me out of the corner of his eye. "You didn't have to come, you know. I was fine."

"I know," I say simply, still without looking at him.

He looks forward again. "I don't know why I followed you out of the gym. I should've stayed and kept working out."

I stop walking to look at him. "Do you want to go back?" I ask, keeping my tone neutral.

He stares at me. For a breath, and then another. Finally, his shoulders slump.

"No," he says, the sound of defeat heavy in his voice. He turns to continue walking.

I don't want to treat him with kid gloves, but something tells me he could use a little positive reinforcement just for that.

I reach for his hand and lace our fingers together.

And even more surprisingly, he doesn't shake me off again. In fact, I think I even feel him squeeze me back.

The more we walk, the more tension seems to leak from his stance. Being outside, in the fresh air, without anyone speaking to him or wanting something from him, I see Kane finally start to come down from the panicked headspace he was in at the gym. And even if we don't say a word to each other for the rest of the day, I feel more relaxed knowing I at least got him out of that situation.

The only time we pause our walk is when we pass by a man with a particularly friendly dog. The German Shepherd goes right up to Kane, his tail wagging happily, and he gives him a look that is very obviously a demand to be pet.

We pause for a few seconds to do just that, then we continue our silent walk. But the run-in reminds me of something, and I immediately reach into my bag.

"I meant to give this to you the next time I saw you. It's nothing huge, but..."

Kane's gaze is curious as he waits to see what I'm rummaging for. When I pull out a dog toy in the shape of a motorcycle, his lip twitches with the hint of a reaction.

"I saw him sniffing your bike the other day," I explain with a shrug. "He seems to be fascinated by it, so I thought he might like his own mini version. Although you might have to get him a side car soon."

Kane's face remains expressionless as I hand over the toy—I can't tell if he's pleased, annoyed, frustrated, anything. I watch as he inspects it.

After a few seconds, he raises his gaze to look at me. "You bought this for Oscar?"

I try for nonchalance with another shrug, hoping it makes Kane more comfortable. It's not a stretch to assume he's uncomfortable with gifts, even if the gift is for his dog.

"I saw it in the store and thought of him. It's no big deal."

For a moment, he just stares at me. I don't break his gaze—instead, I let him read whatever he wants on my face.

That I like doing things for him.

That I'm here for him.

That I like him.

Finally, his shoulders slump and he breaks our eye contact. He hands the toy back to me with a silent request to hold on to it for him, which I do without comment. And when he turns away from me and starts to walk again, his hands dug into his pockets in a clear sign of wanting space, I force myself to not let his reaction dissuade me from being there for him.

So, I follow behind him.

And a few steps later, he starts to talk.

I DON'T KNOW why I'm talking to her.

I *shouldn't* be talking to her.

Nothing good has ever come of telling someone the truth about why I'm as fucked up as I am. The last time I tried to talk about it, I was with a friend in middle school, and all I got was a blank stare and a suggestion to "maybe call the cops?"

I never opened up to anyone else ever again. For twelve years, I've been bottling everything up and releasing the valve with fighting and alcohol.

Isabella *really* shouldn't be another release.

I take a deep breath and force myself to start talking. I don't know which part is harder to admit, the one about my mom or all the rest, so I just launch into it headfirst and hope that getting it out helps the perpetual tightness in my chest.

"My mom called me last night," I start simply.

And sure enough, the second my first words come out, the pressure in my chest eases, and I feel like I can finally breathe again.

"She's an addict," I say, staring forward as we walk along

the river. "She prefers alcohol, but occasionally she'll go for an upper to keep the buzz going. I have no idea who my dad is. She probably doesn't either. But my whole childhood, all I knew was my drunk mother and her revolving door of alcoholic, scumbag boyfriends."

I take a deep breath. "She wasn't physically abusive. Her fucked up parenting had more to do with manipulation and neglect, like I think a lot of addicts tend to fall into. She was always more worried about her next buzz than anything else. It didn't take me long to figure out she doesn't love the way a parent should love their child."

I'm silent for a moment, suddenly lost in the thoughts that always revolve around memories of my mom. The *does she or doesn't she* question that has been filling my head for as long as I can remember—when I'm trying to figure out whether she actually loved me, or if she was just using me to get to her next buzz. The memories of how any positive, motherly act was always followed by massive heartache when I realized she had only done it because she was either drunk, or because she wanted something from me.

My trips to the park weren't the same happy memories that most kids had; for me, those days are tainted with the knowledge that she had to be shitfaced in order to do something for her kid. Or if she offered to do my laundry for me when I was older, it was only so she could dig through my room and steal the stash of money I'd made mowing the neighbors' lawns.

Motherly acts from her weren't done because she loved me. They were just a way to manipulate *me* into loving *her*.

"I would've been fine if it was just my mom's bullshit," I

continue thoughtfully. "Probably still a little fucked up, but plenty of people grow up under an absent parent and turn out fine. I could've survived just that."

I take a deep breath to admit the part that people always guess anyway. "But her boyfriends liked to use me as a punching bag. I can't even remember when it started, or why. I don't think I can remember a time when I *wasn't* getting beaten or thrown around by her scumbag boyfriends."

"I learned to toughen up pretty quick, and to keep my mouth shut so I didn't make it worse for myself. Most would get bored of me if I did that. But then they would dump my mom, and she'd find a new guy, and then it would start all over again."

I can *feel* Isabella stiffen beside me, but I refuse to look at her. I just keep my attention forward.

"I was fifteen the first time I stood up for myself. I had looked up a few self-defense videos on YouTube, and thought I could take on Mom's newest asshole boyfriend the next time he hit me." My chuckle is flat and humorless. "He beat me so badly, I had to stay home from school for a month." I don't add that I had to ice and bandage myself because I was too scared to go to the nurse and get my mom in trouble. By the time I went back to school, I was so far behind that I ended up dropping out a few months later.

Isabella puts it together as quickly as I expected her to. "Those are the flashbacks you get, aren't they? That's the reason you started training MMA."

I nod. "Fighting helped me take control of them. Made me feel like I was actually doing something to fight back, even years later."

She's silent for a moment. I don't know if I expected her to yell or cry or run away, but she doesn't do any of that. Even out of the corner of my eye, I can see her expression is shut down. That she's taking in everything I'm telling her and deciding how to respond.

"How long did you live in her house?" she eventually asks, her voice quiet. A quick glance at her shows me her hands are squeezed into fists, but I can't tell if she's trying to control anger or discomfort.

"I was sixteen when I ran away," I answer.

She stiffens. "Did you have to go into foster care?"

I'm already shaking my head. "No, I managed to lie my way through the next two years. I already looked older with my facial hair grown out, so I just got whatever jobs were available to me." I don't tell her that those jobs were usually fast food restaurants so I'd have something to eat.

"So then where did you live?" she asks.

I clench my jaw, hating having to admit this next part to Isabella. Not because I know she can't possibly understand it, but because despite knowingly being an asshole, I never wanted her to see me as dishonest or a thief. Unfortunately, at sixteen, with no money and no one to help me, there were just things I had to do to survive.

"When I first left, I slept in parks and public places. But eventually, I had to hotwire a car, just so I'd have someplace safe to sleep." I'm not quite ready to admit the details of the next few years, so I glaze over them and say vaguely, "Eventually I saved up enough money to talk my way into renting a shitty apartment. I was there for a little bit but ended up moving around for a few years. I lived where I could, worked where I could. I was basically a nomad until I moved up to Philly three years ago."

Isabella doesn't ask any more questions. She seems to sense that I'm not quite ready to bring this conversation into the present. It's enough that she managed to pull me out of the fucked up headspace that I always fall into after conversations with my mother.

I exhale a heavy breath, one that I've probably been holding in since the last time I vomited all this shit. I feel lighter, definitely less stressed, but I also have no idea where to go from here. The last thing I need is for Isabella to play therapist right now. So, I dig my hands into my pockets and risk a glance over at her to see what she's going to do.

She doesn't say anything. She doesn't try to convince me it'll be okay, doesn't say my mom didn't mean it. She just continues to offer silent support by walking beside me and just *being* there, her hand sometimes brushing against mine.

Slowly, so fucking slowly, the remaining tension ebbs from my muscles. Everything that bottled up inside me after the phone call last night, and everything that exploded out of me during training today... all of it is gone.

Because of one girl.

Because of Isabella.

I start to turn toward her, determined to say something, *anything*, but before I get the chance, I notice that she's looking around, clearly in search of something.

"I know it's here somewhere," she murmurs to herself. She

must spot what she's looking for, though, because she lets out a victorious whoop. Turning to me, she explains, "There are a few hammocks over the water that apparently no one knows about. I have no idea why they built them so far from the park, but you get an amazing view of the river and city, so I like to come here when I need a break. It helps that it's always quiet since it's so hidden away."

I quirk an eyebrow and look over the dock to the hammock below. "Are you sure that thing can hold us?"

"Are you calling me fat?"

My lip twitches with amusement. I don't think anyone has ever made me laugh as much as Isabella does.

"Yes, it's your hundred pounds that are going to make us drop into the water, not my two hundred plus," I say dryly.

Something about my response emboldens her, gives her the green light to move past the need for seriousness. I knew she'd make the vibe light and fluffy again at some point, but seeing the way her eyelids lower and her gaze travels over my body, it looks like she's emboldened for an entirely different reason.

"Two hundred?" she asks in a purr. "You were looking a little more than that today. It looked like you've grown a few extra muscles since the last time I saw you shirtless."

I quirk an eyebrow. "Didn't realize you were checking me out then *or* now, princess."

"It's pretty impossible not to," she whispers, her cheeks heating.

I take pity on her and step forward to lower myself into the hammock below. I'm focusing all of my energy on not breaking this fucking thing and falling into the river, and I'm not even a little surprised when I hear Isabella giggle.

"Don't you dare laugh," I growl, freezing in place the second all my weight is on the hammock. "If I go down, I'm dragging you with me."

"And here I thought chivalry was dead," she says on a laugh.

"Trust me, princess, my brand of chivalry is a little different," I say as I finally work up the nerve to lean back into a comfortable sitting position. It must shock Isabella into silence because she doesn't respond, just climbs down onto the hammock beside me.

We don't talk. For a few minutes, we're done with talking. We simply sit with each other, staring out at the city, and take in the sounds of the waves and the feel of the wind on our faces. It takes me those few minutes to work up the nerve to ask what I want to ask.

"Can you do me a favor?" I ask eventually, my voice like gravel.

"Anything," she whispers, without even a second's hesitation.

I swallow roughly, swallow down all the doubts and fears and nerves. "Can you tell me what it was like growing up in a normal family? Just… a happy memory or something."

I see her close her eyes for a moment, breathing through who knows what kind of emotion. I force down the worry that it's pity.

"Well," she starts, opening her eyes and smiling happily out at the water. "My favorite memories were always when my whole family would go to the pool in the summertime. My mom would usually take me, but the best days were when my dad would come with us, too. He'd play with me all day, and throw me around in the water, and then when we'd stop for lunch, my mom always brought a picnic basket for us. The three of us would sit and eat and then I'd pass out on a towel in the shade, feeling blissfully happy like only a kid can. Those were my favorite days."

I try to imagine what that's like: not just having a parent that wants to play with their kid, but having a parent that actually takes steps to take care of them.

I can't.

Eventually, the only thing I can get out is a quiet, "That sounds perfect."

"But I had bad memories too, you know," she continues, as if *that* doesn't drive a chill through my body. I stiffen and turn toward Isabella with a frown.

"This one time, Allie Mendoza invited me to her eighth birthday party at a nail salon," Isabella chirps, oblivious to my mounting rage. "But my mom said I was too young to have painted nails, so she didn't let me get mine done. So, I'm pretty sure my trauma is worse than yours."

For a moment, I can only blink, thrown off by the story whiplash. Then, once her comment registers, every muscle in my body relaxes and I let out a deep laugh.

Isabella peeks up at me with a smile from where she's sitting with her arms wrapped around her knees. She seems relieved.

"That's definitely worse than mine, princess," I say with a chuckle. "I'm surprised you survived that. You must've been the strongest girl in first grade."

"Well, obviously," she says with a proud smile. And when she leans her head on my shoulder, it doesn't even occur to me to put space back between us.

We talk for a while. Longer than I've ever talked to anyone. We talk about everything, and nothing. We talk about unimportant details, and embarrassing memories.

She tells me about the time her lemonade spilled on the school bus seat when she was in first grade, about how the sixth grade boys saw and teased her for 'peeing on herself.'

I tell her about the time I asked a girl in my elementary class to be my girlfriend, and she thought I was joking.

I listen more than I talk, but Isabella seems to be okay with that. And it gives me the chance to just sit with her and enjoy her company. There's no rush to get anywhere, no pressure to act a certain way, I can just… be with her.

Because when I'm with her, I don't have to think about the past, don't have to worry about the future, I can just be here, in the moment, with her.

After a while, I stretch out my stiff muscles and say, "Not that I don't like this secret meditation spot, princess, but these ropes are cutting into my ass and the wind is seeping into my bones."

She cocks an eyebrow, her grin mischievous. "Is a little chill too much for the big bad wolf?"

My eyes narrow at the taunt. I think a growl sounds from my mouth, but I'm too busy rolling on top of her, my bulk trapping her in place and my hands pinning her wrists above her head. She lets out a shriek of giggles as she's knocked backward.

"Has anyone ever told you that you're quite mouthy for a sweet little ballerina?" I drawl, pleased to see a shiver run through her body. I smirk when her smile drops and she sucks in a sudden breath.

"I'm still a sweet little ballerina," she says, but her voice is too breathy for the clapback to be effective.

"No, you're not." I cock my head and study her for a moment. "You play the part, but it's just an act, isn't it? Underneath all that lace and sweetness, you're actually a tigress. You're strong, and passionate, and you're so fucking sexy." Her chest starts to heave with rapid breaths, and I love knowing I can affect her like this. "How many people have seen that deep, Isabella? How many people know the real you?"

She swallows roughly and it takes everything in me not to press a kiss to that perfect neck. "N-not many," she stammers. "People always just see the ballet dancer."

"A travesty," I murmur. "They're missing the best parts of you."

"But you've never seen me dance," she blurts out, a confused look on her face.

I shrug. "Doesn't matter. You could be the greatest dancer that ever lived, and I'd still think the rest of you was more valuable."

Her eyes go wide at that. Something about that is triggering something in her brain, though I have no idea what because it's the most obvious thing in the world to me. My brow furrows as I look down at her, the unspoken question in my eyes.

She opens her mouth to answer, but suddenly, there's a

loud groaning sound from where the ropes of the hammock are tied to the wooden support beams.

Our eyes widen at the same time. We both freeze, too scared to move even an inch.

"Princess," I growl slowly. "If I end up smelling like fish today, I'm going to be very upset with you.

She bites down on her lip to stifle a giggle.

My eyes dart toward the wooden beam that we stepped on to get into this contraption. Slowly, so slowly, I let go of where I had pinned Isabella's wrists and I shift my weight back a bit. We hear another groan, but thankfully nothing that suggests we're about to plummet into the water.

"You go first," I murmur. "*Slowly.*"

She rolls her eyes at my bossy tone, but the flush in her cheeks gives away how much she likes it. I give her a knowing look that makes the red deepen. But then she's rolling to her knees to follow orders.

She starts to tentatively move toward the edge of the hammock, keeping her weight spread out so she's not heavy in just one spot. When she reaches the wooden beam and climbs on, I let out a breath of relief.

Then I start the crawl of terror myself. Every time the ropes groan, I expect to blink and end up in the freezing water. I have a death grip on the ropes every time I shift forward an inch.

I'm so focused on getting off this thing that I don't realize Isabella is stifling her amusement until I finally reach the dock and hear her say with a laugh, "Of all the things I expected you to be scared of, a faulty hammock was not on my list."

My attention finally snaps to her, and my eyes narrow when

I realize she's grinning. So, without giving her the chance to prepare for it, I pull her to her feet and throw her over my shoulder, heading back toward my bike.

"I'm just kidding!" she shrieks with a laugh. "You're absolutely right, a little water is terrifying."

I spank her ass with a sharp, sudden hand, and I'm pleased to hear her startled yelp.

"You're getting way too comfortable making fun of me, princess," I growl, then spank her again. She doesn't respond, but I feel her wiggling in place. When we finally reach my motorcycle and I slide her down my chest to plant her on her feet, I see a shiver run through her.

Frowning, I reach for my motorcycle jacket in one of the compartments. Without a word, I settle it on her shoulders, then I reach for the helmet and strap that on her, as well. She stands obediently as I do it.

I swing a leg over my bike and then gesture for her to hop on, which she does with a happy grin. When she settles on the seat, she slides right up against my back and wraps her arms tightly around my waist.

I don't want to admit to myself how nice it feels to have her lean on me to keep her safe. The only thing I allow myself to do is drop one of my hands to wrap around her thigh and begin rubbing a soothing pattern with my thumb.

The trip home feels way too short. I almost want to ask her if she wants to take a ride around the city, just so I can spend more time with her, but then I realize that we've been together for hours. Not to mention, she probably skipped out on her plans today to come get me at the gym.

I park my bike in front of our building. I can't tell if her moves to get off are as slow as mine, or if it's just in my head because I don't want this day to end. But when she reaches up to pull the helmet off, I beat her to it, and gently tug it off her head. By the time I put our helmets in the storage compartment and turn back to give Isabella my full attention, she's giving me a look I can't decipher.

A gust of wind blows her hair into her face, and I automatically reach for it to tuck it behind her ear. Her breath catches at the gesture, and I realize just how close we are. How right this all feels.

The obnoxious sound of a car horn has us breaking apart. With the moment broken, I sigh and gesture up the steps of our building.

"After you, princess."

Except, the second we're at her door, and I'm standing in front of her, and I'm trying to tell myself I need to leave her alone, but I'm failing so fucking badly–

Isabella sucks in a breath, looking like she wants to say something. Her eyes are filled with… *want.*

And it hits me that I'm not the only one that wants this. Not by a long shot.

My gaze darts down to her lips. I don't look for the excuse of a gust of wind to touch her, I just brush my fingers over her ear, down to her neck, and curl my hand gently around the back. Only then do my eyes lift up to meet hers again.

There's a silent question in my gaze. I want Isabella so *fucking* badly, but even the thought of her doing something regrettable makes me want to puke.

Thoughts of doubt are suddenly at the forefront of my brain. That dark little voice is telling me again that I don't deserve someone as pure as Isabella, that she'd never want someone like me, especially after everything I told her–

Those thoughts disappear in a wisp of smoke the second Isabella's lips land on mine.

Her movements are eager, her hands coming up to fist in my t-shirt and pull me down to her level so she can kiss me deeper. And I'm helpless to give in to her demands.

With a groan, my grip tightens on her neck and my tongue sweeps over her lips, silently asking for entry. She opens without hesitation. And the second I slip my tongue inside to tangle with hers, she's whimpering against my lips, and I'm fucking *gone*.

I wrap my other arm around her waist so I can pull her onto her toes and flat against my body. Her hands slide up my shirt to wrap around my neck, and I groan into the kiss when I feel her trying to get even closer.

I don't know how long I kiss her for. It could be ten seconds, it could be hours–I have no sense of time, or reality, or anything that isn't *Isabella*.

But eventually I pull away, and I realize we're both panting like we've run a marathon. My grip around her waist tightens when I realize she's clinging to my shirt, trying to hold herself up.

"*Fuck*, princess," I growl after a breathless moment. I want to say something else, but Isabella's short-circuited my brain. She looks just as stunned as I feel.

I want to kiss her again. I want to go inside with her. I

want… *more of her.*

But I don't know what *she* wants. This could very well have been a spur-of-the-moment thing for Isabella, that quick ride on the wild side that I suspected she wanted in the beginning. So, there isn't a chance in hell that I'm not taking her lead on this.

Thankfully, she doesn't make me wait long.

"Do you… umm, do you want–?" is all she's capable of stringing together.

"Yes," I say on another growl, pulling her forward until our foreheads are almost touching. "Whatever you want, *yes.*"

A shaky breath leaves her lips at my response. "I was going to ask if you wanted to come inside," she whispers.

My grip tightens on her neck. "God, yes. More than anything."

She looks up at me, her gaze equal amounts earnest and hungry. She wants this. She wants *me.*

And without a word, she opens her door and tugs me into her apartment.

CHAPTER 19
Kane

THE SECOND I have her inside the apartment, I'm pressing a desperate kiss to her lips. I grip her hips, pulling her as close to me as possible, and devour her mouth.

I didn't consciously realize it, but I've been dying for Isabella's taste for longer than I want to admit. And it's every bit the perfection I thought it would be.

My hand sinks into her hair and angles her head so I can deepen the kiss. I fist the strands and slide my tongue across her bottom lip, hoping to God she's as hungry for this as I am.

And if I had any doubts about how much Isabella wants me, they're silenced immediately in that moment. Because the second my tongue touches hers, Isabella lets out the sexiest fucking whimper I've ever heard and fists her hands in the front of my shirt. Then she spins me and pushes my back against the door, pressing up on her toes so she can get even closer. When she bites my bottom lip, I'm the one letting out the groan.

The sound must trigger something in her because her hands immediately drop down and start to scrabble at my jeans.

"Isabella, wait—"

My words end on a groan torn from my soul, my hands squeezing into fists as I attempt to stave off the sudden and shocking sensation of Isabella dropping to her knees and sucking my length into her mouth.

"Isabella, I—" I choke on my words again when she wraps a hand around the base and squeezes. "*Fuck*, princess, I'm the one that's supposed to be on my knees."

She's completely oblivious to my protests. Her hand pumps my shaft and her lips suction around the tip of my cock, and I realize that I'm completely powerless with her right now; powerless to the sight of her, kneeling before me, so eager to get my cock in her mouth that she goes too deep too fast and gags around my length.

My head drops back against the door on another groan. I can't control my hand as it slides into her hair, not to hold her against me, just to stay connected to her as she takes me deep again.

"You look so pretty like this," I murmur in a haze, watching her from under hooded eyes. Her moves aren't graceful, or practiced, they're just... *hungry*. Like she can't get enough of me, and like her only focus is on giving me as much pleasure as possible, and then tasting it on her tongue.

And *fuck*, but the sight of her dazed, lust-drunk expression, combined with swollen lips, still shiny with spit...

It occurs to me that this might be the beginning of my obsession.

Eventually, she has to pull away to suck in a much-needed breath. But even then, the heat never leaves her eyes as she continues to pump me with her hand. "You taste so good," she whispers, tucking a loose strand of hair behind her ear. But before I can respond to *that* surprising and sexy confession, she's sinking her mouth back onto my cock.

I'm not going to be able to take much more of this.

It's impossible to tell Isabella that, though. Not just because she's sucking me so good, I'm barely able to string any words together, but also because she's showing zero signs of wanting to stop.

And then it really does become obvious that I'm not going to be able to stop her, because I realize only a few seconds before it happens that I'm about to finish in her mouth. I let out a sound of surprise and tug on Isabella's hair, trying to signal what's about to happen, but she just looks up at me with a mischievous smile and tries to take me even deeper.

I manage enough control that I don't come down her throat, and instead pull back just enough to come on her tongue. The orgasm rolls through my entire body, giving me a high I've never felt before and that feels like it goes on forever.

And when she swallows every drop and pulls her mouth off me with a proud smile, I'm a fucking goner.

She's still smiling as I pull her to her feet and press a hard kiss to her lips. She doesn't fight me when I spin her around and back *her* against the door this time.

"You seem pleased with yourself," I murmur against her mouth.

"Maybe a little," she admits.

I let out a hum of affirmation and kiss her again, sinking my tongue into her mouth so I can taste that pleasure. When she moans and fists her hands in my shirt again, I slow the pace by pulling back enough to press kisses along her jaw and down her neck.

"Well, now it's my turn."

I take my time with this part of her body. Her skin is so smooth, her scent so intoxicating, that no part of me wants to rush this. I want to taste every inch of her skin, starting with the sensual curve of her neck and making my way across her shoulder.

By the time my tongue has reached—and slid under—the shoulder straps of her leotard, she's practically vibrating in my arms. She's letting out soft whimpers and bumping her hips forward into me, silently asking for more, and faster. I still her with my hands on her hips.

"Tell me, Isabella," I drawl. "Am I right in assuming you have way too many of these ballerina outfits?"

I straighten so I can see her eyes widen at the question. She nods quickly, biting into her lower lip in anticipation.

"Good. Then I can destroy this one."

And then I'm reaching under her skirt and tearing her tights at the seam.

Her shocked gasp is swallowed by my starving kiss.

With my tongue stroking into her mouth, I nudge her leotard and thong to the side and slowly, teasingly, rub my fingers along her pussy. She's drenched, her wetness making my touch slide easily through her lips.

"So wet, princess," I murmur against her lips. "Are you always this wet for me?"

She only whimpers in answer and bumps her hips harder against my hand.

I continue to run my fingers over her, but purposefully avoid where I can sense she wants my touch. It isn't until she lets out a sound of annoyance and nips hard into my lip that I zero in on her clit with an amused chuckle.

Gripping her waist with one hand, I start to rub circles with my thumb. She lets out another whimper, this time sounding much more desperate and needy.

I debate taunting her again. But with Isabella's taste in my mouth and the perfect feel of her in my hand, I think *I'm* the one that can't wait any longer. So, I sink one long finger deep inside her.

"Let's see how hard I can make you come when I'm actually trying," I tell her with a grin.

And then I slide another finger inside. She gasps and starts to ride my hand.

I'm torn; I want to kiss her, to taste her gasps and feel her moan, but I'm also mesmerized by the sight of Isabella taking control of her pleasure. I look between us to watch as she rolls her hips, and after a second, I put my thumb back on her clit. She must have already been on the edge from everything before this because just that makes her moan and drop her head back against the door.

"Are you going to come on my fingers like the good girl I know you are?" I growl, driving my fingers harder into her. I feel her walls clench around me, and I know she's close. I settle in on the spot that makes her start to shake, my thumb never stopping its circles.

Isabella nods, her eyes squeezed shut. My words don't seem to startle her, but they definitely catch me off guard. I've never been much of a dirty talker—I've always been more interested in the physicality of sex than the verbal and mental part—but with Isabella, I think I'm desperate to blow her mind in every way possible.

I'm just about to scold her to open her eyes when I feel her tighten around my fingers at the same time that her eyes pop open with a gasp.

And then she fucking *shudders*.

She's coming too hard to control the way her hips want to roll with the release. I don't mind though, I'm too mesmerized by the sight of her pleasure. The pleasure that *I* gave her.

If there's one thing in this world I'll have ever done right, it's this moment right here.

Her dazed expression zeroes back in on me. For a moment I can only stare at her, watch her come down from her lust-high and fantasize about how quickly I can drive her back there.

Holding her gaze, I lift my fingers. Her eyes go black with desire, her bottom lip bitten between her teeth as she waits for me to slide my fingers into my mouth to taste her.

Instead, I nudge down the top of her leotard and place my slick fingers on her nipple, rolling them in a lazy circle.

Her gasp is loud enough to bring a satisfied grin to my face. I don't look up at her, though, I simply take my time spreading her wetness over her skin, waiting until she's breathless and vibrating with anticipation before I lean forward and suck that same nipple into my mouth.

My eyes slide shut as a groan tears through my chest. "You taste like candy," I growl, sucking her between my lips again and feeling myself harden instantly. I can't get enough of her. I could drop to my knees and lick her for hours, could kiss every inch of her, and it still wouldn't be enough.

But something tells me we both need a different kind of connection right now. So instead of tossing her on the nearby couch and doing just that, I quickly straighten so I can reach behind her legs and haul her up into my arms.

By the time I reach her bedroom, I'm so desperate for the taste of her that I practically crush her beneath my weight when I drop her to the bed and come down on her lips. I start to lift off her, to adjust my weight so I'm not hurting her, but then I realize she's moaning into my kiss and wrapping her legs around me to pull me closer. And when I settle on top of her the way that I want to, I'm rewarded with a breathy *yes*.

It takes me forever to pull away from her lips. For seconds, minutes, the only thing I want is to kiss her and be close to her, to feel her hands scrambling to touch every inch of me and to taste the hunger on her tongue.

When I do finally pull away from her, I only get as far as her neck, and then the neckline of her leotard again. When I pull the straps off her shoulders, fully intending to strip it from her body so I can finally see her naked beauty in its entirety, I get distracted by the sight of her breasts, and the memory of how she tasted when I spread her pleasure over them.

Which immediately sends me down her body, down to the skirt she has knotted around her waist and the tights I ruined out in the living room. I shred the tights from her body as quickly as I can, intending to reach for the top of her leotard again, but then the sight of the wet spot between her legs freezes me in place.

"Goddamn, princess," I murmur in awe, rubbing a finger slowly across the drenched fabric. I vaguely hear her breaths start to come faster, but I'm too riveted by the sight before me, as I slide my finger under the leotard and pull it aside. When her perfect, pink pussy is revealed, I think I stop breathing.

I couldn't stop myself from leaning down to taste her even if the world was ending around us. After the first lick I'm groaning, after the second I'm wrapping my arms under and around her thighs so I can hold her tightly against my mouth. She tastes like fucking nirvana.

"Oh my God, *Kane*," she chokes out, her hand sliding into my hair and her thighs tightening around my ears. I think she wants to say something else, maybe give in to the urge to say something filthy like I'm hoping I can tease out of her sometime, but the words are swallowed up by her moans.

It doesn't occur to me until later that I'm already planning for a next time with her.

It takes her longer to come this time, but even still, I'm almost sad when she does. I groan when her pleasure spills on my tongue, and when I eventually pull away, it's only because she tiredly nudges my head away from her oversensitive clit.

But then she's grabbing the front of my shirt and pulling me down to her lips, and any lingering unhappiness is immediately driven away by the lust between us roaring back to life.

"So sweet," I whisper against her lips, sliding my tongue in her mouth because I already know she's filthy enough to want it.

Sure enough, she sucks her taste off my tongue with a relieved moan. And again, she's pulling me closer, silently telling me she wants me as close as possible, as connected to her as two people can be.

I half expect that I'll have to be the one to stop the kiss, but then she nudges me back just far enough that she can say with a gasp, "Take your clothes off. I want to see you."

Fuck, but the sound of this girl desperate for me is intoxicating. I reach behind my neck to grab the hem of my shirt and pull it over my head.

Immediately, her eyes go black. Her hands shake the slightest bit as she reaches up to place them on my chest. As she lightly scrapes her nails down my inked skin. Her expression is dazed as she traces one of the designs, and that's even before she lifts up and presses a kiss to it.

I groan and cup the back of her head as her lips start to travel across my chest. Her touch is like fire against my skin. It's only when her eager hands drop down to my jeans that she stops kissing me.

"Off, take them off," she says breathily, fumbling to get my button undone. My zipper's already down from her blowjob in the living room, so it doesn't take her long to push my pants over my hips.

I lean back on my knees and only pause long enough to grab a condom from my wallet, then I kick my jeans the rest of the way off. I start to place the condom but fumble through the motion when I catch sight of the woman splayed out in front of me.

The now-naked, squirming woman with her hand between her legs and a look of pure need on her face.

My hand drops to my cock and starts to slowly stroke. I'm

mesmerized by the sight of her before me like this, and that's even before I issue the command that feels perfect for Isabella.

"Touch yourself," I tell her, my voice like gravel. "Show me what you like, Isabella."

I knew she'd give me a response that would blow my mind, but nothing could've prepared me for the sight of Isabella biting her bottom lip as she arches her back and spreads her legs wide. One hand cups her breast, her fingers pinching the hard bud, while the other slides down her stomach and settles right over her pretty pink pussy. Her self-satisfied smile growing, she starts to rub in circles.

"Fuck," I breathe, hypnotized by those little circles. "Let me see, princess."

Without an ounce of hesitation, she places her fingers on either side of her lips, and spreads just enough that I can see her swollen little clit.

I fall forward with a groan torn from my chest, bracing on a hand beside her hip. I have *never* felt hunger like I do right now, never been this intoxicated by another person in my *life*. I can't move, can't speak, can't do anything other than spit on the perfect, pink cunt she just exposed and thrust all the way home in one rough motion.

Her shuddering moan is drowned out by my own muttered curse. Because if I thought she tasted good, it's nothing compared to how she *feels*.

"*Fuck*, princess, you're so tight," I say through clenched teeth. It's taking everything in me to stay still instead of driving into her, because I know it'll make me come immediately.

It doesn't help that she's wriggling underneath me. If it

wasn't for her eyes blowing black and her hands scratching at me to start moving, I'd think she was in pain. But then I hear her breathe, "Kane… *God*, you're so *big*." Her dazed expression meets mine. "Move. *Please*."

I drop from my hand to my elbow with a pained groan. "So fucking polite," I choke out, pulling my hips back and then immediately driving into her with a hard thrust.

She smiles, a sigh falling from her lips. Part of me wants to swallow the sound, but another part of me is mesmerized by the sight of Isabella looking *relieved* that I'm inside her. I can only brace above her and stare, fucking into her harder and harder.

After a minute, I realize she sucks in a breath every time I grind into her. Determined to feel her fall apart from my touch, I settle in on her clit on every hard thrust.

I sense when she starts to get close. It's not just the feel of her muscles tightening, it's also the fact that her eyes look wild and her breaths are coming in short gasps. *That's* the sight that I'm addicted to.

"Fucking give it to me, Isabella," I growl.

She comes on an aching cry, her back arching and her pussy constricting around my cock as the orgasm takes her under. I ride her through it, completely mesmerized by the feel, the sound, the *sight* of this gorgeous woman finding her pleasure.

"Oh my God," she hiccups when she finally slumps back on the bed. "And I thought your mouth was amazing."

Despite the heated moment, and the fact that I'm dying holding back my own orgasm, I let out a huff of laughter at her comment.

But even though my thrusts had slowed, they didn't stop. And her pupils are still blown, her nails still digging into any part of me she can reach, so after a second, I up my pace again.

She sucks in a breath. "Oh God… I don't think I can take any more."

"Yes, you can," I growl, reaching back with one hand so I can hook under her knee and hike it up over my arm. But she bends so easily that I lift it even further and hook her leg over my shoulder.

"So fucking flexible," I groan.

"You're so d-deep," she stammers, her eyes widening when she realizes that yes, she *can* take more.

It takes longer this time, but I force myself to hold out, knowing it will be worth feeling her come again. When her breaths start to come quicker, I lean down to kiss her, because the more her muscles squeeze me, the more I feel the need to be connected to her. Swallowing the moan she lets out, I slide my tongue in her mouth. I want to taste her pleasure the same way I want to feel it—I want my senses to be completely overwhelmed by her. And when her breaths start to take on a whine, that's exactly what happens.

I'm completely absorbed in her when she comes for me again.

She cries out into my kiss. I thought I'd be able to last through it, to pull another, and then another, from her body, but with that sound ringing in my ears, I have no hope of holding out. I come with a groan.

By the time we come down, we're both shaking from the overwhelming sensations. Her legs and arms still wrapped tightly around me, I drop my face into her neck, already not wanting to pull out of her.

But then she lets out a happy hum and presses a kiss to my neck. When I lift my head so I can look down at her, she's smiling.

For some reason, the moment I come down from my orgasm-high is the moment I see her, looking sated and happy.

And it hits me that this didn't feel the way that sex usually feels. Not even close. We were too good, too in sync, too… *perfect* for each other.

Sex has always ever been a physical release. That's it.

This wasn't that.

The thought is a stab of fear in my gut. I'm out of my element here and I don't know how to handle it. I need out.

I push onto my hands and knees, quickly disposing of the condom and then reaching for my clothes.

"I have to get going," I say absentmindedly as I pull on my shirt.

Isabella doesn't say anything, but when I'm fully dressed, and I finally lift my gaze to hers, I find an uncertain look on her face that has regret tugging at my chest.

Despite wanting to get out of here so I have enough space to breathe, I'm not blind to the fact that Isabella doesn't deserve to be made to feel like I'm abandoning her. Definitely not that I just used her for sex.

I take a knee on the bed so I can lean down to her. "I have to feed Oscar, princess," I say. Which isn't a lie, but it's also not the whole truth. "I would stay if I could. I wouldn't just fuck you and run off."

Isabella studies my expression for a moment. She knows I'm lying. She can *see* my inner freakout, but she doesn't look even the least bit mad.

She just looks understanding, in the way that Isabella always does.

A warm, honest smile appears on her face, and then she nods. "Okay," is all she says.

I press another kiss to those tempting lips, the touch like a brand.

"See you at yoga?" she asks when I finally pull away. But I'm already shaking my head.

"I'll see you before that," I vow, already regretting wanting to leave. "I'll text you. Here, put your number in my phone." I reach into my back pocket where my phone is still stashed and hand it over to her.

She bites her lip, but it does nothing to get rid of the giddy look on her face. It only takes her half a second to type the number in and hand it back to me.

I should just leave at this point, but I can't stop myself from leaning down and pressing another kiss to her lips. "Night, princess," I murmur against her mouth.

Her smile stretches against mine. "Good night, Kane," she whispers.

And for the first time in my life, I don't want to push everyone away. I don't want to keep Isabella out any longer. And even though this is inevitably going to end, if this is all the time I get with her, I want all of it.

CHAPTER 20
Isabella

"Nice work today, Isabella, that arabesque on your left side is looking really strong."

I give Mrs. Martin a grateful nod. "Thank you. It's starting to feel good, too."

When she turns to the next class of dancers, it occurs to me that I didn't have my usual reaction to a dance compliment. Usually, a compliment would come with an overwhelming sense of relief—a confirmation that I'm actually good at this thing that I do. That I'm living up to my potential.

Right now, the only thing I feel is happy that I got a compliment.

They're missing the best parts of you.

Kane's words from yesterday suddenly appear at the forefront of my mind.

That moment, that simple comment, shook the very foundation of my world. Because he wasn't trying to sell it to me, or convince me that *ballet isn't everything*, the way that everyone did after my accident. He wasn't lying just to seduce me—he was just being comfortably honest.

And it hit me, then, that I've been searching for that validation ever since my accident.

And he gave it to me, accidentally, during a playful moment between friends.

I knew Kane was a caring, genuine person even before yesterday. I guessed when I saw the defensive walls he put up, and I knew when he rescued Oscar. Seeing how he acted with me during and after the mugging only solidified that knowledge in my brain. Even without knowing everything he told me about his past, I'd still have the same opinion of him.

But now, hearing what he thinks of me…

You could be the greatest dancer that ever lived, and I'd still think the rest of you was more valuable.

It just makes me appreciate him even more.

So of course, he chooses that moment to text me.

KANE

Princess

Immediately, my heart rate starts to accelerate. How does one word, one *written* word, make me react like this?

Because it turns out that Kane can play my body in ways I didn't even know it was capable of.

Suddenly, my brain is flashing back to memories of last night.

Of Kane kissing me, touching me, *fucking* me–

I rush to distract myself by typing a response.

ISABELLA

Hi :)

My phone vibrates almost instantly.

KANE

Are you at the ballet studio? I'm in the area

ISABELLA

Yea I just finished

KANE

I'll pick you up in five

I slide my phone into my purse, fighting the urge to squeal like a teenage girl.

I'm pulling a thin, off-the-shoulder sweater over my leotard when I hear the sound of Kane's motorcycle out on the street.

I've never slept with someone I wasn't seriously dating, so casual-sex etiquette is completely foreign to me. Will it be awkward? Am I supposed to be playing this cool? I don't even know if he wants it to happen again, especially if the way he left is any indication.

Even though my intuition tells me that was just a scared gut reaction.

Taking a deep breath to calm my nerves, I toss my bag over my shoulder and exit the ballet school.

But it doesn't work, because the second I see Kane, in all his heavily muscled glory, with his tattooed hands wrapped around the handlebars and eyes hidden by his helmet, those nerves flare right back to life.

I take a tentative step toward him.

Kane seems to have no such hesitation. He takes his helmet

off so he can hang it on the handlebar and free his hands by the time I reach his side. I open my mouth to say… *something*, but I never get the chance.

Without a word, Kane grabs the bag from my shoulder and drapes it over the closest handlebar. Then he wraps an arm around my waist and pulls me up against his body.

And takes my mouth in a blistering kiss.

He tightens his grip around me and swallows my gasp. When he slides his tongue across my lower lip, silently demanding entry, it's all I can do to clutch his shirt with shaking hands and comply.

Kane mauls me in a way that leaves me breathless, that short-circuits my brain and turns me into a gasping, needy mess. I'm no longer a participant, I'm merely trying to survive.

I'm panting by the time he pulls away. He seems reluctant as he does it, nipping my lip once, twice, before he pulls back.

"Hi, princess," he rumbles in that gravelly voice.

I'm far too well-kissed to respond to that.

Kane chuckles at what is likely a dazed look on my face. Keeping his arm wrapped firmly around my waist, he reaches for my bag with the other hand and skillfully fits it into the compartment behind him.

"Come on, I'll drive you home," he says finally, handing me my helmet as he reaches for his own.

I pull it on, practically vibrating with excitement as I hop onto the seat behind Kane. I immediately wrap my arms around his waist and plaster myself flush against his back. And I realize that unlike the other times I was on Kane's bike, he's not wearing his black motorcycle jacket. He's wearing dark washed jeans and a simple—but tight—black t-shirt.

I couldn't stop myself from running my hands over his abs even if I wanted to.

"Isabella," he growls, his body stiffening. "Go any lower and we might not even make it back to the apartment."

I hide my smile in his shoulder but obediently move my hands away from where they had started lazily sliding along his waistband. In response, he revs the engine and slowly pulls away from the curb.

I drop my cheek to his shoulder and watch the buildings pass us by. I'm beginning to think the back of Kane's motorcycle is my safe space, because I feel most at peace when I'm here. No thoughts about dancing, no worries about my career or future, no panic about feeling like an outsider in this new city. My brain is silent, and my body is wrapped around the reliable and comforting presence of Kane.

I wonder if driving the bike feels this therapeutic. Maybe it's therapeutic and empowering.

"Have you ever let anyone drive your bike?"

He cocks his head in thought. "No one's ever asked."

"Who would have the balls to ask?" I ask with a chuckle.

"Your balls are plenty big, princess."

A proud smile stretches across my face.

"Do you want to learn?" he asks after a slight pause. "I can teach you."

"Really?" I squeal, the idea of spending more time with Kane immediately shaking away any lingering fears of his motorcycle. "Oh my God, I would *love* that. Yes! Please!"

I only get a grunt of affirmation in response.

A few minutes later, he's pulling into an empty parking lot and turning the engine off, then dropping the kickstand and tucking his helmet into one of the side compartments. I excitedly scramble off the back of the bike.

"Alright, I'm going to slide back and have you sit in front of me so I can keep control of everything," Kane explains. "I trust you, but not that much."

"Thanks," I grumble, sliding my leg over the bike and settling in front of Kane. I reach forward to grip the handlebars.

"Okay, now how do we get going? I want to feel the wind in my hair."

I feel a sharp nip on my shoulder. "Easy, princess. We're not going fast enough to feel the wind. You're going to take it easy today."

I'm pouting, fully expecting my expression to be invisible to Kane. But the bastard must sense it, because I feel another chuckle against my back.

"Alright, the key's already in the ignition, so I want you to start the engine. Just like that. Now, *gently*, I want you to rev it."

I'm beaming as the loud roar cuts through the sounds of the Naval Yard. I have a huge grin on my face when I turn my face to look back at Kane.

He's looking at me with something akin to affection. His eyes drop down to my lips, the urge to kiss me obvious in his expression. Instead, he presses a kiss to my bare shoulder.

"Sweet like candy," he says quietly.

But then he's focusing his attention back on the bike, and mine automatically follows. I'm turning forward when he says, "Okay, now we're going to let the clutch out and practice braking before anything else. Slowly, *start* to let the clutch out, just until the bike starts moving. Then I want you to hit the brake."

Carefully, tentatively, I do as he says. I relax my grip on the clutch, and as soon as the bike starts to move, I step on the brake and squeeze the brake lever at the same time.

"Good," Kane praises. "As long as we know how to brake, we're good. Now let's put it into gear, and start to let the clutch out again, at the same time that we gently turn the throttle. You have to do it slowly, in parallel, so that you don't stall the bike or launch it into anything. Have you ever driven a stick shift car?"

I don't admit that I've barely driven *any* car. That I had a driver living in New York and only drove because I enjoyed long road trips when I needed to clear my head.

"The goal is to turn the throttle just as much as you're letting go of the clutch—the shifts need to be identical. So as you *gently* let the clutch out, you also gently turn the throttle. Got it?"

In theory, yes. I nod.

"Good girl. Let's see it." And then he's moving his hands from my hips to the outside of the handlebars, clearly readying himself to jump in if he needs to.

I swallow nervously and do as he instructed.

I slowly let the clutch out, and I'm just starting to turn the throttle when…

The bike stalls out.

"It's okay, stalling is practically a rite of passage," Kane soothes. "Try it again."

I set my jaw and start the bike again. Then I let out the clutch again, this time turning the throttle at the same time.

Except this time, I'm too ambitious with the throttle, and suddenly there's a loud revving sound as the bike shoots forward.

I let out a loud yelp as the momentum snaps me back into Kane's chest. I somehow manage to keep my hands on the handlebars, but I'm not entirely sure I would've been able to do something about it if Kane hadn't quickly put his hands over mine and taken over. In an instant, we're back to being stopped, the engine rumbling quietly.

"Oh my God," I breathe. "That was terrifying."

Kane's chuckle soothes my nerves. "Another rite of passage," he laughs. "Now you're ready to do it the right way."

"Now I'm kind of nervous," I whisper.

He presses a kiss to my shoulder again, once, twice.

"You're doing great," he reassures me. "One more try."

Taking a deep breath, I ready myself to try again. I let out the clutch, turn the throttle, and…

The bike starts to slowly roll forward.

"Oh my God!" I shriek. "I'm actually doing it!"

Kane's laugh rolls through me.

God, I love the feel of him laughing.

"Speed it up a little. *Slowly.*"

Gently, with 100% of my focus on the throttle, I drive us a little faster.

"Perfect. Let's do a few starts and stops like that, and then we'll loop around the lot."

And as I do a lap, and then another, around the parking lot, wind in my face and Kane's warmth pressed against my back, I know this is truly my paradise. *This* is what peace feels like.

My heart feels like it's going to beat out of my chest by the time I stop the bike and drop the kickstand. I'm smiling from ear to ear, and I almost can't breathe around the happiness expanding in my chest.

"That was so much fun," I say breathlessly. "I totally get how people get addicted to this."

"You did great, princess," comes Kane's voice. "I'm impressed."

My smile, impossibly, grows wider. I can't exactly turn around but I twist in my seat so I can aim it over my shoulder at Kane. I come face to face with his lightning-filled eyes–and they're focused on me.

I can't exactly kiss him since I'm still wearing my helmet, so instead I say, "Thank you for teaching me. That was incredible."

I expect him to tease me about my eagerness, but there isn't any part of Kane's expression that's laughing right now. His stare is hard, his gaze traveling over my face until they land on my lips.

When my tongue darts out to lick them in self-consciousness, his eyes immediately blow black.

"You're welcome," he says, his voice so gravelly it scrapes over my bones. "Now drive the bike over to the side of the building where no one can see what I'm about to do to you."

I suck in a surprised breath at his words. My gaze darts over his face, looking to see if he's teasing, but the glance is useless—Kane isn't really the teasing type. I turn forward to start the bike again and do as he asks.

Kane guides me to park beside the building, where we're hidden from the street and from anyone that might be passing by. It's not completely secluded, but because the Naval Yard is closed and the building is abandoned, there's very little chance of anyone seeing us.

Seeing whatever it is that Kane is planning.

I park the bike and go to shut off the engine, but Kane stops me before I can do that.

"Leave it on," he murmurs, his hands settling on my waist.

Confused, I do as he asks. I take my helmet off and try to turn so I can get a look at his expression and maybe guess what he's planning, but his grip on me stops that, too.

"Tell me, princess. If I make you come right now, will you think I only want to fuck you?"

"What?" I squeak, once again caught off guard by Kane's bluntness.

"You heard me. Answer the question."

My hands fidget where they're folded on the tank in front of me. "I–I don't know. I haven't thought about it."

His teeth nip at my shoulder in admonition. "Beautiful little liar. I saw the look on your face when I left last night. Did you think that was a one-time thing?"

I exhale on a hard breath and force myself to be partially honest. "I don't… expect anything from you. I liked last night, obviously, but I didn't think you'd want–ohhh…"

My words trail off on a moan. Because Kane chooses that moment to slide his hands to the front of my body and dip his fingers beneath the waistline of my skirt.

"You should always wear these cute little skirts when you're on my bike," he murmurs, his lips so close to my ear that his words cause a shiver to run through me. "This whole lesson, all I could think about is whether or not the vibration of the bike was turning you on."

I swallow roughly. I *had* noticed that the vibration feels good between my legs. I'm wearing my usual tights-over-my-leotard and wrap skirt combo, so there's not much between me and the rumbling bike, and it's definitely making me wriggle in the seat. Kane's greedy touch and rough words aren't helping.

I try to get back to answering his question, try to see around the fog of lust surrounding me, because something about Kane's question feels important. I just don't know what it is.

"Kane, I–"

But he cuts me off with another nip to my shoulder. "Here's what's going to happen. I'm going to make you come on my fingers, and then on my cock. *Then* I'm going to take you out to get food before I have to go to work. Because I don't just want to fuck you, Isabella. I know exactly what you were thinking last night, and I'm telling you right now, you're not just a convenient piece of ass to me. Understood?"

I huff a laugh despite myself. "Only you could tell a woman she *isn't* 'a convenient piece of ass' and call it a seduction."

Kane's answer is to reach between my legs and rip my tights at the seam.

"Tell me you understand that this isn't a one-time, sex-only thing, Isabella," he says, sliding his fingers under my leotard and over my slippery clit. "Tell me so I can fuck you without worrying about seeing that look on your face again."

"Okay, okay," I gasp. My hips bump into his fingers, silently asking for more. "I understand. Please, just… *please.*"

I can feel his lips curve into a smile against my ear. "You beg so prettily, princess."

And then he's not talking anymore.

He slides two fingers inside me and starts to drive them in and out. His thumb settles on my clit. The pleasure spikes so suddenly that I have to brace forward on the handlebars just to be able to hold myself up and suck air into my lungs.

And that's even before Kane's other hand slides up the front of my sweater so he can cup one of my breasts through my leotard.

"Oh, God," I moan. "That feels so good, please don't s-stop–"

"Never," he growls, his fingers inside of me driving even deeper as his other hand takes my nipple in a hard pinch. "Now come all over my hand so I can fuck you on my bike like I've been dying to do."

His fingers hitting the perfect spot inside me, another hard pinch, and Kane biting that spot on my shoulder is all it takes to drive me over the edge. I shudder through the orgasm.

Eventually, I slump back against his chest with a sigh. When I feel his hard length pressed against my ass, I let out a purr of satisfaction.

Kane doesn't wait for me to recover. He simply reaches between us and starts to undo his belt. "Lift up for me, princess," he orders. "Feet on the pedals, hands on the handlebars. Hold yourself up for me so I can settle that sweet pussy in my lap."

Delirious, I do as he asks. I grip the handlebars, then somehow manage enough brainpower to brace my shoes on the pedals of the bike and lift my hips so I'm not sitting on the seat.

I hear the crinkle of a condom wrapper, and then he's yanking my ass down into his lap and impaling me on his thick cock.

I let out a cry of surprise as he fills me. He doesn't bother trying to muffle the sound, he just tightens his grip on my hips and starts to pump up into me, spewing filth between us as he does so.

"Shhh, quiet, princess. You don't want everyone to know how hungry you are for my cock, do you? That you're not the good girl everyone thinks you are?"

His words, and the gravelly voice they're spoken in, cause the pleasure to start to rise again. I'm already trembling from the first orgasm Kane wrung from me, but when he starts to drive even harder into me, I know this is going to end in me coming again.

Kane must sense that I can't hold myself anymore, because after a few minutes, he slides me forward so I'm sitting on the seat instead of in his lap.

"Lean forward, I've always wanted to try this," he growls from behind me. I automatically do as he says, and lean forward so my upper body is flat against the bike.

I ignore the pang of excitement that tells me I'm giving Kane something he's never done before.

I think I've leaned forward far enough, but when I feel Kane's hand between my shoulder blades, I realize I'm not where he wants me. It takes no encouragement to put me in the position he wants me in so he can slide back inside me.

But it isn't until my clit touches the vibrating seat and I cry out that I realize what he's doing.

"*Fuck* yes, that's what I was waiting for," he groans from behind me. "You should feel how hard your pussy just squeezed my cock."

I expect him to remove his hand now that he's put me in his desired position, but instead, I feel it slide into my hair.

I removed my usual ballerina bun after class, but only to throw it up into a loose, more comfortable, messy bun. Which means Kane only has to tug on it once for it to tumble down around my shoulders. And when he fists his hands in the curls with a whispered curse and starts to use it as leverage to thrust even harder into me, a second orgasm starts roiling inside me.

I'm lost to the sensations. With the bike vibrating between my legs and Kane driving ruthlessly into me from behind, I don't have a single coherent thought in my head. It's all I can do to hang onto the handlebars and desperately try to suck air into my lungs.

"Give me one more, princess," Kane growls into my skin. "Come all over my bike for me. I want it to be the only thing I can think of every time I ride it from now on."

That's all it takes. Kane's touch and the idea of him *wanting* to think about me.

I shudder as the orgasm tears through my body. And when the last wave rolls over me, I finally collapse forward onto the bike.

"*Fuuuuck* yes," Kane groans, riding me through the last of

it. After a few seconds I feel his hips stutter, and I know he's found his own release.

"Beautiful," Kane murmurs, his touch trailing down my sides to rest on my hips.

"I don't think I can feel my legs anymore," I mumble.

Kane lets out a chuckle at that. Squeezing my waist, he seems to enjoy simply touching me for a moment. And when he eventually drags himself away from me and swings his leg over the bike to stand beside it and right himself, he seems hesitant to put the space between us.

It hits me again that this might not be as casual as I had originally assumed.

"Let's go, princess. I want to feed you before I have to get home to Oscar."

His words immediately shake me out of my thoughts. Enough to glare at him and say, "You make *me* sound like a dog. I don't need you to feed me."

He smirks and leans forward to nip my lip before soothing it with a kiss. "But I like feeding you."

When he pulls away with an odd look in his eyes, I almost wonder if that translates to *I like taking care of you.*

CHAPTER 21
Isabella

KANE DRIVES US to his choice of dinner location, much to my dismay. But apparently one riding lesson isn't enough to make Kane let me drive.

"A cheesesteak?" I ask in confusion when I see where Kane pulls up. "That's what we're eating?"

He gives me an amused look over his shoulder. "Would you rather a fancy steakhouse, princess?"

I turn a glare on him.

He swings his leg over the bike to dismount, then extends his hand to me. Except when I let him help me off, he pulls me flush against his body as soon as I'm standing.

I suck in a startled breath at his close proximity. And that's even before he leans down to whisper in my ear, "I figured you wouldn't want to go someplace nice with shredded tights and a wet pussy. But if you want the thrill, I'm happy to take you to a fancy restaurant just so I can get you off on some expensive velvet chair while we're being served by a guy in a tux."

I can't stop the shiver that runs through me, and Kane zeroes in on how I immediately squeeze my thighs together.

He smirks, and I know he knows exactly how much his words are getting to me.

"I—You—" I try to get the words out. "I—oh my God, you're so *overwhelming*," I finally blurt out.

A loud laugh bursts from Kane. A smile spreads across his face and his eyes twinkle with happiness. Grabbing my hand, he tugs me after him.

"Have you had a Philly cheesesteak yet?" he asks once we're standing in front of our destination. I shake my head.

"I figured. These aren't the best in the city, but they're something of a classic Philly cheesesteak experience, so I thought it might be fun to start you off with it. Plus, you need two people to do it."

I wonder if this is the first time that Kane's been a part of a *two*. And I don't know if I'm imagining the pleased lilt in his voice when he says it, but either way, it makes me grip Kane's hand even tighter.

"I've heard of Pat's and Geno's, but I never knew they were right across from each other," I comment.

Kane nods. "We'll get one of each, that way you can try both and make an official pick about which one you like better. It's tradition."

It takes us only a few minutes to get the cheesesteak from Geno's. When we cross the street to Pat's, though, there's a line wrapped around the building of people waiting to order.

"Is that a… is that a *sign* on how to order?" I ask when we take our place at the end of the line.

Kane chuckles. "Yeah. Welcome to South Philly."

I squint and lean closer to read the sign.

• Specify if you want your steak wit or without onions.

• Specify plain-cheese whiz-provolone-American cheese or a pizza steak.

• Have your money ready.

• *Practice all of the above while waiting in line.* **If you make a mistake, don't panic, just go to the back of the line and start over.**

"This can't be real," I say with an incredulous laugh. "Will they really send me to the back of the line if I mess up?"

Kane shrugs. "I don't know. I've never seen anyone mess up."

It only takes us a few minutes to get to the front of the line, but in those minutes, my nervousness starts to grow. New York isn't exactly known as being a calm, sweet city, but the places I've spent time in and the people I've been around were never this outwardly brazen. I absolutely love Philly, but the bluntness is taking some getting used to.

"What can I get ya, sweetheart?" the sweaty Italian man behind the counter asks. Kane nods at me to order what I want.

"Uh…" Nerves tighten my throat, and I have to force the words out. "Um, can I get—wait, what was the first question again? Cheese type? Um—"

"Jesus, lady, get it together," comes a slurred voice from beside me. I glance over to see a drunk guy swaying in line behind us. "It doesn't take a college degree to order a fucking cheesesteak."

"Watch it," Kane bites out. Gone is the twinkle of happiness that's been on his face since he picked me up. In its place are flashes of irritation.

"Then tell her to hurry the fuck up," the guy snaps. "There's literally a sign telling her how to order. How dumb do you have to be to fuck this up?"

I turn back to the Pat's employee to place our order and try to dissolve the tension. "I'll just order a cheesesteak with onions and whiz—"

"Why don't you back the fuck up and go back to the sewer you just crawled out of," Kane snarls, stepping into the guy's face and staring him down. I see his hands squeeze into fists and I know he's seconds away from throwing the first punch.

"Kane, it's okay. Let's just—"

"Get out of my face," the guy barks. Then I watch in horror as he shoves Kane away from him.

Kane looks almost… *relieved.*

Relieved that he's now justified in pushing back? Or does fighting by itself relieve something in him?

My blood turns to ice at the realization that that's exactly what's about to happen. I've seen Kane in a physical altercation, both in the cage and on the street, and he *enjoys* it. He'll take any excuse to engage in it.

Sure enough, I watch in horror as Kane grabs the guy's shirt with two hands and pulls him up on his toes, ignoring the employee's outraged shouts. He's inches from the guy's face, staring down at him with hatred I hoped I would never see again. He opens his mouth to say something, to express his fury verbally before showing it physically—

But then he meets my eyes.

And he stops.

Slowly, miraculously, he sets the guy down and loosens his grip on his shirt. His jaw clenches with his barely restrained anger.

But thankfully, it *is* restrained. Even if he does shove the man away from himself, never taking his eyes off me.

"Get the fuck out of here," he says to the drunk. "Before I change my mind."

The guy doesn't need to be told twice. He does it with a glare, but he turns around and marches across the street to Geno's for his cheesesteak.

Kane pulls a wad of cash from his pocket and gives the guy behind the counter more than he needs to. "Sorry," he says stiffly.

The employee gives the cash a skeptical glance, but ultimately, he takes it and jerks his head toward the end of the counter to pick up the order.

Kane and I are both silent as we grab the cheesesteak and take a seat at the outside tables. I want to say something, to break the tension and get back to the fun time we were having before everything happened, but I'm not sure how to do that.

Kane somehow figures it out before I do. As he starts to unroll the paper-wrapped sandwich in his hand, he shoots me a hesitant glance and says, "I noticed you ordered onions on this one. Was that on purpose, or is that your way of saying you don't want me to kiss you for the rest of the day?"

A surprised laugh bursts out of me. I'm so relieved at his effort to salvage our time together that I stand up from where I'm sitting across from Kane and lean over the table to show him my appreciation. Still laughing, I press a grateful kiss to his lips, not even a little bit embarrassed about the way I take my time and tease him into a deep, sexy kiss. By the time I pull away, I can't help feeling a little smug about the fact that he's sucking in rapid breaths and looking like he's two seconds away from demanding another one.

"Such a pretty little tease," he murmurs, his gaze darting down to my kiss-swollen lips.

I bite down on my lip to hide my smile as I take my seat again. "So which one should I try first? Which one's your favorite?"

"Uh-uh," he says, shaking his head. "I want an unbiased opinion from you. Try them both, and then I'll tell you my favorite."

I have to work hard not to smile at Kane's fiercely focused expression as I bite into first one, then both sandwiches. I take my time making my decision, if for no other reason than to hold on to Kane's attention.

"Pat's is better," I finally decide. And I know I've made the right decision when his face splits into an excited grin.

"It's the cut of the meat, right?" he asks, reaching for the other half of the Pat's cheesesteak.

I nod my agreement, then take another bite of the sandwich. This time I let out a moan at the flavorful bite.

"Easy, princess," Kane growls. "If you get that turned on from cheese in a can, I might start to feel like I'm not that special."

I let out a snort at that. Almost immediately, my eyes go wide in shock and mortification, my hand coming up to cover my mouth.

Kane chuckles at my reaction. Then he's digging into the sandwich, ingesting almost half of it in one bite.

"I'll take you to Dalessandro's sometime," he says once he's swallowed the bite. "Personally, I think that one's the best in the city, even though it's a little outside of it."

I take another bite of my sandwich to try to cover up my glee at Kane already planning another hangout.

"So how long do I have you for?" I ask after a few minutes of us eating. Immediately I wince, realizing how clingy that just sounded. I open my mouth to clarify, to ask what time his work shift starts, but Kane's already checking the time on his phone and answering my question. He doesn't seem to even react to the way I phrased it.

"I don't start until nine tonight, which is why I had time to bring you down here. Usually, I start at seven. Depending on how long we're here, I might even have time to take Oscar for an actual walk before I head down to the club." He glances my way before adding, "You should come with us. If you're not busy."

I don't bother hiding my smile this time. "I'd like that," I tell him.

Kane nods and goes back to his sandwich, his expression unchanging—except that I can read his tells now, and I can see the gleam in his eye that says he's pleased with my response.

"So, what are you doing tonight?" he asks after a moment. "If you work and dance all day, what does a night for Isabella look like?"

I let out an exaggerated sigh, wiping my hands and

dropping the napkin on the table. Kane shoots an amused look at the empty wrapper where a cheesesteak was sitting only a few minutes ago.

"It's a big night in the Brooks apartment," I start. "First, we have an everything shower on the agenda, which I am entirely too excited for. Then, I *was* going to try a new recipe, but now I think I want to live on the taste of this cheesesteak for a few days. So that's out. I'll probably just dig into the pint of Ben and Jerry's I still have in my freezer and convince myself that I'll run it off as soon as I'm done. But realistically that won't happen until tomorrow because I'll probably get way too sucked into that new serial killer documentary on Netflix." I shrug and fold my arms in front of me on the table. "So basically, I'm going to sit on my couch with a mask on my face and ice cream in my lap and stare at horrific crimes that I have no business being so interested in."

At first, Kane can only blink at me. Then he says, "That was… a lot of information."

I laugh at his confused expression.

"So… true crime, huh?" he asks after a moment. "Every time I think I've got you figured out, you surprise me with something."

"What do I look like I'd be interested in instead?"

He shrugs. "I don't know. Sweet, romantic movies?"

"Why, because I'm a girly girl?" I ask with a laugh, expecting the tone of the conversation to stay light.

But the way Kane looks at me is anything but.

"No. Because you see the best in people, not the worst."

My laughter catches at the sight of his earnest gaze. And if there was any remaining doubt in my mind that Kane deserves a chance, it wilts in that moment.

I don't know how to respond to him without coming off as a completely obsessed and lovesick girl, but thankfully, Kane saves me from having to do that. He reaches for the other half of the first cheesesteak as he asks, "So why true crime?"

I fidget with the wrapper in front of me as I answer. "I like the psychology of it. I always think the reasons that people have for doing things are fascinating. I—" Swallowing roughly, I hesitate to add the next part. But with the encouraging way that Kane is looking at me, it feels like the most natural thing in the world to keep talking. "I always thought if I ever went to college, I'd pick psychology as my major," I eventually admit.

Kane doesn't even hesitate before he nods in agreement. "That doesn't surprise me. You're too good with people to not be successful in that kind of field."

I'm pretty sure I'm beaming at him. I've never admitted that dream to anyone, too scared to say it out loud, and yet, once again, he's supporting me without any hesitation. The same way he did when I admitted my fears about only ever being seen as a dancer.

I don't think this is just a crush anymore.

I force the terrifying thought down before I do something embarrassing—like admit that out loud. God knows I still don't know where this thing with Kane is even going.

"Have you ever thought about going to college?" I ask instead.

He winces, but doesn't shy away from talking about himself the way he would have a few weeks ago. "College wasn't really on my radar," he admits. "I didn't even get my GED until I was twenty-one."

I debate pushing him a little further with a dreams and aspirations type conversation, but I can tell by the tension in his shoulders and the stiff set of his jaw that admitting even that much was hard for him. So, I take pity on him and lighten the conversation.

"So, no psychology, and no true crime. What do you like to watch then? Sitcoms? Docudrama? Oh my God, are you a reality TV kind of guy?"

The corner of his lip twitches in amusement. "I think that cheese whiz went right to your head, princess. What kind of reality TV could you ever picture me watching?"

I shrug, biting my lip to tamp down on my smile. "You seem like you might enjoy a good cooking show."

He chuckles, and I think I'll never get tired of that sound. "I do actually enjoy a good Hell's Kitchen episode. But no, that's not my go-to."

When I only wait expectantly, he finally says, "I like sitcoms. Animated sitcoms, preferably. But anything funny, especially if it's smart humor. It's my favorite kind of… distraction."

Humor. I should've guessed that's what Kane would gravitate toward. And as much as it makes my heart hurt all over again that a twenty-six-year-old man has to watch TV for a little bit of laughter in his life, it just makes me even more determined to make him smile outside of that.

"So, then you like Family Guy over the Simpsons, right?"

Kane freezes in his bite and turns a glare on me. "Blasphemy. Take it back."

I let out a loud and happy laugh. Which makes a half-smile appear on his face.

"So, what have you been watching lately?" I ask, leaning forward to swipe a little bit of cheese that's dripping out of Kane's sandwich. His gaze follows the path of my finger, and when I pop it in my mouth, his eyes blacken.

"I've been doing a Rick and Morty rewatch lately," he says slowly. His attention moves up to my eyes. "Ever seen it?"

I shake my head.

"You should watch it sometime," he says.

I open my mouth to say something that hopefully isn't *I would absolutely love a Netflix and chill date with you*, but thankfully, I'm stopped from embarrassing myself when my phone chimes with a text message.

"Everything good?" Kane asks when I check my phone before quickly putting it away.

"It's just my mom," I answer with a sigh. "She's been checking in with me a lot since I moved down here. I guess she's having a hard time letting go. I'll call her when I get home."

Kane's voice is stilted when he says, "It's nice of her to be worried." He starts to wrap up the last of the cheesesteaks and collect all the trash from our table.

He seems to be mulling something over in his head as he does it. I think he's going to say something else, maybe reveal more of himself, but suddenly, he's standing up and throwing our trash away.

"Let me get you home, princess."

I want to tell him I don't want to go, that I want to spend

more time with him and get to know him better, but I also don't want to push him further than he wants to be pushed. So, I stand and press a chaste kiss to Kane's cheek before saying, "Thank you for dinner."

His expression softens at that. "So polite," he murmurs.

And when he takes my mouth in a kiss, there's none of the chasteness that mine had.

I'M STANDING AT the front door of the club, clicking the pen in my hand, when Marcus finds me.

"Hey, man, Crystal's finishing up with her guy now, so we should be ready to flip for who closes with Bobby in a few minutes."

I give him a gruff nod and go back to glaring out of my head.

I've been pissy all day. I almost got into a fight with a patron earlier that was a normal level of drunk, but I felt like punching someone and he just happened to light the fuse.

It's an odd switch from the past few days. Up until today, I've been pretty much the opposite. I haven't gone after anyone at the club, haven't wanted to snap at anyone in public—I even managed to focus on technique instead of brute strength at the gym. For days, I haven't been my usual angry self.

Since I saw Isabella.

That was the last time I had a late shift. The club has security working extra lately, so the fact that I got even a late start is unheard of—forget having a day off. I've worked every day for the past five days, and I'm on for the next seven straight.

Unfortunately, that also means I haven't been able to see Isabella again. It's not just that she's an early bird and I'm a night owl, it's also that while I'm free, she's working or dancing. And by the time she's free, I'm heading off to work. We have complete opposite schedules, and it's making me pissy as fuck.

Marcus shakes me out of my thoughts when I see him waving from the other side of the floor. The two other bouncers are already standing there, staring glumly at the straws in Marcus's hand.

Closing with Bobby is undisputedly the worst part of working this job. He's the only manager that takes hours to close, all because he re-counts the cash multiple times before he's satisfied. And we have to wait while he does it. So anytime he's closing manager, the bouncers draw straws to decide who gets to be the unlucky bastard that doesn't get home until 5 a.m.

But then I realize something as I'm walking over to the group. The last time I closed with Bobby was the night Isabella knocked on my door at 6 a.m. because she heard me walking around.

An idea hits me just as I reach the guys. Before they can each grab a straw, I shove my hands in my pockets and say in an attempted casual tone, "I can close with Bobby tonight."

The guys stare at me like I've grown three heads. Rightfully so. No one in the history of the club has ever offered to stay *later*.

"You sure?" Marcus asks, his tone skeptical.

I nod stiffly. "Yeah, it's no problem." I think they want me to add a *why*, but they know me well enough not to expect it.

Marcus sighs. "Alright, well I'm not going to say no to that. Good luck getting to sleep at dawn."

I'm counting on it.

I wait at the front desk while Bobby goes through his closing tasks. Normally when I do this, I'm counting the minutes, feeling my annoyance mount as my tiredness does, but tonight I'm counting the minutes as my excitement builds. I pass the time with memories of the other day with Isabella, of how it felt fucking her on my bike and then listening to her talk when I took her out to eat after. I've realized I could listen to her talk for hours—not just because there's something incredibly soothing about her voice, but also because I like getting inside her brain. I *like* that she's chatty.

I'm smiling to myself when Bobby finds me. He gestures to me that he's done and ready to go.

I rush to grab my jacket and helmet.

It's 5 a.m. when I finally walk into my apartment. After greeting a sleepy Oscar, I decide on a quick shower, wanting to wash the stink of the club off me. But that only takes a few minutes, and when I walk back into my living room, I realize it's still only 5:20 a.m. And I don't hear any sounds coming from Isabella's apartment.

I start to pace, trying to figure out how long I should wait before I knock on her door. I make myself a cup of coffee in an effort to stay awake, but I'm so wired with nerves that I don't even really need it.

What if that was a one-off and she doesn't usually get up at six? What if we really do have total opposite schedules and the only time I get with her is hurried greetings in the hallway and a rare night off?

Oscar gives me a confused and grumpy stare as I pace a groove into my floor.

Just when I'm about to give up, I hear a cabinet door slam in her apartment.

I'm out my door before the sound has even died down.

My knock on her front door sounds loud and desperate to my ears, but I'm beyond caring. It's been five days since I've seen her.

When she opens the door, her brow is creased with worry. "I'm sorry, did I wake you? I try to be quiet—"

I cut her off by stepping forward and pressing a hard kiss to her lips.

I only mean it to be a single peck, but the second I get her taste in my mouth, I'm a fucking goner. Sliding my hands into her hair, I tease her lips open with my tongue as I try to get more of it.

When I eventually pull away, we're both gasping for breath. Leaning my forehead against hers, I say in a gruff murmur, "Morning, princess."

She's too surprised, too busy trying to get air into her lungs, to respond. The only thing she eventually gets out is a confused, "What...?"

I begrudgingly remove my hands from her hair and take a step back. "I heard you up, so I just wanted to see you before you left for work."

Her confusion doesn't fade. Her gaze darts over my face, taking in the tired look in my eyes. "You just got home from work?" she guesses.

I nod. She doesn't need to know that 'just' is a stretch.

Her expression becomes worried. "You should go to bed, you're probably exhausted."

I shrug and admit, "I wanted to see you."

She visibly melts at that, and her cheeks pinken as a happy smile appears on her face. "I've been wanting to see you, too," she whispers shyly.

I take that as the confirmation I needed and take a slow step into her space again. Wrapping an arm around her waist, I pull her against my body, letting out a pleased hum when she braces her hands on my chest.

"Our schedules don't really seem to align," I muse.

"No, they don't," she agrees quietly. She pauses, then adds, "I'm glad you came over this morning."

I swallow roughly. "Yeah?"

She nods immediately, the want on her face obvious as she stares up at me. I decide that's all the green light I need.

"I was thinking maybe I could see you in the mornings before you go to work," I suggest tentatively. "I could make you breakfast, even."

And *fuck*, but every single shred of nerves and doubt and worry that I had evaporates at the sight of the bright smile that appears on her face. She almost looks *relieved* that I offered.

I decide then that I don't care if I'm being needy or pussy-whipped or a fucking idiot for wanting to be with a person that will undoubtedly wise up and leave me in the end. If this is all the time I get with her, I want all of it.

"Are you sure you're not too tired?" she asks hesitantly. "I know you have long days with training and working."

I have to smother the grin that wants to appear on my face. "I'm sure."

Relief fills her expression. But then something occurs to her, because she asks, "What time do your work shifts start again?"

"Usually 7, sometimes 9. Why?"

She bites her lip before saying nervously, "Because I was thinking about it too, and… I usually get done dancing at 6. Maybe I could see you if you pick me up from the school? Or was the other day just because you started late?"

"I can pick you up," I respond, not caring how quickly it comes out.

Her smile is blinding. "Okay, great," she breathes.

And then I can't *not* kiss her again. With my arm still around her waist, it's easy to drop my head and take her mouth.

It's *not* easy to pull away before it escalates.

But I'm determined to spend the morning with her. And I don't even care that I've been up for almost twenty-four hours, because hearing Isabella sit at the counter and happily chirp away about some book she just picked up now that she has free time is enough to fill my chest with contentment. I merely listen, and occasionally hum in response, as I make eggs and bacon for our breakfast.

And when I leave her apartment twenty minutes later, I'm not even bummed that I only got a little bit of time with her. Because it's more than I had yesterday.

After a few hours of shut-eye, I head to training. I've been bringing Oscar to the gym with me, since not having enough time for him was one of my biggest concerns about keeping him, and because I just hate leaving him at home by himself. Thankfully, the gym is walking distance from the apartment. It helps, too, that Coach brings in his bulldog that he named the gym after, so the two dogs even get a little bit of socialization while the rest of us work out.

I anticipate my workout being shittier because of the change in my sleep schedule, but the opposite seems to happen. Whether it's because I don't have any energy, or because I'm so tired that I don't have any room for stress, but my technique is on point at the gym today. My rolls during jiu-jitsu fall into a relaxing rhythm and I don't have nearly as many aggressive outbursts during sparring. And the most shocking part? I don't have any flashbacks when I get hit.

I expect it to be a fluke, but a few days later I'm still feeling good. Still feeling relaxed when I train, and calm when I spar. I feel like I'm on a whole other level of fighting.

I'm hitting the heavy bag, working a new combo and trying to get my weight distribution right, when Coach approaches me.

"If you want to fix your balance, step further to the left before you throw that kick," he says without my having to ask.

I try it once and instantly feel the difference.

Coach grunts his approval. I just wait for him to say what he's here to say.

"I can get you the Chevlin fight," he says suddenly.

I quirk an eyebrow. Yoga deal aside, I was fully expecting him to never think I was ready for that fight.

"But I want you to do something for me if we agree to that matchup."

I stare at him for a moment. "Okay…"

"No sparring."

Both eyebrows shoot to my hairline. "What? No sparring *at all?*"

He nods. "No sparring at all. I want you to beat him with jiu-jitsu."

I wince. "That's not exactly my strong suit, Coach."

He gives me a knowing look. "I know. That's why I want you to work it for this fight. Because it's *his* weakness."

I'm still not convinced, and I'm sure it shows on my face.

"Kane, if you get into a boxing match with Chevlin, you *might* win. Toe to toe, either of you could beat the other. And I was prepared to get you that fight and let you have at it. But now…" He sighs and looks off to the side. "Look, your training has gotten way better. I'm going to blame it on the yoga so that I can take credit for it, but your breathing is better, your control is better, and you're definitely more present mentally. I want to build on that. I want *you* to build on that. I'd much rather see you be an athlete than a fighter."

And for the first time, it occurs to me that there's a clear difference between those two things.

"So… what would my training look like then?" I ask, still hesitantly. "Everything the same except no sparring? Can I still hit the bag?"

"Sure. Hit the bag all you want. But when we're prepping for this fight, I want you to work more wrestling and take more jiu-jitsu classes. And keep doing yoga, if that's what's helping your focus. It'll probably help even more with the jiu-jitsu."

I don't tell him that the yoga *has* helped with both my breathing and flexibility, or that he'd have to pry me away from that class with the jaws of life. But that's for a different reason that he doesn't need to know about.

"Okay, I'm in," I agree. And even though it was his idea, he looks surprised that I signed on so quickly.

"Good," he says with a stiff nod. "I'll set it up. It won't be for a few months because Chevlin's gearing up for a fight in two weeks, but that just gives us a little more time to get you ready."

"Okay." And then, a little gruffly but with a lot less struggle than it used to take… "Thanks, Coach."

His gaze softens at that. As much as a guy like him can soften. He claps me on the back before walking away, and it occurs to me that if I ever had a real father figure, Coach Dominic would be what I would imagine.

To say I was elated when Kane suggested we hang out between our work schedules is an understatement. I've never known someone with such an opposite schedule to mine, and if I'm being honest with myself, I was getting a little cranky about it. Seeing Kane once a week on a rare night off wasn't enough— not after everything exploded between us. I wanted to get to know *him*, not just have a quickie every once in a while when we had time.

Not that I don't enjoy those. Because *God*, do I enjoy those.

Even the thought of the hungry look on Kane's face when I open my door in the morning is enough to make my face heat. He doesn't always fuck me as soon as he pushes into my apartment, but when he does—

I shake the memories of the past few days from my head. Kane's about to get home, and although it's obvious that we both love the physical aspect of this… whatever this is, I hate that he thought I only wanted him for sex. I've been making it a point to greet him with coffee the past few days for that reason.

I glance at the clock on the wall. 5:16. Kane should be here any minute.

It didn't take me long to figure out that he gets home way earlier than he originally let on. Six is my usual wakeup time, but when I realized that he was knocking as soon as I started making noise in my kitchen, I started waking up earlier and earlier. Sure enough, I found him walking up the stairs to our floor at 5 a.m. yesterday.

I don't even mind, I'll take all the time with him I can get.

And if our mornings together weren't enough, he's also been picking me up at the ballet school every day. I don't even mind that it means I have no use for my car anymore, I'll happily trade it for a fifteen-minute bike ride with Kane where I have free rein to touch him however I want.

When I hear the knock on my front door, I grab the fresh coffee from the Keurig machine and try, unsuccessfully, to tamp down on the excitement bubbling in my chest. I thought for sure this schoolgirl crush would eventually die down, but it's become obvious that isn't the case at all.

The more I get to know Kane, the more I want to be around him.

My smile is about to split my face when I open the door. He looks tired, the way he always does after his all-night shift, but there's still that twinkle in his eye that says he's happy to see me.

"Hi," I all but squeak.

"Hi, princess," he says in that deep voice that never fails to make my knees weak.

I extend the coffee so as to keep myself from throwing

myself at him.

"How was work?" I ask, walking over to my own cup of coffee. "Any rowdy patrons?"

"I think you have the wrong impression of the excitement level at my job," he answers, his voice giving away his amusement. When I turn to look at him, he's stepped into my apartment and the corner of his lip is lifted in a half-smirk as he goes to take a sip of the coffee.

"I think I have exactly the right vision of what bouncing at a strip club is like," I quip, turning on the espresso machine. "Drunk, feral men everywhere that can't take their eyes off of the hottest women on earth doing incredible acrobatics on stage. I think that's the definition of excitement."

Kane's amusement only multiplies during my description. "Remind me to never take you to the club if *that's* what you think it looks like," he says, taking a seat at my little kitchen table.

"How far off am I?"

"You're not even in the same realm."

I take my cup of espresso in hand and walk over to my fridge to grab some ice. But when I open the freezer door and come face to face with the vanilla ice cream, I'm momentarily distracted.

I bought the gallon yesterday when my week-before-period sugar cravings started up. I rarely ever ate sweets when I was dancing, but if I *did* eat them, it was always with the excuse of my period. It became somehow ingrained in me that I could only eat them during that week. And since I'm still a few days out, I haven't touched the container yet. I just stare at it and drool every time I open the freezer.

I drop an ice cube in my espresso and close the door with a wistful sigh. When I turn around to return to my conversation with Kane, I realize he noticed my pause.

He quirks an eyebrow before his gaze darts back to my freezer. Then he stands up and walks across my kitchen.

"What're you—?"

He doesn't say a word as he opens the freezer and takes the ice cream out. Or while he takes a spoon from my drawer and uses it to scoop some from the container and drop it directly into my glass of espresso.

The only time he talks is when he presses the concoction into my hand and says by way of explanation, "You didn't look like you'd be open to scooping right out of the gallon at 6 a.m."

I can only stare at the glass in my hand.

"Try it, it's delicious," he says, settling back in his seat and reaching for his own coffee.

Tentatively, I take the spoon Kane left in the cup and scoop up some of the already-melting ice cream and caffeine mixture.

"Oh my God, that's so good," I moan as it melts on my tongue. "How have I never thought to do this?" Taking a seat across from Kane at the table, I immediately dig in for another spoonful.

By the time I've eaten the ice cream and drank the last drops of espresso, it's been a few minutes of nothing but the occasional sigh of pleasure and the sound of my spoon scraping the bottom of the glass. When I finally move my attention back to Kane, I find his heated gaze glued to me—specifically, to my lips.

I swipe my tongue over them as I feel my face heat in embarrassment. Hurriedly, I place the glass on the table and slide it away from me. But before I can try to gloss over the fact that I just inhaled an entire scoop of ice cream first thing in the morning, Kane's already grabbing the spoon from my hand and jabbing in into the still-open gallon container on the table.

I'm only confused for a second, because then Kane is immediately scooping more ice cream onto the spoon and lifting it to my lips.

"We're eating ice cream for breakfast?" I ask with a nervous laugh. "I thought we were going to make omelets today."

He shrugs and eats the bite himself. "Ice cream sounds better, don't you think?" Digging into the container, he lifts the spoon to my lips in offer. When I hesitate, he says, "Come on, princess. Live a little."

That thought has me melting faster than the ice cream. I wrap my lips around the spoon… and almost purr in pleasure when the sweet vanilla bean graces my tongue.

And when Kane leans forward and licks into my mouth, I *do* purr in pleasure. Then I'm kissing him back, tangling my tongue with his, and I don't even notice that I've climbed into his lap until he pulls back and I realize I'm straddling his waist.

A whimper escapes me when he ends the kiss, making Kane chuckle. But he doesn't move far, just enough that he can load up with more ice cream.

"Such a tease," I whisper.

His expression becomes amused as he holds another spoonful of ice cream to my lips. "That's not something I ever thought you'd accuse me of."

I take my time licking the ice cream off the spoon, feeling proud of myself when Kane's eyes blacken. And yet, he doesn't kiss me again.

It takes me a second to pull away from Kane's intoxicating touch. But even then, the only thing I can really manage is to not lean into it. "You're working tonight?" I ask eventually.

"Mhmm."

I start to squirm in his lap. "So, when do I get you next? When's your next night off?"

"Not until next Monday. So, you're stuck with early mornings and end-of-the-day bike rides for now."

"What if I come visit the club this weekend?"

He doesn't even hesitate with his answer. "Absolutely not. It would take the owner two seconds to offer you a job. And you're not taking your clothes off for anyone that isn't me."

I can't stop the pleased smile from appearing on my face. I haven't seen jealous Kane yet, but I think I like him.

"You wouldn't pay to watch me strip?" I tease with a pretend pout.

I'm met with a hard look. "Princess, I'd give my left arm to watch you strip. But I'd pay ten times that to make sure no one else ever gets to."

Kane's words drive heat through my body and dampness between my legs. I can't stop myself from rocking closer.

"So possessive," I whisper. When I start to absentmindedly trace the tattoos on his shoulders, I love that I can feel the shiver that runs through his big body. He doesn't respond, he just tightens his grip on my waist. He's like a leashed animal, waiting on my signal to pounce.

I don't give it to him. Yet.

"I have a better idea, if you're interested," I say. "Well, better for me. You might choose the strip club option after you hear my idea."

"Impossible."

His immediate response makes me giggle. Which makes him raise an eyebrow.

"Well, now you have me curious. What's the idea?"

I bite my lip in hesitation. Kane's gaze immediately drops down to it, before reaching up to tug it free with his thumb.

"These lips could make me agree to anything," he says thoughtfully.

I huff a laugh despite the sensual tone of the words. "Hold that thought."

I get another eyebrow lift in response.

"There's a yoga thing I want to try," I finally say. "It's on Sunday morning."

Kane shrugs. "Okay. Let's do it."

I bite into my lip again. "It's goat yoga."

"Absolutely not."

I shift closer and wrap my arms around his neck. "But it'll be so much fun, it's just yoga with baby goats. They're like puppies! And you love puppies."

He gives me a hard stare. "I love Oscar. There's a difference."

I pout. And laugh internally when Kane visibly softens at the sight.

I press a kiss to his jaw, my hips involuntarily shifting closer. "Please? I've always wanted to try it."

His grip tightens on my waist as he pulls me closer. "You're playing dirty, princess."

I feel emboldened, in a way that's become familiar since I've started spending time with Kane. I lean forward so I can nip his earlobe and blow gently into his ear. "I can play even dirtier, if you'd like," I whisper.

A growl sounds in my ear. "Yeah? Show me."

I drop my kisses to his throat as I unwind my arms from around his neck so I can lower my hands to his jeans and start to unzip them. In between kisses, I ask, "And then you'll come with me this weekend?"

"Show me and I'll agree to whatever you want, princess."

And even though it's obvious that Kane would've agreed to my date idea from my first plea, I don't hesitate to do exactly what he wants. Because I'll look for any excuse to worship this man.

I slide to my knees and settle on the floor between Kane's legs. When I reach inside his pants to pull out his length, I can't help glancing at his face to see his reaction.

His posture is relaxed, and he's giving me an expectant look. He looks like a king waiting to be serviced.

I huff a laugh and lean forward to take him in my mouth.

His relaxed posture disappears almost instantly. I feel his thighs flex and harden under my hand that's braced on them, and I hear a groan when I swirl my tongue around the head of his cock. That sound just makes me suck him even harder.

I take my time, alternating between taking him deep and playing with the tip. When I feel Kane sink one hand into my hair, I expect him to urge me to a quicker pace, to start fucking my mouth. I relax my throat and wait for it.

But he doesn't do any of that. He seems to be enjoying everything I'm doing, if his occasional groans and breathy curses are any indication, and he doesn't do anything to take over control. He just seems to want to touch me as I suck him.

He brushes my hair out of my face, first on one side and then the other, before taking all of it in his hand at the back of my neck. And then I'm remembering the way he gripped my hair when he fucked me on his bike, the way he liked keeping me close with that connection.

The memory of it, and the thought of Kane *needing* me, in any sense, makes me moan around his length.

"*Fuck*, princess," he groans. "Even your mouth is sweet. You like sucking my cock?"

I look up at him and nod, continuing to suck him. And immediately become mesmerized by the look in his eyes.

His focus is solely on me, his pupils blown black with lust, but it's the look of awe, and of hunger, that hits me. He looks like I'm the only thing he wants in the world right now.

My body heats from his attention. Between the look in his eyes and the feel of his grip in my hair, I'm too turned on to stop myself from spreading my legs and slipping my hand under the fabric of my thong.

Kane notes the move, and tightens his grip in my hair. I watch as his jaw clenches and as he gives in to the lust swirling in his eyes. When he starts to thrust up into my mouth, I almost want to smile.

The quicker he thrusts, the quicker my own hand moves between his legs. My body heats, an orgasm roiling inside me, and I give up trying to suck him. I simply give Kane my mouth and let him take his pleasure.

When he comes, it's with a deep groan. His head drops back, his eyes close, and I taste his pleasure on my tongue. After a moment, his hand drops from my hair and I pull away with a pleased hum.

Kane takes in a stuttering breath, clearly trying to compose himself. My own need for release fades as the moment cools.

And yet, at this point I should know Kane better than to think he would let me go without. As soon as his focus lands on me again, and he takes a second to tuck himself away, he's leaning down to pull me up.

I expect him to settle me on his lap again, but instead, he seats me on my kitchen table. And his lips are on mine before I can even take a full breath.

His kiss is slow, and grateful. Like he knows that the only thing I wanted was to please him. He takes his time showing me that appreciation.

I'm so lost in his kiss that it takes me a second to realize his hands are on my thighs and pushing my silk nightgown higher on my legs. When he nears my drenched center, my breaths start to come faster.

But his kiss only intensifies at that, his hands continuing to bare me to him. When he finally reaches my panties, he takes both sides in his fingers and slowly slides them down my legs.

I'm panting by the time he pulls away and tugs them the rest of the way off. Kane in seduction mode is unmatched.

"Lean back and spread your legs," he says in that deliciously deep voice, his eyes sparking with heat all over again.

I don't hesitate to do as he says.

Leaning back on my hands, I spread my legs and wait with bated breath for him to touch me. I don't know if he meant for me to lay on my back, but I'm desperate to watch Kane do whatever he's about to do.

He doesn't touch me right away. For a moment, he just stares at me, his gaze moving from my flushed face, down to where my nipples have hardened against the silk of my nightgown, and landing on my drenched center. When he drags his hand over his mouth in hungry anticipation, I practically expire on the table.

And that's even before his cocky gaze meets mine and he says, "Look how messy you are, princess. Should we make you even messier?"

Before I can answer, he's pressing my thighs farther apart, opening me to him completely, and leaning forward in his chair to press his mouth to my clit.

A whimper escapes me as soon as he makes contact with my skin. He's thorough in his movements, taking his time alternating between swirling his tongue around my clit and licking the length of my pussy, savoring the taste. That thought is solidified when his fingers dig into my thighs and his groan vibrates against me.

It doesn't take much time for my orgasm to come roaring back from a few minutes ago. When I feel it start to crest, my eyes close on a moan and my head tips back in anticipation.

Except, Kane chooses that moment to take his mouth away. I open my eyes, ready to scold him again for being a tease, but I'm met with the sight of him reaching for the melting ice cream that's still on the kitchen table beside us. And when he scoops a spoonful into his mouth, my brow furrows in confusion.

I'm too surprised to say anything on the first bite. But then he takes another, and another. The corner of his lip is twitching in amusement, which means he knows exactly what he's doing right now. *I* just don't understand what he's doing right now.

I open my mouth to ask him exactly that, but before I can get the words out, he's swallowing his last bite of ice cream and putting the spoon back in the gallon container. Then he's pushing my thighs apart once more and dipping his head to suction his cold mouth to my clit.

I let out a startled yelp, the sensation like a shock to my body. Leaning onto one hand, I reach with the other to push him away. But by the time my hand makes contact with his head, the cold is already melting into a delicious warmth.

Sucking in a startled breath, my hand fists in his hair. The more his tongue continues to swirl, the hotter his mouth feels. Within seconds, I'm not pushing his head away, but pulling him closer.

"Oh my God, you're going to make me come on your mouth," I gasp, surprising myself with the desire to vocalize these intense feelings. But between the sudden temperature shift and Kane's skilled tongue, a rush of pleasure is starting to expand in my body, and I can sense that I'm about to be completely overwhelmed by it.

Kane lets out a groan at my declaration. His tongue starts to swirl even faster, his movements becoming desperate. I'm two seconds away from the strongest orgasm of my life.

And when he slides two fingers inside me, the bomb inside me explodes.

I don't know what sounds I make, I only know that I'm holding Kane's mouth against me and shaking through the sensations pulsing through my body. It might take minutes or hours, I don't know. I lose all sense of myself as it happens.

When they finally abate and I slump back onto the kitchen table, Kane looks reluctant as he pulls away from me. He doesn't even seem to notice that he's hard again, he just looks like he wants to taste more of me.

I possess none of my usual grace as I climb down off the table and settle in Kane's lap again. It feels effortless to lean forward and kiss him, letting out a pleased hum when he grips my waist to pull me closer and kiss me harder.

"Best breakfast ever," he groans into the kiss.

My lips lift into a smile against his. "Agreed."

But when I shift slightly and realize he's hard again, the smile turns into a frown. I enjoy sex with Kane too much to ever let him leave with blue balls, so I don't hesitate to reach down and start to undo his jeans again.

He stops me with a hand on mine. "Don't worry about me, I'm fine. I get hard from even *looking* at you, so this is nothing new, princess." He nudges me back to put a little bit of space between us. "Let's make breakfast."

When I only stare at him in shock, he gives my ass a playful smack and says, "Up, princess."

"What about goat yoga?" I blurt out.

Kane sighs. "You already know my answer is yes."

I can't help it—a grin stretches across my face. Then I'm pressing an excited kiss to Kane's lips.

"Okay, it's Sunday morning at 10am on the riverfront," I

say excitedly. "I know that won't give you a lot of time to sleep after work, but if you want, we could even get an early brunch before we go and make a whole day out of it—"

He cuts off my rambling with a kiss of his own.

CHAPTER 24
Kane

"Alright, everyone, let's take our places on our mats and get ready to meet our furry friends for the morning!"

I have to actively hold in a groan at the overly cheerful yoga teacher's introduction. A teacher that I'm fairly certain is just a crazy goat lady that collects them on a farm and doesn't *actually* have anything to do with yoga. I'm two seconds away from asking Isabella if she can just teach it, but when I turn toward her to shit-talk in a whisper, I find her attention on the helpers as they leave to grab the goats.

Her eyes are *glowing*.

And any urge to shit-talk immediately disappears.

A chorus of aww's and happy squeals fill the air as the handlers bring the goats out. When they reach the gated area that we've all set up our mats in, they place them on the ground. Which the goats immediately take as a starting gun to begin jumping everywhere.

"Oh my God, they're so cute," Isabella breathes beside me. "This is the greatest day of my life."

My lip twitches with an amused smile. Because I've looked

up Isabella's dance career, and I saw the performance that put her on the map of the ballet world. And baby goats are better than that?

"Hi, baby," she coos, squatting down when one of them bounces over to her. It's tiny, barely the size of my thigh, and it's all white. It sniffs Isabella's fingers for a few seconds before trotting right past her.

And then it stops in front of me and stares.

I stare back.

The only thing that breaks our staring contest is the sudden bleat it lets out, at a volume way louder than I ever would've expected.

Isabella giggles beside me.

"Alright, everybody, let's go ahead and get started with some breathing exercises so the goats can settle down, and then we'll move into some stretches!"

We start in on the breathing exercises, during which the goats begin to wander around the area. Most of them hop from one person to the next, but some of them seem fascinated by individual people.

The white one keeps coming back to me.

"I think he likes you," Isabella says after the thing's third pass and fifth bleat.

"I don't know why," I mumble as I lower myself to the mat. The instructor calls for downward dog, but it's obvious the poses are just a formality—looking around, most people are too distracted by the goats to actually care about the stretches.

I, on the other hand, am looking for any excuse to ignore this damn goat. I plant my hands on the mat and straighten my legs, effectively putting my body into an upside-down V so the only thing I can see is the mat in front of my face.

It means I don't see the goat when it boldly walks up to me and butts his head against my shoulder.

My head pops up and I glare at the animal in annoyance. It glares back and butts against me again.

"Fucker," I mutter.

"Let's drop our hips down for cobra pose!"

I follow the instructor's command, relieved to be in a position again where I can keep my head up and my eyes on the little menace in front of me.

He bleats straight in my face.

At that, Isabella's quiet giggles become loud laughter.

"It's not funny," I protest. I try to shoo him toward her. "Go see her instead, she'll actually pet you. Leave me alone."

Instead of going over to Isabella, he takes one jump... directly onto my shoulder.

"*What the fuck*. Leave me alone, dude." I shake my shoulder to try to dislodge him, but it's no use—he's planted on me.

I'm just about to ask one of the handlers to lift him off me, when he takes a flying leap off my shoulder and trots into the crowd.

"Thank God," I grumble. When the instructor calls for a seated pose, I turn over and settle onto the mat with my legs crossed. I automatically start in on the deep breathing that Isabella always calls for in this position, even though the instructor hasn't called for it yet—she's too busy smiling at one of the goats that fell asleep on another girl's back.

"Calling this yoga seems like a bit of a stretch," I tell

Isabella. "This seems more like a petting zoo with mats and—"

My words are cut off when the white goat appears out of thin air and plops down in my lap. I glare at it as his eyes start to drift shut.

"Don't you dare," I hiss. I shift my legs a little, but the goat only settles deeper into my lap.

Sure enough, the sound of snores fills the area.

I look helplessly at Isabella, but she's too busy clutching her side from laughter.

I turn my glare on her. "You're not going to help me here?"

She stands when the instructor finally calls for a new pose. "I would, but I don't think you actually want me to help you," she says with a giggle. She raises her hands above her head. "Am I wrong?"

I open my mouth to say *yes, of course I want you to get this thing off me*, when suddenly I feel a new weight on my shoulders. Turning my head, I spot a second goat standing behind me with his tiny hooves on my shoulders.

"You have *got* to be kidding me."

Isabella dissolves in another fit of giggles.

"You should see if you can adopt one of them," she says as she returns to her pose. "I bet Oscar would love a baby brother."

"I don't know how you were planning to make this worth it for me, but it better be something big," I growl. "At this rate, that blow job was just the appetizer."

That makes her cheeks heat. She gives me a sidelong glance and says in a quiet purr, "By the time I'm done with you, you'll be offering to make this an every-weekend thing."

And looking over Isabella's long, lean legs and the stretch

of her body, I believe her.

I make it through the rest of the class with Goat #1 snoring in my lap, and Goat #2 bouncing around the yard, occasionally popping up onto my shoulders. I can't move to do any of the poses, obviously—not that they actually do any more. By the time the instructor calls for the end, no one's done a stretch in twenty minutes, and everyone is distracted by one or more goats.

It takes one very determined handler to peel the sleeping goat out of my lap. And even still, she gets several angry bleats to the face for her efforts.

Isabella still has a huge smile on her face when we exit the fenced in area. It's been there since I knocked on her door at 8 a.m. this morning.

Somewhere along the way, it became my favorite sight in the world.

Isabella slides her hand through the crook of my arm as we start to walk toward where I parked my bike. Even her steps are happy, and whether it's because of her close proximity, or just the fact that my attention is so focused on her, but her happiness becomes contagious. I find my own lips wanting to lift in a smile.

I don't know if this feeling is sustainable. I don't even know what it would feel like if it *was.*

My life has never looked like this. Before Isabella and Oscar, my life has been only loneliness, anger, manipulation, and confusion. It's been work, and fist fights. It's been a bomb in the shape of my mother dropped into my life, and then immediate relocation and the setting up of a new life.

It's never been… simple. It's never been happy. Even though I'm in the middle of it right now, I can't even picture a normal day where there *isn't* rage or responsibilities.

And yet, when I look over at Isabella, I feel… peace. I feel peace in a way that I've never experienced before. We're not talking about my fucked up life, not dancing around a game of seduction that's solely focused on sex, we're just… existing.

"What do we do now?" I ask before I even realize I've spoken out loud.

Isabella turns her face up toward me with a smile that immediately hits me in the chest.

I can't lose this.

Before the thought can take over and make me spiral in panic, Isabella is moving closer to me and gripping my arm tighter. "We should do what you want to do now. We did enough of what I wanted."

How do I tell her the only thing I want is to be with her?

She sees my hesitation, but must not see the mess of thoughts in my brain, because she's still bubbly as she asks, "What if we go for a ride? There must be a scenic road around here somewhere."

I'm deflating in relief, opening my mouth to tell her that yes, spending an hour with her arms wrapped around me, trusting me and just being with me, sounds like paradise. But then my phone beeps with a text message.

I pull it out with a frown. I never get texts.

MOM

**Change of plans. I'll be in your area
sooner than I thought.**

The text drops a brick of dread into my stomach.

"Who is it?" Isabella asks. She's not accusatory, she's just worried, if the look on her face is any indication.

I debate swallowing the truth and brushing past the moment with a white lie, but one look at this sweet, kind girl beside me has me deciding against it. Taking a deep breath to gather my nerve, I admit honestly, "It's my mom."

Isabella squeezes my arm, silently encouraging me to continue.

I take another deep breath. "Remember how I told you I was bouncing around from place to place and job to job after I left home at sixteen?"

She nods silently.

"It wasn't because I couldn't hold down a life. It was because of my mom. She used to randomly show up in my life, begging for money and threatening me when begging didn't work."

I think back to the very first time she tracked me down. It had been six months since I'd run away from home, yet she looked like she had aged ten years. She was skinnier and had more wrinkles, but she still had that same dead look in her eyes. She was clearly the same person I grew up with. There was no reason I should have let her in.

Looking back, sometimes I wonder why I didn't feel any hesitation before I did.

Maybe that makes me pathetic. I never felt any love for her, never had any good memories of her that weren't tainted by her manipulations that always became apparent afterward, and yet I *still* treated her like my mom. I still made her dinner that night and slept on the floor so she could take the couch.

Still handed over half my cash as soon as she told me she owed somebody money.

And when I woke up the next morning, all my cash was gone, and I got kicked out of the apartment a week later when I couldn't pay rent.

Isabella shakes me out of the memory when she gently urges me to continue with a soft, "So the last time you saw her wasn't when you ran away from home?"

I shake my head. "She developed this routine over the years. In the early days, I'd live in my car until I could save enough money for a new apartment, then I'd move in and live there for a while. And then she would find me. I have no idea how; it almost felt like she had a sixth sense for ruining my life. Because she'd show up—sometimes at home, sometimes at my work—and she'd work me until I eventually gave her the time of day. If I was lucky, she just needed a place to stay. But most of the time she wanted money. After a while I stopped giving it to her, but then she'd get crafty. She'd find my hiding places for my cash, or she'd get me fired at work, and she wouldn't leave me alone until I gave her the money. And she made me cave *every single time.*" I pull in a shaky breath. "She was both predictable and not, because I knew she would find me, but I could never guess what she would do, or how she'd play me."

"God," Isabella mumbles. "That sounds exhausting."

I only nod. I don't add that it also drove away every piece of pride I'd ever felt for finding my own independence. Because I knew I wasn't, not really. Not with her still in my life.

Isabella hesitates before she asks, "So what does she want now?"

I let out a tired sigh as I tuck my phone back in my pocket. "I don't know. She's never given me a heads up before showing up in my area." I don't vocalize that it's likely part of a new psychological manipulation tactic. Opening up to Isabella is one thing, but involving her in my bullshit life is a whole other. One I'm not willing to entertain even the slightest.

"When was the last time you saw her?" Isabella asks, wrapping an arm around my waist. I wrap mine around her shoulders with a grateful squeeze.

"Three years. Longest she's ever gone without popping up in my life." The last time I saw her, she had broken into my apartment and stolen everything—literally *everything*—out of my apartment: my furniture, my cash, even my clothes. I had to sell my car just to keep from becoming a homeless beggar on the street. That day, I jumped on a train and left Baltimore for good. And in the three years since I've seen her, I've finally allowed myself to start to build a shred of self-confidence. That and hope, that I could actually move past the years I'd much rather forget.

I feel Isabella hesitate. "So what are you going to do about her?"

I shrug and nudge her in the direction of my bike across the street. "Nothing. She doesn't exist to me."

Maybe if I repeat that enough times, I can will it to be true. Because for the first time in my life, I actually have a life I want to protect.

CHAPTER 25
Isabella

I'M STANDING IN the middle of a grocery store, staring at a wall of sauces, when I realize that I have no idea what I'm doing.

My gaze flits between a standard, original tomato sauce, and a higher-end, flavored organic sauce. I have no idea which one to buy. No idea which one I *need*.

Hardening my jaw, I look again at the chicken parmesan recipe on my phone. Damnit, I *want* to cook for myself. And I want to eat something that's not grilled protein and vegetables, because for the first time in my life, I don't need to have five percent body fat.

Determined to at least *try*, I reach for a sauce labeled 'Original.'

Half an hour later, that determination has waned a little bit.

Okay, a lot.

Frowning at my first attempt at breading the chicken, I feel my frustration mount. It looks blotchy, with chunks of panko on some parts and flour peeking through on others. It does *not* look like the chicken in the video I'm watching. And that's not even to say anything about my nervous glances at the oil currently heating in my skillet.

Just then, my phone rings. Dropping the disproportionately breaded chicken breast on the plate, I wipe my hands on my leggings and answer without looking at who it is.

"Hello?"

"Princess," comes a deep baritone. I suck in a breath at the way it immediately makes my body heat.

"Hey," I respond, my voice breathy even to my own ears.

"What're you doing right now?"

I frown at my phone. "Um, I'm home. What's going on? I thought you were working tonight."

"I was. But it's dead in here, and they let me go since I've been taking all the late closing shifts. Figured I'd call to see what you're doing."

I glare at my counter that looks like a tornado ran through it. "I'm attempting to make myself dinner." Sighing in defeat, I add, "I would tell you to come over, but I don't have nearly enough faith in my cooking abilities to promise you edible food." I don't admit the part that the idea of Kane watching me struggle through this would be mortifying.

His chuckle sounds in my ear. "At least tell me you're wearing a cute little apron."

I glance down at my flour-covered leggings and tank top. "I can say that and lie, if you want."

"Guess I know what I'm getting you for your birthday."

I bite into my bottom lip to smother my smile even though he can't see it. Because the sound of Kane making future plans still makes me downright giddy.

I force my focus back to the phone call. "It will probably never get used, if this cooking expedition is anything to go by. I'll be lucky if I don't burn our building down by the end of the night."

There's a pause, and Kane's voice has noticeably sobered when he says, "I can teach you how to make something simple, if you want."

"You know how to cook?" I ask, the surprise evident in my voice. "I mean, I've obviously seen you make breakfast foods, but dinner is a whole other story."

There's another pause, and when he answers, the reason for it is apparent. "I had to learn how to feed myself pretty early on."

I sober immediately at the reminder of his childhood. But in the same breath, it also launches me past my cooking hesitation, and reaffirms my desire to give him positive memories to replace his bad ones.

"I'd love to have you teach me," I tell him softly.

"Okay," he answers, sounding pleased even through the phone. "I'm driving home now. Try not to burn anything down in the next twenty minutes."

With timing that only the universe is capable of, the skillet on my stove spits hot oil in my direction. I let out an involuntary yelp and shut off the stove top.

"No promises," I say with a weak laugh.

A knock sounds at my door, and I swing it open to find Kane and a smiling Oscar sitting at his feet.

"Hi," I squeak.

I clear my throat and focus on Oscar in an attempt to appear more normal, and less like I have stars in my eyes. "Hi, buddy."

His tail starts to wag, and he leans down to grab the motorcycle toy that I didn't realize he had set at his feet. Then he's pushing into my house, and very excitedly shoving his nose into my hand to show off his toy. I let out a laugh at his obvious happiness and squat down to scratch his head.

"That's his favorite toy now," Kane says. "He sleeps with it, too. He's obsessed."

My own smile feels like it's about to split my face.

It takes me a little bit to pull away from Oscar, but after a minute, I stand and let them into my apartment. When Kane steps inside, he wraps his arm around my waist and presses a kiss to my neck. I feel his smile against my skin as a shiver runs through me.

"I'm happy to see the building hasn't burned down," he teases.

"I don't think I'm a bad cook, I just don't know what I'm doing," I admit. "No one ever showed me what to do."

Another kiss, this time to my lips. I gasp when he lightly nips my lip before pulling back.

"Then let me show you. We'll do it together."

Together.

Does that word hit him as hard as it hits me?

His tone doesn't give anything away, but before I can try to get a read on his face, he's pushing past me and making his way into the kitchen. I give Oscar one last pat, and then I'm following behind him.

"Chicken parm, I'm assuming?" Kane asks.

I nod. "Yeah. I thought it would be the easiest, but I don't even know if I got the right ingredients."

Kane looks over the breading station I set up, and the sauce I have off to the side on the counter. "We can make this work."

His choice of words makes me skeptical. "You sure? Don't lie to save my feelings, I'd rather know if something's bad."

He's shaking his head before I'm done talking. "It won't be bad, I promise. Besides, this is already way better than what I used to eat. I had to teach myself how to cook so I wouldn't go hungry some days, but I'll tell you right now, a seven-year-old is rarely a good cook."

He starts messing with the different bowls and ingredients on the counter, so he doesn't notice the shock in my eyes or the way I'm staring at his form. He doesn't see the expression on my face that I'm sure is making it entirely evident the way my heart aches for this man.

This strong, capable, extraordinary man who made something of himself after a terrible start to life.

A man who still doesn't see himself as deserving of good things.

In the past few days, Kane has started to drop tidbits like that into our conversations, seemingly without even noticing he's doing it. I'm so ridiculously glad that he feels comfortable enough to do it, but I've also never felt such an intense mixture of emotions. Standing in the center of my kitchen, I feel rage for young-Kane, pride for grown-Kane, and above all, awe that he feels comfortable enough with me to share these pieces of him. My fingers itch with the need to wrap my arms around him from behind in gratitude.

"Next time, we'll get different panko and a better sauce, but you would've had no way to know that," he says, jarring me from my spiral of thoughts. "Not because these are bad, I just know which ones are the best-tasting for chicken parm." He turns around with a questioning look. "Ready?"

I mentally shake myself from my reverie. "Ready."

For the next half hour, Kane and I go through breading the chicken, frying it, and then baking it. By the time we slide the sauce-covered pan in the oven, I've got a huge grin on my face and an excited bounce in my step.

"I know it's stupid to feel proud about something so simple, but this kind of feels like a stepping stone in my Philly life," I admit. "At the risk of sounding spoiled, I didn't realize it would feel this satisfying to feed myself. I thought having a cook in my house and DoorDash on my phone was a better option because it was quicker and easier, but honestly, cooking for myself kind of makes me feel like a self-sufficient adult."

Kane doesn't try too hard to keep the amused smile from his face. "DoorDash has nothing on your chicken parm, princess," he says with a chuckle as he rinses the last bowl.

With everything finally soaking in the sink, he comes over to where I'm sprawled out on the couch and lifts my feet into his lap so he can take a seat at the end. But his tone is no longer teasing when he says, "But you were always a self-sufficient adult, Isabella. Not knowing something you never needed to learn doesn't change that. I'm *glad* you never had to cook for yourself."

He starts to rub my ankle, leaving me to stare thoughtfully at the side of his face. I wonder if he even notices he always massages my left ankle—the hurt ankle.

I want to ask Kane more about his life, but I also don't want to push him before he's ready. So I settle on asking him about the gym.

I've noticed he's started to talk a little more about the gym lately. Not even about fighting—or the way he used to think of fighting—but about the sport itself. He talks more about what he learned, and less about how he wanted to hit someone. Yesterday he even mentioned a conversation he had with his coach about a possible fight, and instead of shaking it off as 'just another fight,' he described some of his goals for the training camp.

I listen to him talk until he runs out of words. It usually doesn't take long, but I'll take any insight into Kane I can get. I *like* learning about him. There's still so much I want to know, but I'm not blind to the fact that it's going to take time.

And I'm okay with that, because, surprisingly enough, Kane's made it more than obvious that this isn't a short-term thing. So, I'll give him whatever time he needs to open up, especially if they're coming as random little tidbits while we cook dinner together.

I fill the rest of the time with my own chatter. Kane seems to like listening to me talk. Tonight is the first time we're not on a timeline, and can actually relax and enjoy each other's company. I debate asking him if he wants to watch another episode of Rick and Morty—turns out I love the show, and I've been dying to lure him into an all-night marathon of it—but the oven timer chooses that moment to go off.

I practically bound off the couch, so eager to see the finished product of my cooking escapade that I almost don't remember to grab oven mitts. I hear Kane's chuckle from behind me as I struggle to pull them on.

"Easy," he says, amusement coating his tone as he pulls open the oven. "I'm going to be very unhappy if you burn yourself."

"What on earth does unhappy Kane look like?" I wonder sarcastically as I lean down to pull the pan out and set it on the stovetop.

I'm so mesmerized by the sight of our cheesy, perfect meal, I don't realize Kane has stepped up behind me until his arms go around my waist. He tightens his grip and nuzzles into my neck, and his voice is quiet when he says, "It's getting harder and harder to remember."

That gets my attention. I want to turn my head and meet his eyes, to really see the full depth of how he feels, but his face is still tucked into my neck and his arms are holding me hostage where I stand.

Sensing he doesn't want to talk about it, I stop myself from turning in his arms to try to meet his eyes. Instead, I place my hand on his forearm where it's wrapped around my waist, and squeeze affectionately, just once. I'm dying to kiss him right now, to show him I feel the same way, but before I can twist in his arms to do that, the oven timer lets out another angry alarm.

It effectively shatters the heavy moment. I squeeze Kane's arm once more, then mumble awkwardly, "We should probably turn it off before it yells at us again."

I expect Kane to pull away immediately, to distance himself from any kind of serious conversation, but instead, he hesitates. His movements feel almost reluctant, the way he slowly unwraps his arms. But then he's pulling away and clicking the Off button on the stove, and that sensation of *something big just happened* evaporates.

"In the spirit of learning new recipes, want me to teach you how to make the spaghetti, too?" he asks.

It takes me a second to catch the teasing lilt in his voice, the emotional whiplash making me blink in confusion. Then his question registers and I'm turning to glare at him.

He merely holds his hands up in surrender and says, "You're the one who said you couldn't feed yourself." A smirk tugs at his lips. "I didn't want to assume boiling pasta was something you could handle."

Another glare, this time with feeling. "I liked you better when you didn't make jokes," I grumble at him. Then, realizing a glare and a growl aren't enough, I punch him in the shoulder. "*Jerk*," I mutter.

A deep, content laugh rumbles through his chest as he clutches his arm.

"No more self-defense lessons for you," he says with a chuckle. "Any more of those and I won't be able to laugh off your shots."

Pouring the spaghetti into the pot of boiling water, I grumble, "Fine, guess I'll just open myself up to more muggings then."

Once again, he sidles up to me without me realizing it.

"Not a fucking chance, princess," he whispers, and presses a kiss under my ear.

A shiver runs through me at the words and the gesture, but I force myself to focus on the pasta instead of the increasingly attractive man behind me. Thankfully, I hear him start to set out plates and utensils at my little breakfast nook, leaving me to prepare the pasta in peace.

"By the way, set two extra place settings. My mom and dad are coming for dinner."

There's a pause, and then...

"*WHAT?!*"

Even I can't hide my sheepishness when I turn to look at him. Poor guy is standing shell-shocked next to my little kitchenette, plate in hand, with big eyes and his jaw on the floor.

"What, what?" I ask dumbly.

That snaps him out of it enough to glare at me. "Don't play with me. What do you mean your parents are coming over?"

I shrug. "They're staying in the city tonight and they wanted to stop by to see how I've settled in. Instead of going out to dinner, I suggested they just come here instead."

I can *see* the moment the urge to flee hits him. I don't even blame him, God knows it took me forever just to get him used to *my* company.

"You don't have to stay," I tell him hurriedly, wanting to give him an out so he doesn't feel like I've trapped him. "I really did want to hang out with you tonight. But..." I swallow roughly as I work up the nerve to ask for the thing I've been thinking about for days. "But I'd like it if you did."

His gaze snaps back to me, looking just as panicked as it did before. "Who are you going to tell them I am?"

I shrug again, forcing nonchalance into my answer. "My neighbor."

Panic turns into another glare, and I can *feel* the heat in his voice. "I'm not your fucking neighbor."

My heartbeat catches in my chest. "No? What are you?"

He doesn't answer, just continues to stare at me.

I turn back to the pasta to give him some space. After a minute, I hear a heavy sigh. "Isabella, I can't stay. I just… I *can't*."

I nod in understanding, already expecting that it was too much too soon. When I face him again, it's with a smile.

"Okay. Thank you for helping me cook dinner. Do you want to try it before you go, since they'll be here soon? Or were you lying about my abilities to cook something edible?"

"I would never lie to you," he grumbles as he walks over to where the meal isn't burn-your-mouth hot anymore. I cut off a piece and lift the fork toward him, but he nudges it back in my direction. "You first."

When my lips close around the bite of chicken, and my eyes widen in surprise, I realize Kane is staring at me with a smile that can only be described as adoring. And he doesn't look away when he sees I've noticed.

"Good?" he asks.

I nod, feeling a blush burn across my cheeks. "I think so. You try it now."

He doesn't make me wait, he just maneuvers a big bite of chicken onto his fork and then lifts it quickly to his mouth.

And even though I'm almost one hundred percent certain that Kane really *isn't* capable of lying to me, I'm still more relieved than I want to admit when his expression softens into the one that people wear

when they're satisfied their food actually tastes good. Which is solidified when he immediately dives in for another bite.

"Congratulations, you just cooked a meal that is not only edible, but that actually tastes really good," he says around a mouthful.

I'm pretty sure my grin is about to split my face in half.

He sees it and chuckles, then leans over to press a kiss under my ear. "I'm going to go. Have fun with your parents. I'll see you in the morning still?"

I nod, then lean in to kiss him again because I can't *not.*

But just before our lips touch, there's a knock on my front door.

My eyes go wide. Kane's go even wider.

"I'm sorry," I blurt. "They're early. I really didn't think you'd have to see them if you didn't want to. I'll just tell them you came over for sugar or something." I let out a nervous chuckle. "Isn't that ironic? That's why I came over to *your* apartment at first."

"Isabella," he interrupts on a sigh. "I'm not scared of your parents. I just don't expect them to like me. Open the door."

That makes me frown. "Why wouldn't they—?"

Another knock sounds on my door. "Honey, we're here! I know we're early, but we couldn't wait to see you."

I'm too flustered by Kane's comment to do anything but

operate on autopilot. Striding over to the door, I open it to reveal my mom and dad on my doorstep.

"Hi, sweetheart," my mom says, shifting the bottle of wine in her arms so she can press a kiss to each of my cheeks. My dad does the same, smiling as he steps past me. "You know, I don't think I gave this part of the city enough credit the first time. We passed the loveliest little hole-in-the-wall Italian restaurant on the way over here—"

She stops talking when she spots Kane. He's standing in my kitchen, no longer looking panicked, but still looking entirely uncomfortable.

"Hello," my mom greets with a smile. "I'm sorry, Isabella didn't tell us someone would be joining us."

"Mom, Dad, this is Kane," I hurry to say, moving beside him to face my parents. "He's a… friend."

My dad doesn't even hesitate. He steps up to Kane with a smile on his face and extends his hand. "Hi, Kane. I'm Jack, and this is my wife Marianne."

Kane respectfully reaches forward and shakes his hand. "It's nice to meet you, sir. I'm sorry to intrude on your time with your daughter, I was just leaving."

"You're not staying for dinner?" my mom asks. "Are you sure you can't join us? We didn't even know Isabella had made any friends down here. She's not really a talker, so we have no idea what she's been doing down here."

Kane pauses before asking with a frown, "She's not?"

My jaw drops as I turn to stare at him. The corner of his lip is twitching in that way that I can always tell is his attempt not to laugh.

My mom lets out a delighted laugh. But after a moment, she sobers and asks, "We won't keep you if you weren't planning on staying. But just answer one question for me, please. And be honest. Is it safe around here? We were so worried when Isabella wanted to move here because we didn't know anything about the area. Do you live around here?"

"Actually, ma'am, I live right next door."

"Oh, good. And it's safe?"

Kane hesitates, rightfully gauging that I haven't told them about the mugging. I was already feeling inadequate when it came to my ability to stand on my own two feet, the last thing I needed is my parents confirming it with parental worry.

Kane reads all of that in one glance.

"To be completely honest with you, it *is* a city, and any city comes with danger. But Isabella's a strong woman, and she can take care of herself. There's nothing to worry about."

Thankfully, my parents don't look skeptical. And when Kane adds, "And anyway, I wouldn't let anything happen to her," their expressions become pleased in addition to relieved.

My dad claps Kane on the shoulder. "Good man. A father wants to hear that someone like you is protecting his daughter."

I can *see* the record scratch in Kane's brain. But I'm too busy biting down on my lip to stifle my smile—the smile that comes from knowing this is exactly the kind of reaction I expected my parents to have to Kane.

And that it's exactly the thing that Kane needed to hear from someone that's not me.

Kane gives a stiff nod at my dad's words, but doesn't really seem to be able to respond with anything. Instead, he says woodenly, "Anyway, I'll leave you three to have dinner. Mr. and Mrs. Brooks, it was nice to——"

"Oh my goodness, who is *this* handsome young man?" my mom suddenly cries out, clapping her hands together. We all turn to look at what caught her attention, and see Oscar climbing off the chair in my living room that he's claimed as his napping chair.

"Aren't you *so sweet*," my mom coos, leaning down to extend her hand to the pitbull when he walks up to her. Almost immediately, his tail starts to wag. And it wags even harder when she pets him.

I turn toward Kane with a smile, expecting him to look relieved that Oscar is being friendly and well-behaved. He mentioned Oscar's seemed standoffish with a few people, and with his breed having the reputation that it does, I know it's made him a little nervous.

Instead, Kane looks… confused. I watch as he studies Oscar, his brow furrowing.

"I apologize, I don't mean to keep you," my mom says after a moment. "He's just too cute and I couldn't resist."

Kane nods his acceptance, but he's clearly still mulling over something. "It was nice to meet you, Mr. and Mrs. Brooks," he says again. When he whistles and starts toward the door, Oscar follows obediently behind him.

"It was nice to meet you, too, Kane," my dad calls. My mom just smiles and waves as she reaches into the cabinet for the wine glasses.

"I'll walk you to the door," I murmur. When he reaches my doorway and turns around, I can't help asking, "Why do you look so confused?"

His brow furrows again. "I can't ever tell who he's going to be good with," he answers. "It throws me off."

I bite my lip to keep from smiling. But Kane sees it and asks, "What? What's so funny?"

I shrug in an attempt at nonchalance. "You never noticed that he only likes the people you like?"

Kane blinks at that.

"Think about it: who is Oscar friendly with? Based on what you've said, it sounds like he's warming up to people at the gym. But beyond that, who else? Just me, right?"

I don't expect Kane to admit *he* likes anyone, either, so I'm not surprised when he avoids the real question and smirks at me instead.

"You think I like you, princess?"

All the air goes out of my lungs at the way he looks at me. "Maybe a little," I breathe.

His gaze roves over my face, probably taking in every ounce of my infatuation with him, but he gives me nothing in return. After a moment, his expression becomes serious and he says quietly, "Goodnight, Isabella."

"Goodnight," I whisper. Then, before I can second guess it, I push onto my toes and press a quick kiss to his cheek.

He's smiling before he can tamp down on it. His gaze darts over my shoulder, I'm assuming at my parents, but he no longer has that deer-in-the-headlights look.

He has that *happy* look.

CHAPTER 26
Kane

WALKING INTO ISABELLA'S ballet studio is no less jarring than I expected it to be—especially when every eye turns to me and goes wide. Clearly, there's a huge difference between my massive, scowling, tattooed presence and the thin, delicate, porcelain dancers flitting around the studio. There has never been someone *more* out of place in this building.

Once again, I swallow the feeling that I don't belong—in this environment, around these people, with *Isabella*. I force it deep down before it can swallow me whole and convince me to turn around and leave her to her perfect life.

But then…

I catch sight of her. She's spinning in circles, her toned legs flexing as she stands on the tips of her ballet shoes, and she's clearly lost in the movement. I watch her spin once, twice, three times, before slowing and coming out of it with a flourish of her hands, a small smile sitting contentedly on her delicate pink lips.

Just as she's coming to a stop, she spots me. And stumbles out of the spin when our eyes meet.

"That was sloppy, Izzy," an older woman nearby says. "Do it again. There's nothing wrong with your foot, it's all in your head."

I tamp down on my smile when Isabella's gaze jerks toward the woman, a blush flaming over her cheeks. And when she looks back at me, questioningly, I lift my chin in a silent message of *go again, I'll wait for you.*

She hardens her jaw and turns back to the dancefloor with a determined glint in her eyes. I move over to the waiting area so I can sit and watch her, never once taking my eyes off her.

This time around, her moves are flawless. Or, they look flawless to me. I don't know anything about ballet, but I know Isabella. And I can tell how she feels about the dance based on the expressions on her face: nervous, focused, pleased, and my favorite: *pride.* It's plastered all over her face when she finishes the final spin, without stumbling this time.

"Very good," the woman says. "Now grab Henry and start the next number."

The entire time they work through the routine, I can't take my eyes off of Isabella. The guy might as well be invisible, because I can't look away from the vision that is Isabella dancing. She's so in touch with her body, so lost in the movements, that I can't imagine how anyone could *not* stare at her when she's dancing. And I know I'm not the only one when the dance ends, and the old woman gives a grunt of approval.

"Nice work, Isabella," she says stiffly. "Henry, I need you to run the dance a little bit more. Isabella still seems like she's leading you too much. But we'll work on it again next time. For now, class is over."

"Thank you, Mrs. Martin," Isabella says. Henry just scowls. "Do you mind if I stay after a little bit to work? I'm still not confident during that sequence in the second half."

The woman doesn't seem shocked at Isabella's request. She must be used to her dancers working overtime, because she immediately waves an approval at the request and turns to retrieve her purse. Henry also takes the dismissal and moves toward the locker room.

Isabella begins to walk toward me. Her gait is confident, despite the slight blush on her cheeks.

"I'm so sorry I'm late," she breathes. "We ran late, and I couldn't even stop to text you. Do you mind if I practice for a little bit longer? I wasn't planning on dancing after class, but that section in the middle is driving me crazy. I should only need another fifteen minutes."

"Take as much time as you need," I tell her. "I'll wait."

As I settle back into my chair, Isabella starts to dance. And even though it vaguely registers that people are packing up around us and leaving the studio, my eyes are glued to her. Because watching her dance is mesmerizing no matter what's going on around me.

She sinks into the dance, visibly lost in the music now playing from her phone. Her movements are graceful and effortless and perfect, and I don't know shit about ballet but *fuck* if it's not obvious that Isabella was born to do this.

I'm not sure how long I watch her for, but when she eventually finishes a spin with a relieved exhale, I'm snapped back to the moment. She looks tired, but pleased. And I know I'm right when she looks at me with a small smile on her lips and says, "That's the first time I've been able to get through that without stopping at least once."

It takes me a moment to open my mouth and actually say something. And even then, all that comes out is, "Fuck, princess. You're breathtaking. No wonder everyone pushed you to dance."

Something flashes in her eyes, but I can't make sense of it until she says quietly, "Still think dancing isn't the best part of me?"

That catches my attention. She seemed affected by something similar I said before this, so clearly, being seen as more than just a dancer is important to her.

It takes no effort to give her that.

I stand from my seat and slowly approach her, drawn to her like a moth to a flame, and completely helpless to fight the urge moving me forward. Her eyes never leave mine.

When I reach her, I slide a hand behind her neck to anchor us together. "Still." I lean in and breathe the words against her lips. "Always."

And then I'm kissing her, stamping my feelings on her skin so she can feel how much I mean that. *She's* incredible, not just her dancing. She's kind, and hard-working, and so goddamn strong for creating a whole new life for herself in this city.

The reminder that this isn't quite her "home" yet—that it might be temporary for her—is enough to ratchet this kiss from sweet to desperate. Suddenly, I'm gripping her neck harder, slipping my tongue between her lips and wishing without words that this isn't the only time I get to touch her. That maybe if I make this good enough, she'll stay.

With me.

But that thought is born on a quiet breath of hope, one I'm not ready to give much thought to, because deep down I *know* I'm not what she needs. That I'm not anything worth keeping her here.

Once again, I force that thought away, and focus instead on the beautiful woman in front of me. And when I slide my tongue along hers and she lets out a moan that immediately turns my cock to stone, I do just that.

When I drop to my knees, Isabella lets out a gasp of surprise. Her hands automatically move to my shoulders, her lips open as she stares down at where I'm kneeling before her. I can't help lifting my hands to her thighs, cupping behind her and soothingly rubbing my hands up and down her legs. I never take my eyes off hers.

"Kane, what are you—" she starts, but her words cut off when my hands drift down, until they land on the ribbons of her pointe shoes. The moment she realizes what my intentions are, she sucks in a needy breath.

Slowly, so slowly, I untie the satin bow behind her ankle. But as soon as I feel the knot loosen, I'm once again lifting my eyes to catalog Isabella's expression.

It's intoxicating, watching her react to me. Because as I unwrap the satin from around her legs, as the heat between us ratchets with every brush of the material against her skin, I watch the heat in Isabella's eyes grow. And by the time I silently urge her to lift her foot so I can slide the shoe off—taking the time to do it slow enough that my calloused fingers brush over the arch of her foot—I can tell she's about to start begging.

"Kane," she breathes once the first shoe has been loosened. But I only shake my head in quiet admonition and reach for her other foot. I repeat the ministrations with her remaining shoe.

"Kane, please," she begs, confirming my thoughts.

I look up at her from where I'm still kneeling on the floor, letting my hands once again slide up the backs of her thighs. "What do you need, princess? Use your words."

She bites her lip and whispers, "Don't tease me."

I study her for another moment, debating how much I want to tease her. But it barely takes a moment for me to decide that *I'm* the one that can't handle the teasing right now.

"Hold on to my shoulders," I order her.

Then I'm pulling her forward with my grip on her legs to push her skirt up and rip her tights at the seam.

"Oh my God," she gasps, her fingers digging into my shoulders in an attempt to hold her balance. And when I yank her leotard to the side to finally expose her perfect, pink cunt, she lets out a whimper.

I can't exist for another second without her taste on my tongue. I bury my face in her sweetness.

I close my eyes at the taste, a groan slipping past my lips. And I feel more than hear the way Isabella gasps at the vibration. Sliding my hands from her thighs to her ass cheeks, I squeeze the supple muscle, groaning into her skin at the perfect feel of her in my hands. Instantly, the hunger in me multiplies by a thousand. I've never needed to taste something as much as I need Isabella's orgasm.

I know she likes quick, hard circles on her clit, so I settle in with my tongue and give her just that. Adding two fingers would speed it up even more, but for some reason, I want the first thing to be inside her today to be my cock. So, I keep my hands on her ass and my tongue on her clit, and I wait for the tell-tale sound of Isabella's breath hitching.

It doesn't take very long. Only moments later, her body locks up in my hands, then loosens with a delicious shudder. Followed by the flood of her pleasure on my lips.

I think I groan through it. I've never in my *life* tasted something as delicious as Isabella's pleasure, and I don't think I'll get enough of it. And yet, suddenly I'm eager for the feel of it.

I stand from my kneeling position, immediately backing a dazed Isabella against the mirrored walls. As soon as her back hits the barre, I'm stamping a starving kiss against her lips.

"You're so fucking sweet," I growl into her mouth. "I could live on the taste of you."

Her hands are clutching the front of my shirt, gripping so tight I'm convinced she would fall if I wasn't holding on to her waist. Her lips are swollen and kiss-bitten, and her expression is drunk on her orgasm.

"I-I want to taste you again," she stammers.

A pleased smile lifts the corners of my lips as I lean down to reward her with another kiss. This one is slower, almost lazy, even as I slide my tongue into her mouth to tangle with hers.

"You want to suck my cock, princess?" I ask once I've put a fraction of space between our lips. "You want to get on your knees and show me how much you appreciate the orgasms I give you?"

She's too dazed to answer with words—she merely stares

up at me with wide, hungry eyes and nods.

For a moment, I pretend that I'm thinking about it. But then I slide my lips past her mouth, brushing against her cheek, so I can whisper in her ear, "Maybe next time. Right now, I want to fuck you while you watch."

And then I'm gripping her waist and spinning her to face the mirrors.

She comes face to face with the sight that I've become completely obsessed with: a disheveled, lust-drunk Isabella.

I lean down to press a kiss under her ear. "Put your hands on the barre."

She sucks in a breath at my order, but dutifully steps forward to brace on the wooden bar.

"*God*, you're perfect," I murmur. I don't mean to say it out loud, but I'm so enamored by Isabella's presence, and her obedience, that I can't stop it from slipping out.

Her eyes dart up to meet mine in the mirror. She swallows thickly when she sees the hunger in mine, but when she doesn't seem scared by the sight of it, I add, "Since the day I first saw you, I've been thinking about what it would look like to dirty up this perfection."

Her eyes widen at the confession. There's a pause, and then a second later, her hips are pressing back into my lap, her challenge barely a whisper. "Then show me," she breathes.

The tether on my control *snaps*. I immediately reach for my belt buckle with one hand, my other hand glued to her waist and my gaze locked on hers in the mirror. I'm not pulling my attention away or putting any unnecessary distance between us, because I need to get inside her more than I need to breathe.

"Leg up on the barre," I growl as I pull my cock out.

She sucks in a breath at my order, but dutifully lifts her leg up to brace on the wooden bar, in that graceful way that only ballerinas are capable of. I want to come from just the sight of her.

"You're going to watch me fuck you. Understand?"

She nods, the soft smile on her face making it obvious how pleased she is that she's driven me to my limit.

After quickly putting a condom on, I reach between her legs from behind, sliding her leotard to the side and moving her shredded tights out of the way. When I stroke her lips and feel her dripping with desire, I line my cock up.

"I'm going to enjoy stretching this pretty ballerina pussy with my cock," I murmur in her ear.

And then I drive into her with a single, hard thrust.

Isabella gasps at the sudden intrusion, yet she immediately rocks her hips with a silent desire for *more*. I don't need to be asked twice—I start to fuck her.

"Oh my God, you're so *deep*," she says on a breathy moan, her eyes sliding closed at the sensation.

Immediately, I slide one hand from her waist, up to wrap around her throat. The second I squeeze lightly, her eyes pop open in surprise.

"I said *watch* me," I growl, my hips never slowing. "Watch as I make you come."

I feel her swallow against my hand. I'm entranced by the sight in the mirror before me, of my tattooed hand against the perfect, porcelain skin of Isabella's neck. I flex my grip once more, just to see her react to the same sight.

"Look how pretty you look like this," I purr in her ear. "You're not the prim and proper ballerina right now, are you? Not with my cock fucking your tight little pussy, out in the open where anyone could see you."

I watch in satisfaction as her chest starts to rise and fall rapidly at my words. It causes a pleased smile to curl my lips, and then I'm asking her, "Want to see what that looks like? What I see every time I fuck you?"

"*God*, yes," she breathes, her tone sounding every bit as desperate as she looks. "Show me."

Slowly, teasing her with my lazy movements, I drop my hand from her throat, down to the edge of her skirt. Since I moved us into this position, her clothes have blocked any view of either of us. But when I grip the hem of her skirt, and slowly tug it up to her waist, we're greeted with the debaucherous sight of her shredded tights, and my cock driving into her exposed pussy between them.

Isabella lets out a whimper when she sees it. Her muscles tighten around me, and I immediately start to drive harder into her, sensing that the sight alone has put her that much closer to an orgasm.

"That's all it took, huh?" I taunt. "One look at the way I fuck you and you want to come?" I pin her skirt between my forearm and her stomach, freeing up my hand to rub circles on her clit. "Go on then, come for me. Show me how much you love the way I fuck you."

Her pussy starts to ripple around my length. I drop my face into the crook of her neck with a groan, never pausing the movement of my hips or the touch of my fingers. I'm just as desperate to extend her orgasm as she seems to be, her nails digging into my forearm and her breath coming in gasps.

"*Fuck*, that feels amazing," I groan into her skin. "You'll never not feel amazing, Isabella."

And whether it's the honest confession, born on the high of pleasure, or the feeling of my own release inside her, something makes her breath stutter. Only, I'm too far gone in the whirlwind of lust to really register it.

After a moment, I slump against her, bracing my own hands on the barre in front of us. "I really hope your teacher doesn't walk back in here," I mumble into her neck.

Isabella's giggle causes a smile to slide across my face. *Fuck*, when was the last time I smiled with such ease? Have I ever?

The thought should be a sobering one, but instead, I just feel... comforted. Soothed by the idea that I feel safe in her company.

Before my subconscious can dig too deep into that, I straighten and right my clothes. Then I turn my focus to Isabella in the mirror, only to see her biting her lip as she studies her appearance.

I take a guess at what has her flustered. I adjust her skirt to hide any evidence of what we just did, and I reach up to tuck a stray piece of hair behind her ear. One look over her in the mirror confirms she's back to looking like a put-together ballerina.

"There," I murmur. "Back to perfect."

A blush lights her cheeks, and so does a smile. And I realize that I'm sick of looking at her through a mirror instead of in front of me, so I take her hand and spin her around.

"Let's get you home before the old lady comes back and sees how naughty her favorite dancer is," I say, pressing a kiss to the corner of her lips. Absorbing the resulting smile like it's a life-saving antidote.

Maybe it is.

THE NEXT TIME I have the night off work, I'm showing up on Isabella's doorstep with a bottle of wine.

She's smiling when she opens the door. Of course, she's smiling. And when she spots the bottle in my hand, her expression turns delighted.

"Is that for me?" she asks, her eyes twinkling.

I hand it over with a stiff nod.

"I think it's the right one, but I'm not one hundred percent," I mumble, rubbing the back of my neck.

Her brow furrows as she spins the glass to look at the label. When she reads it, her eyes widen.

"This is my favorite wine," she says, her tone one of disbelief. Looking up at me, she asks, "How did you know what my favorite wine is?"

I shove my hands in my pockets, still too uncomfortable to stand still. "I saw it was the one your mom brought you," I say gruffly.

For a moment, she only stares at me. Then she's carefully placing the bottle on the entryway table beside her door, and jumping into my arms, wrapping her arms around my neck and her legs around my waist.

"Who even are you," she sighs between kisses pressed along my jaw, my chin.

I chuckle, tightening my arms around her. And I thought I would hate this kind of affection, but instead, I'm suddenly trying to figure out how I can keep her this close all night.

She doesn't seem to be in a hurry to climb down, so I walk us into her apartment and close the door behind us. Wrapping one arm under her butt to keep her braced against my body, I grab the bottle with the other hand and make my way into her kitchen.

She tries to slide down my front once we reach the counter, but I only tighten my grip on her ass. She giggles and presses another kiss to my jaw.

When she tries a second time to unwind her legs from around my waist, I exhale a heavy sigh and let her go. But before she can step away, I stamp a hard kiss on her lips, sliding my tongue in her mouth and kissing her breathless. I don't let her go until I feel her hands come up to clutch my shirt.

The unintelligible sound she makes when I step away makes me chuckle. I have to take a seat on her couch before she can focus enough to remember what she was doing.

"So have you always worked so much?" she asks as she searches for the wine opener.

I shrug and stretch my arm over the back of her couch. "At the club, yeah. My bouncing jobs have always had me working a lot."

"Do you like it?"

"Yeah, it's cool," I answer. "You don't really have to do much, so it's pretty chill. And I'm friends with the DJ, so he plays a lot of the music I like. It's not a bad gig."

Isabella hands me a glass of wine before sitting at the other end of the couch, stretching her legs out and setting her feet in my lap like she knows I like. Instantly I place a hand on her ankle and begin rubbing circles into her skin.

"How long have you been doing it?" she asks.

"Seven years, I think? I was nineteen when I realized I was good at throwing people around."

I take a sip of the wine, so I don't realize at first that she's hesitating, working up to asking something. When I eventually turn to give her a curious look, she's fidgeting, spinning the wine glass in her hand.

"Have you ever thought about doing something else?" she asks eventually.

That makes me frown. I study her, trying to figure out if that question is coming from a judgmental place. I have yet to see Isabella be judgmental, even though she would've had the right to act it a few times.

"You don't like me bouncing? Or is it the strip club that you have a problem with?"

Her eyes instantly go wide. "What? No, that's not why I'm asking. I don't have an issue with any of it."

"So then what's the question you actually want to ask?"

She sighs before admitting in a mumble, "That was my roundabout way of asking what you *want* to do. But in my head, it kept sounding like *what do you want to be when you grow up,* and I didn't want to sound ridiculous."

Her cheeks pinken and she takes a nervous gulp of her wine, but I'm too busy feeling the earthquake beneath my feet to notice.

What do you want to do?

No one's ever asked me that.

I've never thought about it.

And it hits me that at twenty-six years old, for the first time I have someone that cares enough about me to ask that question. Isabella's not asking because she's making conversation and feels obligated, she's asking because she gives a shit. Because even though she's only known me a few weeks, she sees something in me that even I don't see.

I've been stuck for so long in the now, focused so much on just surviving *today*, that it never occurred to me to look at tomorrow. Didn't think I even *could*.

"Kane?" I hear Isabella's soft voice. She's waiting patiently for my answer.

I don't tell her that single question just upended my entire view of my life. Instead, I say, "I'm not sure. Why, what do *you* want to do? Did you ever think about what you'd do without ballet? Or was the dream always to be a ballerina?"

She hesitates for a moment, observing me with a knowing gaze, but in the end, she doesn't push me on my answer.

"I think I'm content as I am right now, which is a victory in itself," she responds. "With dancing it was always go, go, go, get better, be bigger. Nothing was ever good enough. There was always more work to do. But now..." She sighs heavily. "Now, I can finally breathe. Besides work, I'm not locked into anything. I can do things I actually *enjoy*, and try things I've always wanted to try. I don't have to turn down that food, or say no to an impromptu trip, or weigh everything as it relates to ballet. I love dancing, but I feel like I'm experiencing the pleasures of life for the first time. I feel… happy."

She hurriedly tears her gaze from mine and takes a sip of her wine. When she eventually looks up and meets my eyes, her cheeks are pink and the unspoken part is obvious.

I make her happy.

I don't know how to speak around my heart pounding against my ribs.

She starts to fidget with her wine glass again. "I was actually thinking about staying in Philly a little longer."

Hope expands like a balloon in my chest. "Yeah?" I ask in a rough voice.

She nods. "Yeah, I mean, my lease is month to month because that made sense when I first moved here, since I wasn't sure if I was even going to like it, but it really is a waste of money if you think about it. An annual lease makes way more sense. It would be stupid not to sign one."

She's rambling. I know she's rambling. *She* knows she's rambling.

I swallow roughly and force the words out. "You want to stay in Philly?"

Do you want to stay with me?

Her eyes are wide, and focused on me with emotions I don't dare to interpret. Wordlessly, she nods.

My heart expands in my chest. Between her asking about *my* future, and now this sounding like we're talking about *our*—

We're interrupted by the shrill beep of my phone.

I reach to pull it out of my pocket, and when I see the text message and sigh, Isabella asks, "Everything okay?"

Dropping my phone onto her side table, I nod. "It's just work. They asked if I could come in tonight after all."

An honest to God *pout* appears on Isabella's face. It makes me chuckle and drop my hand back to her ankle.

"They really do have you working all the time."

"Unfortunately." I give her an affectionate squeeze. "I'll make it up to you. How about I take you out to dinner tomorrow night?"

That makes her perk up. She's smiling again, and it hits me that I'm going to be a fucking pushover when it comes to what I'm willing to do for that smile.

"Okay," she agrees. "I'd like that."

I have to tamp down on my own smile as I nod.

She seems placated as we settle back into our conversation. "When do you have to leave for work?"

I glance at the time on my phone. "Two hours."

She nods, then comments thoughtfully, "You don't talk much about the club."

I shrug. "Not much to say."

Isabella quirks an eyebrow at me. I quirk mine right back, waiting for her to ask what she really wants to ask.

It doesn't take very long. She opens her mouth once, closes it, then opens it again and says, "You never talk about the girls."

It hits me then, what she's getting at. A slow grin stretches across my face.

"Jealous, princess?"

Because *fuck*, the thought of Isabella being territorial, not in general but of *me*, is intoxicating.

I almost laugh when she glares at me. "Should I be?" she asks.

I'm shaking my head before she's even finished the question. "No, you shouldn't be."

I watch her hesitate, just for a second, then she's placing her glass of wine on the side table. Wordlessly, she takes mine and does the same with it. And before I can ask what she's doing, she's sliding a leg over my hips to straddle my lap.

I grip Isabella's hips and try not to drool over the sight of her taking control.

"You never get dances from the girls?" she murmurs, her hands landing on my shoulders.

I can't even remember the name of another girl. "Never."

She hums thoughtfully, her hips starting to roll in a circle. My dick hardens instantly.

I think I like jealous Isabella.

CHAPTER 28
Isabella

I've NEVER GIVEN a lap dance before. Never even thought about it.

And yet, it feels like the most natural thing in the world to roll my hips to the beat of an imaginary song. A song that I can't be bothered to actually turn on, because I'm *that* eager to touch Kane. I want to say it's the dancer in me that's in tune with even imaginary music, but the truth is… I think it's Kane. Because with the way he's looking at me, with the way he's touching me, it feels like this is the only thing I should be doing right now.

"You don't ever think of what it might be like with one of them?" I wonder out loud. "They're so pretty, I'm sure you have *some* thoughts."

Kane's hold tightens on my hips. "Never," he says again. His gaze, now blazing with hunger, travels over the length of my body, taking in my rolling hips and the way my shirt has slid off one shoulder. When I reach up to take my hair clip out and let my locks tumble free, I see his jaw clench.

"I wouldn't blame you if you did," I tell him, sliding his

hands from my hips up to my breasts.

Tell me I'm the only one. Tell me this is real.

He cups my breasts under my shirt, his thumbs brushing over my nipples. He can't see my thoughts, my silent begging, because his attention is focused on the way they peak under his touch.

I try again, more obviously this time. I start to trace the ink on his arm as I say, "I've never done the casual thing, so I don't know what the rules are here. But we never said you couldn't see other people."

That gets his attention. His gaze darts up to lock eyes with me at the same time that his hands drop back to my hips. For a moment, he only stares. And I have no idea what's going through his mind right now.

I distract myself by dropping my gaze and continuing to trace the tattoo on his arm, holding my breath as I wait for him to put me out of my misery.

Tell me this isn't casual. Tell me I'm not alone here.

"Have you ever thought about getting one?"

The sudden change of topic makes me frown and meet his eyes again. "What?"

His stare is just as hard as it was a second ago. "Have you ever wanted to get a tattoo?"

My frown deepens in thought. "I don't know. Maybe. I just… don't know what I would get."

He pauses, then promptly lifts me off his lap and onto my knees beside him on the couch. And before I can open my mouth to ask what he's doing, he's already moving to stand behind me.

"Bend over, princess. I'm going to mark you."

I suck in a breath, then swallow my hesitation and lean forward, bracing my hands on the back of the couch.

"Good girl," he murmurs appreciatively. When I peek over my shoulder to watch for his next move, I see him reach toward the journal on my coffee table and the black marker sitting beside it.

And then suddenly I'm not focusing on sight, but on the feel of Kane's hands on my body, on the sound of his breathing growing labored as those hands start to search for the perfect place to stain me. They move over my shoulders, along my ribs, down my legs, and then finally, they settle on my ass cheeks. He kneads them for a moment, seemingly unable to pass up the opportunity to touch me there. The movement makes my boy shorts start to ride up, exposing more and more of my ass.

"You're fucking perfection," I hear him growl quietly.

I half expect him to forget his mission—and with every grind of the fabric against my center, I move closer to begging for just that—but before I can make the request, he's crowding me against the couch, his lips against my ear and his arms caging me in.

"You want to know if this is casual, Isabella? Let me answer that very clearly for you."

And then he's moving away to kneel behind me, and I hear him uncap the marker. Suddenly, the cool tip of it is dragging across my skin, right under my left ass cheek.

I think I hold my breath the entire time. It could have taken a minute, it could have taken ten, I have no idea. My brain and my body become singularly focused on the feeling of

Kane marking me.

When he finally pulls away, the place he drew on me feels like it's on fire.

"What did you draw?" I ask in a breathless voice.

But I don't get an answer, even when I ask the question again a minute later. When I glance over my shoulder, I see Kane staring down at my ass.

And he looks every bit the apex predator that I know he is.

Before I can open my mouth to say... *something*, Kane reaches for the sides of my underwear and slowly starts to slide them down my legs.

My breath hitches as the cool air hits my drenched center.

"Beautiful." The last word he utters before his mouth latches onto my clit and my soul leaves my body.

"*Kane*, oh my God," I gasp at the sudden sensation. But then I have no more words, because he's eating me like he's desperate to consume as much of my taste as possible. I don't think I take a single full breath in the time that it takes him to make me come. I can only gasp and moan and claw my way to ecstasy.

And then I'm coming, shaking and shuddering against his mouth as my hands fist in the cushions and I try not to collapse. Because he doesn't stop, even when the waves finally abate.

While I'm still recovering from the pleasure he wrung from me, I feel Kane's tongue slip from my clit, up to the tight puckered entrance above it. His touch feels lazy, like now that he's given me one orgasm, he's got all the time in the world to give me another.

I can't catch my breath enough to dispute his touch.

I've *never* been touched back there, and my first reaction is to protest the dirty touch. It shouldn't feel good, and he definitely shouldn't want to put his *tongue* back there. The good girl in me wants to scold him for what he's doing.

Except… in the time it takes me to suck in my first full breath, I realize… *holy shit*, it feels good.

I let out the breath I sucked in on a long, heavy moan.

"Oh my *God*," I hiccup. "Why does that feel good?"

Kane's tongue leaves me only long enough to answer.

"Because I was made to bring you pleasure."

And then he's right back to tonguing me in that forbidden place, this time with his fingers sliding inside my cunt to double the sensations.

"*Kane*," I choke out, my hands seconds away from tearing my cushions to shreds. "I'm going to—"

"I know," he growls, his fingers driving deeper and his tongue swirling quicker and quicker. "Come on my face while my tongue is in your ass, princess. Show me how dirty you are."

Between his touch and his words, I have no way of surviving another cyclone of pleasure.

I come with a choked cry, my face burying into the couch cushions in an effort to smother the sound. And when I eventually come down, it's to the sounds of Kane's belt buckle clinking and foil being ripped.

"You're too fucking perfect," he growls as one hand latches onto my hip. "I can't look at your body and *not* want to fuck you."

His words alone make me turn my face into the couch and let out a needy moan. And that's even before I feel the tip of him against my entrance, just barely pushing inside before he pulls out and slides it slowly down to my clit. He's teasing me, and it's enough to make a shudder roll through me.

"Kane," I whimper. "Please, I need you inside me."

A growl vibrates through his chest. "And now you're begging? *Fuck*, princess, I'm not going to be able to let you go."

Something in his words tickles at my subconscious, some kind of warning, or something I should be paying attention to. But before I can think too much about it, Kane fucks into me with a single hard thrust.

I cry out at the sensation, but despite the sudden rough onslaught, I'm already pushing my hips back to try to take more of him inside my body. I can never get enough of Kane. Ever.

He doesn't give me a chance to adjust—not that I need it. I'm just as desperate for Kane to fuck me as he seems to be for it. His hands grip my hips hard enough to bruise, and I realize… I want to be marked. I *want* the proof of him on my skin.

"Spank me," I beg in a breathless voice.

His thrusts slow but don't stop. He's almost as surprised by my request as I am.

And then he's dropping a hard slap onto my ass cheek.

I *moan* at the sensation.

"Again," I breathe, pushing my hips back for more.

"*Fuck*, " he groans. Then he drops another slap to my skin. "Look at you, so eager for my marks. That's what this is, isn't it?"

"Yes," I cry, dropping to my forearms so I can arch my back and beg for more. "*Pleasepleaseplease…*"

I lose count of how many times he spanks me. By the time I feel my body tightening with my release, my skin feels like it's on fire. With his thrusts lighting me up from the inside, and his hand drawing my skin with flames on the outside, I don't have a hope of not losing myself entirely when the orgasm takes me over.

I don't even feel Kane come, that's how lost I am in the whirlwind of pleasure. But eventually, when my breathing slows and I can manage a few words, I realize that Kane has already pulled out of me and disposed of the condom. I must have collapsed, because I start to push back onto my knees again.

Except, I hear a click behind me. It sounds like a camera going off. I turn to see what could have possibly distracted Kane so soon after sex, and find him staring down at my ass, his phone in hand.

Silently, he turns to show me the picture he just took. It's of the mark he left under my pinkened ass cheek, the black marker smudged and slightly faded, but still entirely legible. And when I read the word he marked me with, my body instantly lights with another type of fire.

Mine.

By the time I get home from the dance studio, my giddiness has increased tenfold. With nothing to distract me, the only thing I can think about anymore is my date with Kane tonight.

Date. That's not a word I thought I would ever use in regards to Kane. Even a casual physical thing was too much to hope for in the beginning, but a date out to a nice restaurant— even once this thing between us really got going—wasn't really in the realm of possibility. So having him be the one to suggest it last night was… unanticipated.

But so, *so* exciting.

I can't stop smiling as I get ready. I pick a short and simple dark green dress to go with my black heels, but I take extra time taming my wavy hair into the perfect pattern. I'm so used to wearing it in the ballerina bun that I'm always surprised by how long it is when I let it down.

Not to mention, when I leave it up, it typically results in Kane grabbing onto it.

My hair brush slows as thoughts of sex with Kane start to rush back. As *last night* starts to rush back. Of what we talked about, and then what happened after it.

Of Kane *claiming* me.

A shiver runs through me at the memory. There have been so many questions in my mind lately about how Kane feels about me, but I haven't been able to work up the nerve to actually ask him about it. Leave it to him to answer that question so definitively without ever using any words.

An unwitting smile splits my face when I hear a knock on my front door. I grab my clutch as I leave my room and rush to the front door.

I suck in a startled breath when I open it.

I don't know if I'll ever get over thinking Kane is the hottest guy I've ever seen, but there's zero chance of that happening today.

I've seen him shirtless and sweaty, I've seen him padded up with jeans and a leather jacket, and I've seen him comfortable in joggers at home. But I've never seen him dressed up and *trying* to look good.

He takes up my whole doorway, of course, because that's how overwhelming his stature and presence always is. And he's still wearing jeans, because I don't think even a nice restaurant could get Kane into some slacks. But paired with those dark-washed jeans is a simple black button-up, his sleeves rolled up to his elbow and showing off not just the tattoos on his forearms and hands, but also a beautiful silver watch on his wrist. His short, wavy hair looks more tamed than it usually does, and the top two buttons on his shirt are undone, letting his throat tattoo peek out over the collar.

I don't realize I'm staring until I hear a chuckle and feel

Kane lightly chuck me under the chin.

"You're staring, princess."

"*God*, you're hot," I blurt out before I can bite my tongue.

His expression was already amused from my staring, but my words light his face with something else. Bashfulness? Or is it just heat from my brazen compliment?

"You look pretty good yourself," he says, his gaze openly dropping over my body. The track of it is slow, and they linger on my legs. He doesn't even seem to notice when he growls, "Damn, baby."

Instantly, his eyes go black with lust. Then he's stepping into my apartment and sinking a hand into my hair so he can tip my head back and devour my mouth.

It's all I can do to whimper and wrap my arms around his waist in an effort to hold myself up, my knees immediately going weak from the force of his kiss.

"I'm going to do the polite thing right now and give you a heads up that I'm going to steal your panties during dinner tonight," he growls against my mouth. "Because afterwards, I want you to sit on the back of my motorcycle knowing that the entire ride home, I'm going to be thinking about that bare pussy leaking onto the seat behind me—and fantasizing about how quickly I'll be able to lick it up as soon as we're home."

I can't stop the shudder that runs through me at his erotic words. Then it's me that's stamping a kiss to his lips, sliding my tongue in his mouth and silently begging him to own me with his kiss again.

He's the one who pulls back, though he looks like he's mentally trying to remind himself why he wanted to go out tonight in the first place. But eventually he straightens to put some space between us.

"Ready to go?" he asks.

"Umm, kind of," I stammer, trying to reorganize my brain cells after his kiss. "I had planned to push you back into your apartment when I opened the door, but you're entirely too distracting."

Kane quirks an eyebrow. "My apartment? Why?"

"Because you're always in mine and I've never seen yours." Gathering the rest of my courage, I add, "Plus, I thought maybe we could… spend the night together after dinner. And I wouldn't want you to leave Oscar, or uproot him from where he feels comfortable, so I thought we could sleep at yours. If you're okay with that. If not, that's totally okay. I just thought, with last night, that maybe we—"

"Isabella," Kane interrupts, his voice vibrating with amusement and warmth. "Can you stop talking long enough to let me give you an answer?"

"Yup, I can do that," I blurt awkwardly.

He's hesitating, clearly thinking, and the pause lasts for so long that I come embarrassingly close to filling the silence with more of my babbling. Thankfully, he starts talking before I can do that.

"Do you actually want to come over, or are you just trying to be polite?"

That makes me frown. "Do I *seem* like the type of person who would do something she doesn't want to do, just to appear polite?"

"Yes," he says with a chuckle.

My frown deepens. "Okay, fine, that's fair. But have I ever come off like that with *you*?"

The pause is Kane's this time. "Touché," he finally admits. "Okay. My place it is, then."

I can't smother my excited smile as I quickly check the time on my phone. "Can you give me the tour before dinner? I really want to see it, but also I secretly miss Oscar."

Kane's lip quirks with a smile as he puts some space between us and takes my hand. "All of this is just a ruse to spend more time with Oscar, isn't it?"

"Guilty."

Kane barks out a delighted laugh, and at the sound, my heart fills so completely with joy that I think I might burst.

Is it possible for things to be this perfect?

He leads me out of my apartment and into his. But before I can take in the apartment itself, a huge smile is breaking across my face and I'm dropping to my knees.

"Hi, baby," I coo, greeting Oscar with the same excitement he meets me with. His tail is wagging so hard it sounds like a baseball bat is banging against the hardwood floor. His tongue is lolling out the side of his mouth, and he looks about two seconds away from rolling over for a belly rub.

"You better be more of a guard dog than this if anyone else walks in," I hear Kane grumble from behind me.

I giggle at that, scratching Oscar under the chin one last time before standing up. When I turn to face Kane, his usual stone-cold expression has already slid back onto his face.

But I know him. I can see the nerves underneath it.

I turn in a small circle, taking in the space around me. The apartment layout is identical to mine, so I take in the furniture and décor, instead. Kane's put in a single couch and coffee table in front of the mounted TV, and a small makeshift bar counter next to the tidy kitchen. There are no decorations anywhere, but also no clutter. Even without seeing the bedroom, I can tell the entire apartment is very minimalist.

Very *Kane*.

I turn my attention back to where he's still waiting for my reaction. He only quirks an eyebrow when I focus back on him.

"I love it," I say with a warm smile. "It's perfect for you."

He doesn't look entirely convinced. He jerks his head stiffly toward the couch and says, "Sorry there's not more places to sit. I never have people over, so it's never been a need before."

"You mean you don't host house parties on weekends? I'm shocked."

He chucks me under the chin, the whisper of an amused smile finally appearing on his lips. "Smartass," he murmurs.

I glance back at the couch and add in a serious tone, "I kind of like that there's only one couch to sit on. Just means we'll have to cuddle up to make the three of us fit."

It doesn't look like Kane is even *trying* to hide the happiness on his face.

Just then, the doorbell rings. And I watch as Kane's playful, uninhibited smile turns immediately into a frown.

"Are you expecting someone?" I ask hesitantly.

"Besides you, I don't talk to anyone," he answers absentmindedly, his gaze never leaving the front door. Then he's striding across the room and pressing his face to the peephole.

I have an idea who it is as soon as I see his jaw clench and his expression turn shuttered.

"You don't have to answer," I tell him quietly. Hopefully. Desperately.

But I know he's lost to his childhood memories when he reaches for the doorknob.

The door opens to reveal a woman who I could've guessed was Kane's mom even without watching his reactions. It doesn't matter that they look like opposites in almost every way—where he looks healthy, and strong, and as of a minute ago, happy, she looks tired, and gaunt, and mean. No, those things don't matter because I realize instantly that they have the same eyes. Not just the physical color, or shape, but the same gaze. The kind of gaze that tells you they're a little bit skeptical and a whole lot defensive.

But it's not the scared eyes that make me wary of Kane's mom. It's the slimy smile that slides across her face when she sees her son.

"Kane, baby. Long time no see. How are you?"

"How did you find me?" Kane asks through gritted teeth. I hear Oscar let out a whine in the background.

Kane's mom waves him off. "I told you before, you're not exactly hard to figure out. Finding you was easy." She must see our blank stares because she rolls her eyes and adds, "I knew the gym name from the fight poster, and when I showed up there to convince your coach to 'help reunite his fighter with his poor mom who's been searching for him for years,' I happened to see you walking home. Easiest it's ever been to find you, kid." Then her attention slides past Kane to me. The smile on her face grows. "Imagine my surprise when I won two for the price of one. My missing son *and* his rich girlfriend."

I see every muscle in Kane's back tighten when her focus zeroes in on me. I can only see his profile from here, so I can't read his expression completely, but it's not hard to guess that it's making him increasingly upset.

"Don't worry, she's not the one I'm here to see," his mom says. Her attention turns back to Kane, an over-plucked eyebrow rising as she asks, "Aren't you going to invite me in? I've been on the road for hours, the least you could do is offer me something to drink."

I fully expect Kane to refuse and shut the door in her face, but when a few seconds pass and he still hasn't said anything, I turn toward him in surprise.

"Kane…"

He stands there, frozen. Not turning her away, not letting her in.

She takes the decision out of his hands when she shoulders past him and steps into the tiny living room. Her expression is inquisitive as she looks around the apartment, the quick sweep taking in every piece of furniture, every sign of possible wealth or well-being. She doesn't even pause on Oscar.

"To be honest, I expected a little more than this," she says. "This area is pretty nice, or at least nicer than you used to pick, so I thought you'd at least give enough of a shit to make the *inside* look nice, too."

"Does that translate to you're bummed I don't have more for you to steal?" Kane asks tightly.

That seems to surprise her. She turns back to him, her expression looking both surprised and impressed.

At him pushing back at her? Has he really never done that before?

The pit in my stomach, that feeling of foreboding, grows even more.

"Well, well, well, look who grew a backbone in the last three years," she says with a hum. "Is that your doing or hers?"

Kane doesn't respond, he just clenches his teeth so hard I'm surprised I don't hear them crack.

"What do you *want*, Mom?"

She sighs in disappointment. "I told you: I need money. Your piece of shit stepdad—who you never cared about enough to meet, by the way—left me without a home or a penny to my name. And if you hadn't left me all those years ago, I wouldn't have been evicted from our apartment, and I would've had a place to go back to. So, the state of your penniless mother is *your* fault. And I expect you to help me out now, especially after everything I've done for you."

Rage starts to boil in my veins. I've met a lot of entitled, shitty parents in my life, but I have *never* seen anyone as delusional as this woman.

And yet, I can't bring myself to say anything. Not just because I'm too nervous to stand up to a woman like this, but also because I'm entirely expecting Kane to step in at any moment. There's no way he won't set her straight and kick her out.

She seems to notice my judgment, because she turns her attention to me and says, "Oh please, let's not pretend you know anything about responsibility. Your parents have probably done everything for you, I doubt you've ever even had to lift a finger.

What would *you* know about hardships?"

I open my mouth to say I *do* know about hardship, that I know what it's like to feel like everything in your life is going wrong, but… nothing comes out. Because the truth is, I've never experienced anything even close to what Kane and his mom have gone through.

She must see the capitulation on my face, because a smug smile stretches her lips. Her gaze slides over my face, down my clothes, and back up again. I expect her to say something, but instead, she takes a step closer and lifts her hand to my hair.

"Such a pretty little thing," she muses. "I wonder what you would've turned into if you hadn't fallen into such a privileged life. Would you still be pretty? Or would the pain and heartache of a hard life have taken that away?"

I'm caught off guard by her bold touch, too surprised to move away, but I'm even more surprised by the fact that *this* boundary, this physical boundary, is what causes Kane to snap out of his fear-frozen state by the door.

"Don't touch her," he barks. Striding across the apartment, he grabs my arm and tugs me slightly behind him. "I swear to *God*, I will rip you apart if you touch her."

And apparently, Kane's reaction is enough to snap *her* out of her taunting demeanor. At her son's threat, her expression drops every bit of playfulness, and it hardens into one that immediately makes it obvious how serious she is.

"Fine. I'll stop beating around the bush." Her gaze narrows. "I need $5,000 by next week. I need a new apartment, and I need new clothes, since my bastard ex burned most of mine. I'll come by next week to pick it up."

Kane's expression goes from furious to incredulous. "Are you insane? I'm not giving you $5,000. I don't even *have* $5,000."

His mom rolls her eyes. "Don't act like your girlfriend here can't shake that out of her pocket. The bracelet on her wrist alone is worth that much. She won't even notice the blip in her bank account."

I'm now equally shell-shocked. "Why on earth would you think I would just *give* you that kind of money?"

When she turns her attention back to me, an ice-cold chill runs through my bones. Because the look she's giving me isn't just smug, or insane, it's borderline evil.

"Because, sweetheart," she starts, "if you *don't* give me the money, then I'll make sure Kane gets fired from his little job at the strip club. I can make that happen, and it's not that hard to make sure he's blacklisted from bouncing at any other club in the city." She lets out a patronizing laugh. "And then what is he going to do? What is he good for besides punching people in the face when they get out of line?"

"How *dare* you talk to him like that—"

"Don't even get me started on what I could do to *you*, you little bitch," she snarls. "You think his life is the only one I can ruin? You're delusional. It would take *one* phone call to make your perfect life tumble like a house of cards." She takes a second to settle the smug mask back on her face, hiding her hate with a heavy exhale and a smile. "It's too bad about your ballet career—it must've felt like your life was ending when you got injured. But if you think you don't have anything else of value since then, I'd be happy to prove just how wrong you are."

For what feels like the fifth time in ten minutes, my rage again cools to icy foreboding. This emotional whiplash is making an already-volatile situation feel even worse, and I can't quite catch my breath enough to keep up with it.

If she knows my name, it wouldn't be hard to find out what happened to me. There are plenty of articles that explain not just how big my name was before my injury, but also how bad my injury was, and how permanently it ruined my career.

But she can't possibly know that my entire move to Philly was meant to help me figure out who I am without dancing. She can't know that I had exactly those thoughts before I met Kane, that I have nothing of value without my dance career.

What could she possibly threaten me with that's not physical harm?

She watches all these thoughts play across my face, her grin growing with every second.

"I wonder if you even realize how much you're leaning on your ballet legacy, even without an active career. Does your self-worth tie into who you were in the past? Or do you think this thing you've based your entire life on is untouchable now that it doesn't have a future?"

My breaths start to come quicker. I don't know what she's about to say, but I'm already struggling to breathe just from waiting for it.

And she knows it. Her tone is smug when she says, "That phone call I mentioned? It would be to your dance school *here*. In Philly. It's not that hard to drop a rumor—especially in an uptight place like a fucking *ballet academy*—that will spread like wildfire and ruin everyone involved. Turns out, they *really* dislike any kind of illegal activity by their dancers. And with the company you've been keeping lately, I really doubt it would be hard for them to believe it's true..."

The look she slants in Kane's direction implies her true meaning, and my heart drops into my stomach when I see how much it instantly affects him. I watch as his throat bobs on a hard swallow, and as a veil of guilt drops over his expression when he glances my way.

"Kane, that's not—" I start in an attempt to comfort him.

"Don't bother, he knows it's true," his mom cuts me off. "And he also knows I won't hesitate to do it. Don't you, Kane?" She turns her evil smile on her son. "Would you hate being the cause of your girlfriend's shattered reputation as much as I would enjoy causing it? After all, why should she have a better life than us? *She* didn't do anything to deserve it."

And despite her threats against his job, and *his* life, it's the threats to *mine* that cause him to snap out of his frozen childhood fear.

"I swear to God, if you even *think* of hurting her, I'll make you regret ever giving birth to me," he snarls, the venom in his voice so real, even his mom sucks in a surprised breath.

Kane steps into her space, leaning down to get into her face. "You think your boyfriends fucked up your life before? I will fucking *ruin* you if you hurt her."

His mom studies him for a moment, the surprise on her face dulling as she looks over her son. When she finally responds, she doesn't sound worried about the threat.

"I'll be back for the money next week," she says flatly.

And then she brushes past him and walks out the door.

And the fact that she doesn't slam it makes her exit all the more haunting.

I'm rattling with nerves as I turn back to Kane.

"Kane, we can talk about this—"

"Don't worry about her, I'll take care of it," he says sharply. He checks the time before saying, "We missed our reservation at the restaurant, but I don't feel like cooking. Let's just go to a bar to grab food."

I study Kane's demeanor. In only ten minutes, I watched him go from a happy, grown man, to a panicked and scared little boy, and now to a completely blank and frozen human being. I can't read anything on his face. He's very obviously overwhelmed by what just happened, and his reaction is clearly to just… shut down.

He must notice my hesitation because he steps forward to cup my face, giving me all of his attention as he says, "I'll take care of it, Isabella. I promise."

And even though his words are comforting, I can *feel* the distance in him. Kane would do everything to protect me, but I'm not the one I'm worried about.

I don't get a chance to respond because Oscar lets out a whine from where he's still sitting in the living room. Kane and I both turn our attention to the dog, and I'm relieved to see Kane's shoulders relax a fraction. I hold my breath as he walks over to his friend and pets his head.

"Sorry, buddy," Kane murmurs. "I know she scared you. But she's gone now." When Oscar settles at his touch and his slightly-less-tense demeanor, his tail giving a small wag, Kane turns back to me.

He's still frozen, still numb to reality with a twinge of panic threatening to overtake him at any moment, but he looks slightly more in control of himself than he did a minute ago. Enough that it makes *me* relax a little bit more.

"Are you good if we go out? I could use a drink, to be honest. There's a bar down the street from here that has good food, if you still want to eat."

I nod immediately, desperate to put Kane at ease. If hot food and a drink will do that, I'll do it happily.

"Sure, let's go," I tell him with what I hope is a warm smile.

CHAPTER 30
Kane

THE SECOND THE door shuts behind my mom, I feel a door shut inside me, as well.

With the sound of the lock clicking shut, I go from burning with rage and terror, to numb and frozen with disbelief.

It's been three years since I've seen my mom. Three years of silence, of learning how to bury my childhood fears deep enough that I'd be unaffected by any memory involving my mother. I worked hard to wipe her from my mind, and up until her phone call last week, I was convinced that I had done it, and that I'd continue to remain unaffected, even if she appeared back in my life. That if she *did* show up, I'd be able to trample any emotion she might evoke in me.

It took less than sixty seconds for that idea to crumble.

Mentally, I think I black out after she leaves. I'm so desperate to shove those feelings of pure *terror* back where they belong, that I start fumbling to rebuild that wall of numbness. I think I ask Isabella a question, but I'm so overwhelmed by the terror tickling at my subconscious that I'm not fully aware of what I'm saying. I just know I need to get *out*.

"Sure, let's go," comes her melodic voice. I watch as she grabs her purse and her phone from the counter, then she's standing in front of me with a tight smile on her face.

I hesitate for a moment. I know I need to say *something*, but I'm barely holding myself together, and I know that any kind of discussion about what happened tonight is going to lead to a crash and burn. I know I'm going to ignore any talk of my mother tonight.

And yet, I can't bring myself to do that until I tell Isabella just how fucking sorry I am that I brought her into this. That, because of me, she was anywhere even remotely close to the wildfire that is my mother.

So, I croak out a quiet, "I'm sorry." I'm sure the pain and terror are blazing in my eyes right now, but I don't care. "I'm just so fucking sorry."

Before she can respond with anything, I turn and lead us out the door.

Five minutes after we get settled at the bar top, I've already slammed a vodka double and am waving down the bartender for another.

Isabella studies me as she sips her mojito. She's visibly nervous, and I can tell she's working up the nerve to talk about what happened at my apartment, but there isn't an ounce of me that is strong enough to initiate that conversation.

"We should talk about what happened," she finally says in a quiet voice.

I nod my thanks at the bartender as he slides the glass of

vodka in front of me. "Don't worry about what my mom said. I'll take care of it." Then I'm taking a big swig of my drink.

I see Isabella frown out of the corner of my eye. "Take care of it how? Like pay her the money?"

I shake my head. "No, I mean I'll take you out of the firing line. I'll make sure she doesn't call your school." I hesitate, but force myself to add, "I'll stop coming around after class, too."

That seems to startle her. "I don't want you to stop. I *like* when you pick me up after class."

Her reaction is so instant, so raw, that I can't help believing her, even though I don't want to. But I don't take it back.

Which only makes her more determined.

"I'm not ashamed of you, Kane. And I'm not worried about your mom trying to mess up my dance reputation. No one's going to listen to a random stranger over the owners of the fucking *New York City Ballet*."

I almost want to laugh at her hostility. Almost.

She sobers, and says, "I'm more worried about *you*. Can she really get you fired?"

"She's done it before," I answer in a flat voice.

Out of the corner of my eye, I see her frown at her mojito. "There has to be something we can do. Something preventative."

God, I want to kiss her right now. Not just because she used the word 'we' without even realizing it, but because she cares more about my mom's threat against *me* than the one against *her*.

And yet, I can't bring myself to give in to the urge. Because the wall I built up so desperately at the apartment, the wall that's keeping the pain and the hate from rushing back in, is also protecting me from any kind of hope.

And Isabella is the definition of hope.

"Beyond giving my boss a heads up that she might call, I can't do much," I tell her stiffly. "And despite being a good bouncer, I'm not exactly in close enough with the owner to dispute the threat of getting the club taken down for illegal activity."

"So, then what does that mean?" she blurts. "You're going to pay her?"

I let out a sigh. "No. I don't have that kind of money to spare. I have no idea why she thinks I do, unless she really does think I would ask you for it. But it doesn't matter. I'll figure it out."

She hesitates, working up the nerve to push again. "But how—"

"I said I'd take care of it, Isabella," I snap. "Let it go."

I see her swallow nervously. She nods, then goes back to swirling her mojito.

I slam back the second vodka, feeling the liquor burn its way down my throat and settle deep into my bones. It's a comforting feeling—it complements the emotional numbness well. It shoves the bad feelings further into the recesses of my mind, and it lets the feel-good chemical seep deeper into my body with every drop that rolls over my tongue. I start to relax even before I wave for a third drink.

"Do you want something to eat?" I hear myself asking Isabella, still aware of her presence next to me even though I can sense the vodka start to take over my consciousness. I know it's happening because I don't register her hesitation, even though I know her well enough to know she has no idea what to do with this new side of me.

"No, I'm okay," she says in a quiet, hesitant voice. And then there really is a pause before she asks, "Are you… I mean… is drinking that much a good idea?"

"I already have a mom, Isabella," I snap. "And clearly, she's more than I can handle. I don't need another one."

She's quiet after that. I half expect her to make some excuse to leave, since what normal person would want to be around me when I'm like this, but she doesn't. She simply sits quietly next to me as I sink further and further into my alcohol-addled insanity.

I don't know how much later it happens, I just know I'm drunk enough that things have started to blur in front of my eyes by the time it does. It even takes a second to register what I just heard.

"Hey there, beautiful. You look like you could use some better company. Mind if I take a seat?"

My head turns on a slow-motion swivel to take in the guy standing on the other side of Isabella. He's tall, but not exactly big, and he looks like a normal guy out prowling at the bars. Or at least, that's what my brain that's swimming in vodka is telling me.

"Um, no, that's okay," I hear Isabella say. "I'm with my b— my friend right now."

"Your friend that's ignoring you?" he asks with a small laugh. "Come on, I just want to talk."

And then he gets bold enough to physically crowd her. Stepping into her space, he gets close enough to place a hand on Isabella's waist to ensure that he's the only thing she can focus on.

I think it's the alcohol that slows down my reaction time. Because in the time that it takes me to react, Isabella's already putting her hand on his chest and pushing him back.

"Step away from me," she says forcefully. And God, she looks so *proud* of herself. She could've easily fallen into frozen shock again, could have been the same unsure Isabella that first came to this city. The one that got mugged not too long ago.

Instead, she's growing into her strength, and her self-assuredness. She's becoming the person she came here to find.

Meanwhile, I'm moving in the opposite direction.

As the vodka swirls in my stomach, so does my self-disgust. It spreads in my gut, filling my insides until it seeps out through my pores as sweat.

And yet, it does nothing to stop me from acting on my default urges.

"Get your *fucking* hands off her," I bark, standing from my barstool. "She's with me."

The guy frowns at my reaction, but it doesn't register why. "Doesn't look like it, man. She looks pretty lonely to me."

"She's not fucking *lonely*," I snarl, stepping around Isabella. "I'm right here."

He lets out a mocking laugh. "All I'm saying is if a girl like *that* was out with me, I'd actually give her some attention."

And I'm drunk, but not drunk enough that the burn of shame doesn't register after his words. Because I *know* he's right. And that shame just reignites my fury all over again.

I shove at his chest as embarrassment coils with all the

other emotions. "You're delusional if you think a girl like that would ever be interested in you."

He pushes me back without hesitation. "Get the fuck off me."

"Kane, let's just get out of here," comes Isabella's voice from behind me. I think I feel her tug at my arm.

I yank it away.

The guy smirks at Isabella. "You should listen to her."

Rage boils in my chest. I shove him again, hard enough this time to smash him against the bar top. "Shut the *fuck* up."

"Kane, please, let's just leave," Isabella begs. "I don't want to be here anymore."

I can't hear her. I can't hear *anything*.

I shove the guy again, this time crowding him against the bar and gripping his shirt in two shaking fists. "You never should have talked to her," I spit in his face.

"Kane!" I hear Isabella's panicked shout, can feel her urgently pulling at the back of my shirt.

It doesn't matter. Reality is fading away in a swirl of vodka and ice.

"Kane, *please!*" she begs. "Please don't do this."

There are shouts coming from around us, and a bustle of activity. But nothing registers. I can't even really see the guy's face in front of me, because who he is doesn't actually matter. I'm too far gone, officially a slave to the urges screaming inside of me.

I don't feel my fist smash into his skull.

I can't make sense of the screaming.

I don't even react to the cops when they appear in the bar.

It vaguely registers that Isabella is trying to get to me, that even when *I'm* causing the problem, she's still trying to protect me, still begging everyone to leave me alone.

The sight of it shakes loose in me something I haven't felt in weeks. This feeling of shame, of self-hatred, of being so *undeserving* of someone as good as Isabella.

And with that mix of feelings comes the defense mechanism I've been leaning on my whole life: to push away everyone and everything.

It vaguely registers that I'm yelling something, but I'm too far gone to comprehend what it is. The only thing my brain *does* understand is that whatever I said causes complete and total devastation to appear on Isabella's face.

That's the last thing I remember before blackness sucks me under.

I watch in complete shock as the cops haul Kane out of the bar.

I… don't understand what just happened. I don't understand how we got here.

I don't know what to *do*.

"I don't fucking need you to bail me out with your trust fund money."

Kane's last words ring in my brain, leaving me shaking and hurt and so confused. I've never seen anyone get arrested before. I have no idea if cops deal with drunk and disorderly people differently than any other crime, or if they cart them off just to get them out of the environment. Is a drunk tank real, or just something they say on TV? Is that where Kane is right now? Is this something that goes on his record?

My hands are trembling so hard I can barely get my phone out of my pocket. I scroll over my contacts, trying to decide who to call—or even if I *should* call someone. Does Jax or anyone from the gym need to know about this?

I'm so confused I could cry.

I force myself to suck in a deep breath. Closing my eyes, I count my breaths and wait for my heart to settle down. Finally, I feel a little more in control, and a little more clear-headed. Enough that I think I can start to make some decisions.

First question: do I go to the jail and try to help Kane despite his drunk, parting shot?

I feel my heart crack down the middle as I realize the answer.

No. I shouldn't.

Partly because I'm a strong woman that shouldn't crawl after a man that just humiliated me. It doesn't matter that he was drunk, and I *know* he didn't mean it—alcohol doesn't excuse behavior. I saw the look of regret that he wore with that first vodka. Which means he knew exactly what could happen when he started drinking.

But the real reason the shock and hurt cuts through me at the knowledge that I shouldn't help Kane is because I *can't.* If I go down to the police station right now and bail him out, or beg for his release, or do anything for him physically right now, the only thing that would do is allow Kane to not deal with the consequences. Because the fact of the matter is Kane was rightfully arrested: he got drunk, he got in a fight, he got arrested. He *deserves* to be in jail overnight.

So, as much as it kills me not to help him, I'm not bailing him out.

When my stomach roils at the thought, I mentally add, *at least tonight.*

I'll pick him up in the morning.

Coming to a decision, even one as hard as that, doesn't

make me feel any better. In fact, knowing that I can't do anything right now makes me feel ten times worse. Because now, the only thing I have to focus on is how badly this hurts.

I glance around me, trying to figure out where I go from here. Home, I guess. But going without Kane, when I was *so excited* to spend tonight with him, is really going to amplify the loneliness. The sadness. The heartache. I don't want to go home.

But then I remember that Oscar is home alone. I know Kane fed him before he came over, but he still needs to be let out tonight at some point.

And if they really did take Kane to the drunk tank, then he won't be back until tomorrow.

I bite into my bottom lip, surprised to taste the tang of blood. But it shakes me out of my haze.

I scroll through my contacts once more. I don't have a key to Kane's place, so that means I need to call the landlord and have him let me in as an emergency precaution.

Thankfully, he's both awake and understanding when he answers. We agree to meet at the apartment building in ten minutes.

I'm wringing my hands and giving the landlord a nervous smile and breathless *thank you* when he finally lets me into Kane's apartment. Oscar gives me a curious and sleepy look from where he's lying on the couch.

"I assume you've got a list of things you have to take care of until Kane gets back?" the landlord asks from behind me.

I spin to face him. I obviously didn't tell him Kane was arrested, just that he ran into some issues and can't get back tonight like he had planned. But I nod in answer to his question.

The landlord looks at his phone, then out into the hallway. "Normally, I would wait and escort you out of the tenant's apartment, but I know you and him are friends, and I really have to get home to the family. Can I trust you to lock up behind you when you're done?"

Another nod. "Yes, of course. I'm just here for Oscar."

He nods. And then he's gone, leaving me alone with Oscar and more confusion and pain than ever before.

I busy myself with taking care of him. I refill his water bowl, give him some dog food, and then snap a leash onto his collar when I realize he hasn't stopped following me around.

"Come on, buddy," I murmur, double checking that the door is unlocked for our five-minute pee break outside. Oscar just whines and glues himself to my leg.

When we're back inside, there's nothing left to distract myself with. I'm stone cold sober, with no appetite, and nothing to do except get trampled in my head by my own worries. I don't know what to do with myself.

I sit down on the couch when my legs finally give out, and Oscar immediately climbs up beside me.

"Oh, buddy," I say on a sob, wrapping my arms around his furry body.

He lets out a whine and licks my cheek.

"I don't know what to do," I whisper. "I don't know how to help him."

I feel it then: the urge to let myself crack down the middle and sulk in my own pain. The pain caused by the unfairness of Kane's life, and the pain of dealing with the way Kane chooses to lash out. None of it is fair. And all of it hurts.

But it occurs to me then that this is no different than what it was like in the very beginning with Kane. When he was just as hurt and just as defensive, and his pain made him hurt people. This might be a more intense version of that, but it's the same thing.

And yet, I chose to stick that out. I *chose* to see past Kane's walls, and prove to him that despite his worst thoughts, his worst fears, I see him for who he really is. And I'm staying right here.

Because this isn't a schoolgirl crush anymore—I've fallen head over heels in love with Kane Whitaker. In my heart, I always knew I would, and I knew that if he gave me even the smallest opening, that I would happily make the jump. A small part of me was worried he wouldn't feel the same way, but now I realize the real risk is that he *does* feel the same way, but is scared to fight for it.

Curled up around Oscar, I flash back to the look on Kane's face right before the cops hauled him away.

Pain. Regret. Doubt.

I could see the thoughts on his face as clear as day. Even after everything we've been through, everything we've talked about and shared, Kane still obviously believes he's better off pushing me away. Whether that's because he's scared of trying or because he thinks he doesn't deserve me, I don't know. But both options are bullshit.

So, just like I did when I first showed up on his doorstep. I'm not going to let him push me away. I'm going to stay and show him that I *see* him, and I want him. I'm going to show him what it's really like to be cared for.

And if he wants out, then *he's* going to have to say it. Because I'll be damned if I'm the one that gives up on us.

I WAKE FROM my blackout inside a jail cell.

I wish I could say this is the first time it's happened, but that would be a lie. Though, this is the first time it's happened in Philly.

Groaning, I drag my hands down my face before forcing myself into a sitting position. It looks like I passed out on the bench in the cell, with two other guys snoring on the other side of the room. There's light filtering through the windows, signaling that I either slept through the night, or was blacked out long enough to not remember it. Either way, I'm sobering up and can feel the hangover from hell coming soon. Which means I need to get the fuck out of here before it hits.

I shakily push to my feet and near the bars. "Hey, can I make a phone call?" I call out.

For a few minutes, I hear nothing. Then, the sound of a lumbering night cop meets my ears, seconds before he appears at the end of the hallway.

"Well, look who's sobering up," he says, the disgust evident in his voice.

I don't bother responding to that. But he must see my confusion because he clarifies, "You already made your phone call. Clearly, you don't remember."

Fuck. No, I don't remember that. Who did I call? Isabella? *Dear God, I hope not.*

The cop lets out a chuckle. "You want to ask when you get to make another one, don't you?"

Yeah, I do. But I'm too proud to ask that out loud.

Or to admit that I've never had to ask *any* of these questions—despite being in jail for drunken bar brawls three times in my life already—because I've never had anyone to call.

"Take a seat, Rocky, you'll get another call in a few hours. From what I overheard, your first one didn't go so well."

Fuck. *Fuck.* Who did I call?

It had to have been Isabella. I don't even think I know anyone else's number. Or if I did, and I dialed someone else, I doubt anyone would come to get me.

Would Isabella even come to get me? After last night's shitshow, I wouldn't blame her if she didn't. I wouldn't blame her if she never answered my calls again.

I force that thought from my mind—that thought makes me want to vomit more than the alcohol.

Instead, I take a seat and try to blanket my mind with static. I force every thought—every angry, panicked, shameful thought—from my brain. Because all I can do now is wait. And getting lost in that spiral of thoughts isn't going to make this situation any better.

I don't know how long I sit like that. I don't think it's very long, because the light in the jail cell doesn't change much.

But at some point, my eyes snap open, the sounds of a heated conversation reaching my ears.

And unless I'm still drunk, I think I recognize the voice belonging to… Hailey?

Sure enough, a righteously indignant Hailey comes barreling around the corner. Jax on her heels, of course.

"It's absolutely ridiculous that you wouldn't let us pick him up any earlier," she's saying, glaring at the same guard I spoke to earlier. "What's the difference between letting him out at 7 a.m. or 8 a.m.? Clearly, he's already sobered up. I would think you would want to be *emptying* these cells."

"Miss, like I already told you," the guard says, annoyance lacing his words. "We have rules. We can't let them go until they've sobered up." He glares at Hailey. "And if you think he was sober when he called you, then you're just as stupid as he was drunk."

"Watch it," Jax bites out, his jaw hard and his eyes spitting straight venom at the guard.

The guard looks like he wants to toss Jax in the cell just for threatening a cop. But his wants are clearly bigger than his abilities, because it takes one thorough look at Jax to realize he doesn't have it in him.

"Just get the asshole out of here," the guard finally grumbles, reaching for his keys so he can shove them into the lock and open the door.

I don't ask any questions. I just take the exit I've been granted and walk through the door.

Jax and Hailey wait behind me while I fill out my discharge paperwork and accept the citation I've been issued for…

disorderly conduct, according to the paper in front of me.

Sounds about right. God knows my bar brawls in Baltimore used to be messy.

It isn't until I'm given back my wallet and phone that I finally chance a look at Jax and Hailey. Jax looks like he's a combination of angry and annoyed, which makes sense in this situation. Hailey also has the annoyed look, but it seems to be directed at the guard. Otherwise, she just looks… worried. Maybe nervous.

And when we walk out of the building and stop on the sidewalk, that look multiplies tenfold on her face.

"Are you okay?" she asks in a quiet voice.

"Yeah," I say, my voice like gravel. "Thanks for, uh, bailing me out. I'm sorry if I woke you two up." My brow furrows in irritation. At myself. "I don't even remember calling you, to be honest. And I'm not sure why I thought you'd answer. Or actually come down here."

"You called the gym," Jax explains. "Calls get forwarded to my cell afterhours, so we woke up to your call." My words finally seem to register, because he frowns. "Of course, we'd come down," he says. "We're teammates. I'm not going to let you rot in jail."

My head is pounding. From my impending hangover, but also from the muddled thoughts swimming in my brain, because Jax's words make no sense. He hates me. He *hates me*. That's been more than apparent at the gym.

He must see my confusion, because he sighs and his shoulders droop.

"Kane, just because we don't see eye to eye with our

training doesn't mean I want you to get hit by a bus. I keep my distance because I'm not a good training partner for you, but we're still *teammates*. I still have your back. Inside and outside of the gym."

The question slips out of me before I can swallow it back.

"Why would you do that?" I croak. "I've made it obvious I'm only there for myself. Why do you give a shit what happens to me?"

I expect him to sigh his frustration again, but to my surprise, he frowns. In confusion. In anger.

"Because that's what families do," he answers slowly. Weighing his words, and my reaction.

My reaction, which is a blank stare.

The reason for my reaction must click, because Jax's expression shifts instantly to sympathy. But before I can flip out at him for his pity and throw up my walls, he says quickly, "Look, forget what you *think* families and gyms and teammates are supposed to look like. *I'm* telling you that we look out for each other. And I don't give a fuck if it's one-sided and you never give a shit about any of us. Because that's not why we do it. We won't bail you out when things get rough because we expect something in return, we do it because we look out for our own and don't leave each other stranded. Because *that's* what being in our gym is about. And *that's* the kind of family we've built inside of it."

I… don't understand. Jax's words sing in my head on repeat, but they don't make any more sense on the third pass than they did on the first.

I've never had anyone give a shit about me before. And

definitely not a group of people all at once, none of which I've ever helped enough to deserve this kind of response. I'm a fuckup. An asshole. I'm the last person people should be sticking their necks out for.

And yet… one look at Jax tells me he's being 100% honest with me. He's not lying in order to manipulate or fuck with me, he's just… telling it like it is. He's telling me he cares if I live, or if I rot in a jail cell.

"I've never—" I start, but have to swallow the rock in my throat before I can continue. "I've never had…" This time I trail off, physically unable to get the words out.

"I know," Jax says roughly. And in that moment, I'm grateful for him, for seeing through me and not making me say it out loud. "But you'll get used to it."

I can only nod numbly.

"Isabella's part of that family, too," Hailey says quietly.

When her words register, my stomach drops and I feel like I want to vomit again.

Because she's right. *Isabella* was the first one to give a shit about me. With her, I've had a family.

"Did you talk to her?" I force myself to ask, even though I'm terrified of her answer. Of what she might have told Hailey.

Hailey's expression takes on a look of pity. She shakes her head in answer.

"Not since class yesterday. So, nothing about this." She hesitates, then asks, "Was she… with you last night? Did she see anything?"

I try to swallow down the bitter taste of regret and bile, and focus instead on sorting through my memories before the blackout.

My mom showing up at my apartment. Her threatening Isabella. The pain and fear sending me to the bar with Isabella, where that piece of shit hit on her—

I slam back to the moment when my memories cut off at being hauled out of the bar.

"Yeah," I croak. "She was there."

Hailey and Jax exchange worried glances. "Does she know you ended up here?" Hailey asks hesitantly.

I'm numb. I have no emotions. This can't be happening.

"Yeah," I answer.

"You should talk to her," she says quietly.

"I don't think I can," I say, the words tasting like acid. Hating the idea that last night might have finally driven Isabella away from me.

Because clearly, she left me at some point. Whether she tried to save me from the arrest or not, at some point she left. And left me here. Not that I blame her.

"You have to try," Hailey says. "You can't leave it like this. She *cares* about you, Kane. More than you probably realize."

"She doesn't," I say automatically. Mechanically. "She can't. She deserves so much better than me. Than *this*."

Another look of sympathy enters Hailey's eyes. But unlike when it happened with Jax, I don't immediately feel murderous. I just feel… sad.

Sad that I drive everyone away. Sad that when I *do* open up, I'm met with pity.

Sad that I thought for *one second* that I could make Isabella happy.

"Kane," Hailey says quietly. Her voice sounds distant. "*Kane*," she says again, this time tugging on my hand to get my attention. I turn my head to look at her.

The sympathy is long gone. In its place, I see... determination.

"Kane, you deserve to have someone care about you," she says firmly. "You *deserve* to be loved. Do you hear me? Isabella isn't settling for you. She's been *choosing* you. Every day. Because you're *worthy* of being chosen."

My mouth parts, but the words are stuck in my throat. Not that I know what I would say if I could get them out, because Hailey's words...

They hit me like a fucking brick.

They wrap around me like vines, and squeeze until I can't breathe. I can't hide from them behind my emotionally stunted wall anymore—they're too present, too *everywhere*, to fight any longer.

And that terrifies me. Because hearing Hailey's words, and feeling this... this *hope,* is enough to cripple me. But I can't ignore it anymore. The words are out there, born on Hailey's compassion, and I can't hide how much I've been dying for them to be true.

How much I want to be worthy of Isabella.

"I have to go talk to her," I croak. "I have to see—I have to know if she—" I swallow the end of that sentence, still too scared to say it out loud.

But just making the effort seems to be enough, because I'm suddenly filled with a bolt of motivation—of purpose.

"I have to go," I say more firmly.

I glance at my phone to check the time. Isabella is teaching yoga right now, but that's okay, because I definitely need to shower and clean myself up before I talk to her.

The desperation to see her starts to build inside me. But before I glance around for a taxi, I look Hailey and Jax directly in the eye.

"Thank you," I tell them. "For bailing me out, but also for… everything else."

The words aren't nearly as hard to get out as I thought they would be. And they feel even better when a huge smile splits Hailey's face, right before she slips her arms around my waist and squeezes.

I'm too shocked to do anything but let it happen. And then it's over before I can decide if I want to hug her back, Hailey's smile not dimming a single watt as she steps back. I glance at Jax in confusion, but he just looks amused.

The fist around my heart loosens a little more. I think a grin even tugs at my lips, though I'm not confident enough to let it shine through. But Jax sees it anyway, and grins back.

The knowledge that I can share a smile with a friend—one that's not mocking, or fake, or sarcastic—soothes something in me. Something that's been broken for a very long time, but that finally feels like it might be healing.

Slowly, uncertainly, I stretch a hand out toward Jax.

I don't say anything. Neither does he. But I watch as his expression sobers, and as he reaches forward to grip my hand in a firm shake.

My body sags in relief.

The contact only lasts for a moment before we're both

pulling back, as if one handshake didn't just single-handedly start to heal how I think of friendships. But there's another relationship that's starting to press in on me again, and I'm eager to get moving.

"I have to go," I say hurriedly. "You two good getting home? Can I pay for your ride home?"

Jax waves me off. "Go. I'm taking Hailey to the café, anyway. I'll see you at the gym tomorrow?"

I nod. "I'll be there." A pause, then I add, "Hopefully with less anger."

Jax barks out a laugh at that, clapping a hand on my shoulder. "Dear God, please let there be less anger. I could use you as a training partner. I'm tired of playing pattycake with Tristan."

And this time, I'm the one laughing.

CHAPTER 33
Kane

It isn't until I turn away from Jax and Hailey that it hits me: Oscar was home alone by himself last night.

"No, no, no, no," I breathe, giving up on looking for a taxi this early in the morning and simply starting the sprint home. I fed him and took him out before we went out yesterday, but that was still over fourteen hours ago. And I swore to myself that that dog wouldn't know another day of discomfort or pain in his life.

Please be okay, please be okay, is all I can chant to myself as I run. If he's scared, or if he cries when I see him, I *swear* I'll—

My phone beeps with a text message, my notifications from yesterday finally coming through now that I've powered my phone on. And even though my heart is slamming against my rib cage with worry, I chance a second to look at my phone.

LANDLORD

I'm sure she already told you, but I let Isabella into your apartment last night to take care of Oscar for you. Just wanted to get the emergency notice in writing for both of us.

The heaviest breath whooshes from my lungs as I slow to a walk.

She took care of him. He's okay. She took care of him.

And then my chest tightens so hard it feels like I'll never get another breath in again.

She took care of him even though I didn't deserve it. She helped him despite me.

I rub at the ache in my chest. The ache that hasn't gone away since my mom showed up yesterday. The ache that only Isabella has ever been able to get rid of.

I don't deserve her.

I *want* to think I deserve her. I believed it when Hailey said it, and I wasn't lying when I told them I wanted to find out if Isabella thinks that, too. Because I really, *really*, more than anything, want to be deserving of Isabella. And I want to try for the rest of my life to give her everything *else* she deserves.

But I'm scared. I'm scared of trying, and of failing. I'm scared that if I head down this road, it's going to end in heartbreak. That I won't be enough.

I know we're at an impasse right now. All of the time I've spent with Isabella has been under the assumption that it's going to inevitably end—that I need to take advantage of the time I've been given with her and be grateful for just that. Because after everything that happened last night, this is the end of that path. I can't keep going with the lie that this is a casual fling. I can't sell it, and Isabella doesn't deserve it. She's *never* deserved it.

But if this is the end of that path… then this is the end. I lose Isabella. I don't get any more mornings with her, or rides on my bike, or walks with Oscar while I hold her hand. I get no more Isabella.

Unless.

Unless I ask for more.

Unless I push past this fear of failure, and of letting down the most important person in my life, and I actually… try. I try to be what Isabella deserves. I try to make her happy and be everything that she deserves in a partner. And I'll either fail for the millionth time in my life, or…

Get everything I've ever wanted.

I have no idea what my decision is, what the *right* decision is, when I break into a sprint. But with every step closer to the apartment, I feel a little bit closer to the answer.

My hands are trembling when I finally reach the building and grab for my keys. I know Isabella would have taken good care of Oscar, and that she should be at work right now, but my desperation to get to both of them is making my heart pound out of my chest. I just need to see them, to know they're okay, that I didn't hurt them—

My heart stutters and stops when I open my door and find Isabella and Oscar curled around each other on the couch.

I have to lean against the doorframe when my knees buckle at the sight. When a shaky exhale whooshes from my lungs.

When relief suddenly fills my body.

She's here. She stayed.

And it hits me that… *of course* I'm going to try. Of course I want more of Isabella. There isn't a version of this reality where I *wouldn't.*

I wipe the sweat from my mouth with a trembling hand.

Getting to the apartment was what I was focused on, and now that I'm here, I don't know where to go from here. There's so much I have to do, and say, and apologize for, and I don't know—

Oscar raises his head when he notices me. He's curled around Isabella, his head resting above hers, his position both protective and comforting. I have to swallow down the despair that threatens to choke me when I think of Isabella crying herself to sleep with only my selfless dog to lean on.

When I step forward—quietly, so as to not wake Isabella—Oscar's tail moves in a tiny, happy wag.

"Hey, boss," I murmur as I pet his head. "Thanks for taking care of our girl."

I look over Isabella's sleeping form. Asleep, she looks relaxed. None of yesterday's stress shows on her face—none of the hurt *I* put her through. I almost don't want to wake her.

When I swipe a hand down my face in frustration, I realize that I reek. Between the booze, the jail cell, and my sprint home, I shouldn't even be within ten feet of Isabella, let alone standing over her, ready to beg for her forgiveness. I decide to hurriedly shower, brush my teeth, and throw on a pair of gym shorts.

They're both lying in the exact same spot ten minutes later when I step beside the couch again. Taking a deep breath, I crouch down and reach for Isabella's shoulder.

"Princess," I murmur, my voice breaking on the word.

She wakes immediately. With a start, her eyes snap open.

The first thing I see on her face is… *relief.* The second her eyes focus, and she realizes it's me, a relieved smile lifts her lips and adoration fills her expression.

A split second later, that same expression shutters into wariness.

"You're here," she says, pushing herself into a sitting position. "Are—are you… okay?"

It kills me to see Isabella unsure of herself. Unsure of me. I debate sitting beside her, but decide kneeling beside the couch is what I deserve.

"Hey," I say quietly, wanting so badly to brush her hair off her cheek, but forcing myself to settle my hands on the couch instead. "Thanks for taking care of Oscar."

She nods. "Of course."

I hesitate, overwhelmed for the first time in my life by everything I need to say. I don't even know where to start.

So, I just start by blurting, "I'm sorry."

Isabella only blinks at me, her expression unreadable.

"I'm so fucking sorry I ever put you in that situation, Isabella. You have to know I would never knowingly put you in danger. But I should never have taken you out last night after everything with my mom." I pause, shame coating every one of my words as I add, "I never should have drank that much."

She pulls her knees up to her chest and wraps her arms around them before finally asking in a quiet voice, "Do you normally drink that much?"

I'm shaking my head before she's even finished the question. "Not exactly. I drink when the anger gets really bad because it dulls the edges of it. But it's been weeks since I last drank like that." After a moment I add, "I haven't really needed to lately."

The unspoken meaning is clear: *she's* the reason I haven't

drank as much lately. It's definitely not a healthy coping mechanism, substituting one crutch for another, but it's the truth. Isabella makes me want to be better.

"I'm surprised you ever drink," she admits in a whisper. "I would've thought your mom's life would have scared you away from it."

I swallow roughly and nod. "I thought so, too, for a while. I swore that I would never pick up a single drug or drink, that I would *never* be anything like my mom. Because I saw what it did to her, saw how badly it fucked up her life. And my life was already fucked up enough, I didn't need anything else making it worse." Wincing, my gaze drops down to the blanket spread on the couch. "But then one night, when I was fourteen, I just… gave up. I figured, there's no way anything could make my life worse, so why shouldn't I indulge a little? After all, there had to be a reason my mom liked it so much."

I'll never forget my first swig of vodka. For the first five seconds, it felt like the worst idea I had ever had. It burned almost as much as the beating that drove me to it. But then… the pain dulled. Just the tiniest bit. And suddenly, life didn't feel completely hopeless.

"I went through different phases with alcohol," I continue, still not meeting Isabella's eyes. Just wanting to get this off my chest and help her understand *how* I got to this point. "Sometimes I would drink a lot, sometimes I wouldn't touch a drop for weeks. It just depended on what was going on in my life and how bad things were. After I ran away from home, it didn't even occur to me to drink. But the second my mom showed up on my doorstep and sent my life down the gutter again, a bottle was the first thing I grabbed. It just became a natural reaction."

"So, alcohol was a crutch," she says quietly, trying to understand. I nod silently. "What about fighting? Was that a crutch?"

I start to pick at the thread on the blanket as I work through her question. "Fighting outside of the gym was a release, yeah. Getting in street fights helped me deal with everything that was going on at home. But I obviously couldn't just *pick* fights, so that's when I started doing MMA. I thought it would help to always have someone or something to hit." I take in a shaky breath. "It did, in a way. It took my mind off everything. It also kept me from drinking, since I couldn't train drunk or hungover. Fighting was the only thing that made me feel even a little bit in control." Because when I was fighting, I could *control* the things that hurt me, or didn't. It became my favorite release.

"I've heard the guys at the gym say something about training being therapeutic," Isabella offers hopefully "Like it helps them meditate or something? Could fighting become a healthy crutch?"

I wince at that. "I don't know how to do that," I admit. "I don't look at fighting the way these guys do. For me, it really was just a method of self-defense, and then an excuse to hurt other people. I'm sure there's something to what they said, but honestly for me, even yoga feels more meditative."

I feel Isabella's hand brush against mine, her reach tentative. When I finally look up and meet her eyes, I don't do anything to hide the anguish, the *regret,* from my gaze.

"If yoga helps you get away from all the bad stuff in your head, then that's what you should lean on," she says quietly. "Or if you can talk to the guys and figure out how training might help, then maybe you should do that."

I nod. I know I need better coping mechanisms. I *know* drinking and getting in fist fights aren't healthy crutches. Especially when those coping mechanisms hurt Isabella.

"I'm so sorry I brought you into my problems," I tell her, my voice breaking on the admission. "You never deserved that. I *never* should have drank that much around you, or started a fight with you there, or… or…"

I can't get the rest out. The sight of Isabella watching me get hauled away by the cops, of her scared and heartbroken gaze when I yelled at her, is enough to tear my heart in fucking two. I never want to subject her to any of that, ever again. I don't even know how to properly apologize for it.

"Did the thing with your mom scare you that much?" she asks quietly.

Swallowing roughly, I nod and force myself to be honest. "She always throws me off my game when she pops up in my life, but seeing her with *you*…" I shake the terror from my bones at the memory. "I couldn't stand that she was even in the same room with you. I don't even want her breathing the same *air* as you. If she had touched you, or taken her threat to the next level… I swear, if she had hurt you I would have *lost my shit*—"

"Kane," she interrupts, stopping me before I spiral too deep. Her hand grips mine. "Kane, I know her threat scared you, but believe me when I say: *I'm fine.*"

My hand tightens around hers, desperation seeping into

my grip. "I won't let her hurt you, I *swear*. I'll keep her away from you. I'll keep my distance, and I'll get her what she wants without it affecting you, and I'll—"

Once again, she cuts me off. Lifting onto her knees, she scoots forward until she's directly in front of me and facing me. Her hands come up to cup my face.

"We'll figure it out together," she says quietly.

A ragged exhale leaves my lips as my forehead drops to hers. My hands come up to rest on her waist, needing that physical connection.

My throat bobs on a swallow. I almost can't bring myself to say it, but I ask anyway. "Together?"

Isabella smiles at me. And she simply nods.

I can't stop the disbelief from bursting out of me. "You're not running away from me? You're not scared? Because I'm dangerous, and bad news, and I have anger issues even on good days—"

"Stop," she growls angrily. "Just… stop."

I bite off the rest of my self-disgust.

Her thumbs brush over my cheekbones, her touch soothing. "I'm not going anywhere," she says softly. Then she presses a sweet kiss to the corner of my mouth. "You don't scare me," she adds in a whisper.

A breath rushes out of me. With just those words, the fear, the *panic*, that's filled me all morning, leaves my body. She wants to stay.

She wants to stay with me.

"But…"

I swallow nervously at that one word out of her mouth,

knowing this is the hard part. The important part.

"But I think you need to ask for help," she whispers. "As much as I like knowing I make you happy, I can't be a crutch for you, either. I mean it when I say I'm not going anywhere, and I'll help in any way I can, *be* whatever you need me to be, but… I think you need to actually deal with everything in your head."

I can't do anything but nod. I know she's right. I've always known this, I've just never wanted to accept it.

"We'll take baby steps," she says soothingly. "Keep coming to yoga with me. We can do it at home, too, if it helps to get you out of your head. I'll be your own private tutor and critique you as much as you want." That makes my lips twitch with a half smile, and she looks relieved at the sight.

But we sober just as quickly. "I think you should talk to the guys at the gym, too," she says, then quickly adds, "Not about… all this, but about changing up your training a little bit. Maybe Jax can help?"

I nod quickly in agreement, my hold on Isabella's waist tightening. "Okay. Okay, yeah."

She bites her lip, clearly hesitating before saying what she really wants to say.

"And maybe… maybe you could talk to someone. Someone like… a therapist?"

I can't stop the wince before it shows on my face. The idea of talking to a stranger, of forcing myself to verbally vomit all of my problems, doesn't sound appealing *or* helpful. But this isn't the first time someone has suggested I see a therapist— though it hits me that for the first time, the idea doesn't seem as crazy as it always has.

Isabella sees all of that in my expression, and likely expected it, because her smile is sad, but knowing. "We'll work up to that."

"I'll get help, I promise," I tell her, hurrying to assure her that I'm not a total lost cause. "I will. I've always known I need healthier ways to cope with my shit, I just... I never had a reason to try. Or to care."

"I care," she whispers, sinking her hands into my hair and shifting forward on her knees until her lips brush against mine. "*I* care."

My shaky, disbelieving exhale brushes against her lips. I want to kiss her *so bad*, to just get to the good part, but I need to be honest with her.

"I want to deserve you," I admit in broken voice, pulling back slightly. "I know I'm not even close to being good enough for you, but for the first time in my life, I want to be. I don't want to be a fuckup anymore, I don't want to be hated by my coach, or my teammates, or random fucking people in a bar. I'm sick of being broken. And you deserve to be with someone amazing, someone who could take over the world and leave it at your feet. Someone who—"

She cuts me off with a kiss. I let out a sound of surprise, wrapping my arm around her waist and pulling her closer to deepen the contact.

But she pulls back slightly before I can do that, putting just enough space between us to whisper against my lips, "I already have someone amazing."

I shudder at her confession. And then I feel it—hope

begins to bloom in my chest. Hope that, even if I don't believe it myself yet, that *she* does, and that one day, I can feel the same way.

"I know you've had a hard life," she says. "I know you've seen and experienced things that no one should ever have to go through, and I know they've made you a little hard against the world. But Kane, that doesn't mean you're *broken*. It just means you had to load up with more armor than the rest of us. And I don't care that we might have to spend a little extra time creating a safe environment for you. This isn't your 1 last shot to get it right, this is us *trying,* every day. And some days will be good, and some will be bad, but every day, we keep fighting. Together. Because I would rather live in *your* world, with *your* arms around me and *your* heart against my palm, than anywhere else. I want *you*, Kane. Never doubt that."

For a moment, I can only stare at her, my awestruck gaze roving over her face. Then I take a deep breath to gather the rest of my courage, and I take that first step toward being the man I want to be. For Isabella. For *me*.

"Okay," I whisper. "Then I'm yours, Isabella."

OVER THE NEXT few days, I settle into a routine.

Making my peace with Isabella and with my own personal demons doesn't mean I suddenly have a perfect life, but it brings a level of calmness to my days.

I stop taking the closing shifts so I can instead spend my nights asleep next to Isabella. I wake up with Oscar wedged between us at the foot of the bed. Some days I let him crawl up the bed and cuddle Isabella, but other days I trick him out of the bedroom with the promise of a treat just so I can spend the morning buried between Isabella's legs.

By the time I can finally pull myself away from her, she's usually cutting it close getting to one of the million classes she either has to take or teach. Which leaves me to hang out with Oscar for a few hours before going to the gym and getting my workout in, then heading to the strip club to work for the night.

I wasn't sure if it was going to be weird with Jax after the jail thing, but in a way, it was almost comforting to have a worry like that. It meant we had *some* kind of relationship.

I still get the daily nod, the only difference is… I nod back.

A few days after Jax and Hailey bailed me out of jail, it's the day of the week when we spend the entire hour sparring. I assume I'm still confined to heavy bag workouts, so I reach for my bag gloves.

"Kane, go with Remy for a round."

My head jerks up in surprise. I shoot Jax an incredulous look, then turn toward Remy in confusion.

"Dude…" Tristan says through gritted teeth.

Jax keeps his attention on me as he waves his friend off. "She'll be fine."

Tristan's brow furrows in confusion. But he must trust his friend enough to not push it further, because eventually, he turns his attention to me.

His blue eyes trained on me, his stare promises every bit of the savagery that I've seen him be capable of. His voice is hard as he says only, "If you hurt her, I'll fucking kill you."

A few weeks ago, I would have flown off the handle at the threat. UFC fighter or not, I would have gotten in his face and dared him to try.

But… I don't want to be that person anymore. I don't want to be defined by my anger, or my fists. I don't want to be offended by Tristan's accusation—one that's true if he's going by what he's known up until this moment—and I don't *want* to hurt Remy.

So instead of reacting, I merely nod at Tristan and start to wrap up my gloves.

Coach appears in front of me as I'm stretching out.

"You good?" he asks.

I automatically give a quick nod. But then I look across

the room and see Remy warming up, and Tristan murmuring something to her, and the rest of the fighters standing around the cage, waiting for us to start. And I realize something.

"I don't want to hurt anyone," I finally admit on a cracked whisper.

It kills me to say that out loud. But *wanting* to be a better person and *actually* being a better person are two different things. Not wanting to hurt Remy or any of my teammates doesn't mean I'll be able to control the urges and flashbacks that have taken over my body and mind so many times before. Last time was proof of that. And I'm terrified that I'll fall back into the trap of directing my fear and panic at other people.

Coach's expression softens at my comment. He doesn't give me a look of pity, or respond with some kind of bullshit *you'll be fine* comment, he just does what a good coach should and gives me an honest answer.

"Alright, look," he starts. "I want you to work on something for me. In the same way that you've been breathing through bag work and jiu-jitsu exercises, I want you to try to be present in the moment while you're sparring, too. MMA isn't just about winning, or about physically hurting your opponent. It's about technique, and athleticism, and discipline. It's about learning your body and appreciating what it's capable of. It's not… a punishment. Or a survival weapon." He gestures at the cage where Remy is getting ready for our round. "I want you to *enjoy* the fight for what it is. I want you to breathe, and think, and more than that, I want you to be proud of yourself for what you're capable of. Do you understand what I'm telling you?"

I force myself to take a breath and mull over Coach's

words. If I'm being honest with myself, I don't *completely* understand his strategy, but for the first time in my life, I think I can kind of see what he means. Fighting has been about a physical release for so long that I never stopped to look at it as an art—never stopped to actually look at what I'm capable of and be proud of it.

"Okay," I say slowly. "I'll try."

He claps me on the shoulder with a pleased nod. "Good. Now go have some fun." Then something occurs to him, and he sighs. "And if, for some reason, you feel yourself start to lose control, just… do five burpees or something."

My lip twitches in amusement. "Yes, sir."

When I enter the cage, I realize Remy doesn't seem worried as she takes up her stance. She's short, but she's not exactly a small female—she's got too much useful muscle to meet that description. But despite that muscle, she's physically not a match for my two hundred plus pounds, even without anger problems fueling me.

The bell rings, and we start to circle each other inside the cage. She snaps out a few jabs that I easily deflect. I even throw back a few of my own, but I'm hesitant enough that none are actually thrown with the intent to hurt. My frame is stiff, my movements unsure. I have no idea how to spar someone that's not my size.

I watch as Remy tucks her chin and throws a few combos. One of them lands, and when I jerk back in surprise, she lands another. And another.

My frustration starts to bubble up. Not in a way that makes me want to lash out, but in a way that I imagine is the natural human reaction to losing. Biting down on my mouthpiece, I duck my chin and settle into my stance again. I start to look for openings in Remy's movements, and after throwing out a few test combos, I think I find one.

I suck in a deep breath, forcing my muscles to loosen and my shots to become more fluid. I feel myself start to settle into a comfortable rhythm. My punches aren't thrown to hurt, they're thrown to tag, or to set up something else. I suddenly feel so relaxed in this flow state that I even throw a few leg kicks.

Remy lands a punch, I counter with one of my own. We go back and forth, both of us landing a few shots a piece. Before I realize it, it's become an even, competitive round.

And then suddenly it's not. Because just as the bell rings to signal the end of the round, Remy capitalizes on the fact that I have to punch down by landing a huge overhand right on my chin.

I blink in surprise, stepping back to recoup from the shot. As I stare at her, I realize that the entire gym is silent. Out of the corner of my eye, I see every person crowded against the cage, their breaths held as they wait for my reaction.

All I feel is shock. Not because I've never been hit, or because I'm surprised Remy could catch me with something, but because... there's no flashback.

There's no flashback.

There's no anger, no deep-seeded desire to violently lash out. No feeling of desperation or panic that makes me want to hurt someone else before they can hurt me.

And it hits me that when there's no fear, no rage... maybe there's no flashback. No trigger.

On the heels of that realization, and without any conscious effort, my lips lift into a grin.

Collectively, I hear everyone exhale a sigh of relief.

"Nice shot," I tell Remy simply, holding out my glove for a fist bump.

She studies me for a moment, likely trying to decide when I'm going to flip back to my normal angry self. But when she sees that my compliment was a genuine one, she slowly reaches forward to bump gloves.

"Good round," she says gruffly. Then she's turning and walking out of the cage, to be replaced by her boyfriend.

Tristan doesn't say a word, he just finishes tying his gloves as he takes up his stance in front of me. His expression is completely blank. He's got the best poker face in the UFC, which is one of the things that makes him a great fighter.

Unfortunately, it also means I have no idea how he's feeling right now, or if he's about to beat the fuck out of me.

I swallow roughly, taking up my own stance. The second the bell rings, we're circling each other and throwing out jabs. I think he expects me to fly off the handle at some point, and when I don't, he snaps out a *hard* combo that lands perfectly in my ribs.

I grunt at the impact, but don't counter right away. I simply duck my chin and look for a better opening.

I never end up finding it, but I'm surprised to not be mad about it. By the time the bell rings, Tristan and I have gone back and forth for the full five minutes, both landing some solid combos and actually settling into a technical flow. As we separate, Tristan bumps his shoulder against mine in a silent message of *good round.*

"You should follow up that body shot with a left hook," he says simply. "The cross to the body lands well, so build onto it with a level change. Head, body, head."

My eyebrows shoot up at that. Suggestions are rare enough, I'm assuming because I never listened, but having a compliment mixed in is even more so. I can only nod in answer.

From outside of the cage, I hear Aiden's shell-shocked voice. "Did I just step into Bizarro world?"

My brow furrows as I turn a glare on him. I open my mouth to invite him in for a round, but in the end...

I just launch into a burpee. And then four more.

Coach laughs so hard he almost falls over.

And just like that, I become part of a family.

I feel happy when I walk out of the gym. Like I can actually breathe for the first time in my life.

Is this what it feels like to have a support system? Is this what I've been missing my entire life? Because this makes me feel like I could take on the world and win. I feel... *light.*

The feeling continues throughout my afternoon—through my walk with Oscar, my ride to pick up my girl, and during my rare night off that I spend on the couch watching TV with Isabella. And after her repeated glances my way, I realize the smile hasn't left my face since we walked into my apartment.

It hits me that this feeling started bubbling inside me weeks ago, when I first started spending time with Isabella. Thinking back to that time, to the confusion I felt about life being this easy, this *good*, and not knowing what to do with it. Even when I accepted it, it felt like I had to grab on with both hands and hold on for dear life—to hold on to it for as long as I could, because it was only temporary.

And now… now I realize it's not temporary. Now, I realize that this feeling is a part of me. And sometimes it's going to hit stronger than other times, but this strength, this *happiness*, is something I'm capable of, regardless of everything.

I'm still thinking about it when Isabella and I eventually go to bed. And I lie there, with my girl in my arms and my dog at my feet, and I think my chest is going to explode from these feelings.

There's only a single gray spot in the back of my brain.

Pulling up my recent messages, I type out a text.

ME

We need to talk

MOM

I knew you'd come to your senses.
When?

My heart burns at the ill-intent in her message. *Did she ever treat me with a mother's love? Or was it always an act?*

ME

Meet me at my apartment at
noon tomorrow

MOM

See you then, Kane

I'm waiting on the stoop of my apartment building when she arrives. I stand as she walks up the steps, looking just as rundown as she did six days ago when she ambushed me here. Her clothes are ill-fitting and loose, and she's got dark bags under her eyes.

She looks sober, but she's clearly not doing well.

As I search for my key to unlock the front door, I wonder not for the hundredth time in my life if I'm making a mistake by not helping her. Even though I've given into her demands, given her the shirt off my back and every dollar out of my pocket, each of those times has come with ten times that many instances of trying to shut her down and push her away. And every time, every single time for the last twenty-six years, I've wondered if I was making a mistake.

This time is no different.

And just as she has every time before this, she looks smug as I let her in. Like she already knows she's going to win this twisted game between us. Either now, or in another two days after more threats, but she clearly thinks she's going to get what she wants.

We're both quiet as I let her in. As I gesture for her to take a seat on the couch, as I busy myself with getting Oscar some fresh water.

The sadness in my chest deepens when she barely spares Oscar a glance. She's too busy looking around my apartment, probably thinking about what she could steal, to care about this living thing that her son seems to really care about. It's a *dog*, for fuck's sake. She can't gather enough humanity to give even a little bit of a shit about man's best friend? Is she really that self-centered?

But, as much as it saddens me, that thought also solidifies in my brain that I'm doing the right thing.

I place Oscar's water bowl in front of him, steeling myself for a conversation ten years overdue. And then I take a seat on the coffee table in front of my mom.

"I'm not going to give you the money," I start quietly.

She doesn't even look surprised. She merely raises an eyebrow and waits for me to continue the speech she's heard a thousand times before.

"I'm not going to give you the money," I repeat. "I'm *never* going to give you the money. I'm done enabling you."

She rolls her eyes at that, but her stance is stiff as she crosses her arms in front of her. "You always did have such a ridiculous conscience. It's not *enabling*, Kane, there's nothing wrong with me. But if you want to protect your precious conscience and put the burden on me, then don't look at it as enabling: look at it as protecting yourself. Because it would take only one call to get you fired from that disgusting club, one call to ruin—"

"I don't care," I cut her off. My voice is hard, harder than it's ever been with her. "I don't care about your threats, about losing my job, about you following me around like a lost little puppy for the rest of your life and trying to get me fired from every job I'll ever have. I don't care. I've survived being fired before, I can do it again. I don't care."

I pause and watch her expression turn suspicious. I've tried to say no to her before, but never like this. *This* is different.

I can see the moment she realizes that. Can see as she goes from surprised, to flustered, to angry.

"*You* might have experience with being a fuckup, but your precious *girlfriend* doesn't," she snarls. "How do you think she'd handle being looked at like the scum of the group if they found out how she's been spending her free time? If they knew she's been dating a drug dealer and a pimp, a fucking waste of space that funnels illegal shit through his club? Do you *really* think she'd stay with you then?" She barks out a laugh, the sound dripping with cruelty.

My hands squeeze into fists in my lap. *This* is the moment I was most scared of, the moment she would threaten Isabella.

I knew it was coming. I knew if nothing else worked, that she would be smart enough to see this as her ace. And of all the threats she's ever made, this is the one that will make me flip my shit. *This* is the one that scares me the most, the one that is most likely to make me give in. Because *this* is the thing that I hold dearest.

I suck in a deep breath in an attempt to calm myself, to soothe the anger bubbling in the pit of my stomach. The emotion that will likely always be there, but that I have hope I can twist to show as passion instead of hate-filled rage.

I'm vibrating with the need to control it, still not entirely sure I *can*, when I feel a weight press against my leg.

I look down to find Oscar staring up at me with the gaze that only dogs are capable of, the one that says *I know, and I'm here*. And I immediately feel the calmness that I was just searching so hard for immediately seep into my body.

Taking another deep breath, I turn my attention back to

my mom. "I'm not going to give you the money," I repeat again.

Something about my tone registers for her. *Something* finally makes it clear that I'm being serious, that I've finally reached my limit with her. That I'm not going to give in to her, ever again.

Her expression shifts again. She's back to surprised, and then desperate, and finally a bone-deep expression of *panic* settles over her features.

"I'm sorry you've had a hard life, but I'm done feeling bad for you," I say in as hard of a voice as I can muster. "It shouldn't be a child's job to look after a parent, especially if that parent has done nothing but make their life hell on earth."

Panic morphs to guilt, though the emotion isn't blazing nearly as brightly as the others were. Part of me is glad to see she can feel it, but it's obvious that she has a long way to go before she can own her actions and apologize for them.

"I deserve to have a mother who loves me. Who *actually* loves me. Not one who is only nice to her child when she needs something, and who disappears as soon as she's gotten what she wants. That's not love. That's some fucked up version of it that you've latched on to. I don't know if it's because of your addiction, or if it's just your shitty personality, but I deserve more than that."

The accusation in my words is like a trigger. I see the moment she becomes defensive—the moment it all turns to fury.

But I don't wait for the explosion. I brought her here to say my piece, and I'm going to say all of it.

"I don't want you in my life anymore," I finish. "Not until

you can talk to me without begging, or mocking, or *threatening* with something. I'm out. I don't want any part of this game you're playing."

Sure enough, the explosion is immediate. "You ungrateful little shit," she snarls, standing from her seat on the couch. "You think *you* deserve more? You're delusional. You have *no idea* what I've done for you. I never asked to get knocked up with you, and yet I've sacrificed more than you could *ever*—"

"Get out of my apartment," I interrupt coldly as I stand.

She starts to shake, her hands clenching into fists. "Give me the *fucking* money, Kane, or I swear to *God*—"

"Get out of my fucking apartment," I repeat, louder this time. I'd really prefer not to call the cops on my own blood, but I'm so far done with her that I'll do it if I have to.

Her eyes practically bug out when she realizes just *how* done with her I am. She looks like she wants to yell more, or maybe even hit me, so before she can do that, I walk over to the front door. And whether my strength comes from Oscar, or Isabella, or even knowing I have the support of my teammates… something gives me the final push to open the door and stand pointedly beside it.

"Bye, Kara," I say quietly.

Her eyes widen at the name, and all anger melts from her body into a puddle of shock. I've *always* called her Mom. Even in the worst moments of her manipulation and abuse, she was always Mom.

No longer.

It seems to be the thing that finally convinces her I'm not going to change my mind the way I usually do. Whether she stays here and trashes my apartment, or comes back in a few weeks and gets me fired, I'm done.

I see the tiniest flicker of something in her eyes, something I might one day identify as regret or shame, and for a split second, I see a hint of the mom I always thought I had. Maybe it's real, maybe it's not, I don't know. I don't care. Whatever it is, it seems to be the reason she completely deflates in front of my eyes.

When she leaves, it almost feels anticlimactic—she doesn't say anything, doesn't stop to look at me, she just blows past me and out the door.

I don't know when I'll hear from her again. I know this won't be the last time she'll ask me for money, and she'll probably still try to carry out her threats, but for the first time since I was a teenager, I'm not scared to deal with it.

I feel… freed.

A while later, I'm settled on the couch with Oscar leaning into my side when I hear the lock scratch at the front door. I look up to see Isabella walking into the apartment, the key I gave her this week clutched in her hand and a wide smile on her face.

"I was half-worried you gave me a fake one," she says with an adorable giggle.

I don't return the laugh. I can't. I can only stand from my seat and walk across the room to wrap an arm around her waist and cup her face in my hand.

Slowly, the smile drops from her face. She looks up at me with wide, dazed eyes, asking me without words what I'm doing.

I answer her with a kiss.

I kiss her with every ounce of love, and happiness, and gratitude in my body. I don't take my lips off hers for seconds, minutes, hoping that with every press of my mouth against hers, I can somehow convey the gratitude that I have for her.

I know it's an impossible mission. I'll likely never be able to truly show this woman how she helped me—how she accepted me for who I am and opened my eyes to my worth. I can only try.

When I pull away, her lips are pink and her expression is dazed. But there's a smile on her face, and the sight of her happy is like a balm to my soul.

"Hi, princess," I murmur with a smile of my own.

"Hi," she whispers back.

"Did you have a good day?" And *God*, it feels effortless to ask that. It's such a simple question, but I never actually thought I'd be able to use that word to describe any part of my life. Never thought I would *want* to.

"Mhmmm," she hums. "It's better now, though." She seems to finally notice that there's something different about my demeanor, something lighter, so she pulls back just enough to get a better look at my face. "Did you?"

I nod. "It's better now," I parrot. There isn't a chance that I can tamp down on my growing smile.

"Good," she says happily. "Are we hanging out tonight? What are we doing?"

I lean down so I can press a kiss to her neck. "Anything you want, princess," I murmur against her skin. "I just want to spend time with you."

She tightens her arms around my waist, wanting me closer. "I want Oscar to be with us, too. Why don't we watch a movie? I picked our movie last time, so you should pick it this time."

"Deal," I agree immediately. Because I was right about Isabella's smile having the power to make me agree to anything, and I'm not even a little bit mad about it.

She lets out a happy squeak and presses a kiss to my lips before she steps back. "I'll order food for us then. I'm so excited!"

I'm chuckling as I watch her prance around my apartment, over to where Oscar is curled up on my couch. My heart wants to practically burst out of my chest at even the sight of it, and I'm suddenly filled with a gratitude so great, I don't know how to breathe around it.

I can't believe this is my life now. Can't *believe* this is what my future looks like. That Isabella, and Oscar, and happiness are a part of it.

And as I shut my front door, I can't help feeling like I'm closing the door on my past. I'm ready to lean into a future I never thought I could have, but will be thankful for every second of the rest of my life.

"Alright, *TIME!*"

A chorus of groans echo all around the gym, all of the fighters collapsing at the same time.

"You guys are so *dramatic*," Coach sighs as he leaves his vantage spot beside the cage.

"You know, I would love to see him do one of these workouts one day," Aiden gasps as he clutches his stomach. "I know he was some hotshot pro fighter back in the day, but there is no *way* the old man could do these pain camps he puts us through."

"Reeves, I could do two-a-days of these workouts back-to-back and *still* wipe the floor with you," comes Coach's voice from inside his office.

Chuckles sound around the gym as Aiden grumbles, "That's rude."

"If that happens, one of you is obligated to call me so I can get that on camera," Dani snickers from the sidelines where she's taking pictures of practice.

Aiden glares at his girlfriend. "That's even more rude."

She blows him a kiss in apology, which immediately softens his ire and makes stars explode in his eyes.

"You can make it up to me by getting some shots of me beating up Tristan," he says.

Tristan snorts from his place on the mat. "Fat chance, pretty boy."

I can't help chuckling at the back-and-forth banter. It took me a little bit to warm up to the rest of the team, but after I stopped looking at them as strangers that I sometimes punch, and after Jax pulled me into their conversations a few times, it got easier to connect with them. I learned that Tristan shares my opinions on expressing emotions, and that Jax is a great sounding board when I want to talk about fighting as a form of therapy. Remy also turned out to be a great training partner, and has completely changed my fighting strategy with how technically smart she is. Even Aiden has brought something to my life, most of the time being humor.

Even if it is laughing *at* him.

"You would think he'd be a little more modest after we just spent the last two hours kicking his ass," Remy says with a sigh.

Tristan pulls his girlfriend into his lap. "I don't think he even knows the meaning of the word." Then he wordlessly rocks backward and throws his leg over her face at the same time that he captures her arm.

"Tristan!" she shrieks in surprise.

"God, I love when you scream my name," he groans. Then tightens the submission.

There are collective groans around the gym. When I plop

down next to Isabella where she's seated in the viewing area, I realize she's the only one laughing.

"They're so cute together," she says.

"They're weird together," I correct. "I've never seen a couple where fighting is their actual foreplay."

She gives me a coy look. "I don't know, it might be kind of sexy." I raise an eyebrow at that, to which she shrugs. But her blush gives her away. "I remember feeling connected to you during our self-defense lesson."

My thoughts flash back to that lesson, to the serious start of it and to the way I felt during it. To the protectiveness I felt toward Isabella, and then the overwhelming closeness.

I tuck her hair behind her ear, loving that we've reached a point where I can freely touch her, freely relive some of our memories. "You want to do another lesson, princess?" I murmur. "I can add in some jiu-jitsu this time if you want to get to the real foreplay."

Her blush deepens, and *fuck* I want to follow that color under her clothes. I give her an openly predatory look, taking a moment to appreciate the sundresses that she's started wearing around me. She claims it's because I've torn too many of her tights.

Fine by me.

I open my mouth to tell her we're leaving, that there's a good chance I'll fuck her on my bike because I'm too impatient to get her home. But I'm interrupted by the door opening from the heavy bag room across the gym.

"And this is our mat room," Jax says, gesturing at the room in its entirety. "This is where we teach the jiu-jitsu and sparring classes."

When he steps aside, a girl walks through the door and peeks around at the gym. She's young, barely college age, and wide-eyed as she takes everything in.

"And your membership covers both Muay Thai and Jiu-Jitsu classes?" she asks. "Or is it an additional cost to do more than one?"

"It covers both, so you're free to take whichever classes you want," Jax answers. He nods first at Tristan, then at Max. "Tristan is our head Muay Thai instructor, he's a professional fighter who's known for his striking. And Max over there teaches our jiu-jitsu classes. He's a brown belt and one of the best in the Northeast circuit. They'll be your main coaches."

Tristan shoves Remy off him so he can give the girl a professional greeting. Max also gives her a polite wave, but his eyes linger on her a little bit.

Jax points at Lucy, who's stretching on the far side of the mat. "And Lucy teaches our cardio kickboxing classes, if you're interested in the more workout-oriented classes."

Lucy smiles at the girl, but not before her gaze drops over her body for a split second.

Jax finishes the introductions by saying, "I also teach, but I'm usually working the front desk during the night classes. If that's when you're thinking of training."

The girl nods. "It is. And I'd like to sign up for your unlimited option. I'm a big fan of martial arts, I've always wanted to learn. And now that..." She swallows and adjusts the bag strap on her shoulder. "I'm just really excited to get started."

"Great, let's get you signed up then," Jax says with a smile, before leading her toward the front desk.

"I'd like to take a look at your waiver of liability, too, please," she says as she starts to follow him.

I catch Jax's look of surprise. This girl barely looks old enough to read a syllabus, let alone a legal waiver. But he nods and says, "Of course."

"Jax, can you take a look at the signups for—" Coach walks out of the office and stops when he sees them standing at the front desk. "Sorry, I didn't realize you were busy."

"This is the owner and our head coach, Coach Dominic," Jax says by way of introduction. He nods at the girl. "And this is Skylar. She's our newest student."

Coach nods stiffly, in that grumpy way that's his signature greeting. "Welcome to the gym, Skylar."

Skylar gives him a shy smile. "I know who you are," she admits. "I looked you up. I've seen all your fights."

Coach's eyes go wide at that. I know for a fact that he hates talking about himself, so I'm not surprised when he doesn't reply.

Skylar seems to sense that, because she glances back toward the fighters still spread out on the mat. "Actually, I looked all of you up. I wanted to see who I'd be learning from." She turns her attention back to Coach. "Is it bad if I tell you I chose you because you beat the owner of the other big MMA school in the city?"

That seems to crack Coach's mask. A grin appears on his face—that rivalry, and him *winning* that rivalry, is one of his favorite fights. Figures it would be the only thing to get him to react.

"I think that's a very smart reason to pick us," Coach says with a smirk.

"Okay so note to self, Skylar already knows all of our weaknesses," Lucy says with a laugh.

"Guess we're going to have to step up our game," Max agrees with a laugh of his own.

Jax sighs. "You guys are kind of killing my closing argument here."

Skylar chuckles. "I was sold before I walked in here, don't worry. Weaknesses and all."

Guess we've got a new student at the gym.

When Jax gets her started on paperwork, everyone's attention finally strays back to their own individual conversations. Mine snaps back to Isabella like a magnet.

"Ready to get out of here?" I ask, pressing a kiss to her neck. Her intoxicating *Isabella* scent envelops me, reminding me that I want to get her home as quickly as possible.

"Mhmm," she hums, returning the kiss with one of her own. It takes everything in me not to deepen it right here, in front of everyone.

"Who knew not-so-angry man was so into PDA," Aiden comments from outside of our bubble.

I throw him a glare. "What did I say about that nickname?"

He grins shamelessly. "But I like it."

"Let's see if you like it after a three count in the cage," I growl.

"Ooh, I wanna see that," Dani says, lifting the camera up to her eye and aiming it at us.

I open my mouth for another threat, but freeze when I realize what I'm looking at.

"Are you… are you *posing?*"

Aiden very obviously flexes his abs in his girlfriend's direction. "If she's shooting, I'm posing."

I shake my head and sigh. "I can't handle you."

Aiden's smile is very obviously pleased. "Thank you."

I hear Isabella giggle and turn to look at my own girlfriend, raising an eyebrow in question.

"What? He's funny," she says defensively. When I only give her a disbelieving look, she shakes her head, smiling, and says, "Just go shower before Aiden tricks you back onto the mat."

I grab my bag to do just that, but before I disappear into the locker rooms, I wrap an arm around Isabella's waist and pull her against my body, not caring about the sweat because I know she doesn't.

"Just wait until I trick you into my bed, princess," I murmur in her ear, loving that I can feel her heartrate pick up against my chest.

And yet, her voice is steady when she replies. "Kane, I've been infatuated with you since the first moment I saw you. You don't have to *trick* me anywhere."

EPILOGUE
Isabella

KANE TAKES THE scenic route home without me having to ask for it. Taking bike rides together has become a peaceful escape for both of us—until I start getting turned on by the vibration between my legs and the feel of Kane beneath my hands. As soon as my touch starts to stray over his abs and under his waistband, Kane always immediately makes the next turn to take us back home.

I expect him to pull me into the bedroom as soon as he opens his front door, but I'm not even a little bit surprised when he becomes distracted by Oscar.

"Hey, boss," Kane greets him, squatting down to the dog's level so he can give him a proper head rub. "How was your nap?"

I take in the sight with a smile on my face and a warm feeling in my chest, forever amazed by these two. In a way, they saved each other, and the gratitude that they both show makes their love that much more beautiful.

It makes *me* love them even more.

Sometimes I think about my life a year ago, or even six

months ago. When my days were full of first dance, and then a lack of dance; when I was alone with my own thoughts, with no one really filling them or giving me anything else to love or live for. I was lonely.

Or I was, compared to this.

Now, my days are filled with love and happiness and awe. I've watched Kane grow into the person he's always wanted to be, the same way I feel like I've grown into the person I've always been at my core, that I finally have the freedom to embrace.

My face aches with my smile. By the time Kane finally pulls himself away from Oscar and takes a seat on the couch, I think my heart's going to explode with happiness.

Kane notices, of course, and pulls me sideways onto his lap with a small smile of his own. He shows them off more freely nowadays, yet every one of them hits me just as hard as the first one ever did.

"Hey, princess," he murmurs, pressing his lips to my neck.

"Hi," I whisper back. "How was your day?"

"Better now," he murmurs distractedly, his kiss drifting over my skin. It takes him a few seconds to pull away, but when he does, he asks, "Are your parents still coming down this weekend?"

I nod. "If you're still off work."

"I told the club I can't come in this weekend, so we're good. I think my boss is actually *glad* that I have something to do that isn't punching patrons and other MMA fighters."

As he's talking, one hand moves to my waist so he can absentmindedly rub circles on my hip. His other hand drops to Oscar's head and pets him in the same unwitting motion.

An excited grin springs to my face. "I'm excited to actually show them around the city. I think they'll enjoy the personality of Philly."

"I think so, too. Your mom was already asking me about restaurants." Kane gives me a worried look. "Is she expecting something fancy? I could ask the guys for recommendations, but I haven't been to the nicer spots."

I'm smiling as I shake my head. "She doesn't need fancy. She just needs good."

I watch his body deflate in relief as he nods.

We haven't spent a lot of time with my parents, but it's been nice watching them welcome Kane. And seeing him relax around them. Kane's experience with parental figures has obviously been horrendous, and I would never ever want mine to try to replace his, but I think it's softened something in Kane to see what good, normal parents look like.

To see what parental love should look like.

We haven't heard from his mom since she showed up on our doorstep, though neither of us are delusional enough to think we've seen the last of her. Kane thinks he saw her outside of the strip club not long ago, but by the time he went outside, she was gone. And whether she was readying herself to carry out her threat, or lurking for an entirely different reason, we fully expect her to show up again.

But when that happens, I know Kane will be strong enough to set the boundaries with her that he needs to set. I know he believes in himself enough to know he *deserves* to set those boundaries.

I'm shaken out of my thoughts when Kane suddenly says,

"I have a surprise for you. In my jacket pocket."

I immediately begin vibrating with excitement, a grin stretching across my face. I lean over Kane so I can grab his jacket and pull it over to us—both he and Oscar let out grumbles at the disruption. But when I pull the envelope out of Kane's jacket, Kane's frown is replaced by a soft smile.

"What is this?" I ask in confusion. It takes me a second to read over the words, and even then, it doesn't make sense. "You rented a car?"

Kane shoots me an amused look as he tugs the paper from my hands. "Not exactly. It's an RV rental. I would've just bought you plane tickets so we could go wherever you wanted, but I figured you'd enjoy it more if we brought Oscar with us. So, I rented us an RV for a week."

I'm still looking at him in confusion when I ask, "Why? Where are we going?"

He shrugs. "Wherever you want. I overheard you talking to Hailey about the traveling she's done, and it wasn't hard to pick up on the fact that you wished you could've done the same. I'm guessing you've only ever traveled when you were on tour with the company?" He waits for my little nod before he continues. "I figured we could do some exploring around the country, just you, me and Oscar. Take our time, go wherever you want to go. Get a real vacation in."

I feel my heart squeeze at his words. He's so… *thoughtful.* And no one would ever know it if they didn't look beyond his hard shell.

It's moments like this that I feel so unbelievably honored to be the one that he opens up to. That he trusts me enough to open himself up.

He hesitates, as if he's not quite comfortable with the words he wants to say next. "We should probably be back before the fall semester starts, though," he adds.

Pride blooms like a flower inside me. Because Kane picked that particular life trajectory on his own, with nothing but my unwavering support as his boost. He's going in as undeclared because we have no idea yet what he's going to study, but if some of his vocalized thoughts are anything to go by, I have a feeling it's going to do something with helping those with substance abuse problems.

"We can totally do that," I reassure him. "It won't be during the semester, I'll make sure of it."

I feel it, then. The words that are constantly trying to escape lately. I've been wanting to say them for weeks now, but the last thing I ever want to do is force Kane to say or do something before he's ready. And with the impression of love that he's grown up with, I know he has a lot to work through in his head before he feels comfortable enough to say it to someone else.

So, I swallow the words. I force them back down by pressing a grateful kiss to Kane's lips, and I show him my love in the only way I can right now.

"Thank you for the gift," I whisper against his lips, feeling so incandescently happy I think my face will crack.

His mouth curves into a smile beneath mine. I melt all over again just from the feel of it. "So polite, princess," he murmurs.

When I eventually pull away, it's still there on his face. These soft smiles are my favorite because they're when he's the most peaceful. When he's happiest.

Except, there's something else in his expression right now. Something I've never seen before. Something that makes me tilt my head in question.

He slides his hand into my hair and, for a moment, he just looks at me.

"I love you."

The words roll easily off his tongue, and there isn't a single piece of him that looks nervous or unsure. In fact, he looks the opposite. He looks like saying those words relieved something in him.

I, on the other hand, swallow nervously. "You do?" I whisper.

His thumb brushes along my jawline where his hand is still sunk into the hair at the nape of my neck. It almost feels like *he's* soothing *me*.

"Of course, I do," he says evenly. Simply, again.

And there's something beautiful about the fact that it was this easy for him to say. That, after everything, the emotion was so obvious to him, and his heart so full of it, that he could say it to another person, randomly on a Monday night, with no nerves or doubts.

I can barely get the words out myself. But after blinking away tears, I tell him in an overwhelmed whisper, "I love you, too. So much."

And if I thought Kane's first smile was one I'd never forget, it's nothing compared to the one I get right now.

BONUS CHAPTER

"Hey, Kane. Your girl's here."

Turning my head in confusion, I see Isabella walk into the strip club with her usual big smile on her face.

And just like it always does, just the sight of it makes me lose my breath.

She's wearing a short pink sundress, the straps barely covered by the thin sweater she has over it, and her sandals show off her matching pink toes. Her hair is down for once, the brown curls so long they almost reach her waist, and it gives her a slightly wilder appearance than normal.

She looks adorable and sexy all in one perfect little package.

"Hey," I greet. "What're you doing here? It's almost 2am."

She shrugs, closing the rest of the distance between us and settling sideways on my lap where I'm seated in one of the big chairs beside the stage. My hands instantly go to her body, needing to touch her anytime she's close enough to touch.

"I missed you," she says softly, winding her arms around my neck. "And I couldn't sleep. I swear, the more comfortable Oscar gets, the louder his snores become."

I chuckle at that, because it's definitely true. It's been months since I found Oscar, but every day he surprises us with how much more he comes out of his shell. He's still not a people person—which Isabella teases me endlessly about—but with anyone that I seem to like, his full-blown personality comes out. He's playful, very demanding when it comes to belly rubs, and surprisingly talkative when he wants something.

Gone is the scared and battered dog I found in a dumpster, and in its place is a fat, happy puppy.

Who also likes to push us out of bed and snore so loud we can't sleep.

"Did you try to rearrange him? Or wake him up?" I ask.

"I tried both of those things," Isabella says grumpily. "He's getting too big for me to move, and I swear, *nothing* can wake that dog when he's having a good dream." She sighs, a happy smile settling on her lips. "I love him."

My lips tip up in a smile of my own. "Me, too."

The song playing through the speakers switches, and the girl dancing at the end of the stage takes her exit. Another girl steps up to take her place, this time on the pole right in front of us. The DJ's voice sounds out around us.

"This is our last dance of the night, folks, so get the rest of your cash out and show Cherry how much you appreciate her!"

Isabella looks around the club, her brow furrowed. "Who is he talking to? There's no one in here."

I chuckle and rub my hands over Isabella's bare legs. "He's just fucking with us. He knows I've never paid any of the dancers."

Isabella's attention zeroes in on the girl in front of us, her eyes widening as she takes in the way her body starts to sway to the music.

"Why not?" she asks in that beautifully innocent way that she does.

I can only stare at her in rapture as I answer. "None of them ever interested me."

"Dick," I hear muttered from the stage.

I let out a laugh at Cherry's rebuke, though Isabella looks shocked by it. When she turns to me, her eyes have gone wide and her lips have popped open.

"Cherry's just teasing," I reassure her with a chuckle. "Plus, I'm the last person she'd want showing interest in her." When Isabella still looks confused, I lean in so I can brush my lips over her shoulder and whisper in her ear, "She likes girls, princess."

Her lips form an *ohhh* as she turns back to the girl dancing in front of us. Cherry must guess what I said, because she winks at Isabella as her hips continue to move.

We watch in silence as she finishes her dance. Well, Isabella watches. I'm just staring at my girl.

"Alright, folks, that's it for us tonight. Thanks for spending your Tuesday night with us! We'll see you back here tomorrow morning."

The music fades out, and Cherry finishes her set by wiping down the pole. But as she leaves the stage, she looks over her shoulder at Isabella with a sexy smile. "You should try it. You're beautiful, I bet the guys would eat you up."

I aim a glare at her. And when I realize that Isabella isn't nervously laughing it off, that glare becomes a confused stare in her direction.

She's biting her lip in that way that makes me want to bite it for her, and there's a mischievous twinkle in her eye when she turns her attention to me.

"Don't even think about it," I tell her. "I don't feel like having to kill every man that walks in here."

"But there's no one in here," she says innocently. "No one would see me but you." Wrapping her arms around my neck, she slides her body flush against mine and playfully nips my earlobe. "You haven't thought about me dancing for you?"

My grip tightens on her hips as I grumble, "I *only* think about you dancing for me."

When she straightens, there's a pleased smile on her lips. I automatically lean forward to steal a kiss, but Isabella pulls away before I can reach her. Placing her hands on the stage floor behind her, she swings herself up to sit on the stage, and then spins around so she can stand up.

Want to read the rest of this sweet (and spicy)
scene between Kane and Isabella? Visit Nikki's
official website to read it!

ACKNOWLEDGMENTS

No book is easy, but this one put me through the wringer. It wasn't just that this was my first book as a full-time author (which came with its own set of unanticipated struggles), it was also that I've seen so many "Kanes" come through the gym, and I wanted so badly to do their story justice. I hope I achieved that goal.

I have so many people to thank, but number one is, and will always be, my husband. I'll never say this to your face, but none of these books would exist without you. Every day I think it's impossible to love you any more, and every day I'm wrong.

To my beta readers, Amanda, Nicole, Sam, Dora, and Brittany. You've all become an integral piece of my writing process, and none of these books would even slightly resemble the final product if it wasn't for you. Not to mention, I think we need to write 'talking Nikki off the ledge when she gets lost on Trash Island' into your contracts. But beyond that, you've become some of my closest friends and I'm so, so grateful for you.

To my brilliant editor Kenzie, who I can never ever thank enough. Without you, there would be no Nikki Castle, and I stand by that. Your brilliant developmental edits continue to amaze me, and I'll never stop being awed that you can take a first draft (let's be honest, this started as a 2 star) and turn it into a 5 star book that I can be proud of. If I haven't told you enough, you're incredible.

To my subject matter experts: this book tackled some

topics I was flying blind with, so thank you for making sure I was writing them accurately. Caitlen for capturing what it means to be a ballet dancer, and Sami and Emily for the yoga scenes. Thank you!

To Jenn, for proofreading for me in the eleventh hour because I love adding to my manuscripts at 3am the night before they're due. Thank you!

To my family, friends, readers, everyone that has supported me throughout this writing journey, all I can say is THANK YOU! Normally this is the point in my acknowledgements where I make the "without you, a book is just some ink on a dead tree" joke, but this time, I'm going to say… without you, I never would have been able to make the jump to doing this crazy writing thing full-time. Because of you, I got to follow my dream this year. And for that, I am eternally grateful.

TRIGGER WARNINGS

This book contains references to addiction, alcohol abuse, substance abuse, child neglect, child abuse, physical abuse, and animal abuse.

ABOUT THE AUTHOR

Nikki Castle is a wife and dog mom from Philadelphia who writes spicy love stories about alpha MMA fighters and the women that melt their badass, playboy hearts. She's a full-time romance author during the day and spends her evenings running a Mixed Martial Arts (MMA) gym with her husband, who is also a retired fighter.

Nikki has been writing in one way or another since she was a teenager. She pursued an English and Philosophy degree in college, and finally decided to sit down and fulfill her longtime dream of writing a novel when quarantine began in 2020.

Nikki loves to hear from her readers on Instagram or through email. Message her on any social media platform @ nikkicastleromance or email her at nikkicastleromance@gmail.com!

ALSO BY NIKKI CASTLE

The Fight Game Series
Book One: 5 Rounds
Book Two: 2 Fights
Book Three: 3 Count

The Just Tonight Novella Series
The Stranger in Seat 8B

www.ingramcontent.com/pod-product-compliance
Lightning Source LLC
Chambersburg PA
CBHW021335310726
48971CB00001B/140